Tales of the Heart
A Collection of Love Stories

Kd Amidon

Dear Reader,

Welcome to Tales of the Heart: A Collection of Love Stories. This book is a labor of love, crafted with care and filled with stories that speak to the most profound human experiences. Whether you're a hopeless romantic, a seeker of truth, or someone who simply loves a good story, you'll find something here that resonates with you.

Love is a universal language, one that crosses boundaries but unites us all. It's in the shared glances of strangers, the comforting feeling of family, the steadfast loyalty of friends, and the unexpected moments that take our breath away. The stories in this collection are as diverse as the people who wrote them, capturing the essence of love in all its forms romantic, familial, platonic, and everything in between.

As you turn each page, you'll journey through the hearts and minds of people, who have bravely shared their personal tales. Some stories will make you laugh, others might bring a tear to your eye, but all will remind you of the incredible power of love. These are real stories from real people, written with sincerity and vulnerability. Some writers have chosen to reveal their names, while others prefer to remain anonymous, adding a touch of mystery to their tales.

I invite you to read these stories with an open heart. Let them remind you of your own experiences, or inspire you to see love from a new perspective. This book is not just a collection of stories it's a celebration of love in all its beautiful, complex, and sometimes messy glory.

So, grab a cup of tea, find a cozy spot, and immerse yourself in these tales of the heart. I hope they touch you as deeply as they've touched me.

With love,

Kd

My Thank you.

First and foremost, a heartfelt thank you to every individual who contributed their love story to Tales of the Heart: A Collection of Love Stories. Your willingness to share personal and often deeply emotional experiences has made this anthology a true celebration of love in all its forms. Each story is a testament to the power of human connection, and this collection would not be possible without your openness and bravery.

To those who chose to share their names, thank you for your courage in attaching your identity to your narratives. Your stories are an inspiration and a reminder of the diversity of love that exists in the world.

To those who preferred to remain anonymous, your stories are no less impactful. Your contributions add a layer of mystery and universality to this collection, allowing readers to see themselves in your words.

Lastly, to the readers thank you for opening your hearts to these stories. It is my hope that you find pieces of yourself in these pages and that they touch your heart as they have touched mine.

Trigger Warning

This book contains content that some readers may find distressing or triggering. Topics include:

- Suicide and suicidal thoughts

- Arguments and conflicts

- Sexual content

- Profanity and strong language

- Emotional distress and heartache

Please proceed with caution and take care of your mental and emotional well being while reading. If you find any of these themes upsetting, you may want to consider if this book is right for you at this time.

Table of Contents

Mischa

————— ❖❖❖ —————

I had a childhood friend of mine that I was really good friends with years ago back when we was in middle school together back in 2014, her name was mischa and we were good friends, we weren't super close but we were definitely very familiar with each other, we went to the same middle school, rode the same school bus and we even lived in the same neighborhood and every time we talked we always got along during that time she was bullied a lot in middle school, but despite that i actually had a big crush on her at the time, she was my first ever crush and the first ever person i really liked at the time considering we were just kids at the time, she was very beautiful, but due to the constant bullying that she had succumbed to, i didn't realize it at the time, she never told anyone about it, not even me, and to put it simply... in February of 2017 she passed away due to suicide, she was 14 at the time of her passing even though it's been 7 years since she passed i still think about her all the time, i still think about her everyday and not a day goes by where i don't miss her growing up i've always played the piano and to this day i still play the piano and even though it's been several years since she's passed on every time i play the piano it always makes me think of her, if heaven was a person it was definitely her and playing the piano is the closest thing i'll ever get to heaven I still play piano to this day in remembrance of her and our memories we had together, i choose to do good and be good to others despite what others might do to me for her sake, she was the first person i ever really had feelings for and i wish i had got to tell her before it was too late, playing the piano is my way of telling her i love her.. even to this day i still do, it will never fade i'm 21 years old now and despite her passing being several years ago, i will still always love her forever.

-@revengevibesonly

Intertwined Souls

From the moment I met Raon, I sensed something very memorable. It was not like how lovers meet across a crowded room, but like kindred spirits recognizing fragments of their souls in one another. We crossed paths in the first grade, amidst a game of Mafia. She was this quiet beauty, while I was the chatty, high-spirited child. She was the teacher's pet, and I was constantly clipped down to red for my mischief. Yet, when we first played together, I felt an inexplicable sense of peace beside her.

In those early years, I often sought the validation of my peers, feeling perpetually out of place. But in the simple joys of laughing and exchanging childish gossip with Raon on the playground, I felt a rare completeness. Though our bond wasn't immediately apparent, I believe the universe had a timeline for our souls to intertwine.

As the years slipped away, we found ourselves in 2021, in the midst of an online school world. I was struggling to navigate adolescence as I had just lost all my friends and my parents were getting divorced. I sank into the deepest shadows of despair, my spirit dimmed and my days filled with an all-consuming void. One day, when I had given up and surrendered to my misery, I was lying in the bathtub, tears mingling with the remnants of my hope, when I received an invitation to an Instagram group chat that included Raon. In that moment, when my heart was heavy with the intention of ending it all, the universe sent me an angel. Raon's voice became my lifeline, our daily calls dissolving my loneliness. The first time we met outside during the pandemic was a beacon of joy in a bleak summer. We visited a small shopping center, and for a day, the weight of my negative thoughts lifted. With Raon, I found an escape from my toxic home life. I was no longer in fight or flight, and I found someone who not only connected with me but also helped me grow.

In middle school, both of us navigated our own darkness. Raon struggled with extreme social anxiety. Every time she was put in a position where she had to speak, her mind would race with disordered thoughts driven by fear. These thoughts haunted her so much that she found it easier to remain mute and not speak at all. She was always nervous about speaking her own opinions and wanted to say only what the other person wanted to hear. In contrast, I wore my insecurities on my sleeve, compensating with a facade of overconfidence.

Our lives mirrored each other, running parallel yet reversed. I had abandonment issues because my mother was neglectful emotionally and physically, and Raon had an overly strict and involved mother. Raon yearned for freedom, often lost in daydreams of running through open fields, escaping the constraints of her home life. I, on the other hand, was both blessed and cursed by that very freedom. It felt liberating yet hollow, leaving me yearning for structure. I sought a guiding presence, a parental figure to offer direction and care, to infuse my life with order and meaning.

In each other, we discovered what we longed for. When we were together, the boundaries of age and place dissolved. We were re-molded into children again, free from the world's demands, and we found ourselves in a sanctuary of comforting fantasies. I was able to show Raon a glimpse of the freedom she yearned for, while she provided me with a sense of comfort and assurance that allowed me to find contentment in my own company.

By the time we reached eighth grade, I began to heal and grow, and so did she. Despite our closeness, our connection remained obscured by a cloud of negativity. Our mental states held us back from fully being able to love one another. Freshman year, I went to an arts school, a half-hour away from Raon. Though separated by distance, our friendship endured. I made it a point to meet her daily after school at our favorite spot. When we were together, we would sit at this diner and talk for

hours upon hours. These hours after school were the only times I was able to enjoy life without longing for more. She awakened my spirit and reignited my energy when my home and school environment drained it from my soul. Eventually, I transferred to Raon's high school.

Raon used to be fearful of vulnerability whereas i bluntly expressed my emotions. We began to influence each other immensely. Through my own shameless display of love and emotion, I helped Raon shed her fears and embrace the pure beauty of genuine connection. I revealed to her what true love was supposed to feel like in its most unconditional form. It is an endless wave of affection that flows freely with no expectations or demands. Raon does not owe me anything for my love, I love her solely because her existence brings light into my life.

I feel extraordinarily blessed because I was granted the chance to walk this path with her in this universe, in this timeline. Our love is a profound reflection of what it means to be truly connected, like DNA, we are two intertwined strands, a double helix. They don't entangle but grow together, forever linked yet distinct. So are we, two halves of a whole, not diminished when apart but whole in our individual selves.

Nika Momtaz

nikiamomtazz@gmail.com

Rome and Jocelyn

Jocelyn showed me what love was, Jocelyn showed me what a true relationship was. Jocelyn showed me how to love properly. Jocelyn, made me the man i am today. without Jocelyn i think i would never have been such a loving, caring, faithful young man that i am today. Jocelyn and myself; Rome, met in 5th grade. it all started at such a young age. Jocelyn and i were really good friends at such a peak time of age. we felt like we were grown already but we had so much to learn. i caught feelings for the first time, i didn't even know what "liking" a girl was. Jocelyn was known as a really pretty girl in middle school. She was smart, kind, beautiful, outgoing, and so much more, of course she's all those traits til this day. In middle school I was such a class clown, I wasn't taking classes as serious.

One day i shot my shot. and i told her i liked her. this was all in 7th grade, 2 years after i met her. I asked her out, and she surprisingly said yes. a couple of months go by and we had grew such an amazing connection. everyone loved the young couple we were. but it all went to hell with my life. half way through the school year my best friend passed away. the whole school was devastated. but it took such a heavy toll on me, and jocelyn tried her best to be there for me. as stupid as i can be, i started smoking and drinking for the first time. and it all caught up to me, all the consequences were coming up to meet me face by face, and i was diagnosed with epilepsy. epilepsy is a disorder that deals with seizures, and the first time i had one in front of my parents, i died. obviously i came back to life, as I'm telling you this story. people at school thought i had passed away. two losses in the same year, everyone was so devastated at how this world can be. once i had left the hospital after a good two weeks.

I went back to school and to my surprise everyone knew i was coming out of the hospital, and that i didn't die. Jocelyn was by my side as a young lady helping me recover through it all. as we grew passed elementary school, we moved onto freshmen year. but things weren't going the way we liked, so mutually... we decided to end things. Jocelyn, just gone. it was so hard on me because of how much i cared. my first love. the person who was there for me when my life was living hell. two months go by and we reconnect, as we would talk... we picked up a conversation about why we broke up. so told me it was for no reason, but she wasn't thinking right. i accepted her apology of course, as i could never be mad at her.

we never argued, i was never upset, i adored her. we lost connection after sophomore year. and finally picked up again senior year. as we were a bit older, we understood what was happening between us. she told me that she believed we were soul tied. i never really understood... but now i do. after prom, she told me that she was finally talking to someone. i was so happy for her because ever since me and her she hasn't dated, or talked to anyone at all. we were close friends always, especially after our breakup. after her and her boyfriend had been together for some time, she unfortunately had to cut me off due for respect of the relationship she had. my heart shattered, she was there for me at my lowest, and i was there for her at hers. I love her infinitely. i can't let go, but i have to knowing that the guy she finally met after 5 years makes her happy. ever since 7th grade, I've loved her. and we're sophomores in college... and i still can't let go.

If she came back to me id take her back instantly. i now understand why and how she believes we're soul tied. before she cut me off she told me she'd find her way to me eternally. and i for some reason believe her. god has done good to us, as we've loved each other through thick and thin. as she has showed me how to become such a respectful, loving, caring, and faithful young man that i was. i would lay my life for jocelyn... and i wish jocelyn knew how much i cared for her, and about her.

But out of respect, i care to much to try and tell her to please stay. i just can't imagine life without her. she has no flaws, she's all perfection. i now have to learn how to let go, after almost 7 and a half years... it sucks but as long as she's happy. she'll forever hold a spot in my heart, and i cannot wait to tell my children about her.

9/24/21

Three years, an eternity in young hearts,

Laughter echoing down familiar hallways,

Hands intertwined, dreams whispered in the quiet of night.

High school sweethearts,

Bound by the innocence of first love,

Every glance, a promise, every touch, a vow.

But time, relentless and unyielding,

Whispers of change and new beginnings,

Paths diverging, futures calling.

The weight of goodbye,

Heavy on tender shoulders,

Eyes meeting with unspoken understanding.

To move on, to let go,

Is to honor what was,

And embrace what will be.

Memories etched in the fabric of their being,

A bittersweet symphony of youth,

As they step forward, apart but forever changed.

In the silence of their parting,

A quiet strength is born,

Two hearts, once one, now finding their own way.

-@avaa.alvaradoo

Love is…

---◆◆◉◆◆---

Family is love, Family is never ending support, without it, i'm nothing, here's a piece of my heart"

- DJ Scheme

I feel as if everyone thinks they know what love really is, or what family is truly made of. I once thought I knew the meaning of love but at the age of 18, I realized I was…wrong. Love has been being tossed away like filth by those who I am supposed to call "Sister", and being manipulated by someone who I thought was special.

My definition of family has changed drastically, as I've never known what that word means. As the youngest of four, I am the brother of three sisters. For anonymity, their names shall be Shanti, Troya, and Trinity. One would imagine that they would always be by my side, willing to jump anyone who messes with their baby brother, and yet that ideal image burned to ashes throughout my life. Trinity is the youngest of my sisters and someone I thought would be my best friend, my twin flame.

She always bought me toys and snacks, let me have sleepovers at her house, and came to events like my graduation and my Martial Arts promotion exams. These experiences blinded me from the hatred and envy she held for my mother. At the age of 12, I was exposed to her nastiness, hearing her curse out my mother and seeing the disgusting messages she would send via text. My mother did the best she could to hide her nastiness, but only so much could be done. From then on her anger and vile tongue spread from my mother to me. All I wanted to do was defend my mother, was that so wrong that she began to hate me? There were times when she came after me and I became emotionally abused by my sister, the one who was closest to me. I thought she loved me, and I thought we were family.

My relationship with my oldest two sisters was always questionable, Troya being the first. Our bond was always distant, there was never any anger but that changed as I grew up. Her issue was more so with my dad, as we have different fathers. I was the only one who grew up with a dad, which played a part in all of their jealousy. This distaste for him caused her to disrespect him and my mother, and she was nasty about it.

My father has his demons, specifically with drinking, he isn't a violent drinker, he just has his pain and doesn't know how to deal with it. He was born and raised in Mexico, so he grew up hardened and grew to be emotionally immature. This habit however sparked a lot of hate towards him from my sisters Troya and Trinity. Imagine being 15, waking up on a Saturday morning, to the sounds of your sisters yelling at your dad, how would you feel? I forgot a lot of what was said but I can never forget what Troya shouted, "Next time I see you I'mgoing to shoot you, I'll put you where your mother is". That scared me. It wasn't acceptable for me to witness my blood speak to my father like that, I was scared. Troya has always been somewhat violent in my eyes, even so when I was younger, I was scared of her, always scared she would take a knife and stab my mother. She had even manipulated me before to gain information so she could attack my mother and insult her.

Eventually after so many traumatizing incidents, as a family we decided to cut ties with Trinity and Troya, this also included my innocent nieces and nephews. They will never know how much I miss them and continue to hope for their safety and well-being. It felt as if a piece of my heart was snatched away and crushed. To this day I have no idea how much they've grown and what they're up to, and it haunts me. This unfortunately leads me to my mixed relationship with my oldest sibling, Shaniqua.

She has a distaste for my mother from what it appears, there has never been a concrete answer as to why, she simply kept her distance from me and my mom. As a child, I remember asking my mother "Where is Shanti? Why doesn't she look for me?" She responded by telling me to text her and see what she said, and so I did. I was met with retaliation and blame. She mentioned how she wanted to stay drama-free and that's why her distance was kept, I felt hurt. It felt like I was the problem, and that's why my sister didn't want me. As of today our relationship has softened and we text from time to time, but she still holds an unknown distaste for my mother. My love for my siblings left me betrayed, I thought they

14

cared about me, but instead, I had lived a lie. I was in so much pain, I cried so much, I tried to hide it from those around me, I dug my nails into my skin. They didn't love me. I felt alone until I met someone who I thought would change that.

My first love, who I will call *Cynthia*, had changed everything for me. We had instantly felt a spark and our relationship was joyous and filled with romance. She was so attached to me, that I felt like her hero. After many failed relationships, I thought I was the one for her, she felt like the cure for my pain. I remember the many gifts she would make me, they would range from handwritten letters to origami and other little trinkets. They made me feel appreciated and worth something. I trusted her with everything, my insecurities, my pain, and my stories. I had opened up to her about my feelings of abandonment and being emotionally manipulated and abused by my sisters.

She told me that she would always be there, and would erase the pain I had been burdened with. I became close to her family, her brother taught me in high school as he was my Speech & Debate coach, and her mother would cook for me and joke with me, similar to her stepfather. I felt like I had a family again. As much as I love my mother and father, I felt like there was much more that I was missing, and this was the piece to that puzzle. I spoiled her, I gave her letters, custom jewelry and so much more. If she was hungry, I fed her, If she was hurt, I healed her. I did my best to cure her insecurities as she did with mine. We went strong and steady for a year, the three months after were the genesis of our demise. As much as I thought she was honest, she was sneaky. She knew how to hide secrets from me, she dealt with an addiction to weed and alcohol. She was easily influenced by her friends to partake in substances and she could never say no. I found out about it and I told her that I didn't like it, I wanted her to stop, I begged her to. I was under the false belief that she quit, I thought my love was strong enough.

During this time, I was no longer a part of my speech team, I left to focus on my other passions. A good friend of mine was still on that team, we'll call him *Judas*. I trusted him to watch over her on their competition trips, I couldn't be there for her, so I hoped that he would. I trusted him. In February, a little after Valentine's Day, I told her that I loved her and that she wanted a break. I didn't believe in breaks, but I believed in her. That was until the truth was revealed.

She fell in love with Judas and they became intimate on these trips during our relationship. It started around October. They would sneak around to their friend's house and her own. I found out that she had been using me for my money and pleasure. I didn't realize it but It made sense, there were so many times when I said no but she seduced me into intimacy. I felt abused and taken advantage of, to top it all off, she used pictures of herself to get substances from her friends. I felt like shit, like I wasn't enough, only good for what's in my pockets and my pants. The one girl who I thought would ease my pain, amplified it to levels I couldn't imagine.

Cynthia was a heart eater, but despite the pain, my eyes began to open. I started to realize what family is. I had my parents, who loved me dearly, but I also had my friends. Our group name is "The Regime". They were there for me when I needed it most, and for the first time, I felt like my friends liked me, something I struggled with during my previous groups. There was one other person who helped me, I'll call her *Tea*. She's Cynthia's sister-in-law. We grew close as friends during my theater days. She's like a sister to me, we're crazy when together, it's hilarious. She helped me with my self-esteem and always made me laugh.

She offers me advice and I do the same. When the definition of family became clear, I learned that family is not just blood, it is the culmination of individuals who share love. When I felt alone, abandoned, and thrown away, these people came to my aid and made me feel whole. That's what love is, picking someone up when they collapse and supporting someone without asking for anything in return. So thank you to everyone for helping me, and thank you for reading.

- JB

11-28-18

I still believe you are my twin flame.

Squirrel & Wolf

er POV- Love isn't easy. As many people may say... but to me he is what makes everything easy. Love comes in different forms. But to me this, this is all the kinds of forms I could ever ask for. We shall call this boy wolf. While wolf knew my standards, he didn't give up without a fight to let me know he is that man for me. But to me, i let him try a bit harder. As he tried and tried again, i finally let in. Now, since the day of his commitment, i knew he was the one. I'm deeply grateful to have such a beautifully hearted man by my side. A partner I believe every woman deserves in their lives. Although we are exactly 1388 miles away. Distance will never come between us. 3 years have passed and many more are to come. In this book, I'm here to express the everlasting love I have for this boy, named wolf. I love you, and forever on my wolfy.

His POV - What do you call yourself when you're agile, persistent, social, intelligent, full of energy, and maybe even curious? She may call herself a track star, some others may call her a smart person with goals. But to me, she's my squirrel. a beautiful woman with a hard driven heart that wishes nothing but a bright future ahead. She was going to be mine and I knew it. No one wanted her as much as I did and ever since I realized that I was committed to start my love life with her. How with such a goal directed mind could love me back?

I made her realize that love and support is what she needed to continue to drive her forward I was determined to fight with and for her even with distance apart. Even as friends our love for each other became apparent every day. We share the same humor every single day, we show our love, and respect each other. Even with far distances, our love is too strong to never let go. I truly believe I will have my squirrel in my arms for the rest of my life.

Two loves

— ◆◈◆ —

July 6 . I'm only 20. I know I'm young but I've experienced multiple forms of love so far that changed he way I perceive relationships, whether it's friendships or a partner of the opposite sex. I know I have. I've experienced different forms of love, be it familial love, unrequited, lost, first, romantic, found, platonic, unexpected, the kind of love you'd kill someone for, the kind of love you'd die for too. As people we don't show the kind of love, sometimes people will never love and understand you to your depth of understanding, we all love differently and that is what made my definition of love so complex.

Love for me is a risk, you're bearing your heart in someone's hands with the hope of them not breaking it, with the hope of them tendering to that love the same way you will, all because you're genuine. We're all different people with different experiences, different lives, different traumas, different perceptions so it's hard for me to know if someone really is genuine, except sometimes it's soul crushing to go into something blind-sided because everything that's fragile breaks, just like our hearts. Just like anyone else I have trust issues.

I'd hate to dismiss all of the people that I've met too because they were and still are special to me but these two loves impacted me the most, both of them being one and the same: my grandmother and especially you. My mom gave birth to me when she was young, she birthed me when she was 21, still pursuing her degree in college. The pregnancy disturbed her academics and this isn't me saying that I was a mistake but sometimes I tend to ruminate on the fact that she should've maybe had me at a planned age. If she had then maybe she would've been able to take care of me in her own, under a roof full of love. She wasn't able to fulfill her role and be present fully because of her degree and I have a lot of maybes when it comes to this topic because maybe if she raised me then I wouldn't have had to navigate myself through the definition of love by using other people, maybe certain things would not have happened to me if she fully present.

I threw myself to the world and knowing how harsh the world is, it broke me down instead. I only established a relationship with my mom three years ago when I moved in with her after my incident. I grew very fond of and protective of her because during that time framed she healed me, she moulded me into the woman that I am today through soft love and I did not understand what that was at all, until I met her completely. Only then did I understand why she had to do what she did.

I had so many questions. My dad isn't a topic that I like to dwell on too, he wasn't there as well, he's nothing but a blur. I have lived in burden when I had a present yet absent mother and father. It weighs heavy on your shoulders when you constantly go out there to the world seeking the same comfort that they could give to you, only to be backstabbed, betrayed, spat on and not knowing who to turn to all because the same people that made you are not capable to nurture you the same way you need to be. You feel alone. My mom gave me to her parents when I was 6 months of age, completely placing me in their care, allowing me to be their responsibility, allowing them to tend to my care ever since I was of a very young age. My grandmother isn't a good person and I hate to speak about her this way because at the end of the day she played her role in raising me but my understanding of her was different to how people described her to be.

Exterior individuals praised her, they spoke about hoe caring, humble and giving she is. I knew deep down that it was partially true. When it comes to family, there is a certain extent of knowing someone that no matter what people say about them it won't matter because you see this person as if you are looking into a mirror, it's impossible for them to have a façade if you've known them for years. At the end of the day you are the one to visibly see this person as if you are looking at yourself. I'm a first born daughter. My grandmother taught me what love isn't. My grandmother taught me what love is, love in the form of hate, love accompanied by discomfort and pain. I'm still maneuvering around my definition of love when it comes to her.

I know it's something that's there but I'm not entirely sure about it. I developed a love and hate relationship with her during our time together. She's emotionally abusive, manipulative, toxic and constantly made me feel as though love was nothing but a condition. I don't

22

like making it known that my family has money or that I come from money but it does not matter what the person purchases for you, the investment accounts they make for you, the amount of acres that your home has, the branded shoes and clothes you have or the timeless pieces you are gifted, there still is and always will be a void. Exterior familial members only saw us as a good family, with money, and children that are sent to good private schools. No one knew what I had to deal with, living in a broken home will never really make you content as a person.

No amount of money, kind of car, job or size of a house will allow you to truly be content as a person if you can't get to the root of what happened to you as a child, but that's just my belief, someone else can choose to argue otherwise. I had everything but internally I knew I was dying inside. It got to the point of me comparing myself to the friendships I had. I was jealous of poor people that would live in a household with both parents present, I grew envious of them.

It made me angry as a person because I yearned for my mother to come to my parents 'consultation in primary school or my dad to watch me at a soccer game. I was closed off when it came to friendships.

People had questions such as "where is your mom?" or "is your dad going to be at the soccer game today?" and I'd dismiss them and laugh it off as a joke when inside I was raging with so much anger for a person. At the end of the day this is my story and I would hate to make it seem as though I was ungrateful for the things I was privileged to. I thought that love was my grandmother's actions, that the way she would treat me was a reflection of who I am as a person. The thing with abuse, in any shape or form, is that you tend to grow attached to this person, doing anything for them to feel accepted.

I looked at my grandmother as if she was my mom, my mood depended on her. She would constantly beat me down with words, commenting on the way I ate, dressed, spoke, walked and I never felt free enough to eat around her because when I did, she'd mention how skinny I am and how that would never change no matter what I did. When it came to money and clothes, I knew it was conditioned. Grocery shopping would cause her to add comments on how if I wanted something, I'd have to do something for her in return.

I was a baby, a toddler, growing into a teenager so I didn't understand what she meant or why she did the things she did to me. I knew I didn't deserve it. I did well at school too, it still wasn't enough for her. I know I did well. I know I worked hard. I know I did all these things to impress her but ended up being constantly dismissed by this person, constantly and constantly searching for ways to change myself just so I could feel like I was enough for her. It still wasn't enough for her. Nothing ever was enough for her. You can never forget the words that someone says to you, being around them all the time makes it even worse too because it's a wound that is always being stabbed on, never given a break, never given a chance to fully heal. I hated home because of her.

School and friends was my only escape and form of

happiness, but it was only for a small period of time because at the end of the day I still went home to the same thing that I resented most. My family knew the kind of person she was to be around and it made me feel even more alone because I needed help. I needed saving. I needed someone to look at me in the eyes and ask me if I'm okay. I needed someone to understand and acknowledge what I had to deal with in the place I called home. I wanted someone to hold my hand and tell me that's it was going to end. Running away and putting myself in the adoption system felt so comforting.

The movies I watched made it seem like something to look forward to. I didn't feel wanted, more importantly by the same person that made me and the same people that raised me. The void I felt was carved deep enough for someone to place a mountain of rocks inside, eating away at my sleep, my eating habits, my relationships, my perception of the world changed too. I didn't feel deserving of my friends buying things for me, expecting them to want something out of return or wanting them to shout at me when I said something. I had friends at school, of course, but the happiness I felt when I was with them was short felt. My grandparents were old schooled too, asking to go out felt like a punishment. I did it once and they gave me a beating saying that I should stay at school, how I shouldn't like things as a person.

I missed birthdays, dinners with my friends, the late night outs or sleepovers that my friends would have with each other. Relationships became different for me now because firstly I would tell a small lie about me traveling to another province on the day, secondly it developed into bigger lies where my friends stopped inviting me to such things. I felt left out during the "remember when" conversations. I wanted to be a part of it all too. I wanted to have conversations where my friend would send me a funny memory that we had together when going out and how we'd have inside jokes that the rest of the world didn't completely understand, all outside of school.

My brain dissociated at some point because of the amount of pain that it had to tolerate and so I put my walls up to protect myself. I wasn't able to fully express myself or have a space where I could voice out how I felt, every action felt forced and had to be done only because "the other person would say this about me" My friends described me as nonchalant but little did they know that I cared so much that I was suffocating. The dynamics of my relationship with this woman were complicated because I would hear through the grapevine of the good things she would say to other people when they asked about me from her. They made me so happy but I yearned for her to come to my face and tell me the same things she would tell other people but she never did. "Stay in school, stop talking to so many people over the phone so she said" "You're always reading books and you're always on your phone" How would I not if I had no form of escape in that space? The thing about the dynamics of this relationship was how clingy and attached I became to her.

I hated how I enjoyed the way she made me feel and regardless of me crying at the back of the house every day, it was unusual when she didn't say anything to me at all. Silent abuse from a verbally abusive individual will have you thinking that this person doesn't want you anymore, that you're the problem. Who would take care of me if she didn't? but how could I allow her to constantly walk over me? Why did my mood depend on her? Why did I go out there to the world and talk so many good things about her when I knew who she was as a person?

Why did she treat exterior family members more than she did her own? Did I disgust her? Constantly searching for reason in everything is soul crushing. I felt alone, in every aspect. The kind of loneliness that creeps and eats at you at night, never allowing you to grow, never allowing you to aspire all because you are trapped in this environment with this person. But why was I so attached to her? I did things to evoke responses from her all because it felt reassuring. I fed on her reactions and words to keep me alive. She was the only person that I had. I mean she took me in and she raised me as her own, did everything she could to provide for me, she had to love me or at least have a soft spot for me, didn't she? The day I turned 14 was the day that the hate and anger that I had was diverted towards myself, more than the one I felt for her.

Living with the person that takes you in as their own forces you to love them, all in the name of family. I was angry at myself mostly for allowing this one individual to treat me that way and never being able to comfortably open up to anyone about the words she would throw in my face each day. I didn't have anyone besides her and so I clung on to that hate, I clung on to her as if she was my own mother, constantly placing my heart in her hands with the hope of her changing. I had hope, hope enough to last a lifetime. Maybe one day she would realize what all of this was doing to me.

How could she if I didn't speak up? She is a person of her own and maybe that's what she thinks love is., right? It frustrated me how this was the same person I would go to God about and praying for her to change, giving her a second chance, a third one, a fourth one. I lost count. I reached a breaking point, wanting to die and I tried to do it. I overdosed on pills, twice. Back to the money thing again, if there's a problem the first thing my family looked at was what I didn't have. The latest phone? I got it. The latest shoe? The world was mine. No one saw it as a cry for help until I did it again because all those materialistic things didn't matter to me. Everything changed beyond recognition when I repeated it the second time, a year exactly after the first one. My grandparents moved away a week after the "incident" and it felt as though they were running away from the very exact turmoil that they bred themselves.

This was when everything changed, the dynamics, the feelings and the relationships around me too in a way that I thought that it was wrong for me to do something like that. None of my friends knew why I was being rushed to the hospital each year, the family kept it private from outsiders and maybe they were protecting me, or maybe I was just an embarrassment. How do you explain to someone that your daughter, cousin, or sister tried to kill themselves but failed to? Everyone would view you as psychotic or how ungrateful you were for having the things that they didn't have.

However, I don't regret it at all because after that incident a new birth was created. I went for therapy and healing took place, healing through words, healing through someone else understanding your story and not judging you. Healing through a community of people that went through something similar. I realized then that as much as my grandmother did all those things to me, I morphed into her in a similar way. I was so stuck in my head so much that I pushed so many people away. I became manipulative, angry, toxic and abusive to myself and others in a way that I would sabotage relationships and close myself off from people and became so stuck in my head. I know now that they had the best intentions in mind for me but I didn't feel deserving of that because of what I experienced for years. Self-sabotage is a thing that exists but constantly seeking pity from people and self victimizing myself was never going to make things any better for me. I had to take the step to notice all these things about myself and do the work to become a better person, not only for myself but for the people around me.

Healing is a never ending journey and you will meet people that bring the absolute worst out of you. I love myself enough now to walk away from any situation that does me no good and that may be selfish to others but some people aren't self aware and willing to work on their flaws, that's completely okay because someone else prefers that cup of tea but I don't. Healing is like taking a walk down a straight road and bumping into a mountain of boulders that you can choose whether or not to take the courage enough to walk over, for your sake but all I can say is that the walk is beautiful.

When I talk about my grandmother today it doesn't faze me anymore, I know that she tried to do what she thought was best for me, be it the little things that I wasn't aware of or the prayers she made for me behind closed doors. She fell sick three years ago and it keeps on getting worse by the day.

I don't see her as often as I would want to but I miss her, regardless. I still think about her. She lost a lot of weight and ever since she got sick, a part of me died inside too because I know that if I lost her to death I'd lose my mind. July 6th was the day I sat her down and reminded her of something she said to me when I was young and we laughed about it.

She said she was sorry; I know indirectly she's sorry for everything she did to me. July 6th was the day I chose to forgive her, to unburden my heart and let go of all the anger I had for her. July 6th was the day that I realized that you can choose to love someone at a distance. I'm grateful for all the good things she taught me that I didn't mention in this story. Now that I've healed the question isn't why she abused me in that way but the question is why is she that way? What happened to her when she was young? Our fingerprints don't fade from the lives we touch. Someone else could read my story and choose to pity me, someone else could be empathetic because they understand and this story meets them in a way that they relate because they went through something similar.

What matters is that I was finally able gather up the courage and boldness to share it to the world, to be able to express myself to people and that's all that matters. Loving her was hard. Loving her was pain and sacrifice for me, it's constantly seeing the darkness in her and defying the impulse to jump ship. Love is choosing to serve and take care of someone yet being present with them in spite of their heart.

I know that nothing in this world will prepare me enough to lose her. My grandmother was my biggest learning curve because she taught me what love can't be. She taught me what love is. It ends or it doesn't. It can become less or more than the one you felt before. If the sun doesn't come up one day you find a way to live without it. If they're not there you learn how to make tea for yourself alone. Everything happens for a reason. She taught me how to take care of myself as a woman, how to humble yourself to elders and people, how to iron your clothes, how to cook, how to make your place clean, how first impressions matter, how to be strict with myself as an individual as people will take advantage of you if you're too nice.

She taught me a lot of things that I'd name off the top of my head but as much as I've healed from what she did, I remember everything. Today I can speak about her without breaking down. Today I can correct her when she says something rude. It could be her sickness, it could be remorse because regardless of her being the way she did in the past, one thing I can proudly say today is that I know I did my best to take care of her to my fullest potential. She affected a lot of people in the family to the point where no one wants to be around her at all, besides me.

Just because she abused me and certain people doesn't mean that she deserves to be punished. Cups of tea were shared between her and I and she would constantly mention how she only wanted me to sing her favorite song at her funeral. I hope she gets better. Loving someone at a distance.

When I was with her, I never saw the good she did but now that I've healed, I can pinpoint the good about this person. As much as she emotionally abused me, I know my grandmother like the palm of my hand. She's a passive aggressive person. Regardless of her words, when money wasn't there I'd watch her search for her last money in her purse just so I could buy lunch at school.

My grandmother constantly complained but she never allowed for anyone to do anything for her, regardless of her knowing that she suffered too, she still did it at the end of the day, better than anyone ever did. She wasn't good with words. I watched her lose her brother, a phone call from her sister made her collapse and cry, locking herself in her room. Her and I were connected in a way that the pain was mutual, she didn't have to say it because I knew. She understood me in a way too, when I had bad days at school she knew what meal to make, she knew not to speak to, she knew when to leave me alone.

She wasn't open to talking about how she felt. "It's all going to be okay one day" she'd say. I knew that she was in pain but not enough to tell anyone. Her and I shared a cup of tea together each day and while I read a book, she drank her tea and listened to the radio or played with her Nokia 3310 phone. She taught me that going to school is the most important thing in the world. As much as everyone in the family viewed her as a terrible person, no one understood our shared bond.

My grandmother was thoughtful too, she would bring my favorite meal back home for me after coming back from a wedding, or funeral, etc. She constantly defended me too when other people said otherwise. My grandmother is a perfectionist, doing the same thing over and over again until she got it right. She knew how I liked my tea, or porridge, or proportion of food or juice. The hate I had for her subsided and only then was I able to see past the spectrum of thinking that I was in.

Her and I had inside jokes that no one knew, a form of communication that no one was able to pick up but her and I alone. During family meetings she'd hum a song in silence, I'd be able to pick it up and sing along with her while everyone followed after. It's the little moments we had. The advices and lessons she gave to me still live on. I'll never forget her.

Instagram: @luvlupaa / @monicaxno

Email: tshegofatsomonicam@gmail.com

I dated a stranger

*B*eginning of May 2023, this girl and I matched on tinder. We'll call her Mira. Initially, I thought that nothing will happen between me and her. But the same day we matched, we had a few small conversations. The conversation lead into her talking about naps and I jokingly said "pull up to my crib and nap with me then". To my surprise, she said yes and she somehow ended up going to my place.

The same day we matched. Our first "date" or even meeting each other for the first time would be back in my place. Not no restaurant or the theaters. This was my first time inviting someone over. My gullible ass thought that we for real just going to take a nap together. We talked and cuddled and shit and it escalated into her kissing me. I told my homies prior to the meet up that it wasn't going lead to us having sex but it did. It was my first time doing it, and I did it with a stranger. After we finished, we hung out for a bit. For some reason, me and her thought it would be a good idea to make it official then and there. And so in a span of a day, Mira and I officially became a couple. Everything was going well.

She met my family, as I did with hers.

We often went on dates in which I paid everything for since she didn't have a job. My house became her 2nd home as she would sleep over close to everyday. Our little "honeymoon phase" would quickly come to an end as problems started to pop up. I noticed that she never tried to get to know more about me. There was an instance where I was asking questions about her and all I got was "shut up and just cuddle me". Haven't tried since then. We were always together but whenever we're not, she'd never call me on her own which I addressed to her. Nothing changed. We would constantly have sex throughout this relationship and do nothing afterwards.It felt like the relationship was lust-driven and so I distanced myself to give myself some time to think if I wanted to be with Mira. By this point, we barely hung out in person or text each other. Of course Mira noticed and mentioned that it felt like our relationship was ending. Because of that, I told her how I felt. How I wasn't sure if I liked her or not. And asked her to give me some time to think about her and our future together. A week pasts and she mentions if I've reached a conclusion WHILE she's in the hospital. My mistake on this was not talking about it in person, but regardless of that, at that moment, I realized that I was attached to her. After all, she was my first everything. And so I texted her "I like you I suppose". In which she responses "you suppose?". That was my fuck up. At the time, "I suppose" was heavy in my vocabulary.

So I added it on almost every sentence.She started comparing me to her ex. About how her ex lead her on and shit. But I tried reassuring her. By the end of that

35

conversation, I gave her some time to think about "us" this time. Another week pasts. And during this week, she was extremely distant. I was trying to bring this spark back that me and her once had by trying to plan up dates. This would be by the end of August. She had promised me to come over to my place to chill. But it ultimately ended up with her breaking up with me. Some people would stop here. But I was an idiot.We get into a situation ship for the beginning of September all the way to mid November.

After our lil break up, I was obviously hurt. But I haven't given up. Beginning of September, she lost her kitten. The same day Mira lost her kitten, I seen a cat in a park that's posted on facebook. And so I told her about it and went to go look for her kitten. We ended up not finding the kitty. To cheer her up, we got late night ice cream. When I get home from her place, we would spend the night together until 3. During this time, her phone kept blowing up with a bunch of text messages. I try to ignore it but I overseen a text that said "can we call?" from someone. I went home afterwards and that kept me up for the rest of the day.By this point, she had established boundaries. She tells me she didn't like the idea of "friends with benefits". And I said sure. I planned a movie date with her to the theaters the following day. Of course, I tried to be touchy with her, to which she tries to reciprocate but always end up stopping herself and pushing me away. After the movies, I ended up going back to her place and would watch another movie. She would constantly text someone while watching this movie with me.

I asked her if I could sleep over but she said no.

36

Feeling annoyed with my phone dead, I told her I'm going home since I had work the next day. She stops me and tells that she'll let me sleep over if I give her "back rubs". That leads up to us doing the deed. This would ultimately start up the situation ship. Her phone breaks and I proceeded to basically live at her crib for the entirety of September and half of October. During this time, I got very close to her siblings and her mom. And during this time, in a span of a week, during September, I learned more about her than I did during our relationship. During this process, I fell in love each day. Not to mention, we were having sex VERY often. I would also constantly buy her shit like food and materialistic shit that she'd love.

And a lot of these times, she would shut my feelings down completely by telling me that she'd never give me another chance. Or tell me that I deserver better. But you know. Her actions kept showing otherwise.We would fuck, hang out, have fun, and literally act like a fucking couple. So despite hearing hurtful words, I was convinced that if I keep showing my efforts, she'll see that I'm devoted to her. October hits and she gets her phone fixed. She becomes distant and stops doing all this sweet shit wit me. By this point I had plan a trick or treating matching onesies for the both of us for halloween. I would still sleep at her place but not do anything sexual. One day, she had to leave to go to her hometown since she's moving back. I decided that fuck it, I'm gonna look through her phone. I find out that she had been talking to someone else. And the dates goes all the way back to September. I try to confront her about it but she kept lying to my face. "He liked me but I don't like him back really." "I told you I'm not in the right phase of mind to date right now." etc etc. All of which I knew was a damn lie.Now every guy would probably leave her. But I couldn't. Since she hadn't gotten her period.

A week pasts and she gets back home from her hometown. We decided to buy some pregnancy tests and all of them came back negative (thank the Lord). The next day, I find out even more about the guy and that she had been talking to this dude ALL the way back in August when she was deciding on whether she'd stay with me or not. I considered it cheating. And so I confronted her about it that night. I confront her about the guy, and that during our little situation ship, I developed love to her. She did not take this well. She played the victim. "You told me you'd just be friends with me!" you told me this, you told me that blah blah, while crying very hard. I do not like it when people cry because of me.

So I felt extremely bad. This would also be the night where she tried cutting me off. So I say my goodbye to her sisters and mom.I was going to stop here. But that same very night, she lost her aunt. I felt guilt. "Why the fuck did this happen now?". I felt so bad that the next day, despite her not wanting to talk to me and shit, fucking cooked for her whole family to cheer them up. We talked again. But casually. Up until she had to leave to go move to her hometown. Which I helped with moving furniture and shit. She ended up dating that guy she cheated on me with and ghosting me on my birthday on December.I've no regrets on the amount of effort I put in on whatever this was. But goddamn. All I wanted was a 2nd chance. Instead I was constantly compared to her ex. Was told that I was trying to "buy" her off because I constantly bought her gifts even though she knows one of my love languages was gift giving. All I asked was for her to be truthful. She didn't spend a single dime on a single date, not a single dime on our countless meal, not a dime on ANYTHING. Shit I would've loved a fucking handwritten letter but I never received a singular gift. A lot of lessons learned but again, goddamn.

-Louise
@louise.sals

Lasting Heartbreak

W e meet on a "dating app", I was so close to not even replying to you but something in me just wanted to see what would happen. We clicked immediately, we soon started talking on messages. Not that later on we started calling and that turned into FaceTimes, we would stay up talking late, past midnight. We would spend so much time on FaceTime that some people would think we would be bored of talking or run out of things to talk about but it was never a dull moment talking with you. We always had something to talk about or we would just act silly with each other, listening to music, and sometimes playing games. I fell so quick for you.

The only thing that was a problem was that you lived 2 hours away, not that far but it was difficult to arrange when we would meet up. We had talked for over a month before actually seeing each other for the first time. When we did meet up it wasn't awkward because I felt like I knew you so well that it seemed so easy to talk to you and be around you. You were my first for a lot of things, I don't regret having my firsts with you because I really loved you and I trusted you. I really think you are my first LOVE. You saw the most vulnerable parts of me and also saw the most happiest moments of me. You made me so happy, really made my world so bright and full.

I think that was my problem, I let you control my happiness, take over it really. We connected in ways that I've never had connected with anyone and I got so attached to you, my eyes and soul and heart belonged to you. A little after three months of us talking you started to disconnect, the "three month rule" happened. When I started to realize what was happening it was too late, you eventually ghosted me. It hurt so bad, I really believed you when you said you loved me, which I never said it back in fear of what would happen and in the end it did happen.

You "love bombed" me, you made so many promises and put ideas in my head that we would be together and travel and do so many things together. It's about to be a whole year since we first started talking and I still miss you, I've tried moving on and forget about you, sometimes in the wrong ways, but till this day I can't. I think some part of me will never forget you or unloved you. You really fucked me up, and I hate you for what you did but I also can't help but still love you. I miss you so much. I can't stop thinking about you. I hate you but I love you at the same time. I always think of what happened and why everything went down the way it did. I wonder if I did something wrong or if I wasn't enough for you.

You were my everything, you never leave my head, I think about you every single day of every single minute. I really thought we had something special, you made me think we did. How could you say so many things to me that made me think you really loved me, did you really love me?? If you didn't then why, why did you do me like that, I'll never understand what and how you could've done me like you did. If you did really love me then what happened?? Why did you just leave me without saying anything?? You broke me in so many ways I didn't even know was possible, my heart still aches and craves for yours. I just wanted you to love me like I love you. I gave you everything I could've given you at the time.

I know "long distance" was the biggest challenge for us, but I thought that would never separate us. I was learning how to drive so we could meet halfway at least and you wouldn't have to drive the full 2 hours here. I still can't understand, every night since you've left my mind always goes back to the question, why aren't we still together, what happened to us?? We were so happy, I was so in love and happy, you were such a big part in my happiness.

I even told my dad about you, I eventually told my mom and sister and my brothers about you but sadly after you broke my heart. I wanted you to be part of my family, I wanted you to meet my family bc they mean the world to me and my dogs omgggg I would spend HOURS talking to my dog about you even though he's a dog and doesn't understand anything I say. He's heard more things than I've ever told anyone else about you. I let you in so easily so fast, I was so vulnerable and bare with you, I really showed you my bare true self because it seemed so easy to. You were so comforting and easy to open up to. I was so desperate to have your attention and desire that I did anything you asked me to even if I wouldn't be comfortable with it, I just wanted you to be proud of me and I wanted to give you everything I could've given you. That was my mistake, I gave you so much of me that I didn't have anything left of myself when you left, you took everything I had and I've been trying to get myself back. I really defended you to my friends and my brother and dad, I should've listened to them, I should've been more careful. But how could I, I was so in love, I didn't listen to anyone because I really thought what we had was so real and I thought you could never mean me any harm because you swore it so.

I'm not going to lie I've tried to move on so bad, talking to guys, going out on dates, isolating myself from everyone, trying to change myself. But nothing has helped, every guy I've talked to or went out with I was always trying to find a part of you in them, always comparing them to you. I wanted to find you in a different person, I just wanted you, I still want you. I think? If you ever called me or texted me I think I would answer you immediately, I would really want to try to fix what we had and be happy again. But now that I'm really thinking about it, it will never be the same, my heart will still be broken, my heart will never heal from you. People tell me time will heal, i will find someone else that will make you seem like a silly little fling, a puppy love type relationship. But I know you will always have special place in my heart because you were my first LOVE, the one that broke me in a million little pieces and changed my whole perspective on love and relationships and the idea of men. I've been so angry at myself for being so stupid and so angry at you for being so stupid too, I gave you everything I had, I was working to give you more, I would've done anything for you and yet you threw that all away for what?? For another little relationship that didn't last?? Yea I found out about a girl you were with, it's funny because I found out about her a few minutes before going out with a guy I've been talking to for a little after we stopped talking and I self sabotaged that relationship because of my trauma you left me. And now you have a new gf, idk exactly how many girls you've been in relationships with or been talking to after me or even during me.

But I really hope that you won't forget about me, I really hope I did mean something to you. I hope you still find a little part of me somewhere. The Maria's?? I hope you never forget the memory of us listening to their album, CINEMA, while we were kissing. Or maybe even all the late nights we would stay up on FaceTime just talking about anything and everything and every single little memory we made. I'm pretty sure our record is 12hrs of being on FaceTime. I let so many parts of me become associated with you, my favorite songs, artists, food, movies, tv shows, literally everything. I wish I can talk to you one more time, one more time hearing your voice, maybe even your laugh, or see your smile and your beautiful green and hazel eyes, how I loved your eyes and lips and nose that you would always hate because it was "big". You were so perfect in my eyes, after meeting you I never set eyes or looked twice at any other guy while talking to you. My eyes and heart was always looking at you. I still have your boxers, I wear it to sleep sometimes. I just want to be as close to you as I can be. I did end up deleting all the pictures from FaceTime and videos and all the cute little texts you would send me, I do have some saved that I've sent to my friends and I sometimes look back on them. You really fucked me up but you also loved me, I felt so loved by you. Even if it was fake I still felt loved and I loved every part of it. I hope I find something like that again someday but better. I try to have an open mind, trying to heal and get back out there, but I'm so traumatized and hurt by the ghost of you and your actions.

I self sabotage everything and my mind is my own enemy. I overthink so much, overthinking with you though was something different, I was right in the end to overthink, even after you would reassure me I shouldn't. I just wish you could've told me, I even told you to tell me whenever you felt like you didn't wanna talk to me or just wanted to talk to someone else to tell me and I would leave you alone, but instead you just talked to someone else or maybe more people and just left without saying anything.

Making me think I did something wrong, and even then after I sent you a long paragraph to reach out to me and tell me what was happening because I was so worried something bad happened to you or idk I just wanted you to say something. Omg I spent almost 3-4 months after you ghosting me getting drunk and smoking to just forget you, and I still do, not going to lie, but it doesn't work, it makes it worse, your memory and everything about you is so buried deep inside my mind

45

and heart that I would always think and talk about you whenever I have the chance. I just hope you're okay and I hope you find what you're looking for. I wish that could've been with me but things happen right. Just know I love you still and I am here for you if you ever wanna talk or if you ever need help with anything because even though you broke me so much and completely destroyed me, my heart will still be a little strong enough to give you love and to help you out. I love you, don't forget that please, I hope in another lifetime we did turn out happy and live a happy long life together until death did us apart.

This is just a little bit of what I wanna say to you and what I'm thinking about right now. There's still so much more I wanna say and explain and ask but this is enough for right now. There's also so many things I wanna update you on my life, like where I'm going to college and how I finally got my license literally 2 months after your bday. I'm glad overtime I've had less and less tears to cry for you, but everyday I have enough for a little because my heart still ache for you my love. But there will come a day where I will think of your name and I wouldn't have the urge to cry or to kiss you so much, I will just smile of the memories we had but that's it, just memories, and I will move on with life without a second thought because that's how life works. Even now I still think of so many little things that we used to say or do and listen to or even play, I still cry at those memories, and almost every single little thing reminds me of you, but again one day those things won't remind me of you and that's when I will know I have moved on, I wish that comes soon because I'm so broken and I need to heal and move on into adulthood, I hope this pain will flourish into something so beautiful one day, it will make me grow as a person and maybe even change me in better ways. So as my last act of love for you I leave you this letter and as my first act of love for myself I will heal, move on, find and love myself before anyone else.

-c.v

The Love That Remains

I wish you knew just how much I really loved you. The love I have for you was so authentic and unconditional. I wish you knew just how much not being with you hurts me. I cry in your absence when I'm alone at night. I've slowly made peace with knowing that we won't ever be like how it used to be. If I'm sincere with you. You were the only person I felt really happy with. I really did love you and it's hurts me that we aren't together anymore. Still hurts even after 6 months have passed. Even after all the pain, I still have so much love for you.

We tried to make things work for us even after the breakup. We both just couldn't stay away from each other. But you kept hurting me, especially when you wouldn't text me for days, when you could go without me for days. When I couldn't. I tried to cope but it hurt that you didn't put any effort in making it work. We both knew trying and eventually after months. Only I was trying to make it work. I would drive 2 hours to go see you even if it was for 2 hours did that for you without any commitments, Because I loved you. I would risk everything just to be held by you one last time. Every single time I tried you would stay and things would go well for us. Then you would go back to your old ways again and again. But I stayed because I kept trying to force myself to believe that with time things will be fixed. But time has opened my eyes. Your actions made me feel very unloved. I really tried my best to love you. To keep you in my life. But at some point I realized that it was for the better that I leave the waiting room. That I finally stop begging you to communicate with me. Even thought you said you still love me. I eventually started to go crazy.

I really did think, things between us were getting better but after theses 2 months where communication went out the window. Your life got busy and I waited for your text back. I was patient. But I slowly realized, You weren't even afraid to lose me. So I honestly, I don't even know where we stand as. I don't know if we are friends.

I waited and waited. Each day for a message from you. You would ghost me consistently Even after promising to stay and never leave my side. I cried because I missed your old love you had for me. I just started to get sick from the pain I felt of this one sided love. When I went to your house. You sat in my car, and lie to my face about how you never wanted to lose me, that you loved me. You would hold me tightly and kiss my forehead. I would feel that warmth again and I would fall for your cheap lies again.

But after so many times. The very last time, I didn't feel the same. I genuinely couldn't believe the words that came out your mouth anymore. Even when you said you love me so much. I just couldn't anymore. I just started crying. I cried because I finally realized you never loved me. Especially when it was my birthday and you said we were going to spend the whole weekend together but you stopped texting me all week. So when the day came. I had already told my family not to do anything for my birthday. Because we had plans. I didn't want my parents to be disappointed in me so 1 still drove to your house. Just to find out that you were working.

I still went and waited hours to see you. When the time came it was 12 am at night and I was excited to see you even after my feeling were hurting. I remember pulling over and crying hard. Just feeling all my emotions on how stupid I was for coming. You didn't even get me anything for my birthday. You didn't even buy me a present. When I left your home. You kept telling me your cheap lies on how we will see each other again.

The last time I saw you. I genuinely broke down crying on how shitty you were treating me. I cried and admitted how you kept hurting me in so many ways. How you drained me and my happiness away. It hurts me when all I ever wanted to do was love you and for you to do the same for me. But you just ignore me. I don't deserve to be treated this way. I will admit I was afraid to lose you in the beginning. I was scared to let you go. But with time and clarity I noticed through your words and actions that you didn't love me anymore. You just didn't want to lose me.

Because I was the only woman who has ever cared about you beyond your sisters. I checked up on you constantly after you got into a car accident. I asked you about your day. I called you when you were sick. I always looked for you when nobody would.

I let you be vulnerable with me when you needed it. I gave you roses when nobody ever has. I always prayed for you when No one else would. I always showed you physical, emotional and words of love. I showed you your worth and I valued you for who you were. But I guess that wasn't enough for you. You never valued me because ppl never value the people they use. So I hope when your therapist makes you feel awful about how you chose to treat me when I love and accepted you for all you had.

But how can you love me when you didn't even appreciate me anymore. Yet you continued to say you did. All to time point that you said we were official again. But you lied. You lied to me for 5 months. You never processed your feelings. You never told me the truth till I wouldn't stop asking.

Each time you kept hurting me by not answering my question. You kept hurting me when you said you were never going to hurt me again then turn around and do all the stupid things again. You never cared about my feelings and the effort died. You stopped trying because you gave up on us.

So I'm glad your going to therapy. So you can figure out why you couldn't appreciate me. I guess the only thing you did do right was letting me go when you finally realized you were hurting me. That I didn't deserve the shitty "love" you were giving me. If you had never told me you didn't love me that night. I would've probably still be trying today.

I'll never find someone like you ever again. I'm happy though. I couldn't see myself ever meeting someone like you or who you once were. I know deep down inside, I will be looking for the old you where ever I go.

YOU were an amazing man to me through all the time God gave us to live together. We both were so full of love and we shared the most beautiful moments. I'll remember them forever.

When I frequent the places we went to. I only see shadows of the glimpse of what once was there. I walk down the park where we first fell in love and I remember how you held me tightly when I was cold. I still replay the night that we first kissed.

Remembering all the deep and emotional conversations we shared about our dreams. Us staying up all night, chasing down stars. Talking about our dreams and loving each other. I'm going to miss the late night calls, texting, the FaceTime calls and the game nights we used to have. But most importantly, I'm going to miss you the most. Before you were my lover, you were my best friend, I'm going to miss the way we both were together. I miss just being able to call you randomly on snapchat and you instantly picking up.

I'm grieving you even though I know you are alive and well. Things have changed and I know you simply just don't care about me anymore and it hurts to know that. One day I'll be in someone else's arms and I won't think about you anymore. I just be thinking of him and how he makes me feel. I hope one day I reach forgiveness with you.

I can't forget how our love was a painful love but it was the most purest love I've ever experienced. It was delicate, sweet and beautiful. I saw so many beautiful things being together. You bought the light back into my eyes. Light that I haven't seen in such a long time. You was there when I needed you. I would do anything just to please you in anyway you needed it. I adored every single rose you gave me. I still adore them to this very day. I love everything you gave me. I still have your polaroid pictures on my bedroom wall. I admire your beauty everyday. I hope you still admire the ones I gave you too.

I remember when you loved me you would drive long distances for me, just to see me for only 5 mins. Your reminder lingers in my mind daily. I still see your Jetta in the streets around town. When I see angel numbers, remember you used to ask me

"What did you wish for?" And I would say "I can't tell you, or else it wouldn't come true.

Truthfully all of my wishes were all for you. To be happy, healthy and safe. I wished that we would love each other forevermore.

I really wanted it to be you. I really did. And sometimes I still do. You will always be my carinito, and I hope I will always be your bebey in another time line. I miss the tender love you gave me, and all the patience you gave me even when I was stubborn and I would get sassy. I'm grateful you gave and showed me the love I deserve to be given. I know I deserve to be with someone who loves and adores me for who l am.

And I'm sorry Armando for not being the best girlfriend to you. I'm sorry for overwhelming you. I'm sorry for not being more supportive when you needed me to be. I'm sorry for overly caring about your safety. And most importantly I'm sorry for be jealous, and over calling you. I'm sorry for being so much. If only I knew you didn't like it I would've stopped. I hope that through my love, I was able to show you that you were loved by me unconditionally.

I wanted to show you that not all woman take advantage of your kindness. I never once did that. I treated you like a prince. I gave you roses. I bought you birthday gifts, Christmas gifts, surprise gifts because I knew you would love them, I would seriously go dig for hot wheel cars when ever I saw them to find the ones you loved.

It was all worth it to see you happy. But most importantly, I showed you how it is to accept love. That you are so worthy of it. That your past doesn't make you unlovable. That you aren't a disappointment or a mistake. That you deserve to be alive and well. Despite you breaking my heart into pieces. I still admire you for all the struggles you been through growing up.

So the next girl who gets to be in your arms, I hope she loves you the way you need to be loved. That she listens to you when you need it. That she strives to make you happy and smile every single day. That she enjoys all the flowers you will gift her. That she appreciates the little kisses you give, The way you will hold her hand. That she loves the way you caress her when she is sad.

That she adores the laughs from you when you tell her a stupid joke. That her heart beats fast when she sees you waiting for her. That she snuggles up with you in bed. That she feels like a princess when you open all the doors for her. That she loves the way your face scrunches up when you make your silly face. That she admires how you show and give gifts. I hope when your favorite songs plays, she sings it with you and you smile at her and you sneak in a small kiss on her hand like how we both did once. I hope you take her on all the trips we planned together. That you will go back to universal studios and wrestling events.

I hope both of you are happy driving and cruising through the night. Just like how we once did. That each time you guys are together, you fall in love with her deeply. That you keep your promise in loving her in every single lifetime you will have. Like how you once said to me. That you learn to adore her. That you never lie to her. That you will make it your mission to make her happy and smile every single day. I hope that she treats your family with so much love and appreciation. Your parents are one of the most sweetest people I've met. Your sisters are amazing. It shows just how much you love them. I hope she helps you heal from the pain and helps you bring your light back into your life.

That she treats you the way you deserve to be treated. That she doesn't treat you like garbage. That she shows you that you are worthy of sincere love. That you are so capable in fulfilling your dreams. Because know you can.

You can and will finish college, you will fix your car, you will see both sisters graduate high school. You will find another job that will pay you better. That life will bless you in a better situation. That you will feel better. It hurts letting you go, because I really didn't want this ending for us. I wished you still loved me like before. Because I don't understand why you stopped loving.

Especially when despite the breakup, my love for you only grew more for you. I'll always love you. In every single lifetime I'm blessed with. I'll always fall madly in love with you even if it means it will end exactly the same. I wish you didn't mistreat me in the worst way. I wish you knew how to appreciate my love. I wish that your mentality wasn't the way it was towards the end. But the heart break was worth

experiencing that love we had. And I'll never regret it. Loving you was never a waste. It was a pleasure to love you even when you didn't love me.

-@_marleyyy_

Lessons

———— ❖❖❖ ————

So it started in my freshmen year when I met this really cute girl in orientation, I didn't see her ever again after that until sophomore year I still thought she was very cute so I decided to go for it and ask for her instagram, she gave it to me and we started talking for a couple of months, but it was on and off so I didn't really think she was interested because I was putting all the effort in, but one day I just said to myself "fuck it if I don't tell her how I feel someone is gonna beat me to it" so I told her and she said she didn't expect it but at the time she said she wasn't looking for someone, fast forward like a week, and she now has a bf, I was like wtf why she say she doesn't want a relationship and then she gets into one, so for months I was hurting because like every time I try to get at a girl they either stop talking to me for no reason or I'm Too slow and I don't tell them how I feel fast enough, so I was just overthinking myself to sleep for like a month thinking About what is wrong with me or what I did wrong, but then I realized that it wasn't my fault, It was like a sudden realization that this new generation of girls don't give a fuck about what type of guy you are as long as you have money and take them out they are happy.

@jc_.510

I Hate It All

I hate it all I hate how i've put you on a pedestal i hate how you've changed me I hate the person i've become because of you I hate that you are on my mind at all times I hate how I wanted nothing to do with you a few years ago and now you're all I ever think about I hate how all of this is irreversible I hate how we never dated and it's affecting me this much I hate how I let this affect me I hate how attached I get I hate how much I want from you I hate how I stay I hate how I keep going back knowing it's not benefitting me I hate how we say I love you I hate that I love you I hate how I lose sleep over you I hate this all I hate how you know all the right things to say I hate how I accept your apologies without a second thought i hate how you know you should treat me better I hate how I know I do deserve better I hate how I don't want better because I want you I hate how I find comfort and familiarity in you and the way you treat me I hate the way i've normalized the shitty treatment I hate that I look for you in everyone I hate that there's no one else like you I hate that I want to move on but I cannot for the life of me I hate the thought of starting again with someone else I hate how I only want you I hate it all but I don't hate you.

-Anon

The One I Always Wanted

━━━━━━━━━━ ◀▸●◀▸ ━━━━━━━━━━

I t all started with him.Back in 4th grade I met this boy named Rob, he would listen to me talk for hours and he wouldn't even get tired.He loved me to the point where he will do anything for me,We started talking the night of July 5th 2020,I opened up to him about my my SH and depression at such a young age and he was with me at every step I took, we would call, we would laugh together ,we would make jokes, we would do anything together even if I didn't feel like getting up in the mornings he would always be there calling me and telling me to get up and go eat something.

A year later we started 5th grade together, same teacher, same homeroom, same everything.We were still the the same old duo everyone knew and shipped together but I never caught up that he developed feelings for me ,He was my ride or die.I never told him I had feelings for him cause I was scared he didn't like me or he thought I wasn't pretty enough or just not good enough for him so I forced myself not to fall for him again, until one day everything changed.

A boy named Amir transferred into our school he

immediately caught my eye so we started talking for a couple weeks and one day he just asked me out.I said yes because I liked him but something just felt so wrong My heart would shatter when Rob stared at me and him together so I knew I made a mistake so I broke up with Amir because I realized Rob was the only one I wanted, he understood me, he was always there for me, he helped me and most of all he healed me. Me and Amir broke up because it felt so wrong and Rob was what I really ever wanted but one day everything changed, my life changed. I finally decided to tell him I had feelings for him and I was so sorry for everything that happened but right as I told him I was in love with him he told me he found a girl he really liked and he thought that was the one for him.

Fast forward we enter middle school 6th grade I remember the first week of school I wrote a letter to him saying how I was so sorry about choosing Amir over him,I felt so bad I wrote him a whole paragraph.The next day in class he gave me a letter saying "You played a really big role in my life, you were there when I needed you but I wanted to tell u that maybe we can try in the future but right now i have to stay loyal to my girlfriend I'm sorry but I love you" I immediately started to overthink everything at that moment of how I really messed up but fast forward a couple months later we were in class and we would just stare at each other like if we wanted to tell each other something but something was holding us back.

That moment in my life I knew I couldn't go back and fix my mistakes so I decided to keep things to myself from that point on but then we moved to 7th grade and he changed.Rob changed he lost interest at even looking at me, being around me, and interacting with me. I loved that boy so much with all my heart but I knew I hurt him, I wish I could go back in time and fix things but I know it isn't possible but if he ever gets across this just know it was you that I ever really wanted. I always loved you Rob and I still do.(Ps:"The night we met" will always be your song.)

Katie The Girl From Meridian

When COVID started I thought the world was going to end because I was 11 and I thought I might as well make sum new friends from around the country so I downloaded this app called wink (they have now rebranded to soda) and I started trying to get new friends. I found this one girl Katie. She was from Meridian Idaho which I thought was pretty cool because I'm from a place with another town nearby called Meridian.

So I added her I said hi all the normal stuff and I asked her (because her bio said 6'0) if she was actually 6'0 and she said yes and I responded with that's slightly taller than me. Fast forward 2 years I completely forget about that app on my phone and I find it again and decide to look through it one last time before I delete it forever I see that Katie has her Instagram linked to her wink account so I add her on Instagram and we don't really talk for another 2 years just meaningless conversations swiping up on each others story every few months till. January 4 2024 I see sh.. Posts on her story that she's in the hospital for a low potassium levels and being the smart ass that I am I swipe up and say "1 singular banana could have prevented this" which she send replies "apparently it wasn't because my potassium was too low it was because of something to do with my illness. And we talk about her unknown illness till like 2 am my time 3 am her time. I tell her that I have to go to bed and that I'll talk to her tomorrow and she says ok and I go to bed. I wake up and text her good morning she replies almost immediately good morning how did you sleep? I tell her that I slept amazing and she says that's nice and we continue to talk but now it's getting more interesting things like what do you do for fun, What would do if you won the lottery, Favorite hobbies, shit like that and this goes on for a few more days thinking nothing of it just normal conversation stuff.

Then I tell her that I'm going on a trip to Japan and tell her about kanji structures, how One symbol could mean whole words and she sends me a voice message saying "that sounds like a pain in the ass" which I reply "yeah it is, but you have a really soothing voice yk that" and then from that point on we just start flirting day and night for 10 days straight calling for hours at a time then on January 15th after one of our calls end I tell her "love you sleep well" and she replies "Goodnight love ttyl" my heart soars at this moment because I didn't think that she liked me at all I thought she was just tolerating my presence but the funny thing was is I don't think she remembers our old conversations on wink so she doesn't know what I look like and my Instagram pfp isn't me and I reply "really? You don't even know what I look like" she replies "I don't care you're the sweetest most kind person I've ever met and I'm so sad that I can't be there in person with you to be able to give you 100% of my love and affection but when I do see you in person you better bet I'm gonna make I call her back immediately and ask her if she means it and that if she actually loves me she says "ofc baby I love you limitlessly and endlessly" I start crying happy tears but she doesn't know that and she says "what's the matter baby" I reply through my tears " I didn't think you actually cared about me I thought you just tolerated me and that you were flirting with me because you felt bad for me" she replies with " and why would I do that my love " I reply through sobs " I don't know some people are cruel and mean" she replies with "not me I'm a complete lover girl" I reply with "I love you so much" she replies with "I love you too baby " and with that we started dating Everyday we would call from 7 pm to 7 am PST sometimes we could talk for hours other times we would just sit in complete silence and fall asleep in each others presence and sometimes she would sing for me to help me go to sleep because I have in person school while she has online school her favorite song to sing to me and play on her guitar was fade into you by mazzy star and she had the voice of an angel it never failed to make me fall asleep within 2 times of her singing the song.

That's how life was for 2 months till her phone got taken away I didn't know that and I thought she was avoiding me I got blocked on Instagram which I didn't know I thought it got deleted for some reason so I got nervous I started texting her number texting her Snapchat trying to see what was going on and what I did wrong for her to act in such a way. She got her phone taken away on a Thursday and next Friday she got it back and texted me back saying "sorry my mom took my phone away" I responded with "thats Fine but I wish you would give me a warning so I don't have to stress". She responds with"sorry it was out of the blue so I couldn't warn you" I responded with "okay that's fine why did you get her phone taken away " she said "I don't want to talk about it" and me not wanting to push her I never mention it again and I started she was being more and more distant as time went on it got so bad that she wouldn't talk to me unless I started the conversation and every time I wanted to call she had a reason to not to. So on March 14 2024 I told her "happy 2 month anniversary" she replies with " I didn't know we were still dating" at this point my heart is already crushed into a million pieces and I text her "why would you think that" she text back with "I was gone for a week" and I text back with "why would I move on after we never broke up and you were gone for a week?" She texts back with "idk" and at this point I don't text back for a few hours trying to clear my head and think about what To say and I come back to a screenshot from my friend on her Instagram story calling another boy cute and my heart was even more broken I thought she had just lost feelings for me which is fine but she had cheated on me I texted her the screenshot and asked her " why didn't you tell me that you didn't like me anymore and why did you block me on Instagram" at this point she said it plain and simple that she didn't have any romantic feelings for me anymore and that she couldn't do long distance anymore (even though we were only 1 state away from each other (Washington and Idaho) I said ok and said some things I shouldn't have said but it was the heat of the moment and I wasn't happy in the slightest. So we broke up and she blocked me on everything over the next few weeks I cried for hours per day crying myself to sleep my grades dropping dramatically and my teachers started to notice

67

and asked me what was going on and I told them what was happening i told my friends never told my family except my sister who thought Katie was a really cool and good person for me. The school year ended with my grades going from all A's to 3 D's a c- b- and A-. It still hurts to this day that someone I cared for so deeply could do me this dirty is such a short period of time.

-@gabriel._.snyders

Self Worth Over Heartbreak

I added this guy and we started talking he was so sweet we went out together and i loved him he always understood me my friends told me it was a love boom i didn't believe that cuz no way he would do that but now I know they were right i went with my friends to the mall n he already told me his at home but then i found him in a mall with another girl i saw him but didn't go to him i went home and i was about to cry but I remembered i shouldn't be crying over a man who cheated cuz I know my self worth cuz once i feel disrespected you will never see me again.

The Right Person Wrong Life

In summer 2022 I fell in love with this girl she was my first love I had relationships before her but she truly changed my perspective on what love is on what it feels like to have someone care for you and what it's like being in a actual like serious relationship to actually have a partner in life and not just a "girlfriend" she truly taught me what it meant to have a significant other she helped me through things no one else has after we broke up she texted like a month later and she told me that she had been thinking of me a lot during that week and I remember that I too was thinking about her more then usual so in a way I think that maybe we were something special but for some reason it just never truly did work out the way we wanted it to but as they say she was the right person but I met her at the wrong time when I met her I was going through stuff that made me not be able to settle down into a relationship we where off and on for months and unlike other relationships I never truly got bored of her in a week from now we've been broken up for 2 years and for some reason I still think about her almost ever day if not everyday she's in a new relationship and I truly am happy for her you know at least she's happy.

One Week In Vegas Love That Almost Was

***

L imerence". A word that I never understood until i had it happen to me a few months ago... anyways, my name is Marc and this is my story about how I fell in love with a girl within a week... the story starts with me and my family in Las Vegas, the city that never sleeps. We were on vacation to visit some family and bury my dad next to my grandparents. Plus we haven't been on a vacation in years so it was perfect timing... we had already been in Vegas for a couple of days when my uncle decides to rent a hotel room for the night at the very well known MGM grand, the place where most boxing ppv happen. Anyways, We head there that same morning he booked the hotel room and arrive shortly in the afternoon, after grabbing something to eat along the way. This is the part I'll always remember... we head through the entrance to the cave, which was a mini shopping mall under the MGM grand hotel, and I saw a Harley Davison store which by the way is my all time favorite motorcycle brand and as I was looking into the store and quickly looking through as we walked past. there she was. A pretty Latina girl who I never would have guessed have so much significance to my growth as a person... all I can remember is walking past and seeing her and catching myself kinda staring at her as we walked past. I'm pretty thankful that she didn't catch me this time, but hold up there's more.... We finally arrive at the check-in desk and waited in the lobby while my uncle sorted out the room. All I could think about was how pretty she was and how I would actually like to talk to her... Shortly after, my uncle meets up with us and we head up to the room. I wasted no time, I was scared she was getting off soon so 1 dropped my stuff and I mean literally dropped it and headed right back down to the Harley Davison store... It was almost too perfect because it was just her in the store when I got there, but I'm not gonna lie, it took me a good 15-20 minutes until I finally "picked out a shirt"... nah I was actually prepping myself to go and talk to her and so I found my shirt and went up to pay... I kinda forgot how we started talking but I could remember saying I was on vacation and that I'm from Canada, I also remember how I dropped my money on the ground like a dumbass in front of her but I managed to recover by picking up a Canadian dollar and gave it to her and said "here's a souvenir from Canada" and I remember her taking it in such an adorable way. So I bought my shirt and left without asking for her number because I was too scared and wasn't thinking but before I left I told her my name, she tells me hers and I head back up to the hotel room. remember getting back to the room and my sister asking me about what I bought and I show her the new Harley Davison shirt, but she noticed I looked a bit cheery inna way and asked what happened and so I tell her about who 1 met. I also tell her about how I was scared to ask for her number and yeah my sister laughed and said I'm dumb but she said to go back.

I was too scared and embarrassed at this point for not making that move so 1 planned to go back the next day to go "buy another shirt" and which I did but this time tho, she wasn't working, it was a nice man who looked in his late 50s who helped me out on finding a new shirt. I went to pay and we end up talking a little more about motorcycles and during the conversation I managed to slip in and ask about the pretty Latina girl I met the day before. I asked him if I was able to leave my number and Instagram for her which was totally he said was cool, "we have me some scrap receipt paper you can write it on" he says. And I wrote both my Instagram and number down on it, he took it and put it in a sealed envelope and said "I wouldn't wanna get her all embarrassed but I can't promise not to tease her" and he did keep that promise I'm not gonna lie. I left the store and went back up to mv hotel room and that was that.. so lets fast forward a day or two, my family and I were leaving Vegas and was heading out to California for the other portion of our vacation. After a long 5 hour car ride, we arrive to west Covina, California where my uncle lives... we had spent the day there just wondering around the city and we eventually stop at the Filipino food market to grab some goods for our bbq tonight. Shortly after, we got back to my uncles spot and he starts whipping up the best carne asada's, I mean I'm from Canada, we don't have nothing like California does sadly. But anyways. We all ate shortly after and now everyone is now drinking. I don't really drink myself so I was just chilling out on the porch with my uncle and smoking a little and that's when I got a notification on my phone from Instagram saying I have a message request. I opened my phone to see who it was, when I checked, it was her, the girl from the Harley Davison store. When I saw her message, was honestly so scared to reply to her, so yeah. It took me about 40 minutes until I replied and "actually saw her message". I still remember the smile I had on my face when I replied back to her. After exchanging a few messages, I finally said to her "I'm sorry if this is weird, but I thought you were very pretty" | thought it was endgame and I was just gonna be left on seen but nope, she tells me that she was thankful for my comment and how she was actually hoping I'd come back to give her my number when we first met, and teases me a little about it. After a little, she then says she would like to see me again. So I finally gained my confidence and asked her out on a date, and of course she said yes... So I'm enjoying my time in California, her and I were texting each other mostly every day after that night she first messaged me. After a week passed, I was headed back to Vegas for the last 3 days of my trip and also to go on my date with this girl. Before we left. We made a stop at a cemetery in long beach to bury my dads ashes alongside my grandparents, which was what he wanted. I kind of find it a little ironic because at the time, I felt like my dad was the one to send this girl to me. But I never thought he was actually teaching me a lesson through her. Ok back to the story. We head out in separate cars and I decide to ride in my other uncles Subaru! And there we were, on another 5 hour car ride back to Las Vegas.. the girl and I were messaging back and forward trying to figure out what we could do on our date so we both agreed to walk around the Fremont strip and maybe grab something to eat... arrive at my uncles house where I didn't waste a second and got ready as fast as I can. The rest of my family finally arrive when I just had hopped out the shower and my sister was waiting on me to get ready so that we could go. I remember that the girl messaged me saying that she was ready and that she's good to go any time, so my sister and I head out to go pick her up. We finally get to her house and I walk up to her front door where she meets me and we both walk into her house so I could meet her mom. Her mother greets me in Spanish, I managed to respond in Spanish, thankfully because French and Spanish share similar words. And I managed to make a good first impression on her mom, I had noticed her brother watching hockey, to be honest, I still feel like he was watching it because he knew his sister was going on a date with a Canadian. Anyways, him and I talk a little about hockey and how I use to play back in high school during my off season for football and so I think I made a good first impression on her family. Thankfully I wasn't awkward as I usually am... After her family and I were done chatting, I say my goodbyes and thank them for their hospitality, her and I walked to the car where she met my sister, they introduce each other and we head off to the Fremont strip. We got there and decided to have my sister drop us off at the golden nugget, I say thank you to my sister and my sister wishes me good luck and so my date with this pretty Latina starts... We were walking into the middle entrance of the Fremont strip and we both noticed how crowded it was that night, i mean they weren't lying when they said it was the city that never sleeps. As we were walking, we kept getting split up by the crowds walking and also watching the buskers perform their act, i remember grabbing her hand and leading the way until we finally got through all of that foot traffic!, I noticed her still holding onto my hand and I said "it's ok if you don't wanna hold my hand anymore" and she replied with "no, it's ok, I like holding your hand" so I just went with it knowing full well my heart was racing for the past 30 minutes. We decided to find a quiet area to sit down for a little so we could figure out a place to grab something to eat. We never ended up settling on a place to eat which was my fault because I got lost in our conversation and having a little fun teasing her because she would hide her face every time I called her cute or beautiful, it was just adorable. I also gave her a power keychain from chainsaw man and after all the laughs, we walked to a nearby cvs to grab a drink because I guess we laughed ourselves to dehydration, not literally but you know what I mean. Anyways, I pay for our drinks and we decide to walk around again and look for another place to sit. We find a place on the second floor of the strip shortly after, it kinda worked in my favorite because I kinda wanted to find a place where not many people would walk past so it was perfect. We decided to sit on the stairs leading up to the third floor and we talked and joked with each other for another two or three hours. While I was kinda teasing her, I ask her if she was ok and if she was bored in which she reassured me that she wasn't and that she was having fun. As a joke I kept repeating "are you sure?" And she would sarcastically say "actually yeah, Iam" and let out a cute giggle right after. And at the end I finally asked her if I could kiss her. And she replied "yeah, I think you can" and both of us shared a kiss that I will never forget. It was almost straight out of an Anime. During the kiss, I noticed that she kinda was off rhythm which I found adorable by the way and later I found out that I was actually her first kiss and that this is her first date when I asked about it, but I asked in a nice but teasing type of way but I really wanted to know! Another hour passed by and I noticed that she was getting a little tired when she yawned, I asked if she wanted to go home and she nodded but also said "I also don't wanna leave". I said that it was ok and that it wouldn't be the last time we saw each other and so we ordered an Uber to pick us up and bring us back to her house. We both got up and head down to the location where the Uber would pick us up and funny thing was that the Uber pulled in as soon as we got there! We hopped in and cuddled in the back and she fell asleep in my arms for majority of the ride. It was cute, she would wake up and smile at me because she was a little embarrassed. After a 20 minute car ride back we arrive at her house. She asked me if I wanted to come in while I waited for my Uber, I was kinda iffy on it so l asked "are you sure your mom would be ok with me coming in?"and she said that it would be fine because "I pay rent" she says, I laughed and said okay and we head into her house and straight to her room, but had to be super quiet because her brother was passed out on the couch watching TV... So when we got to her room, I sat on her bed while she cleaned a little, which by the way, her room wasn't messy at all, but anyways, she sat down on the bed next to me and we kinda sat awkwardly in silence for a good minute but kept laughing when we met each others glance. I grabbed her hand and gently pulled her closer to me and then placed my hand around her waist. I looked into her eyes and just couldn't stop myself from falling at this point, yes, I was falling for her in that very moment. I slowly went in for another kiss but this time, the kiss was a little more passionate, I had to stop myself from taking it further knowing it would also be her first time so l didn't want to rush that, we stopped and I laid on her chest for a little and I mumbled "I think I love you" hoping she wouldn't hear, then she replied "I love you too" and I smiled while she played with my hair... After a while, it was about three

AM in the morning and she was getting really tired so I called an Uber, I hated that the Uber was only 3 minutes away from her house but I made the most of it at least, because I didn't think this would be my last time holding her. I wouldn't let her go and kept telling her how much I'm gonna miss her when I have to go back to Canada in two days and she would say "I'm gonna be here when you come back, I promise", i wish she never promised me that. The Uber arrives and she walks me out and to the car, I gave her one last kiss and went back to my uncles, of course I was sad during the car ride. I was wishing I had more time with her... Alright so this is where the plot of my story starts to twist. Two days after our date, I was at the airport waiting to board my flight, her and I were on the phone with each other and I was talking to her the whole time I was waiting. We were kinda having a deep conversation about how I felt about her and that I really would like her to be my girlfriend. Oh I forgot to mention. I asked her to be my girlfriend when we were in her room and she said she would be happy to be mine. Anyways.I asked her if she was really sure about being in a relationship with me especially knowing it would be long distance for the first part and she replied with "I knew what I was getting into, so of course of sure" she also went on to reassure her feelings towards me and more. I also remember her telling me that she was also going to EDC that following weekend. I told her that sounds really amazing because I've always wanted to go to that festival and so we went on talking about how we wanna go to so many EDM festivals like Tomorrowland and ultra music festival!. After an hour, my flight was called and we started boarding the plane. Thankfully I was sitting next to my siblings this time because I had to sit next to random stranger on the way there. I was still on the phone with her but I had my camera on so she knew I couldn't really hear her. After we sat down, I had to end the call but I remember her blowing me a kiss before hanging up, I texted her before we took off "I love you" and put my phone on airplane mode... A few days have past since I've been back home in Canada and everything between her and I seemed pretty good and we kept communicating back and forward, she tells me that she might not be able to message me during the weekend coming up because of how bad the cell reception is at festivals, which was EDC weekend. Which I was okay with but of course I had that feeling in the back of my head that things would change between us after the event is over. she was kinda messaging me and sending me pics of her outfits before she would have to go, she looked so amazing I'm not gonna lie. The weekend passes and we're now on the Monday after the event, she doesn't text me the whole day so of course my mind started to race a little but I was also tryna give her the benefit of the doubt. I let it slide because I thought that maybe she was just tired from the festival and she's been sleeping! But it kept kinda going on the more the week would pass on. I finally decided to ask her about it and I guess I worded my message pretty straight forward, so l felt like I messed up a bit, she replies hours later saying that nothing had happen at EDC and that she hasn't done nothing in that aspect, but she now started feeling like we rushed things. I called her and we moved the conversation to the phone. I tell her that it's my fault if she feels that way because I am the one who asked her to be my girlfriend so quickly in the first place, she reassures me and says that she's also one to Blame because she was just excited to have her first boyfriend, she then suggested we breakup and take things slow but still have the same relationship but just without the labels but she also adds how she would like to get back together when she's ready. I understood and agreed because I wasn't trying to force her into something she wasn't ready for. I was glad we got to talk that out because I was just super confused about what was going on, and really thought we were gonna break up... A week had passed since that conversation and things felt kinda off. we weren't talking as much as we use to, I mean she would message me, but it just didn't feel the same and more like she felt forced to. To kind of break the silence, I asked if she wanted to hop on Gentian Impact with me, and so she did. Things felt kinda good and like how it was when we first met. She was teasing me about my low level and I was teasing her about her adorable accent. But I didn't know that this would be our last genuine moment as two strangers who fell in love with one another. After a long three hour session, we told me that she was getting tired but to call her so that she could fall asleep on the phone with me. She wasn't even in her bed for more than ten minutes, she was talking one moment and then in a split second, she's passed out. I laughed and said "I love you" also not knowing it would be my last one she'd ever hear it come from my voice... as the days passed by, she grew more distant towards me, I'm not saying that she's obligated to but she went from not letting a message hit an hour to leaving me on delivered for hours, and even wouldn't get one until she's going to bed. Again, she's not obligated to by any means, tend to me nor message me as soon as possible! But due to my past relationships, I started to grow a little bit suspicious that things aren't good between us and in my head, all I could think about how maybe she did meet someone at

EDC but that's because I tend to overthink things... I test the waters by letting a few days pass by and just giving her space. After that few days, I gained some confidence and asked her if things were ok between us and kinda told her about how she's been really distant with me this past week. The first thing she reassured me on was the fact that she didn't do anything or met anyone while she was there and that she was being loyal, I kinda found it reliving even though it may have not been true, but I only say that because it was a question I was gonna try to follow up with. She then also explains to me that she's been having realizations about herself and that she "may not be attracted to men" and how she may have found that out through me, she didn't really say much beyond that and just kept her message short, so then I asked "did you want to just end things between us?" And she said that she doesn't want to but she also doesn't want to keep leading me on, my heart sank to my stomach and I kinda panicked, I asked to call her because I was just having a hard time trying to process things when just a week ago, she was asking me if we could take things slow and how she would like to get back together in the future. After I sent that text, she didn't respond. So I kinda took it as she was ignoring me, and I'll admit it, I bombarded her a little by blowing up her phone with long and short messages. I gave up finally and stopped trying to push so I threw in the towel. The next day she doesn't reply until the afternoon, which is morning in Vegas. She replied a short message basically replying to only one of the many messages I sent the night before, and says that she's ok. I kinda took it as she didn't care. And didn't care that we just ended our relationship literally the night before. And till this day, I feel like this is why she left. My dumbass left her on read because I felt like my feeling weren't

82

being reciprocated. And now we're at the beginning of the end of my story with this beautiful girl. We stop talking, and she unfollows me on pretty much everything. Fortnite included sadly. And so my mind starts to race again, It was starting to settle in that were just gonna become strangers again... and so 1 would try to message her and win her back, knowing damn well that I lost already. After a week and a half of trying to message her and being left on seen, she finally replies, "I'm sorry but there's not much I can really say. You said you didn't want to be friends so I think it's just best we both move on, I'm sorry but this will be the last message I send you but I thank you for all of the memories" I didn't reply back because I didn't think she wanted one and so I just left it at that... after 2-3 weeks 1 finally decide to message her a finally goodbye and wish her well in life and whoever she finds later on, I told her how beautiful our memories together are to me and how much I will cherish them forever. I told her that I loved her even if she never felt the same and that I'll always be thankful for having her, even if our time was short lived. After I sent the text I left to my nephews football game and 2 hours later, I get back home and check my phone. She blocked me, she drove the last nail in and left with no reply... closing the final chapter to a story about how I fell in love with a stranger I met at a Harley Davison store at the MGM grand, in one week... I'm not sure if this is even a case limerence after fully writing this all out or if this is just a case of "the right person, wrong time" I wish it was her in the end, but life doesn't give you what you want. But it does give you things you do deserve... It's been 3 months since the whole heartbreak and I can't really say that I'm happier but I also can't say that I'm sadder about the whole situation. But I think I'm finally just learning how to accept my defeat. I'm learning how to love myself again and being alone in general. I want to fix the many things I need working on so that I'd be more prepared for later on... As a way of me letting go, I released a single on all platforms and named it "VEGAS GIRL (RUNAWAY)" which portrays the emotions I faced during it. My name is TOKYOXO if you

were wondering by the way. And I plan to take my music far. Call me hopeless but I do hope my music reaches her again and maybe in a small glimpse she'll think about me. But like in my song "I'm a ghost wondering up in your mind"... Ps. If this reaches you, just know that I love you and that I hope you've been doing good. I miss you so much but I know it isn't my place to reach out. I don't blame you nor do I hate you but i won't lie and say it didn't hurt so much. It broke me in a way. I think you took that loving side of me with you when you left. Because I feel like I can't love anymore like I how I fell for you... I hope you stay true to whoever takes your heart and I hope they love you just as much as I do. You will always be that beautiful Latina girl who was pretending to fold shirts just so I wouldn't notice her looking at me... I love you white. Promise me you'll see Japan...

-Marc

Love?

——— ❖◦❖ ———

The strange concept of romantic love always rattled me as a child. Not having a definite demonstration of romance at home as my parents split when I was young. Gratefully I did experience familial love with my parents and sister, always saying I love you and never going to bed without a kiss goodnight but I always daydreamed of a perfect "love", a person to claim as my lover and be my happily ever after.

Believing that love was only accessible to a lucky few, as the beautiful princesses on screen married their princes and had no issues at all happy they were and little did I know there was much more to love than one glance and a fancy carriage… growing up I think I didn't feel like the prettiest child, all people my age already being in relationships and I was left wondering when my turn would come.Waiting, imagining, yearning till when I stopped searching It came unexpectedly.Freshman year of high school my best friend and I had signed up for tennis as a joke, we began getting more involved and getting to know our team I met someone, a girl.

A girl? I thought.I was always open to the idea of

experimenting with my sexuality as I have two moms and it was an accepted concept in my family, however the opportunity never presented itself to me.Little did I know it was going to be the most life changing experience of my young years.The excitement of being wanted was so healing to me, I felt like I was in a fairytale, sharing beautiful moments like my first kiss, my first date and so much more with her. In my parents eyes I became rebellious and for a time damaged my relationship with them, 1 didn't care because I was happy but after a while I realized I had to balance my family and my relationship.After balancing my relationships I thrived in a fruitful time.

The most important thing I learned however was that love can be misinterpreted as a perfect union however that couldn't be further from the truth, love is messy, it's the willingness to forgive, the willingness to put one's pride aside and the willingness to be accepting of another's imperfections. It truly is an unmatched experience everyone on this earth deserves to feel.As the saying goes "it is better to have loved and lost than never to have loved at all"for the time it is present cherish it as everyone thrives of love, whether it be self-love, familial love, platonic love, romantic love. Love makes humans well, human and it is crucial and amazing.

-Arlene @arlnfp

The Heartbreak of First Love

First day of middle school, the day had passed and it was time to go to fifth period, as I was walking towards a group of boys only one caught my eye. the most handsome boy I've ever seen. as I continue walking around them in the hallway I hear one of them say "where's your girl?" so I lost interest but I had a feeling that my heart still belonged to him. a few weeks pass by and I decided to tell my best friend. We've been best friends since 3rd grade so I trusted her.

After class a ran up to her and told her that I liked him. She seemed shocked..but I thought it was because I told her I liked him. I ignored it and asked her to put me on with him because he didn't have a girlfriend anymore and I've liked him for such a long time. She did and turns out we both liked each other! I was so happy. Soon enough he asked me out in the hallway. I'll always remember that day. We started dating but it was really awkward because i didn't know how to communicate, my best friend was really interested in our relationship but I thought I was because she was my best friend and that's what best friends do.

Everyday after school we would text and ask each other how our day was. He was always dry and seemed like he had no interest or energy into talking to me but i didn't really notice because of how much I wanted to talk to him. We didn't really talk at school because I was really nervous and shy. After Halloween we were texting each other but we were both really dry. The spark wasn't there anymore. I knew that he had lost interest. The next day of school as I was leaving third period all of my friends from a different class keep asking me if we broke up or if anything happened between us and I said no, I asked them why.. they said because he asked out my "best friend" and that he was saying he broke up with me.. my heart dropped. I was so confused. We didn't even get to break up!. I froze when I heard those words coming out of my friends mouths. As I was turning to another hallway I saw him.

We made eye contact but I froze even more than I already was. My "best friend" was walking with him but quickly walked beside me acting like nothing had happened. While I was walking she was comforting me, saying how sorry she was for him breaking up w me. During class my eyes were watering, I wasn't paying attention to the class nor the teacher. I was zoned out thinking about what had just happened. My eyes started watering even more so I asked to go to the bathroom. Once I got there I started balling my eyes out, I tried to be silent but I couldn't. I was so hurt I couldn't hold it in anymore. I hear footsteps walking towards my stall.

I realize it was my best friend Erza. She started asking me if I was okay which just made me cry even more. I told her what had happened and she let me cry in her arms. After a couple minutes we had to go to class.When I stepped foot in class everybody was asking me if I was okay because my eyes were puffy and pink. I tried to hold in my tears as I said yeah. I would always see them hugging and talking to each other.

I was so sick and tired so I told her that we should just stop being friends. I missed her so much but I would always tell myself not to because of what she did. A few months go by and I'm over him I just miss him a lot and they're still dating. She texted me, she said how much she missed me and how sorry she was for doing what she did. But that didn't change the fact that she did what she did. I told her that I missed her to but I don't know if she meant it by "I'm sorry".

She told me that she is breaking up with him to save our friendship. I didn't know if she was saying the truth but she was. She sent me a screenshot of the breakup message so I believed her. We started to be friends again and I was so happy. It felt like I didn't have a knot in my stomach anymore. The rest of school was normal and me and him started to be more comfortable with each other and I knew I didn't hate him I just hated what he did. We became close friends and school ended so during summer i didn't text him or have any contact.

I decided to look at his repost and it seemed like he was at a low point. I decided to text him since i worried about him. He told me about how he wasn't feeling really good and how no one ever texted him but me, he said how he deleted everyone's contact except mine, it made me feel some type of way... We kept on talking and I realize my love for him never ended. I made video about him and he saw it. He knew it was about him. He texted me later that day and said how he also has feelings for me, and he wants to try again. I said yes because he meant so much to me and I'd love to try again with him. We started dating and everything went well.

He was always telling me how much he loves me and how I he wanted to go places with me. I was so happy. He was like the person that was keeping me together. I decided to check his repost one day and I see he reposted a girl. It bothered me but I didn't confront him. The video was repeating in my head. She was pretty, prettier than me. I confronted him and he said that it was just because of the sound, I knew it was just an excuse because he's told me how beautiful and pretty she was when we were friends. I shamed it off. I didn't want it to affect my mood but it did either way.

I decided to take a nap. I woke up to a message. "hey. I'm sorry about us. You know and how I've been treating you. I'm sorry. I really am you don't deserve me. you deserve better". My heart sinked. I couldn't believe it, I texted him repeatedly but he never answered. He finally answered and all he said was "hi" like nothing happened. I asked him what he meant by that even though I clearly knew. He said that I know what he meant and I deserve so much better and how he isn't in the position to date anyone. I didn't respond because I was confused. How is he gonna get with me and then say that??.. He said he just needed some alone time. I left him alone. We didn't talk for days which killed me. He texted me and said "well this is where our road ends. love you Camila talk to you soon" "I love u more. bye." I thought that was the last time we were ever gonna talk, but he texted me later. "I miss you" I hearted it.

I missed him too but i didn't want him to know that but I told him I missed him too either way. He was being flirty with me and he was complimenting me. He said that Godspeed by Frank Ocean reminded him of me. My heart melted. I couldn't stop smiling. He was so sweet. Then he said "I don't say this a lot but I want to keep you around forever". I believed him. I loved him so much at the moment. I said I wanted to keep him around forever and lock him in a closet so he won't leave me.

We kept on talking and he said this Halloween we could go together. I said yes and we kept talking about us and how even though we're not together we'll always be there for each other. He kept texting me and he was saying how beautiful I am and how he can't stop admiring me. "thank u baby". I told him. I had to go to bed so I told him "I have to go to bed baby good night sweet dreams I love u " he said it back. I remember still smiling. I had gone to bed expecting the same energy the next day. The next day i didn't have my phone so I couldn't text him. I tried texting him but he never answered. The only time he did answer he either took hours to respond or it just felt like he didn't want to talk to me. It affected my mood a lot. I tried texting him because I was at my worst at that point, the message turned green. He blocked me. I was so confused and angry. I left it alone. A couple days after that I realized he had been dating someone. He lied to me. That night I had cried myself to sleep thinking why he had been flirty with me one day and acted like he never knew me the next. I decided to text him, but I couldn't so I told my best friend to tell him to unblock me. Once he unblocked me he said "why did you want to talk to me?" I told him that I needed an explication.

"I just need to know why u lied to me." I didn't get an answer. My anger built up and I started to type faster and faster with tears building up in my eyes. I told him how I've always defended his name no matter what terms we've been on. I defended his name while I was blocked. "no one will ever love you like how I did." He couldn't even text me back because he knew i was saying the truth. "i was at my lowest. i blocked you so that i can forget about the past. you don't know what I've been through Camilla".

We kept arguing. I told him something i didn't wanna say but I had to. "I don't wanna say this but…. I thought we would work out. I really did.." I couldn't anymore. I was so angry and exhausted of all the lies. Then he said something that shattered me. "and I can't go back to you, I just can't" "k I'll leave u alone, something I should've done in the first place." I fell for it again. It repeated, the same thing.

-@cmila.xx23

Emotions of Young Love

I saw this girl at the gym, I have been seeing her for years but something about her, her energy was completely different and extremely attractive last year. I decided to talk to her one day and my only intentions were to get to know her. We had a lot of small but interesting chats in the gym and eventually i found her I guess.

I decided to ask her if she wanted to grab ice cream. And it was just not gonna happen (she's a brown girl and is not allowed out once its dark). I understood but i really wanted to get to know her and honestly i just wanted to see if we click, i had no bad intentions just wanted see if we can have a good connection between us. I personally don't like chatting a lot and i focus on spending time in person with others so i decided to ask her to come do little things like get boba, ice cream, walk with me but all the time the answer was no bc if studies and parental issues.

We had been talking quite frequently for a long time over insta and i could see that she's starting to get attached and then one day she randomly asked me "yo bro what are your intentions" bc i had been asking her to hang quite a lot of times I let her know that im just trying to get to know her. And she sent me multiple paragraphs talking about how she could only marry guy within her religion and that she had been mistreated in the past. And she also mentioned that she believes a guy never wants to hang out with a girl alone just as friends. At that time i was not too clear about my feelings bc it felt like i didn't know her enough. But i let her know that i have no bad intentions w her, i just wanted to get to feel her vibe and see where things can go cuz personally i feel like theres better things than a relationship out there, even friends are totally cool and can sometimes mean way more than a relationship.

And after that i feel like she felt some refreshing energy bc she got a lot more closer to me and wasn't hiding her soft side anymore. After that for 3 and a half months straight, our friendship was unreal. And I was finally beginning to have genuine feeling for this girl, not in a completely romantic way but i genuinely cared for her and just wanted make her the happiest she could be. And it was clear that she had feelings for me, always wanna spend time with me, always around me in the gym and all. And everything was going good but then the sexual tension between us increased like crazy.

Me personally i just knew about her family beliefs and everything so i never bothered to make a move in any way to try get her be in any sort of relationship w me. But from time to time she took flirting to the next level, and threw clear signs at me that she wanted me. She messaged me one day saying that she was about to message me and hang out earlier that day but she was

94

glad that she didn't. She was home alone and her devious thoughts were going crazy. Even tho it felt good hearing that i was low key scared bc it felt like these thought can lead up to something big and that could potentially ruin the beautiful connection that we have between us. So i decided to have a heart to heart convo with her address my concerns and i actually miss those interactions old days bc sometimes we would stay up till 4 am working everything out and making sure we were on the same page.

That day i told her that we either do something about this tension or just forget about it. She's always been confused about what she wants and she's flipped out on me couple times but it never affected me negatively and lmao it actually made me adore her even more. She ended up saying that she will just forget about it but nothing rlly changed haha the tension was still there and about two weeks later she asked to meet up as she wanted to talk about something.

She asked if we can take this a step further and try friends w benefits and i was honestly so chill w that but we spent about an hour and a half talking about everything and all the possibilities and we made a promise that no matter what our friendship will never die. We did our thing twice (no sex) and second time we did it, she actually got caught driving w me by her family friend. And they let her parents know straight away, she had a hard time w her parents at home and ended up making up an excuse. The next day ofc we decided to end this act of physical intimacy as she had told me that she felt bad doing things behind her parents back and honestly i didn't feel bad but i wanted to end things just cuz i didn't want her living a lie at home. Me personally I'm really transparent w my mum cuz i don't like hiding things from her and i don't want that sense of guilt out of anything i do.

And she's actually really chill about everything excluding addictive things like porn, alcohol and drugs. We broke it off but decided to stay normal as friends and i honestly just wanted to support her through everything and also allow her to have some fun time where she can just relax and wind down. But then the next day she messaged me saying she's about to block me for a while bc everything at that time was too much for her and honestly i supported her through that was and let her do it but it felt super rushed and i felt like our friendship now could've been a lot different if we actually talked about it that day.

I get blocked and i see her almost after 2 weeks for the first time and damn her body language was screaming "get the fuck away from me" she seemed uncomfortable and she had a very repulsive energy around her. This honestly hurt and i just wanted to talk to her about it and i somehow managed to get in contact with her and i was told that she's doing good and that i should be working on moving on. It was confusing and this negative energy lasted for 4 months. In those 4 months i avoided talking about my feelings a lot bc i knew things are bad for her at home and i just wanted to be supportive and be a best friend she would need at that time and ofc I didn't wanna add more worries on her shoulder by talking about my feelings. But i didn't end up talking about a dew things and i was told to just move on. It was strange, sometimes she was really rude and unpredictable which was quite unlike her and i knew she always felt bad after being that way towards me as she apologized to me quite a few times.

To me she was just a little baby and i just want to look after her and decided to be understanding rather than being responsive to negative situations. After sometime things get back to normal at her home and she decides to unblock me and i was hoping for us to get back in that form of friendship we had. But the vibe from her was completely off, and i low key felt heartbroken. She wanted to just be normal friends, i gave her that and she wasn't happy w it. I could just sense that she wants us to be close friends again and i decided to be that way and she loved it.

But now that everything is going completely perfect for her, she decided to start leaving me on seen and opened quite often. I asked her wassup and she said that she's just trynna lower her screen time and social media time. After all those months having to deal w her emotions, i finally lost it. I didn't yell at her or anything but i let her know that its not okay. You have no right treating me like shit from time to time and then come up with a bullshit excuse. I did in a very calm manner rather than being violent bc i just couldn't do her like that. But i let her know that she can treat me however she thinks deserve to be treated and i left it at that. She decided to message me twice in 2 weeks and always ended the chat short and left me on seen. And i had no problem w that i already had a lot of other problems to deal w and a lot of shit had me busy and i also felt like i had detached from her in that way like i still love her like crazy i would be there for her if she ever needs me but if theres nothing to talk about theres no point trying to spark a convo. She messaged me like 5 days after we had last spoken saying hi and i replied saying heyyy luv bc i was actually so excited to talk to her and she was confused, she was like "lmao ur funny dude, u disappear outta nowhere and then u call me luv" and i found that quite offensive as i was the one keeping convos alive. And it slowly turned into an argument, and i was so heartbroken bc it quite unnecessary and she was saying things that i knew she would regret saying later on but once again she said that she had a mood swing and that she was quite out of it.

My way of looking at it is that we are super young and we gotta learn a lot of things. She's just a baby and she needs someone that she can embrace her soft side around. I can forgive her for almost everything and she just messaged me last night saying sorry about how things were recently and that she's so grateful to have someone like me by her side. I feel proud of myself that I don't let a lot of negativity get to my head and allow it to change my perspective in life. Idk like even after a lot of bad times i still love her? And genuinely just want the best for her and I also know that the best for her doesn't necessarily have to include me.

Izaiah<3

—— ◆•◆•◆ ——

I wanted to write a short story about me and my boyfriend he is the absolute love of my life and he gets me through so much without knowing it just being with him makes me blush we have a soul tied connection even though we both fucked up and did some bad things to one another at least once we fixed things over the last few months and those bad mistakes of mine I feel strengthened us yes we still argue because no one is perfect and we definitely have some things to work on but we can't stay away from each other every argument only last maybe a hour we just can't stay away what I'm mostly trying to say is I found the love of my Life even though we are so young and don't know what the future holds I wouldn't want to share this life with anyone else.

-@onlyforhim95

The Thin Line

T he line between love and heartbreak is as thin as this piece of paper. A boy lost in his emotions; lost in his journey finds love in two people. Both change his view on love and both impact his heart. Its the end of February. Kai who's 19 doesn't have any drive or passion in anything he does. Now Kai has a friend, named Shayne, someone who he's been friends with since the 9th grade. And she's in college and she has it all figured out. She like a walking ray of sunshine.

But one day Kai saw something that just didn't feel right. Almost as if she was hiding her tears and cries behind her smile and laughter. She brushes it off as if Kai is just "looking into deep into things"and asked him "why do you care anyway". He says because you're my friend and i love and care about you. Over the next couple of months Kai and Shayne really looked out for each other and really have a love for each other but not in the romantic form.

It was so beautiful and warming that it healed both of them and they were so open and supportive of each other that they found a romantic love with other people while still being platonically in love with each other. In October that platonic love was tested when Kai met a girl named Sade, and Sade was the female version of Kai. They were the same person and they started dating in November. But every relationship has its up and downs, and in December. Kai and Sade got into an argument, one that required the guidance of his friend Shayne who said " if you love her, you will find a way to work things out, and if she loves you, she will find a way to work things out. But i don't agree with what she did and she shouldn't make you feel this way." The problem with Kai and Sade's relationship was that they were too much alike and it caused issues because there stubbornness would make them bump heads...a lot.

But when Kai and Sade weren't at each others throat, they were so happy, so so happy. Shayne could see this happiness and something started to change in her attitude towards Kai and Sade. She started to say things like "i would never do that to you." or things like "maybe you and her aren't meant for each other."Well one day she she made a slick comment about Sade and it bothered Kai to the point he told her never to talk about her again. He told her if she doesn't have anything nice to say don't say anything at all.

But sadly in February everything came crashing down between Kai and Sade. Her and her brother were moving back home and Kai was getting ready to start Med school. These were things that they talked about before they even started dating but when the time came things just didn't go the way they planned. They stopped going out as much, they stopped talking as much, and they seemed to be distant with each other. Kai had asked

Shayne for a word of advise on the situation and she was helpful. She said " whats meant to be will work itself out naturally." Kai took what she said and thought about it, so on valentines day he left her a basket of her favorite candies flowers stuff animals and perfumes bug also a card, and the card was more of an apology, then a love letter.

And later that day Sade called him and they talked for hours and hours and hours. But by the end of this call Kai asked Sade, "if she's ok?" Sade says "yeah"but with a weak sound to it. She then asked if Kai was ok, he had a pause and let out a sigh and said " yeah, im ok." He then asked her "are WE okay." And with tears flying through the phone she said "i don't know" and she cried.

And hearing her so upset made him upset and she went on to say with everything going on with her moving back home and work, she's just been stressed out and its overwhelming for her, so they they decided to take a little break just to get everything that had going on straight. (They never saw each other again) Kai then tells Shayne what happened and she was so upset, because she saw i was happy but was so supportive in telling me that she's there for me "because i'm your friend and that I love and care for you."

The same way that he was there for her. Love to me isn't a feeling or an emotion it's an act. When you love someone you will always want what's best for them even if you don't get to experience that happiness with them. Love can always change forms and you can never realize it. When Sade had moved back home, i wished her nothing but the best. I had wanted to see the girl that i loved succeed and be happy in a place that she was happy in. Now she's got her own apartment, she's now ay a higher position for her job and she's now found someone who she's able to experience this new stage in her life, and I'm so happy for her, because she deserved it. Now I'm starting my medical career, I'm talking to someone new and i've been looking for a 1 bedroom apartment, and she hopes that I find one, because she also wants me to find happiness the same way that she did. That what I think love is.

-@k_williams

Illusion of Love

I will tell a story about a girl I met in a Snapchat group. This happened in 2022 when I was 15 years old in The Netherlands. Let me first tell you something about myself a little bit. I am now 17 years old I don't believe in love I don't believe it now and I didn't believe it when I was 15 years old. I come from a Moroccan family I've been through a difficult life I had a hard childhood.

I was a happy child and everything was good until my parents divorced. I saw my father hitting my mother they where fighting a lot and I also was getting hit very hard at the age of 3. My father used to hit me a lot for every small thing. I was getting hit for accidentally letting a cup of water fall I was getting hit for not walking normal for crying to fast for wanted to play a lot and for wanting attention bc that is what 3 year old kid's do.

I was getting hit for literally every small thing you can imagine. So when my parents divorced I moved from Belgium to the Netherlands when I was 7 years old with my little sister and my mother . I left my best friend I lost literally everything. that's where life started to feel useless. We we're homeless for 3 years we had to sleep at my mothers friend house the other day at my aunty's house. I remember one day that we we're in the macdonalds until 4 am figuring out where to sleep that night. I was getting bullied because of my Belgium accent and that's where I started to have anger issues. I wasn't the same kid anymore who was happy and loved school I was a kid who the school saw as " a danger for our school ". I would be very aggressive with very small things I would fight every kid that just looks to long at me I would fight teachers I would fight outside my school I wasn't the same kid anymore. Everyone was afraid of me because of my anger attack I failed my school I failed everything.

When I got older it was still the same still the quiet angry kid who would fight everyone everyday on high school even the teachers. but is was worser I started doing bad things outside. Those things really hurt me I was good with everyone I never bullied someone in my life nobody was scared of me I was laughing with everyone. Yes I have anger issues but I cannot control it. They hated me they always had something to say to I had the feeling like it was always me. That was just because another organization was helping me before high school. They knew about my situation but they still thought that I was a monster or something.

They kicked me out and sent me to a school full of crazy kids. My classmates were all criminals one beaten someone to death one stabbed someone the other one was not 100% they sent me somewhere like a am a psycho or something this is not who I was. Everything changed i never got in trouble ever again. But I was and

I am still that quiet kid with anger attacks. But right before I got sent to that school I met that one girl on a Snapchat group who I thought was the one who changed me and everything around me. Snapchat groups is or was a trend in the Netherlands where you join random groups with random people. Once my friend sent me a link to join a group. I clicked on it and joined a group. As soon as I joined the group I started talking and getting to know the people in the group when I saw a girls name that got my attention. I don't wan't to say her name for her privacy so we will call her *girl*.

So I asked *girl* how she was and how old she was and started talking with her inside the group. I was flirting with her (as a joke). The people in the group could see what I was trying to do so they where shipping us (also as a joke) that is what they do in the Netherlands as soon as they see something between a boy and a girl they will start shipping them. As soon as we start talking more and more and getting closer I asked her to add me so that we can talk in private.

And of course she did. So I was asking some more personal questions. I am talking to a girl but I don't even know how she looks like I asked a picture. That's the moment that will decide our future will she say yes and we continue the talking of will he say no and is this the end. And her answer was yes. She sent the picture and she was the most beautiful girl I ever saw. I sent a picture of me and she gave me an answer that I never heard of a girl a answer that I would never thought I would have. She replied with "je bent een mooie jongen" ("you are a pretty boy"). On that day my life changed I got a little bit of hope in life. I was saying to myself

106

"maybe there love". So after talking and talking we started calling for the first time. We called everyday until we finally met for the first time. There was a fair somewhere in our neighborhood. So I decided to meet her there. I was nervous but at the end of the day it was all good.

I really thought that there was something between us we weren't dating but we also didn't like it if we talked to someone else. So there was something between us. I fell in love with her and decided to confess to her I told her how beautiful she was how much I loved her and how much she changed me and my life we called and hangout everyday. I told my friends about her I was so happy I was the little happy boy again from Belgium that loved school that loved life. Some women/girls don't understand what they can do with a man/boy how much they can change him and everything around him.

My life was black before I met her. I started fighting since I was 5 years old. I did taekwondo (a Korean fight sport) I had almost my blue belt but I moved to the Netherlands. When I turned 7 I started doing kickboxing and when I was 16 I started doing MMA initial now. So when I turned 15 I had my first ever kickboxing tournament and I won. I got €350 and spent all my money to her. I bought her a cheap chain and a lots of gifts. I really thought that she was the one. But it ended very quickly. Her account disappeared so I was waiting for weeks and weeks. I asked her friends "what is going on with "girl" he account disappeared is she okey?" They replied with "yes everything is okey Snapchat blocked her account she has a new one so you wan't me to give it to you?" I said "yes of course" they gave me

107

her new account. But we weren't like how we used to be. We didn't call that much like bef2 ore we never saw each other after that. It was only a little bit of talking and that's it. I didn't felt what I felt before we weren't so close anymore she didn't text me anymore I was the one who started every conversation.

And then her account disappeared again until 2 weeks she came back and I asked her if everything was okey. She said "yes but my account is doing weird here I give you my other account. So as soon as she gave me her other account I stared waiting until she would text or call me. But she never did I texted her and was waiting for her to answer but she didn't respond. I was checking I see on my Snapchat "delivered 1 week ago" "delivered 2 weeks ago" she just didn't texted me back.

I started to never open my Snapchat again. Until I really started missing her. I opened my Snapchat and saw "opened 10 weeks ago" so I started to have hope again. I started texting her and texting her but answers for months. That's where I realized that she is ghosting me. I lost hope again my life was and is black again I am the quiet kid with angry issues again but this time with a broken heart the only thing that I have of her is the pictures and videos that she sent me. I thought" maybe there is love" but no there isn't this situation happened in 3 months so I had to tell a little bit about myself to make the story a little bit longer but it all happened in a short period. I still don't believe there is love I still don't believe that someone will love me. I think that this is just it for me. Thank you for reading my story.

-R.I.

A Storm and its Stars

To Marissa-

how come you still glisten so bright, even after all this time

i'm in the eye of the storm, which is fueled by the thought of... you.

this storm so dark and twisted. I need out..yet I can't move.

I can, but..won't.

what would you think? what would you tell me... does it even matter anymore?

I ask myself so many questions, and sometimes I have an answer.

sometimes...l don't.

either way I want your answer. I'd be lying if I said i didn't.

life is in my hands and it's going to continue with or without you right? right.

I wouldn't change anything for the world..and for all that has, and all that will be, thank you.

forever & always.

but my god..when things get tough, just look up at the stars. I'll make sure to glisten extra bright.

..maybe then it'll be too late..

I also wonder if you'd do the same...

a piece of me truly believes you would, just as I.

thank you, and until next time~

- Amine Amri

Legos

There was this one time when my girlfriend and I were building a mini Yoshi lego character at her house. We were laying on her bed having such a great time, but I accidentally made a mistake and she got upset because I didn't understand how to build mine. I felt so embarrassed and wanted to cry. We finished but I wasn't happy. She got on her phone and I just laid down crying silently. My girlfriend noticed this and immediately put down her phone and laid down and comforted me. She wiped my tears away and held me tight with one hand on my cheek, saying 'shh, "It's okay baby, everything is going to be okay, I'm here". In that moment, I felt a wave of love and gratitude wash over me by the way she wrapped me in her arms and made me feel safe and cared for. I've never felt like that by anyone. Not even my own parents. I couldn't even remember why I had been crying in the first place, as her presence made everything better. Though it was a simple gesture, it meant the world to me. It was as if all my worries melted away in her embrace. It was that moment, when she comforted me in my vulnerability, that I knew

111

without a doubt that I was completely in love with her...

   -A.M.T<3

A wish

L ove is beautiful," they say, but it truly is only when experienced.

Some think this way, yet my mind whispers different thoughts.

If asked what emotion I'd cherish forever, I'd say limerence without a second thought.

Limerence is love, yet not quite the same;

Love is a feeling, but limerence-a state of mind derived from it.

It blends the good with the bad, from beauty to unwelcome thoughts—

Intrusive, melancholic echoes that love often brings.

From this introduction, I move to my wish:

When I love, I love deeply. Though I don't feel it now,

I cast this wish to the future, hoping it comes true:

I wish you'd love me as I love you.

I wish you'd speak to me as you do to him.

I wish you'd call me as you call him.

I wish you'd hang out with me like you do with him.

I wish you'd ask me out, invite me over, to watch a movie or play games.

I wish you'd introduce me to your parents, and I'd introduce you to mine.

I wish you'd hold my hand during long walks, Share your secrets with me, whispering late into the night.

I wish you'd laugh with me at our private jokes,

And comfort me in moments of despair.

I wish you'd plan adventures with me, Dreaming of places we'd explore together.

I wish you'd see me as your confidant, your partner,

The one you turn to when the world feels heavy.

I wish you'd remember the little things about me, The way I remember every detail about you.

I wish we could build a life filled with shared moments,

With joys and sorrows, and everything in between.

I wish... I wish... I wish...

We could love each other eternally, and find our happily ever after.

Stop.

Cycles of Heartbreak

fter my first love I was heartbroken. no matter who i went to or what i did i couldn't get over him or what we had. although truthfully, i was the reason why we ended things. i couldn't get over him with all of the guilt i was carrying and finally came to terms that i was still in love with him while he was now with someone else and getting with other guys would fill the void and i needed to heal first.

looking back, I don't think i was really heartbroken, maybe just lonely and missing what we had, but not him. it was like i wanted to love him more than i actually loved him, and it was like now that the relationship was over i mourned it and wanted to love him more than i even loved him in the relationship anyway. i finally got over him but not quite moving on or ready to get with anyone else. that was until i met my second love.

(I'm leaving him unnamed so feel free to use whatever name or just refer to him as second love) now this was super unexpected and almost like it was unreal. we immediately clicked in a way that felt so right like we were a true match. he made me feel so loved and made me forget about my first love, and not like i was intentionally trying to forget about him because i felt truly healed and past him but it was like now i believed that i could love again, like now it was possible. after talking until sunrise countless nights and talking for hours on end i found out he cheated. it was like the same heartbreak but way worse. it was like an unbearable pain that i could explain. it was my heartbreak relived and 100x worse. it felt like my first heartbreak was puppy love and this was a whole new level of heartbreak that i never saw. like something beyond words he cheated on my with HIS first love and i felt betrayed because even though i had a first love i was now over him and committed to this guy just for him to cheat on me with his. i felt like i was so in love and now i knew what love felt like just to find out he was still looking back at his first love. it caused an entire personality shift for me.

Almost two months later i found out they ended things. apparently they were off and on for a long time and i was nothing but a filler for while they were on break even though i thought it was love. the more i uncovered the truth the more heartbroken i would get and it would almost reset my healing process. after they broke up he came back. i was so angry now knowing everything and i promised i wouldn't let him back in. but of course i fell for it again and got back with him.

Never fall in love with the same person twice because it is not the same person. i tried to get passed it and but now i was sitting in a relationship that i had to carry guilt with each day because of what he had done, now knowing that no matter what i do I'm going to get heartbroken and knowing that i will just have to let

117

things be the way they are supposed to, but if things were the way they were supposed to be then why did he come back? i feel almost as if things are meant to play out this way. i prayed for nothing but peace and then he came back and i could've kept my peace by not letting him return to my life but instead i did because i believe in second chances even though deep down i know its going to happen again. i question why i wont leave because i do have self respect and i know whats right and wrong for me but its like im stuck. now i wonder if this is all about love or because i just wanted reassurance.

-Rose

Reminiscent Remedies

I was eight and a half years old when I first saw her, she was my younger brothers friends 'older sister. Her and I were a year apart in age and in school. I longed to know her, she was friends with everyone, always playing with the boys too. Something like that was unheard of, the girls all played with girls at the school I went too, so to go home and play with the neighbor kids and to have a girl join in was truly something special in my eight year old life.

She was a very sore loser though, she kicked me in the nards after I won a game of twenty one. Shortly afterwards, life happened. My family had to move away, and I thought I would never see her again. Then suddenly, there she was eight years later, on my recommended friends list on Facebook. Her profile picture was captivating, and I knew it was her, I would never forget that smile with those dimples. I befriended her, in hopes she would remember me. I was amazed when she did, and accepted my friend request. We immediately caught up.

I found out her family moved as well, and they lived

five minutes away, a five minute walking distance that is. Both of us were excited to meet up so we did, at the park across the street. That was my summer of '69, in 2010. We talked a lot, walked around a lot, and spent so much time together. I was truly amazed that what I thought I once lost was right in front of me. We spent Fourth of July together, and watched the fireworks illuminate the sky. When her family went inside, we stayed outside and just talked. We talked so much it felt like our souls were catching up from the past life. Like we knew each other forever, but still had so much to share. Well, our teenage years were split into relationships, and melancholy between us.

She was always with a boyfriend when I was single, and I was with a girlfriend when she was single. Life separated us once more, and we went our separate ways. She went on to be with her high school sweetheart, as did I. Both relationships ended in disaster. Hers ended with her having a baby girl. Mine ended with addiction to alcohol spiraling me into a seven year abyss. I climbed myself out of that abyss, and was a year sober, then covid hit.

I had been reading self help books, trying to improve any aspect of my life I could. After the covid ban, it was August when My mom approached me to share my childhood friend was asking for my number. I couldn't believe it, of course give my number to her! I thought this has been what the past year has been for. It's been preparing me for this moment, this future with her. Finally, I could have my shot with the one woman I've always wanted to be with. She reached out and we caught up.

She had two more kids with her ex husband, after her high school sweetheart and her separated. Now she has a total of three kids. I didn't care, I was willing to be the best stepdad I could, I was more than ready to raise kids with her, and we could all be together as one big happy family. She was ecstatic. I shared if she needed sometime after leaving her ex husband she should take it now to make sure this is truly what she wants. She assured me she was ready. We dated for four months, then I met her kids.

After being with her for seven months, I was able to afford an apartment for us to be living in. This was great because we were staying at her aunts house, and now with more room we could have the kids full time. Took me seven months to get her family back together. After this, there were signs. She developed a really nasty habit with smoking marijuana. Her reaction to most things was filled with anger, everything was a bother to her.

It affected the whole family, and primarily the kids. We talked about having a child together, and she was happy to go through pregnancy again for me. She gave up smoking marijuana while she was pregnant. I felt honored, and I made it a mission to give her the smoothest pregnancy she ever had. She was grateful on many occasions all that I would do for her, for the kids, for our family.

Our daughter arrived, all the kids were happy to have her home and meet her, I couldn't believe that I had a daughter with my crush since I was a kid. Everyone was excited for the future, with my raise at work we were going to be able to afford a house. With our family

121

growing bigger, that's exactly what we did two months later. Got into a house, on the very neighborhood we grew up on. Life happens though, this isn't a story about how two people become strangers. This isn't a happily ever after or tall tales. This is a once upon a time... Once upon a time we were kids. Kids who grew into friends. Friends who grew into partners.

Partners that came so close to marrying. Partners that ended it all, at the last sign of disrespect, at the last time repeating oneself. We had it all together, and everything we planned to do, I kept on doing afterwards. I want to live the life I was working towards, I just wanted her and the kids to be there with me as well. She didn't want to live the life we spoke about, because as soon as she was single, she went back to all the things she had given up.

Something in her, since she was a little girl, was broken so she went around breaking hearts. I wasn't anyone to her. I was only another heart she could break, so she did it slowly. The worse part about it all? I'll let her do it again in the next life. This is my perfect nightmare.

-@uhohjosh

Lasting Pain

———— ◆•●•◆ ————

This story might sound weird but, I met him off of TikTok.. Ik might be funny but he sent me a request and I accepted it, he found my social media and dm me, I had no idea who it was the dm went on by saying. "hi I found you pretty and I saw you at ….. basket ball game was it you? I was too scared to ask for your social so I asked someone from your school" I didn't think much about it since it was new to me talking to boys, I was always judged by looks so I was surprised someone found me pretty.

We start talking in the beginning it was really good and it was my actual first love, which is young love. we t started talking through the last days of may going into June. everything was going out smoothly by the 2 weeks we hit I came to my mom and told her, I was too scared when we first because she always said to never date a boy at a young age which I can see where she's coming from by saying that, but it's all different for other people.

Throughout last year I was depressed and had a lot of stress going on with my life since I will say I didn't have a father figure since he has recently left us at that moment.and I would express my feelings and anger by self harm. i will say it's not good for yourself or anyone, it's better to seek for help, but I know it might be hard I try anything possible to not do it anymore. But it's different for other people so I don't judge. I was the closest one too him and I always felt more love to him and attached. Ever since he left I've been feeling weird because now I don't have no family that's really close to me. me and my mom.. we get into a lot of arguments because we have the same attitude, which is why I had more favoritism for my dad.

we were dating for about 2 months at this point when it was July going into August , I did self harm once again, and ended up seriously hurt which I had to be in a mental hospital, the boy I was dating did not know about this. My mom wanted to keep it private for her image and our family image. She took everything away once I was enough time in the mental hospital which we came back home. I can remember in the car it was raining and everyone was quiet.

I didn't have my phone or any devices, so I wasn't able to reach out to him. once we got home I went straight to my room and locked me up, my mom called me out I was too scared to go. I was scared, my mom came banging on my door. after a while I opened the door n I fell to the floor since I knew something bad was going to happen. but she teared up and started crying and yelling, I was too embarrassed looking at my scars.

I knew my mom would definitely not support it. so when I came out to my aunt about my self harm I told her to not tell no one. eventually she did, I don't blame her neither. she was just trying to do what's best for me and help me out. when my aunt came out to my mom about me. I had to stay by my aunts house for 2 weeks my mom did not want to see me. Which is why I would have to sneak in the house to get my clothes and my stuff when my mom was at work or away. which is when later on I did it again and was leaded on to the mental hospital. My mom had lost trust in me so when school started I would ask my friends to let me use their phone and check the boys socials and text him. later on I found out he had a new girlfriend.

I get that I ghosted him but I couldn't do nothing about it. Months pass I didn't contact him in those months when I had my phone. He saw me at my volleyball tournament, once I saw him every little thing came rushing back about him, memory's, and ab his new gf, later on I found out he was there for his new girlfriend tournament, once we went against his girlfriends team, he kept looking at me and I couldn't stop thinking and shaking. so I brushed it off and played on, when the game finished. he was trying to talk to me but I shoved him to the side I heard in the distance he said "good job on winning." I had lost it once I heard his voice. I couldn't stop crying. and thinking of why would he do that to me. a month later he followed me on socials.

so I did back and he texted me by phone number and I would just leave him on read. I know it's not his fault I don't blame him. but after all we talked things out but I couldn't tell him about why I ghosted him. so I brushed it off and said I had my phone taken because I sneaked out. he believed it after that he broke up with his girlfriend and he wanted to talk again, so it took a long time for us to start dating again. since I was always hesitant about it but he asked me out, obviously I still missed him so I proceeded to say yes. But this time it was different, he would be toxic over the most smallest stuff.

But yet I still stayed with him because I know if I lost him it would be the same like before so i made sure to stick with him, after that we got back together, turns out he cheated again. he had a girl best friend which i knew and trusted, at first the relationship was going smooth and well we rarely got into arguments and we would hang out in the weekends or whenever we could.

I loved and appreciated every single time with him, we were almost into a month in, at that time i was on vacation. I remember being in the with my grandma, aunt and little sister, when i got a dm from insta which was his cousin following me it seemed weird and I never follow people back right away so I just wait a few minutes and follow them back. once I followed him I realized I had gotten bunch of messages from him on instagram saying how he had to show me something, so I told him to show me, he had sent me a screenshot of my bf and his girl best friend chats. his girl best friend and his cousin were talking at this point. so the girl best friend took a screenshot and showed the cousin. which he proceeded to show me. I started tearing up after this happened. I felt lost confused wasn't thinking straight. I remember crying the whole ride to the store and back. I couldn't let my grandma see me so the whole ride I was looking at the window. I was overthinking everything. was it me who had caused him to cheat. why would he do this. why would he. I was lost. I loved that boy so much that I was too scared of giving him all my love that I knew if he did something bad I will end up hurt.

I ignored my thoughts because I knew he would change. but yet. I still manage to see the best in him. he did say sorry at the 3 days this had happened since he acted like he didn't care. 3 days pass he text me late saying I'm sorry for everything I've done you don't have to forgive me or respond I wont do that again. yes. I did go back to him but I realized I was more than that. last time I texted him, begged for him, was April.24.24 , I miss him. more than I thought I know it's almost 3 months yet he still views my story's and I miss him.

He will always be my first love. I will never forget about that boy. I know im stupid for doing that but I will always see the good in him. my first love e ,, and just so you don't worry if you ever read this. yes I am doing better and with my mom better we have our own therapist so we will have a better relationship so you don't have to worry about that !! and ab me I'm also doing fine I've figured writing my stuff down is a better way to express myself and feelings. sorry if it came out sloppy!!! I was crying while this writing!!

The Perfect Love

For the last 5 months after a breakup I've been trying to find myself. Soon as the last week of may arrive I met a friend and we talked and i asked her if she knew anyone that was single as a joke and then she presented me one. She told me that she's single after a bad break up with her ex which she still misses him. Soon after work I message her and I was kinda nervous at the same time and we texted to get to know each and from there it changed. I remain loyal to her and waiting for her and she did the same and soon on the last day of school I drove to her and went on a small date and we enjoyed it together. Later on we started to become a little more serious and I've always send her good morning text which she loved and we stayed on the phone when we were about to go to sleep and every time I have interaction with her I've always been very calm and grateful that I met this girl, she did so much that she fixed me and that I'll always love her. I hope she'll be my wife one day.

-@el._.chuyy

Moving on

I met My first love around middle school after her cousins passed me off to her and at the time nobody knew who I was and wouldn't know till later, me and this girl broke up many times before but it was middle school, she was my first kiss and the first girl I ever thought I felt love for at that time. She eventually moved on and found another lover but due to my inability to let go i stayed with her as friends, i would text her when my nights were dull or gloomy or sometimes when they were better and she'd return a text talking about her feelings and her problems and I always gave her a blunt and straight forward answer.

Her and this guy dated for around a year until they broke up, I was ecstatic especially since he had been treating her poorly and I couldn't stand to see her going through it. In the time frame that she and him were together I got to know her family better down to the great uncles and great grandmothers I'm still friends with her cousins to this day, they're both Awesome and I'm glad I'm able to be apart of their lives and journeys, I attended her quince instead of my first hoco because I was so love struck, even though I left early. Her parents and I had a very good relationship and I they trusted me, however I don't think she cared about me like I did for her. About four or so months later we had went on a date that ended pretty great and I invited her over to come see my parents and she didn't really say anything. Again I mocked it up to her being shy or not knowing what to say, I was blindsided by the fact that she had went on a date with me for the first time in two years.

I asked her if she'd like to be my girlfriend again and gave her a blanket to ride home in since she was cold and she said yes, I started applying myself into my school work since she went to alternative school and was going to graduate early and i wanted to catch up so I could come with her. A week or so later we went on a second date to the library, did some work Ate Girl Scout cookies that were a little past expiration date made out and went home, at this point I seriously felt like my life was at its peak. Later I mean like a day maybe two later I can't get a response out of her, she had previously mentioned something about her graduation date so I prepared a list and bought her favorite cereal a bone for her dog blankets her favorite drinks everything that I knew she'd love.

After i finished work I would send a message, before I went to work and when I'd get to the break room. I wasn't trying to overbear her since I knew she was busy with work so I tried to lay off but still check in as much as possible. Eventually she Texts saying she's tired and that was it, so I wait awhile hoping for another text and I view her story to find out I was just the first of many that she had done this to. I was brutally devastated, I remember I stopped eating for a few days, I stopped smiling at school with my friends and I was known to make people laugh. She had ripped a hole in my chest and I felt as though I was never going to recover, I gave my dog the treat so it at the minimum didn't go to waste and i couldn't stand to look at everything else. I deleted her contact and prepared myself to forget the sound of her voice. Eventually my friend made me realize that she wasn't the one for me and I felt better about myself. However to this day a year and a half later when I get slightly or remotely under the influence I still think about her like I'm waiting on a text or call that will never come, even if I haven't thought about her in months she makes a surprise appearance. I've stopped looking or pursuing girls about four or so months ago as I just don't want to be in a relationship unless they want to put the effort in to be with me and actually want to be with me and not just for a temporary reason.

-Mikey

Long distance is for the weak

─── ◆◆❖◆◆ ───

I saw a girl online. It was on Wizz, an app where u can meet people. I texted her some super bold/corny shit (not saying what it was) but it worked and see seemed like she really liked me so she sent me her number. Everything was amazing about this girl from her looks to the way her brain works I was getting obsessed really early but I hid it.

Not only was she he was so beautiful she was the sweetest girl I've ever met but nobody else saw that in her not even her but no girl has ever treated me like she did. One thing I didn't say was we were long distance, when I first texted her profile said Illinois (where I'm from) but she was just visiting and really lived in another state right next to mine though but still the down side of that is nobody had a car. We were texting/ face timing back and forth a whole bunch for a month and a half then she ghosted me for like a month I was pissed I started taking to some one else someone not long distance.

That's didn't work out anyway I was too nervous but then... she came back!? Idk what came over me I thought I was so completely over her but deep down I really missed so I forgave her immediately. She apologized and said she was scared of the feelings she had for me so she pushed me away and I genuinely understood. After that our situationship was better than ever before she sending random pictures of her I got more possessive and and she ghosted me again but not for long she came back saying it was a lot of stuff going on with her family I said "whatever okay"... yeah i still took her back..smh. A little bit after that, and get ready for this she ghosted me again I was pissed i was done this time like really But um she told me she was raped which really fucked me up because i can't do anything about it this was when i realized i would hurt someone for her and I'm not violent. But anyone can be. Now ofc I'm not mad at her that it's just whenever goes through something she pushes everyone away but she's never trying to hurt me but it does ofc. But anyway we were back to being happy again and then ig it just started to be a relationship. At this point it was around the end of October (side note we met the year before in the beginning of December) and i kinda fucked up I texted that other girl I met when she ghosted me but only like friendly convo but I told her cuz I didn't want to keep things from her and that really hurt her so I immediately stopped she started to act all nonchalant and not responding to me but we worked that out we were back to being happy until later in December she went back to being a little nonchalant not as much as before but still it was weird and kind of scary... I'm sorry I couldn't

133

finish in time but this is really heavy on me and I guess it's just too soon.

-@noahnvo_

Right Person, Wrong Time

———— ✦✦✦✦ ————

Her name was Karina, I met her at Mexico at a basketball court when I went for vacation 4 years ago. She was a shy girl and quite, but invited her to play with me and some friends because she was sitting alone days past and her and I became friends, and we texted at night until like 2 in the morning Then her and I started flirting with each other and we become girlfriend and boyfriend. Then for the past 4 years we been on and off of our relationship since I live in Arkansas and she lives in Mexico 1,567 miles apart And long distance relationships don't work out for me and I was doubting myself if I should stay with her or break up with her so her and I could find someone for us back home.We are friends now, and we miss each other a lot. I miss everything about her, she was my other half. Right person, wrong time. I hope she finds someone that'll take care of her and love her for who she is. All I want is for her to be happy. Her future is bright. We agree to be friends and find our true soulmates.

-Kevin

Demure Effort

Love can be unexpected, and sometimes it can end the same way that it came. If I could write about our story I would, but I would end up with my own book. Being a rebound wasn't the best and sometimes I wonder if what I thought we had was ever real. Making her cry tears of joy brought happiness to me. I genuinely felt happy at some point, and now I have gone back to the numb feeling I once had. She was my first everything and I gave every amount of effort that I had. I won't forget the first time we expressed our love to each other on a 9 hour call. Or all the times we played Roblox on call daily.

Even though what she did was wrong, I still forgive her. Leaving the day after my birthday and telling me you slept with your toxic ex of 3 years who has a gf was crazy. But what was even crazier was me looking like a homeless person asking for answers. If I ever beg for answers again then shoot me. I don't think I will ever be blinded by love again, especially after all those red flags. I don't know if I ever wanna sing to someone again and just be treated as if I meant nothing. I never got an answer but I was forced to believe what I was told. At the time that I'm writing this I have school tomorrow, and I hope that I don't see her, but I want to see her at the same time... sorry if my story didn't make sense, I just didn't wanna end up yapping even more. I do miss who I though she was and even though our story is over, she did make me the happiest person at some point. I hope she's okay and that someone will treat her well, even tho they won't since I exceeded her standards (me being delusional). One thing that I did learn is that no matter how much effort you put in, someone else will take her without any effort. Thank you for reading my nonsense and I hope that you live life to the fullest even if you want to give up, remember it's our only time here... If you somehow see this, then I forgive you Vicky (Lily).

-@alex_417

All That He Was

Ok so my story is about my friend Timmy, sadly he killed himself my junior year of high school around December, he jumped to his death and I loved him dearly.Timmy was not only my friend but acted like a older brother to me and a mentor, when I was doing drugs my sophomore year he would take care of me and made sure I was eating and staying hydrated but he was also there for so many people. But I was very selfish and didn't really appreciate him as I should have.

When he died it was the first time I felt a real heartbreak in my life I was so deeply affected by his death I was never truly the same again. For the next few months I was completely numb to anything, I shunned a lot of people in my life. Looking back at it, I reacted like that because he meant so much to me more then I realized in that moment. Because as I reflected more and more i realized that he didn't need to go out of his way to make sure I was ok but he did when I essentially had no one or wanted anyone to help me.

Before he killed himself I always thought about hanging with him again I missed having him around school during a football game as I was with my friends I thought about calling or texting him to go out the next day but I decided on texting him later cause I was talking to a girl I liked, sadly that same night he would never go back home. I was devastated when I heard he died a part of my heart died with him, I always blamed my self after that. So all those months self isolating I was upset at myself because he helped me so much in my life more then he probably understood , but sadly I was too late, but at his grave I swore I'd live for him and try to live why his example and help people out in whatever way possible. Even as I'm writing my story out I still love Timmy for all that he was. Not a day goes by that I don't think about him, someday I hope to see him again.

-Armando .E

Metamorphosis

I'm in the beginning of a relationship, and there's something to say about 2 people being aware of the excitement that clearly exists, but also the patience needed so we can move forward without having any mistakes or accidents derail what we've accomplished so far. And I'm not just talking about what we've accomplished together, but more importantly individually. The inner work, which should always continue, where we need to support when possible. The deeper layers that one needs to feel safe with. To be vulnerable again and feel free. We've been been in relationships where we each thought and felt we had our person. And life, God, the universe, shows us different, and we both chose to work on ourselves instead of blaming another person, working hard on not holding resentment. We loved these people in our past. And despite the pain that went into those relationships and the rips, our hearts learned to love so much better. We embody love now, instead of looking for it in others. We are becoming the best versions of ourselves, and I pray we see our story through. We trust the process, we communicate, we listen, and do the work, we are passionate and compassionate, all the makings of another great love story.

-Jose

Lovers to friends

I met this girl and me and I were going good and then we started arguing and then she ended up losing my trust and I took her back and we broke up again and again and again and then she lied to me and lost my trust again and I miss her and I still love her and me and her friends, but it still hurts because I really like her and I feel like me and her being friends is gonna hurt me more. She's not over it too but I'm just really hurt right now

-@standard_

Lovee<3

———— ◆•◆•◆ ————

L ove is such a beautifully, complicated, complex feeling/emotion. I thought I knew what it was at a young age, but as I got more older, i realized that it's this constantly changing, ever lasting feeling that evolves as you do. It's truly what's brings us all together and it's the only reason we're out on this earth today. Love is so much more than relationships, love is a mothers kiss, love is in home cooked meals, or a smile from a stranger across the street love is found in unexpected gifts, love is found in notes/poem, it is found in songs/frequency, it can be felt all the way across the world and can be felt in the palm of a hand. it is found deep in the heart/mind/soul And I am sure that it can travel across the universe. love is found everywhere if you're looking for it. love is patient and love is kind, love will hurt and love will heal, And most of all it is beautifully infinite. Ki2MySoul has taught me about love.

-Nicolas Tologanak

Now

———— ◆◆●◆● ————

I want to talk about my current relationship. I met him last year we had a class together and I felt and instant click with him, we got along so well and always had something to laugh about I felt comfortable and like I could be myself around him. During summer we didn't talk because I had no way of contacting him but I still thought about him so when we got back into school we fell right back into that friendship.

He helped me through some hard times when I was struggling and I considered him my best friend throughout that friendship I started to get feelings for him but I didn't say anything for a while to protect our friendship and then he asked me and I didn't want to lie and I wanted to know how he felt about me and the feelings were mutual so we started talking and then he asked me out, we've been dating for 8 months now and they've been both the best and worst months of my life.

He's been nothing but good and patient with me but my family isn't accepting of the fact that I have a bf and that's really messing things up. During those 8 months we've only seen each other during school and haven't ever hung out or gone on a date or anything and it's draining and depressing but he's been so patient even though I know it's hurting him too and I hate myself for putting him through all this but he doesn't want to leave and I don't want him too because I know we can have the most amazing relationship once we're given that chance. I graduated this year so I won't even be seeing him at school anymore and I don't know what I'm going to do, I've tried talking to my dad about things but he doesn't listen any just ignores me.

I have my full license now and can leave but when I get back from hanging out or doing anything I know it'll be a big fight and I can't deal with that mentally, I'm so drained I can't enjoy things with family or friends anymore I haven't even seen my friends all summer. I've also talked to my mom about things and she understands and is trying to help but my dad doesn't listen to her either I don't know what I did to deserve all of this.

The love me and my bf have for each other is so strong and he treats me like I'm the only girl in the world I don't deserve him and he doesn't deserve this relationship he deserves being able to live and enjoy spending time with his gf and I've told him that but he doesn't want to leave he says that he knows what we have is special and he knows I'm the one.

Fading Echoes

This is about a boy I met 2 years back. I was the type of girl who didn't believe in love much I got played a lot and what they say hurt people, hurt people so I kept myself away from finding love. But little did I know I would fall In love with him so quickly. I met him while i was volunteering for face painting at this fair.

And he walked up to me and complimented my skills you know. I said my thank you and everything and he walked off. I saw him later on and walked up to him we started talking, exchanging numbers and instagrams. Time went by we got pretty close. But we were just friends but not really friends. I really liked him and I wanted to be more but we wouldn't have worked out if we argued over tiny things which resulted into not talking or hanging out.

Then there was no way we would've been a good couple. But our arguing would constantly repeat over the most tiniest things. Until one day we stopped everything no contact. I saw him again at a party through a mutual friend. We had small talk and got close again I missed having him to talk too. We left the party earlier. Went in his car. And just caught each other up on what was going on. He was pretty high and drunk at the same time. He was slurring his words and saying the most random shit. And that's when I said I didn't like the fact we would argue a lot and that I really liked him and every time we fought it made me sad. He said he really liked me too from the start, when he first met me. And I hadn't felt like that with anyone in a long time. I never knew I would fall in love with someone and connect with them so fast. But after what he told me, he kissed me. And it was the happiest moment of my life. We started talking again but as a situationship not friends.

And god he was the sweetest most understanding kindest man Ive ever met. I have a lot of mental problems. I have bpd too. One of the reasons I stayed away from getting romantically close to anyone. But he was so understanding he would solve my problems with me. Every time we argued he would help me fix it.

We fight we fix and that's what we did. He made me feel so appreciated and happy. One day he asked me to be his girlfriend. And all he ever promised for was to not break his trust. And I promised I wouldn't. But I did 4 months after. I eventually broke his trust. I lied about such a small thing it caused us to end. I broke his heart so bad it hurts. I never wanted to hurt my baby. I loved him so much. I apologized and I cried and I promised I wouldn't have done it again. And he understood he gave me another chance but I did it.

I did what i said I wouldn't do all over again. I did it more than once and twice. And I broke his trust I broke his heart, I made him sad. When all he did was ask me for one tiny thing. And I don't know what and why I kept doing it. It was hard. And he loved me, he loved me so much. But I couldn't do one simple task. I hurt him. I couldn't fix it and I knew breaking up would've been the best and he did too. Even though he loved me dearly and I did too. We broke up. I couldn't bear the break up. I would constantly go over to his house.

I would beg and I would cry to get back. I knew it was my fault. I fucked it up and I ruined it for us. But god I love this boy and I still do to this day. I can't move on and I don't know why. He was my everything. He made me feel appreciated and I have never felt that. And he was the only one that made me feel like I was loved. And I'm so happy he's living his best life. And moving on and just enjoying it. I love him. And I always will. From the bottom of my heart he will always be my soulmate. I love you to the moon and back.

A Lost Love

It started when this random girl followed me because I had stolen my best friends phone and posted on her story some funny things that caused this new girl to follow me I accepted and followed her back and life went on as normal until one day I saw she had posted something sort of sad and I was like damn let me check if she's okay plus she was kinda cute so it gave me an excuse to talk to her anyways so I messaged her asking if she was doing okay and she literally just poured her heart out to me she said things that broke my heart and made me feel so bad for this poor beautiful young women who didn't deserve what she was getting But as we talked more and more we both started to realize how incredibly natural it was and instantly how comfortable we felt together it was one of the weirdest yet amazing feelings I had ever felt in my life never have really gotten anywhere with girls and especially one as beautiful as her , we can call her Sarah , Sarah was everything I wanted and still want in a person keep in mind she had her problems she had some drug abuse and addiction but that's not something that was really stopping me from loving her if anything it pushed me to love her more because she deserved it people in her position deserved to be loved and cared for not just casted aside And as our friendship grew and grew some of her problems such as drinking got slightly worse because her situation had gotten worse And because of this when she got drunk whether I'd be there in person or FaceTime with her the whole time to make sure she was safe , and one night in her drunken state she confessed romantic feelings for me she said she loved me so much that I was the only reason she was still here because I was her constant that I gave her a reason to want to stay on earth the next day after she had sobered up I asked her if she had remembered what happened the night before and she told me no she did not and probably in one of the stupidest most fucking unknowingly dumb decisions I've ever made I decided to not tell her anything that she said moving on from that night our relationship had only started to get stronger and stronger until one day she tells me this guy had asked her out and she said yes. And of course because I love and care for her I told her I was happy for her I mean I genuinely was I felt as long as she was happy even if it wasn't with me I could live happily knowing she wasn't alone and sad which sounds like a sad thing on my part but I sometimes js want the best for others even if it means I'm left alone and sad. As time went on this new dynamic was going fine with me we still hung out and talked all the time as friends of course. Until one day we spent the day together hanging out walking around a park doing random shit towards the end of the hangout we got into deep conversation about the future and our pasts and how we feel what's going on in our heads and I told her that she was the most amazing wonderful person I knew not only beautiful on the outside but

150

inside too I told her all her problems her self harm scars everything was beautiful yes were they bad for you but she overcame them and should never feel ashamed of them I could see her start to tear up and I told her I loved her more than just a friend while she has a bf yes ik dick move but you just know when the moment is right , the way we felt in that moment was undeniable we knew we had real love or as much as we knew how to love we gave it to each other she looked at me and confessed her feelings back saying she felt the same and I had always been there for her seen her at her worst and never left her cared for her even when her own family wasn't there for her and she loved me more than I could every know and we actually cried together because it was such a relief to say. But after she actually got picked up by her boyfriend. And reality hit back. That she didn't know what to do. I told her it's okay and you know stuff happens forbidden love go crazy but she felt horrible Because even tho she did love me she also did care for her bf which is understandable. And the next few days we discussed what to do. And it was in favor of me basically 99% of the time until the fateful day we were talking and she hit me with " Billy I love you so much but I can't " I remember the exact moment I was actually in orchestra practice waiting for the director to turn to my section , and she went on to explain that she loved me and I really had been there for her the last two years more than anyone in her life. She didn't want to do that to her boyfriend that she loved him as well and keep in mind her boyfriend was a much better looking man than me so that day she chose her boyfriend of two months versus her Closest friend and love interest of two years and I know it's my fault too so I have no one to blame but myself for this lost love relationship and I still mourn

151

it to this day. So the moral of the story is don't let past things stop you from making the most of something that is given to you and it's clear what was supposed to happen but you let doubt make u choose the cowardly way It'll only lead to heartbreak.

-B.E.W

14/3/24

It's been 5 months since me and my girlfriend started dating. We met in grade 8 of our school year we're now in grade 12. We've been in each others classes every year since that first time we met but would never really cross paths to much or speak to each other, Until the beginning of grade 11 after we both failed two of the same classes resulting in us being in back to back classes first semester which brought us really close to the point we were best friends. We had really good chemistry and never had any issues talking to each other. we could never runout of things to say to each other we'd be up all hours on FaceTime talking about anything or just simply playing Roblox.

We never really knew we both had feelings for each other it was more an assumption due to classmates pointing it out. We were always just distracted by each other and then i asked her out to valentine's day and we went to laser tag shared gifts then got a happy meal together because we wasted all our money on games and laser tag. Fast forward to march break and i invited her over to my house and we played minecraft and watched movies. We kissed on that day for the first time and started dating. Since then we've seen each other almost every day at school and after. she's ultimately my best friend and i love her so much. We have an amazing relationship with really good communication and i genuinely know we will get married. It's like that scene from hotel Transylvania when they first saw each other that's how i would describe us and even now she's laying next to me as we watch dead pool. i enjoyed everything about the school year and i feel there's nothing that could go wrong with us. we have one year left until we graduate and i can't wait for her to be my wife and the mother of my kids.

-J&B

Un ángel

I met this girl on the bus , she was crying cause her and her boyfriend broke up and I was just tryna comfort her and make her feel better , after I got home my friend told me that she wanted my number and I was like yea that's okay, after that the girl texted me and we started to call for hours and hours , and after a few weeks pass by we just idk clicked in and started dating , we had our first kiss on the bus , we went out on our first date to the mall, we made cookies together during Christmas, it was perfect and everything I ever wanted , I've never been treated this nicely before , but then she started getting less talkative , and idk she just got really dry with me and we went on a break and this was before valentines and I had made plans for her and me and I had to cancel them all , and during the break she just starts talking bad about me to other people and making fun of me, from what I heard and I didn't know if it was true but I was hoping it wasn't. After a month passes she texts me apologizing for everything and how she wants to get back together, and I was stupid to say yes and accept her apology , I was really in love with her, idk if it was because she was the first one to treat me right or actually showed that she loved me , but I said yes , and it started off well , we were gonna go watch a movie together and everything, and I got her a rose and everything but then she stopped caring about me , she didn't wanna sit next to me , talk to me , just forgot about me , but then it was summer I was planning to go somewhere and the minute I went , she started being more dry , and leaving me on delivered for days and I was worried I did something wrong , and then I heard something from my friend that she was cheating on me and yk at first I didn't wanna believe it , cause I really loved this girl , yea we did have our arguments sometimes but I still loved her even though sometimes she did manipulate me in those arguments. But after she had left me on delivered for more than a week I decided to break it off, and we got into this huge argument and she was saying how I manipulated her and how I treated her badly , and yk it hurts alot hearing that , after treating her with care and all the love I had in my heart, I'd always tried to get her out of trouble, I'd always protect her , buy her food , be there for her when she was sad , I never left her side I was always there , and it hurts hearing that cause after all I did for her she tries to manipulate me into thinking I treated her bad and that I manipulated her , but after the argument calmed down , she apologized , she said she was sorry that she said that stuff and that I never did none of that and that I was the best boyfriend she ever had and we decided to be friends , we talked as friends and I got at a really low part of my life and I was just really just not happy at all , now she has a boyfriend , she graduated from high school and I was really Happy for her , but now it's been more than a year and I've been still single , I've worked on myself, Im definitely happier now , and I did start talking to other girls and it was going really well but I messed up cause I got scared of getting hurt but now I've just been yk minding my own business enjoying life.

-@nomames_maxi

Love of Intricacy

To be honest, it was quite a love story with a lot of interesting circumstances It all started eighth grade year. I was a kid that really didn't get the attention. of my parents when I was home so I always showed out at school until the day I met her. I was in class causing trouble as I usually do it around that time. The next thing you know, I feel a hand tap on my shoulder and it was her.

With her gentle eyes she said to me, please stop getting in trouble. I actually like you. And from that day forward, I became a better student started giving my teachers less of a hard time. All because of a girl, I knew nothing about ask me to it's truly something mind-boggling I don't know what it was about her, but it just felt like I can trust her so I did, but she was a very confusing person because even though we now hang out and are very close to the point that she's jumping on me every time she sees me And she made me feel a way that I never felt before it was a truly surreal experience.

Until I find out, she had a boyfriend and I won't lie to you. I wish I did the right thing and distance myself when I found out, but I was young dumb and in love so I continued to entertain the idea that this was OK even though I know it hurt boyfriend but I was just too blinded by the affection that I was receiving that I just didn't care and so this is how it continued us flirting but nothing ever official and has time passed on when it was freshman year of high school we end up going to two different schools, but try to stay in contact and everything was going great until about two weeks and she stopped texting and responding saying that she was too busy to chat or respond to my good morning. Text and to be honest I was Okay with that then I found out that she had a boyfriend someone that she fell for at her new school and that was the reason why I wasn't hearing from her, so I decided to match her energy and respect her relationship so I cut all ties as to not intrude into their relationship. I decided to spend time and reconnect with the friends that I've neglected while I was spending time with her.

And she saw that I was posting a lot with these people and I don't know what it was but she started texting me and she kinda sound hurt that I was talking with these other women but mind you these are my friends that I grew up with so they like sisters to me and she knows that but I guess something about somebody else for once must've triggered something to the point where we had an argument why I told her I can't keep doing this is either we all in or not and she said that she loved me and I say that you said that before, but yet you always seem to love another also so I told her to enjoy life and we went our separate ways fast-forward two years now junior in high school it was my birthday and I don't really like to post anything for it But this year, I decided to post a thank you to everyone who said happy birthday 12 o'clock the next day so my birthday would be officially over and then I went to bed and woke up to a text from her saying that she's sorry she forgot my birthday and I said it's all good she said it's just been so long. It's hard to remember. I told her that I never forgot your birthday and I'll prove it to you.

And that I did the day that her birthday hit as soon as it hit 12 o'clock I was the first person to say happy birthday and from there we kind of started texting again nothing too crazy just post back-and-forth and checking in until two weeks later she tells me that she loves me at first I didn't know how to take it so I kind of played it off as nostalgia from how we used to be until the day we hung out and she kissed me. Something about that changed me it's like my heart felt something that it hasn't a felt in a long time. And just like that, I was hooked it was love real love The type of love that had you up till six in the morning, just talking about our future and the family that will create the type of love that just being with each other's presence is enough to satisfy the heart, and to be honest it was a wonderful relationship one that I learned so much from I truly wouldn't change it for the world and this relationship continue for a beautiful six months until August 1. we were on the phone and my mom started panicking because they said my grandma had passed away now me thinking that this is some type of sick and twisted April fools joke. I didn't take it seriously until I made it to her house and saw the ambulance outside there they rushed her to the hospital what we set for an hour waiting for any news, hoping for the best that's when the doctor can tell us to say our goodbyes It's something inside of me just died right there with her looking at her for the one last time. I just couldn't keep it all in. I was so hurt but didn't know how to express it because she was my best friend. I always spent time with my grandma because my mom was always working, she was want to spend time with me even up to that point every time I go to our house I just sit in her room and enjoy her presence while I have it Not knowing that that was going to be my last time seeing her alive, I'd play so many things differently I spent all the remaining moments with her and that's still wouldn't be enough to make up and thank her for all you've done for me. so when I got back home I let her know that my grandma passed away and she asked me that I need space and to be honest she was my safe space one I could be vulnerable around And so she stayed with me and it was helping a lot with processing everything and everything was going great until the following month after losing my grandma, I lost my car in a car accident where the police officer said. I should be dead and doesn't know how we all made it out alive with no injuries. But I know by the grace of God And for that I am eternally grateful for my Lord and savior, but after the accident, I fell into a depressed state one that I never been in before and I didn't know how to react so over the phone she said you don't love me no more you're not the person that fell in love with this is somebody else and all I can say is sorry because over the phone had my sadness was hard especially with her because I didn't have to have my guard up with her. I felt like I could let my emotions slow and she'll be there to help me process, but I guess it was too much for her to the point Or she said she couldn't live anymore at least for a while and I completely respected it because she never encountered this and her friends were telling her that this is happened with them before and that they end up breaking up so she decided to go down the same route so two months after losing my grandma and one month after losing my car I lost the love of my life to be honest life was at an all-time low and I had nobody to talk to because we decided that telling my friends wouldn't be best for the relationship because a lot of them didn't really like the idea of us getting together because they've seen our past entanglements so with no one to talk to I overcame it on my own and ever since then that marks the end of my life now I won't say forever because I never know but right now I don't even know anymore if it's something I want because opening up to somebody new is not something I'm ready for But I'll tell you I still love that woman even to this day it's never hatred negativity towards her Because if I'm being honest, we could've all played it better so I choose to remember her by the good memories that we shared instead of the tragic end that came to be.

-henny

The Light That Faded

T he love I used to have it was great she was nice at first the things we do together and chill an stuff or being on the phone just talking about life and stuff this apart of my life was in a dark area but there was a light I did took it she herself told me I was that light idk something within that I have myself have to change and then she left to go to Cuba for while that when my life idk hard not being with you other person ngl i knew that she wasn't gonna be the same after all because there was less communication it suck for while I myself was kinda talking to someone too and idk but when she came back idk something about her changed life was weird because I was focusing on my stuff yk going on bike rides taking it all in that whatever life holds for me but when she came back yea her love was there but it wasn't how it was when she left i knew or felt like she was doing something behind my back and she was yk life continue make you humble who you are where you wanna be at in life.

-@crumdropn

162

I gEt iT, I wAs YoUr FiRsT lOvE"

eginning of senior year, I didn't have many friends, and i wasn't really close with my parents. I had left my mothers house to live with my father. I had met a girl online, met her in a chat room and we became friends. At nights i would go for runs to clear my head and eventually as we started talking more, she called me while i was on a run one night. She knew i was running from something i could never actually run away from. she said "stop it you dumbass", granted that is not so romantic, but thats when i realized, she cared about me.

That was our beginning. On our 1 month anniversary, we both decided to meet up. She was absolutely gorgeous! our first date was at Dennys. Our story to our parents was, we met at a UIL competition for band, i was on drum line and she was a color guard dancer. and we exchanged information and had been talking since. We would visit each other once every month or every other month at least. We even went to my Prom nightI wasn't a people person, so we ended up of ditching and going to the river walk. Her feet began to hurt so i got down on one knee, and slipped my shoes on her. we like to tease each other on occasion, so i left a hickey and a bite mark on her thigh on the inside of her slit dress. we continued walking as i held her heels in my hand. till eventually we were alone, where i placed my hands on her waist, hers on my shoulders, and we slow danced in the moonlight. we watched the sparkle in each others eyes till we eventually got closer, and closer. and we shared our most romantic kiss i could remember Me and my parents always had a shaky relationship. My dad would always say ugly things about my mom and would push them onto me. Saying things like "She will leave you for someone way better than you" "she's gonna cheat on you". and i would push them down, ignoring it, though i knew that she could do so. she was absolutely gorgeous compared to me, most beautiful girl ever.

I didn't tell her because i didn't want her to resent my dad. i wanted her to be an addition to my family. She was nervous about it because she felt like she wasn't good enough. but we had been working on it together. Around 9 months into our relationship, i asked my parents if she could join our beach trip, they agreed and we had been super excited. the day started off with my and one of my sisters going to pick her up from her house.

On the way from her house to my house, mentioned she had been having cramps so i offered to get her an Advil when we got home. My dad watched me get her an Advil and a cup of water... ... on the way to the beach, me and her sat in the back seat of my dads truck and she leaned on my shoulder and we watched a show on netflix. my parents were doing their thing. at the beach i was trying to get her out of her shell, get familiar with my family. but me and her ended up playing in the water together. on the way back, i sensed a tone change aimed at us, shooting from my parents. after we dropped her home, my parents were furious with me, for spending time with her, and not the family. for treating her special.

For being in love. thus driving the wedge my dad built deeper. he sat me down in front my whole family as he told me to break up with her. till finally after 3 days, i couldn't bare anymore. i wasn't allowed to show the hurt from it because of i did, lectures were sure to follow. me and her went back I'm forth for days, i tried telling her to let go. till finally she did, and found someone new her new boyfriend started encouraging her to skip classes to smoke, he would have intimate interactions with her and more. i didn't find out about that part till a year later, i reached out to check on her.

Come to find out she had been with a few guys and they didn't treat her the way she was meant to be. what hurt more was she want satisfied with since of it, she just went along. nobody had taken the time to learn her the way i did. i could've written a book on who she was, from her features to her personality. we had a chance to have a do over. but i couldn't, she isn't the girl i fell in love with the first time. and I'm no longer the guy she deserves.

Trial and Error and the pursuit of something special

Very often at times I find myself pulling inspiration from your videos. You have wisdom beyond your years, and you make emotional maturity feel so effect you basically give out therapy for free with your wisdom and videos. So I hope this story helps; Because this love story although not tragic, is still in its own way tragedy at its finest. Like La La Land (if that makes sense) May not be exactly what you are looking for but with a good ending I hope it can be of some use. For this is my story and I have faith that your prospective is something that I'd welcome. This is my story 4 years ago in the season of spring, redemption was the immense feeling that primarily held me accountable.

It was my senior year and graduation was upon me. So many footsteps in the halls of my school yet very often in different shoes. A pair of Nikes, Jordan's, vans, converse. Either way, they were my footsteps and soon my feet would know longer track in those halls. Unfortunately I never got to go back to school after spring break, for the world was under attack by the pandemic that was Covid-19. Nevertheless, my spirits

166

were high and after graduation online I was ready to begin my life. In a pandemic, nobody was outside. Still new and alarming, the pandemic made it close to impossible to see my loved ones a lot; My childhood neighborhood isolated with only the wind pushing the swing sets. And after a boring summer little by little the world got a little more open. Tinder, my utter demise but only hope for dating during a gap year. It wasn't long before I matched with her. At sundown she picked me up, I had no plan and no idea what she looked like tonight. So I improvised, played it safe, and pointed out an open chick fil a parking lot. Not that it mattered, all restaurants lobby's were closed, and I'm not having my first date in my family's living room. She parked, and turned on the lights in her car.

She wore a blue sweater, straight brunette hair to the shoulders, brown eyes that ultimately became my weakness. Her voice soft, nevertheless her demeanor was quiet yet sweet. And there we talked for hours. It's all we could do in a pandemic. And so our next few dates We're simply just talking. She cared about me, asked me more than I even know about myself. When we weren't together I'd call her after work, her voice like a soft piano. Always calmed me down from the stress of working at a time where everyone ordered fast food and nobody wanted to work. A few months in we went on real dates as the world opened up more and more.

Never had a met a kinder soul, so gentle with my heart until the changes started. We fell hard for each other. I was determined to make her happy. The least I could do for her genuine care for me. But she started changing. She pursued makeup, dyed her hair blonde, and ditched the warm sweaters for a more fancy aesthetic. I noticed but at the end of the day she was still the woman I loved. I just figured she was evolving, finding her new comforts and style. But she developed an intensity, this tainted attitude of entitlement. Figured I was a man who could do everything for her and I should. Money got tight so I worked two jobs. My legs yearned for I had no car still and I worked at least one job everyday. Fights spawned out of nowhere, as if our love was a garden that all of a sudden had weeks infiltrating my desires to keep her happy and content. By summer I proposed.

A fake out ring at first, I used my genuine humor to throw her off and proposed with a ring pop, only to walk her down to a heart shaped bridge, decorated by our memories together. I used the real ring this time, planted a photographer, and ultimately she said yes. After taking the most iconic pictures I had dreams that things would get better. After all I loved her and she loved me, what could possibly go wrong. She ran hot, not by a temperature that can be cured by soup and rest, but a fever that could only be cured by a child.

She had baby fever, the kind that took the joy of making a family and turning it into a chore; Constantly trying start a family but never any results. I was torn. We had no place to live yet, I still needed a car, and waited patiently for an overdue promotion. But I couldn't give her what she desired despite trying anyways. Never putting my own priorities first. She dumped me, delivered everything to me except the engagement ring. One week later, she posted her 4 month anniversary with some guy. I was confused, we had just broken up. We were engaged. Immediately close friends and family started calling me, rapidly and too a point where I was lost. I had no explanation, no context. We met up one last time, I needed closure. No, I needed answers. She had been cheating on me with a past boyfriend, she was already moving in with him, and he had more to offer.

I felt used, disregarded myself. Punched brick walls into my knuckles turned purple, couldn't identify my hands as purple given all the blood that covered my hands and fingers. Worried for my mental and emotional health, I got help. Therapy was kind to me, offered me a closure I wasn't sure existed. Closure that eventually I'll find love again, and I should keep my priorities in mind. Closure that made it easier to breathe, after all I was realizing I devoted so much to her and couldn't see the signs. I kinda knew she was fucking another man, I just led with my heart and made the bet to not assume anything. That was a mistake and through therapy I developed self confidence and love.

I spent over a year swiping on tinder, bumble, hinge. After therapy I knew I wanted to date again, but the right way. To find companionship with a best friend and a lover all in one. I was too nice but my kind heart was never my weakness, my weakness was not realizing how she had me do everything for her just to cheat on me in the end. After swiping for a year I became tireless. Like a machine, open minded yet swiping as much as I could. The more time passed without going out on a date the more I questioned if the love for myself that I had was earned. It's easy to love myself but gets a lot harder to maintain that love for myself when nobody will give me the chance. Eventually I met someone new After swiping for a year I became tireless. Like a machine, open minded yet swiping as much as I could. The more time passed without going out on a date the more I questioned if the love for myself that I had was earned.

It's easy to love myself but gets a lot harder to maintain that love for myself when nobody will give me the chance. Eventually I met someone new. Both of us heartbroken, we kept it casual. Went out for really nice burgers and talked about our lives. Driving to the date I kept asking myself am I really ready for this. And the second I saw her I knew I was. Unlike my ex fiancé who took a while for me to have genuine feelings for her, my date for the day I felt something instantly.

She was energetic, had the most amazing laugh I'd ever heard. Brian hair, and brown eyes that looked upon me like I was actually there. And I was, she was just amazing at keeping eye contact and listening to our conversations. She had these round glasses that I instantly crushed on. I never dated or even had a crush on someone with glasses but hers only brought out the gold in her eyes. While my ex fiancé went from quiet to demanding, my new date fully embraced who I was. I didn't have to hide a piece of me. We needed out to music and anime together, we had the same goofy humor, and we had hearts of gold. Her job was taking 911 calls also she could help save people. Unlike my ex I was finding what my standards were. Compassionate and honest, with the genuine respect to be yourself and be goofy every once in a while. To bond over our interests even if we haven't tried or heard of them. She didn't know who my favorite artist was so I made her a playlist and within two weeks she had listened to it.

She didn't pretend to know, she took a chance on my compassions. Even when I was in between apartments she let me stay at her place. Through our memories of compassion and laughter in my eyes, she became the most beautiful woman I've ever known. More beautiful than any song I've listened too.i wish we could have lasted, for a had found my best friend, my second half, and the person that took a chance on me and actually liked me. We fell apart. Doesn't make any sense right!? Like I bet anyone reading this was thinking that the story was over, and that I earned a happy ending.

Unfortunately, no. I told her loved her and she never said it back. I respected that, but she went on to claim that I wasn't right for her. That I deserved better. If only she knew how perfect I thought she was, so perfect if someone better is out there I truly don't want it. Everything about her was perfect and she didn't feel the same. I made the mistake of going to see her when she requested time to think. I was panicked, I didn't want to loose her. And I did. I was devastated. I started throwing up, felt like someone kept hitting me in the core. I'd cry randomly. I'd be doing something and all of a sudden: tears. She possessed my routine, was constantly reminded of her or memories I made with her if I heard a random song, or saw something random at the store. To this day it still happens.

I reflect to the night of the super moon, we were at a concert and I loved over at her. She was dancing, laughing. Genuinely happy, an emotion I wish I could make her feel on my own. If heaven is really your favorite memory on loop, that memory is what I'd choose to be my eternity. Back to therapy and that was brought up. I inherited my mother's legacy but I'm pretty sure our hearts are the same model, just with different mileage. My mother was amazingly compassionate and put many other's needs before her own. My heaven is literally someone else being happy, so I had to find my own sense of self love. I found it in music but that's just a hobby/interest.

I really found myself in long walks around the nature that is Colorado, and in the gym. Where my head would clear and only my own goals would be the priority. I'm not one for masculinity despite being really really strong for my height/weight ratio. So the gym isn't for other people to notice me, it's for me to appreciate me and learn more about my physical and mental health. Since we broke up I haven't been on a single date. I went from hours of screen time on dating apps, to hardly scrolling at all. And that's the cycle. First love didn't work out, second love was a real love and unfortunately it didn't work out, and now self love. The most important kind of love. Cause now I feel free being myself at all times. I gained a sense of self confidence and maturity through spending time with myself. I hate feeling alone but I'm never alone. My past won't define me, it'll just keep pushing me towards my future. Love is scary, heartbreak hurts. But I'm not afraid of it. I will find love again and even if I lose it, I'll always find it again within myself. Why? Well because: "Genuine love is something that should not be special but too often is.".

-Braeden

First Love, First Heartbreak

ould I have thought 2 years ago, one person would have shaped my whole perspective on love? He was my best friend's brother. I knew him for a while but after a year me and his little sister fell out of our friendship. The summer of 2022 I spent getting to know people that I thought I could look up to. I added him on Snapchat and asked him if he sold because I wanted a reason to talk to him. He ended up scamming me, but a month later our county fair was coming up.

I told him I could get alcohol for his friends and asked if it was okay if I hung out with them. I got the alcohol and it was in my bag, it had been 2 years since COVID hit and I was standing in line for the zipper with kids I last saw in elementary school. (I was an upcoming 8th grader.) I saw him walking up and I pulled out my vape and the alcohol and my old friends looked at me confused because I used to be this innocent little girl that they used to pick on. I felt, powerful.

I walked away from that group and was with him and his friends. We walked by his little sister and I didn't even make eye contact with her. It felt wrong, but at the same time I felt good about myself. How I didn't let one person ruin my chances at meeting more people. That night, it was his cousin, his cousin's girlfriend, him, and me. We were messing around and he pulled me by my jean loop because I had his sunglasses. I fell onto his lap and I got immediate butterflies. Throughout the night he showed more and more interest in me and had all of the group laughing. After fair, I asked him what it was about and he told me, "I think I wanna fw you, my cousin told me to go for it if I felt this way, so here we are." A couple weeks went by and he invited me to little get togethers with his friends. I was happy.

One day, he invited me over to the same house and wouldn't tell me who was there. I walked in and it was his sister. We both were mad at him, and his friend that was our age left with him to get alcohol. (He was an upcoming junior, but we were a year and a half apart in age.) It was awkward between me and his sister, but we made up and realized the drama we had going on was stupid.

After 2 months of talking, we went to the bowling alley in a big group and he was all over me. We walked 30 minutes in the group to our Safeway and we were sitting outside at the benches. Everyone was distracted and we were laughing and he turned my head and kissed me. After that he asked me, "Do you wanna be my girl?" I immediately said yes and told my close friend that was with us. I was happy. A month went by and he got in trouble at a football game at the school he went to. His cousin, his cousin's girlfriend, his little sister, and I all followed the golf cart he got picked up in.

He got in trouble and his parents drove me home. My grandma hated him after that, refused to let me be with him. Lucky for me, she never saw his face and he lived with my best friend, (his little sister.) I went to their house for every holiday.

I went to six flags with them and this became a problem when him and his little sister argued who I should hangout with. On halloween is when I realized he wasn't the best person when he was drunk and I balled my eyes out. I was sad. In December, is when I lost my virginity to him. This brought us closer, but not for long. It became an almost everyday thing.

We didn't start having problems until January, 2023. He started drinking way more and hanging out with people who hated we were together. I couldn't leave, at least I couldn't let go of what we used to have. Around this time is when my grandma found out we were together. On New Year's, we walked down to this party that was two houses down from the family get together, and there was so many girls asking him for his vape and trying to talk to him. I wanted to cry, I was stressed out and realized what the possibilities were.

What if he's cheating on me? This became a huge problem. In February, his cousin and him texted me asking if I could pick them up and bring them to my hometown that they lived a 15 minute drive from, but a 3 hour walk. I immediately convinced my aunt to pick them up and he was being an asshole to me all night. We got food at a restaurant and he didn't get me anything which I wasn't bothered by, but was just being a drunk slob shoving all his food down his throat staring at me.

His cousin gave me one of his chicken strips, and I was happy with that. I snuck them into my grandma's house and he wouldn't stop arguing that he had to go somewhere else. If his cousin was staying, he wanted to leave. If his cousin was going to a girls house, he wanted to go with him and got all excited.

He also left his phone at home. I was just trying to calm him down because it was 2 in the morning. They ended up staying another night and he wanted to do the "deed" while his cousin was asleep on my floor. He stopped texting me. He face-timed me the night before he decided to break up with me. The conversation was very short. I texted him the next night at 3am and asked him what was wrong. We had a deep conversation and I was telling him what we needed to fix if we wanted to keep this relationship going and after a while he said, "Idk" and I left him on open. 10 minutes later he texted me and said, "I think I'm done with you." My heart stopped. I couldn't breathe. It's like my whole world stopped and my lungs gave out. I swiped out of our chat and he blocked me. I go to text him on Instagram, he blocked me.

His TikTok, he blocked me. Messages, he blocked me. I ran out of my room and it was one of the only nights my aunt stayed over. I was crying my eyes out like someone died. It felt like it, it felt like I lost the only person keeping me going. What was the point? My aunt told me to go to sleep and I left and went up to basically my mom at their apartment in the same complex.

I walked in balling my eyes out still. They comforted me and ending up making me laugh. I went back home and I don't remember the rest of that night. I had to go to a family dinner the next day. I didn't wanna talk and couldn't make myself eat. 2 weeks later I cashapped him $1 asking him to unblock me. He told me it was because he was talking to his ex that came before I talked to him. I broke down crying again like it first happened. I stopped texting him.

Why? What did I do wrong? I did end up seeing the chats with him and her, and it was from the last night we were together. That he didn't bring his phone. Turns out I lost the love of my life, and my best friend in the end. He is still with the same girl and I am happy that he found his person, but there is so much more to the story that happened months later that I cannot include because it would mess up a lot of people's lives and the story would go on forever.

It took me months to move on from him and multiple rebounds. I learned a lot from him and even after all that happened between us I'm thankful for how it turned out. There is still endless possibilities on what happened and what went through his head, but the blame cannot be put on either one of us because it was my first time loving, and he didn't end up wanting something serious after he realized what came with it. Learn from it, don't yearn on it.

-Delilah

We Always Make Our Way Back

W̲e were 6 and 5 we we became best friends ever and couldn't be away from each other then we didn't see each other for a bit and again at 9 and 10 we saw each other at a snow trip and we got into like buddy system and we got next to him and didn't want to leave his side and then he called me his gf and we didn't leave each others side and sad each other ever week and then we went our separate ways again then again at 12 and 13 and now we were more aware of what we were and we started hanging out again as best friends and then he said he liked me and I liked him and we hung out he took me out to a place and we walked around and we started dating and we were the couple everyone wanted to get together and then he moved so we lived about an hour and a half away or 2 hours and we were still together we would see each other every two weeks or month I would go to his soccer games and go see him and then my birthday came up and I went over there and spent it. With him and my cousin and then for my gifts he got me two rings and I had my first kiss that day and then about in February we split up because of rumor but

178

it was getting toxic we started fighting a lot and he didn't want me to go out and he was getting manipulative and then a month before we broke up he was talking to other girl and he canceled our plans to go see her and then I realized what was happening we stopped talking for a while about almost a year and after we broke up he posted the girl a week later saying "happy 2 months" and I was broken and then after about almost a year he texted me around my birthday because they broke up and when I saw that friend request my hear sank he told me he texted me because my brother was coming up it was about a week and a half before my birthday So now I was about to be 15 then he apologized and told me how much he loved me and I fell for his trick so we got together again and I went over there again and saw him and then he told me he was busy and then I got that feeling again he had said he changed and he few what he did was wrong and then we talked about it and I fell in love again and everything was great until 2 weeks before I was about to go I felt off and then he started changing again and when I did go I had found out he was talking to another girl and I didn't want to believe it but then I had proof and then that broke my heart again about after all the fighting and arguments I forgave him and then I just went thru it again so that broke me and we blocked each other and then 5 months after his friend sent him a screenshot of me at a tournament and completion and he said that he felt bad about what happened and then he unblocked me but was still with the girl and he changed the way I look at guys because he was my first love first everything and most traumatic.

-    Santi

My Forever

O n Monday 8th of January 2024 at 20:08pm i had my first ever girlfriend and everything was going so well we were so in love with each other, she was THE most beautiful woman in the world she took so much pride in herself, her hair was never out of place, her voice so soft and smooth i'd listen to it forever, her eyes her face i'm telling you i'd stare at that woman for a life time. yes she was my girlfriend but she was no girl that really was a woman, a strong woman, a proud woman, MY woman she was all mine and i was hers.

She was into me first and so many people told me her friends my friends even just mutuals but i never listned, we had one massive group chat with everyone else included and her way of flirting with me i thought she wanted to just argue with me so i never payed her any mind but i was convinced in the end, three of my friends said to give it a try and so i did.

Our first ever conversation between us started off as her sending me a picture of her feet it was weird at first but the more we spoke it just kept getting better like as if she was me but just the complete opposite gender, in fact she was SO into me she initiated our first date and it was put together like this "you, me and iceskating" and so we arranged a date and time and i fucked up, i fucked up real bad i had an argument with my mom before we were supposed to leave and because i had a slight bit of attitude where i asked her to drop me off she dropped me off 30 minutes away from there as she assumed i knew my way to the iceskating rink and i had to walk but i was lost and i called my mom to give me directions and so i missed every single call from her and in the end we never got to go ice skating, eventually we met up even though it was too late to fix things we still went to wingstop and i bought her the food she wanted, while waiting in line we never spoke once it was an awkward silence but understandble i was just late to our first ever date but i lied to her i didn't tell her i had an argument with my mom.

I didn't tell her i had to walk there and got lost i didn't tell her the reason i missed all her calls was because i was getting directions i kept quiet about it because i thought she'd judge me and i didn't want to lose her an so everyone and i mean everyone her friends and my friends they all thought i played her, that i was just another guy manipulating girls for fun. despite our first date coming to ruin she still wanted to talk to me she still wanted to pursue what might of been there and she forgave me but i still never told her the truth i just couldn't so i kept it to myself.

Afterwards everything was going so smoothly valentines day came around and i bought her a really nice bear that she wanted and i bought myself one as she wanted us to match but the only downside was that we

181

couldn't really arrange any plans because exam season was approaching so we both had to focus on ourselves and to of course pass our exams but we still kept in contact and spoke every day, i first told her i loved her on the on the 25th of march, we had a bit of an argument the day before it was a silly one i told her i was watching some weird vid and as a joke she asked "are you gay ??"

Because of the vid i was watching was about LGBTQ+ and i knew she meant it as a joke but i took it personal in the moment and said i don't want to speak to you right now and told her goodnight but while laying in my bed i realized i was the one at fault i let my emotions get the better of me over a simple joke but it was too late to message her as she was sleeping since it was late, so i woke up in the morning and i apologized for how i acted and treated her the night before and i told her "i love you" and she said it back she told me she loved me and i was the happiest guy in the world.

I knew then we were perfect for each other and from the 25th of march to the 31st of May we were in love SO in love i was hers and she was mine of course we had arguments but we kept resolving them we spoke about how we felt although it was hard for me she brought out a different side to me where i could express myself and there wasn't an argument we had we never fixed because i loved her and she loved me but may was when exam season started the exams that would decide the first part of our future so we were a lot more distant and conversations were shorter and felt less exciting but i still none the less felt the love from her. June hits her birthday month the 2nd to be exact i bought her a gift it was a silver bracelet with 6 charms to represent we had been together for 6 months and every month after that we would go together and buy a new charm until we hit 12 to represent we would have been together for a full year but that wasn't her actual gift it was just so she didn't see what i really had planned for her which was for us to see SZA.

We had been talking about it before and she said she'd have wanted to go so without her knowing i bought them and i got my best friend to lie to my mom and say how he and i wanted to go but he's pay me back as i was the one buying the tickets and my mom agreed and i had them and i was so excited and we even had SO much planned for the summer to do together i honestly couldn't wait but then the day after her birthday she began to ignore me constantly over and over again and said she was just studying and said to me " i can't believe you'd think i'm lying about studying" and i said you know what you're right its exam season we can focus on our relationship.

After exams but i still wanted to clarify if her feelings for me where still there and so i asked her whats really going on between us and she said " i just don't care anymore" was the key highlight out of all the messages she sent me and on Thursday the 6th of June she broke up with me said she had been ignoring me on purpose for weeks and that she wasn't studying that it was just an excuse because i talk so much and i fought for it of course i didn't want to believe it was over but she wouldn't hear me out she didn't want to fight for it like how i wanted to and that was it i'd just been abandoned by the person i said i'd marry , the person who said i should call her my last name instead of her name the person who told me she'd never leave, the person who told i was the best boyfriend ever i'd just been left our entire summer plans had just been crushed.

I cried for 2 days straight but i put on a smile every day and said i'd be okay and i was getting there slowly but surely i was feeling like myself again but then 2 weeks later on the 24th of June she randomly messaged me she said she was checking up on me and we spoke it was mostly a dry conversation as i came to terms that she didn't want to save our relationship so why must i show all this affection again and the conversation got the point where i said i was going to leave now and she said "no messaged you for a reason" and asked her what that reason was and she said " i just miss you, not this not like i'm ready for this to happen again but i miss you", and from then onwards i was drawn in, i didn't pay attention to her actions only her words her false words that drew me in again and we kept talking until she told me she knows in herself that i'm the one for her but that right now she needs to find out what she wants for herself and then she told me she loved me and i got pulled in even further and we started speaking again and it felt so good even though we weren't together it felt good like i had my person back, she was back to liking all my instagram stories she was back to being MY woman but its not like we spoke 24/7 we'd leave each other on open or seen on read whatever it was because we both knew we couldn't but we still kept talking she updated me on her life and i did the same.

She kept getting jealous if she thought there was another woman in my life when there wasn't i was waiting for her waiting for her to be ready but she would never listen to me she gave me one worded answers told me she didn't care and then she dropped everything and said "i just don't have feelings for you anymore" after dragging me back in after telling me you miss me and you love me you stopped everything again for good and i don't get why i was told i was perfect i was told she was so lucky to have me i kept getting told everything.

I wanted to hear she told me she promised she'd change but i kept hearing the change but i never looked for it and now i hate you i hate you so fucking much but oh i love you more than anything because how are you able to just move on so quick, i did everything i could i how do you just forget about me like that how do i all of a sudden mean nothing to you anymore i hate you, i fucking despise you i want you to receive all the pain in the world i want someone to break you so fucking bad you realize what it is you left, i want someone to call you the ugliest person they've ever seen so you can remember when i continually called you the most beautiful woman in the world, i want someone to leave you on delivered all day and tell you they just don't want to talk to you so you can realize how it is you treated me, i want someone to ruin you're perception of love so that you can remember all the love i gave to you, i want you to be ruined so you never feel like you can be loved again.

But even though i'm behaving like this i want you and i need you because i'm in love with you still i want you to be MY woman again please just stop reposting about him and come back to me have you're love return to me come back and genuinely apologize to me tell me how bad you fucked up tell me how sorry you are for ruining what we had tell me that you love me again but mean it mean it with you're heart and you're soul but right now i'd give anything for someone to ruin everything for you so you can just come back because you will NEVER find me in someone else you can look all you want but the one you want is me isn't it ??

When will you realize it was me all along in this very moment i hate you i can't help but hate you but i also love you i love you so much more than anything so i want you to die i want you to die and then come back to me i need you and i want you its you and me i'm yours and you're mine thats what you told me right these are MY feelings so you wouldn't get it but just hold my hand again lets love each other just one more time because i know we can do it right so what do you say because i don't want to lose you again i don't want to lose you anymore my love you are still so beautiful trust me i've seen you're tiktoks but i can't comment anymore i can't like them or favorite them i can't do anything until i'm with you again because... i love you.

Elegance Of Affection

⬥⬦⬥

Prologue: its June 2018, the first time I saw her, she had very attractive eyes that's all I've been able to figure out at that point. we 17 and went to the same high school where we had almost every class together. one class period we had a project and we both got paired. I was so nervous inside, then when we both started to talk my nervousness started to go away little by little.

Hardness: once after we done with our quarterly examination, I was eagerly waiting for the results as I did , pretty well for the first time and expected to be in top 10 among 9th standard for which we are rewarded with medals I never had one for studies though. when results were out , I missed medal this time too but rank, guess what? she stood in the tenth place. I was more frustrated when I came to know both secured the same amount of marks, but they preferred a girl over a boy, kidding actual reason is she secured more in math which is considered for ranking if totals were the same.

The change- Cupid entrance: I felt bad she used to struggle as hard as I did. but she never disappoints and

187

happy as if she stood first in school. I was surprised and thought of communicating with her , but all the nervousness came back then I was least bothered about marks, ranks etc and started concentrating on her my whole 10th standard unknowingly I might fall for her, dreamt of her every time. she was the only reason I even attended school on Saturday. it was magical days I used to buy everything she bought including pink colored water bottle facepalm I used to stare at her most of the time. when I saw her attractive eyes everything went to vain , I didn't have enough guts to go up and talk to her as she was with her friends. Being Dumb: somehow I finally managed to get her number In my slam book through one of her friends (female).

Coming up is the dumbest thing I've ever done. or its better if I say anyone would have ever done. so I text her stating "I LOVE YOU TOO" thinking she might have sent me those but that was her mother number and then the next day her mom called my phone yelling saying how you get the this number, luckily her mom didn't revel the actual messages so I was able to manage the most embarrassing situation in my home pretty well.

But I got to know that her mom scolded her a lot as I sent "LOVE YOU TOO" very foolish and I thought she wasn't never going to come back ever again I'm pretty sure I'm going to miss her a lot. every time I think of her I feel hyped, delighted,blushed and even energized. The Unexpected part: after years past one of my school friends created a group chat for our school batch on December first week of 2019, though which I got her number her real number, pretty sure my nerves wasn't there anymore, so I dared to wish her a happy new year.

Me:(12:00AM) Hey happy new year its been a while since we talked. She: hey hi, happy new year I'm so happy to hear from you. Happiness- The best part since then we've been together and we both love each other a lot and we are more happy then ever. This is my story on how I found my unexpected magical love of my life THE END) 1. What I've learnt is first love never dies, no matter what 2. whatever happens in life it happens for a reason. 3. sometimes ignorance is better than acceptance. 4. there is a perfect time for everything to happen, all we need is patience.

-@vibe.withty_

Unfortunate Events

I met this person during an internship where she worked, and I was an intern. We quickly became friends and talked every day. After the internship ended and I no longer went to the workplace, we continued to hang out on weekends, and I would sometimes stop by to see her. Over time, I developed feelings for her and started to have a crush. I kept it a secret for about a month, but eventually, I couldn't hold it in any longer. Even though I knew she didn't see me that way, I decided to tell her how I felt. When I confessed, she said she only liked me as a friend. I felt hurt and embarrassed, so we didn't text each other for about two weeks. After that time, I sent her a message explaining that I was too embarrassed to reach out earlier and needed some time for my romantic feelings to fade. She responded with a short "ok." After that, we didn't text each other.

-Oscar

A Love Once Held

In the summer of 2022, I first went to summer school. I had no friends and not much of anything. Until I met her. She was beautiful—so beautiful beyond the universe and stars. I wanted to talk to her, yet I was scared. I messaged her, and that's when everything started. We fell in love during that time.

We first started getting close when school began again. We hadn't hugged or called each other until November, a couple of days after her birthday. I remember calling her; she sounded so sweet. The next day, we hugged and talked for the first time. I loved it so much. The way she held me made me feel so happy. That's when I knew I had to be her everything, to be the greatest person for her. She had been hurt and broken by her past, so I helped her and loved her through it all. She became my reason for focusing, for changing myself physically, mentally, and spiritually.

We created so many memories together. I remember playing guitar for her favorite songs, even when I felt shy and afraid. I almost had an anxiety attack, but holding her for so long made everything better. Walking her to work and meeting her mom were moments that filled my heart with happiness. Her mother's kindness, the thoughtful birthday gifts, and the embrace she gave me made me feel like part of their family. Douglas, the stuffed animal dog we shared, became a silent witness to our love.

But love isn't always easy. The year 2023 was tough. We lost each other a few times, but each time we found our way back. I would walk miles, driven by my love for her, just to see her. Walking ten miles to church to see her in her beautiful dress is a memory I hold dearly.

As school ended, she hugged me tightly, holding on as if she knew what was coming. Misunderstandings and doubts began to creep in. I believed that she wanted someone else, and my heart broke. I distanced myself, thinking it was the right thing to do, but the regret stayed with me.During summer school, I wanted to talk to her but kept my distance. On the last day, I told her how I felt and apologized. She forgave me, and for a moment, it felt like things could go back to how they were.

Then, the messages stopped. She was moving, and the fear of losing her forever settled in. Every day felt heavier without her. I missed her—the warmth of her hugs, the way she played with my hair, our laughter. It felt like losing a part of myself I turned to prayer, asking God for strength and wisdom. The physical pain I put myself through at the gym was nothing compared to the emotional pain inside me.

But through the heartache, I began to grow. I learned about vulnerability and the importance of trust and communication. I realized love is about more than just joy; it's about enduring the tough times together.

Days turned into weeks, and I slowly started to rebuild myself. She was my reason for growth, my everything. I changed for her and promised to be better for her. Through her, I found myself and became who I am. I love her and always will. But I know I have to let go, even though it hurts. Maybe someday, maybe not, but I'll always love her. She will always be my special girl. I love you forever I will always my star.

-Caleb

Love Lost

Ngl I've been hurt so much in the past by countless boys, my dad, my mom, and my own family, and I do feel like I hadn't fully let go of the past but mostly overall I had. I've never had luck with boys or love Yk they give you the world and then end up telling you they need a break or they can't be with you rn and that they'll come back, and I think you know the answer to if they ever did.

But when someone leaves you with nothing and no closure or words of peace. You have 2 choices which are to bed rot every day and constantly be sad over it and never let it go and keep living in the past or take some time to rest and when ready get back up and put yourself on your own 2 feet again even though it's hard and trust me it's hard......So I got back up, and I comforted myself I healed the wounds they caused And I found my happiness And I found the peace in being okay with being alone And I can't tell you how great it felt to achieve that And I had told myself I was done with love But 5 months later...I meet him.

He was like this big bright light that could shine all

the darkness away. He never cheated. Never was disloyal. Made sure I was taken care of before he was but I ofc made sure he was in return I never take without giving back. He would drive countless nights to come to see me. He'd help me fall asleep when I couldn't he'd even play with my hair most of the time bc he knew I liked how it felt. He would hold me when I wanted to be held. Let me cry when I needed to. Never judged me for being me. Took showers with me which I loved bc he would always wash my hair for me and give me little scalp massages would help rinse it all out but the best part was when I would hug him and we'd just stay that way and I felt the hot water running down my body and at that moment I felt nothing but peace. He listened to me, he understood me.

He always would try to make sure he could help in any shape or form. Took care of me when I was sick. Used his own money on me bc he knew I didn't have a job ofc but he said that didn't matter. He made me laugh and smile. And this was the first time I didn't feel anxious with someone.I didn't feel uneasy, Or like I wanted to throw up 24/7 I was just calm. And honestly, this was also the first time I felt comfortable with someone sexually and I felt like they enjoyed embracing me and praising every inch of me and making me feel good in my own body He was patient Even if I would yap for hours he'd still listen and he ofc gave excellent feedback.

And each time I had a negative thought he was right there to reassure me no matter how many times he had to he would. Ik there were also times when he would slip up it wasn't common kinda of like rare. But nobody's

195

perfect I can't expect him to be perfect He's human and so am I. My job is to help him learn not to bash him constantly for his mistakes and that was his job too But a month passed and it was the beginning of August like the first week. And we're talking in my room it's past midnight at this point And I'm asking him what he wants to do with his life bc I ofc am curious like any girl would be. And he tells me he's leaving for school in 4 days.... I can't tell you in that instant my heart sank...And he knew the whole time.

But he said the reason for not telling me was because he didn't want me to be anxious the whole time, He didn't want me to worry about him leaving So he kept it from me even though that's no excuse I understood kind of but I also was just too upset at the time to try to understand and I also knew he should've just told me and that's final. And I didn't move for a good 20 min I sat there frozen and the whole time he kept trying to get my attention whether it was trying to comfort me ask me what was going on in my head or what I was thinking and I just looked at him and I was like " why" and then he ofc added on how long distance was hard for him and that space was gonna be good here and there and that it wasn't gonna be the same.

But I couldn't even take any more information in right bc my head was spinning and my stomach felt like I wanted to throw up. And I told him to leave which I'd never done before. I looked at him with so much anger and told him to get out And the tears just started falling, but he didn't leave...He sat right next to me and kept trying to comfort me but each time I pushed him away. Kept trying to get me to talk. But I didn't move I just sat there in shock and the tears just kept rolling I swear like a waterfall but my face was blank like there were tears but no emotion. After a while he did leave bc he had to...and i ofc let it out that night. The days after that were hard bc I only had a few days to decide whether I wanted to see him one last time. It's hard when the thing that makes you feel better is the thing that's causing you to hurt in the moment. But I knew I'd regret not seeing him one last time so I did and I wish I had hugged him tighter or looked him in the eyes and told him how much I loved him even more He told me he'd come back...which wouldn't be till Thanksgiving break which is 4 months originally I thought it was only 4 months that he was gonna be away at school.

A week went by he'd already left by now he kept telling me how sad it made him when he had to pack bc he didn't want to leave but it's school something that's gonna help him build a career and a future and I can't simply tell him to give that up. But the reality starts hitting me. Last night were on the phone and idk a small disagreement came about and I found out it's not 4 months....he's gonna be in school It's 4 years he's gonna be gone. He comes back in 4 months for a break though.

I can't tell you how bad it hurt I just kept crying and trying to catch my breathe bc my chest felt so tight. He wasn't gonna leave though he said he did suggest some space to make it easier for the both of us bc we both have our own lives still and we can't be constantly focused on each other especially when we're both gonna start school soon and I'm gonna get a job and there's just opportunities coming my way and his and if we're so focused on each other we'll miss those opportunities. He said he'd never cut me off though and that he'd be right there always. But a girly has trust issues so it's not easy trusting that ever.

He said he'd always love me no matter what and that his love would never change for me. He said it was up to me on what I wanted to do. Personally trusting that someone can go to college for 4 years and stay faithful is hard, especially with how boys are nowadays. But I also know it's hard letting someone go that I fell in love with and who gave me the love I've always wanted and even gave me peace in being with someone and also being able to focus on me as well Idk how many times he's apologized...I couldn't even count if I wanted to. But 4 years...4 whole years and he kept that from me All bc he wanted to make me happy and not worried.

But it also felt like he was being selfish in some ways bc he really wanted this to the point where he didn't wanna bring up something that would potentially cause me to not talk to him or to have different thoughts. I guess now he realizes that was a terrible mistake bc it ended up hurting me which really fucked with him. Even on the phone I could tell me crying like that hurt him bc he wasn't there to comfort me and there was no amount of comfort he could give me at that moment to help me bc he wasn't here and I couldn't even focus on what he was saying anymore. I just felt my chest sinking inward more and more every time I tried to calm down it just kept coming back. And it wasn't that regular cry It was that gut-wrenching cry where you just want to scream. What hurt also was I told everything All the pain I was caused in the past and the lessons I learned from them.

198

He still chose to do it this way.

And I just kept saying "I didn't wanna do this again" and that it hurt I couldn't even finish a sentence bc my voice kept breaking. After hours of talking and me finally being able to explain to him how I felt I knew he was getting tired but he kept fighting the urge not to fall asleep bc he didn't wanna leave me alone so he asked "Do you wanna fall asleep on the phone" I said yes ofc he said goodnight and that he loved me not even 5 minutes later I hung up Idk why but I just couldn't...I thought I could but I couldn't even be on the phone with him anymore and I just let it all out LIKE ALL THE WAY didn't matter how loud I was or how long I cried for I just knew I had to let it out rather than keep it all in It went on for hours until I eventually wore myself out and passed out.And now it's tomorrow.

I did wake up feeling better which is why I love to sleep of course my face was puffy and my eyes were a bit swollen which is due to the fact your girl was going through it last night. I texted him I didn't wanna speak to him until I was ready and I didn't know when that was gonna be I said what I wanted to because I knew he wanted to know how I felt. This is what he had to say. "Ima be real with u u right about saying a lot can change in 4 yrs. Its a possibility I go fw another its a possibility I don't. Idk what the future holds.

Knowing that it's up to u on what u wanna do whether that's completely cut me off keep talking, u need to do what's gon be right for u rn. Im not gon feel a typa way ab what u decide ever. I also didn't think we was gon move as fast as we did. I feel like shi was js going so fast and going good and I wanted to keep it like that for as long as I could which was obviously a mistake ian mean. I'm sorry I hurt u it obviously wasn't my intention Lilly." And now I'm stuck.

Because I couldn't cut him off completely but that means I'd never speak, see, or know him again or I could push through the hard times right and hope everything turns out well and risk knowing if the consequences turn out bad or good for me. Both hurt equally the same It's like I can potentially choose to lose him forever or have hope and trust things will work out but still take space for me and my life and focus on the opportunities coming my way.

And it hurts bc it's like I'm in love with someone I can't fully have. I'm not weak you can ask anyone and they'll tell you I'm the strongest most loving person you'll ever meet I always no matter what time of day or who it is I'm always offering advice or help any way I can because it feels nice to help others heal and learn from my mistakes I never want any type of pain or hurt to change me I always want to be loving and kind and patient and forgiving with others. I know it can be hard to forgive some people but remember you forgive them for yourself not for them. I'm the therapist of the group because even at the age of 17 I've been through hell and back my whole life basically but always made it out alive which is why I say I'm strong. That doesn't mean I want to be strong 24/7 it's not easy.

But if I'm not strong then I know that's me giving up on myself and I can't do that. So I guess I'm just stuck right now on what I want to do....I don't plan on speaking to him today anymore and idk when the next time gonna be it could be days or even weeks from now. I just know I rlly am trying to be positive right now and focus on living in the present and focusing on my opportunities coming up but I also know I'll eventually have to make a decision..whenever that is. I pray to god every night that no pain changes my heart no matter how cruel or how evil a persons has done me I never want it to change my heart. But I feel the thing that sucks the most is. If shit goes sideways and it doesn't turn out in my favor if I choose to still keep him apart of my life....I'm gonna have to be one to leave which hurts even more then having someone leave you. I already know he's not going to. I just hope eventually I'll figure out my plan.

-Lilly

The first person I ever fell in love with there could never b anything wrong with this girl ever to this day she's beautiful but as much as she was beautiful her soul radiated out of her I've still never met anyone like her and we tried our best the relationship was beautiful and I fell in love with her more and more every single day but she wasn't happy in her life n who she was as a person and as much as it hurt I let her go I miss her everyday and I think about her often I'd still give her the world if she called I'd drop anything go to her if that's what she wanted I see her on social media sometimes and as far as I know she's happy I'd give up anything for her even if that means giving up her I'm happy she's happy I'm satisfied I still love her n hope she's okay n I wish

nothing but the best of the best I can't give her the world
but I hope the world gives its self to her.

   -@4lyssa4._

In The Shadow of What ifs

———— ◆•◆•◆ ————

I t all started on a rainy Tuesday. I was behind the front desk, dealing with another tedious check-in when she walked in-Lena. New face, and honestly, I didn't think much of it at first. She seemed aloof and disinterested, but that was just me being my usual judgmental self. It wasn't until I noticed we had something in common that I started paying attention. One day, during a quick break, we ended up talking about weed. It's funny how a shared interest can change everything. Suddenly, Lena wasn't just another coworker; she was someone I could actually talk to. We started hanging out more, and one day she asked if I could give her a ride to the dog grooming place. I didn't think much of it-she seemed more like a favor than a date. After the grooming, we grabbed boba and watched a movie. The evening was relaxed and fun, but I couldn't shake the feeling that she saw me as just a friend. Maybe it was my introverted nature or my overthinking, but I convinced myself that she wasn't interested in me. My friends, however, had a different take. They urged me to ask her out, saying that I was just being too cautious. Four years without a girlfriend had made me hesitant and nervous. The idea of rejection played on my mind constantly. Finally, mustering all the courage I had, I asked her to a movie. She turned me down. I started to distance myself at work. I didn't want to face the awkwardness, so I withdrew. But weeks later, she started reaching out again, joking around, and laughing with me. I was confused. She mentioned wanting to watch the new Deadpool movie and that she didn't have anyone to go with. I wondered if this was her way of giving me another chance. That night, I couldn't sleep. I overthought every possibility until I finally decided to ask her out again. To my dismay, she rejected me once more. It was like a punch to the gut. I decided it was best to keep my distance, but deep down, I knew it wasn't just about timing. It was about my own fears and insecurities that had held me back. After writing this, I realized it's not a love story at all. But this is the closest I've experienced it. One-sided.

-@zamiryx

The vampire lady

The vampire lady. For the first time in my life, it felt like that thing many refer to as "true love." From the very first day we spoke, it clicked. We connected like we've just always known each other. Whenever we interacted, it was our souls bonding with each other. Feelings of pure nostalgia, that almost felt like they were from a life that I've never lived before. All though, we couldn't see each other. It wasn't the right time. I wanted to wait. Funny, right. The vampire lady. It only took her so long. Because the way I felt wasn't reciprocal. After all, she's a vampire. It wasn't me that was interesting to her. It was my blood. I was falling in love with the very thing that was going to kill me. How silly.

-@genkidev

You can see the best after the worst

——— ◆◆◆◆ ———

So, this girl, she was my first love, first ever girlfriend, my first ever experience in a relationship. We had known each other a while before we started dating, but I had always kind of had feelings for her. Then one day she sat next to me in class, and we just started chatting. After a few weeks, I could tell she was acting differently towards me than she ever had before. So one night, I texted her, and I told her how I felt, and asked her to by my girlfriend. And she said "I'd like that".

We proceeded to be together for the next 11 months, I loved her with everything I had, I don't know if it's just Because it was my first experience with love, but I gave everything. I was always there for her, felt guilty when I couldn't be, she was always on my mind. And I started to notice that she couldn't do the same, but I just brushed it off because I didn't even want to think about not having her in my life. As months go by, our relationship felt the strongest it had ever felt.

206

Then, she told me about a guy, and she told me about how he acted kinda weird around her, and tried to find ways to touch her a lot, he even invited her to lunch. And I asked her to please tell him. That you have a boyfriend, she then proceeded to tell me she didn't want to "make it weird". Even then, I still trusted her. And then about one month later, there was one day. July 7th. She was texting me super dry all day, it made me feel physically sick. And I had to ask if she was losing interest, she then told me it's complicated, and to call her. So I did, and she was crying, and explaining how she couldn't handle a relationship at the moment, and just needed to work on herself. And I was like, okay, that's fine isn't it? People need time, people need to heal alone.

So I was like, I'll wait for you, I'll still be there. But she was very stern on telling me. Not to wait, and to find someone else, which was strange at the time. But we broke up that day, and I didn't shed a tear, I was stunned. I couldn't think, I just wanted her to be happy. Then, one day a friend of mine, who is also friends with her, told me. She saw her making out with another guy And the words startled me, and at first I had no belief that it was true. But then he started to explain more, and I knew it was real, and I started uncontrollably shaking, I felt freezing, and my heart hurt. The image in my head of that happening was driving me

Insane. After she cried to me, told me she needed to work on her self, and could handle a relationship, and weeks after that she's with someone else. As the weeks go by I start to hear more news everything that happened, it was with the guy she told me about before, the one she told me not to worry about.

They were doing things I never did with her, because I am a Christian and waiting for marriage, and wanted to be respectful. And she was vividly describing what she did, to me, like she got some rise out of it. She was going on and telling people behind my back that I was "too sad" and mocking me.

This the same girl that I loved with every bit of my heart, that I dreamt about being married to. After all of this though. I have learned to much. I realized all the red flags I missed, I realized that I may have love bombed her, I realize that I was not the perfect partner, and neither was she. But most importantly, I have learned how to grow by myself.

I still think about her to this day, and I probably will for the rest of my life, but I know that I'm not chasing a relationship anymore. I know that god has it all in his hands, and when I meet the one god has for me, I'll know It. But I just want to love someone, feel loved, feel needed. I want to have picnics, and I want to play with her hair, and I want to rest my head on her lap. I have hope that I will someday. And whoever is reading this, if you don't have this yet, I believe that you will, and I'm exited for you.

-42clouds

Whispers of Goodbye

◆◆●◆◆

When i first saw you i wasn't looking for love but at the time i didn't know what it was but i felt it in my soul something about you charmed me. As the time we spent together passed the more my love for you grew i didn't instantly fall in love with you but the more i got to know you the more in love i grew with you it was the happiest i've ever been i enjoyed every second being around you, you made the most boring things feel so lively just the thought of you made me instantly happy just by being around you, you made me want be better as a person.

Unfortunately i was young and foolish i didn't appreciate what i had in front of me until i lost it. there was a time when you asked what i liked about you specifically but i couldn't answer but if you were to ask me now i would be able to rant about everything little detail about you for hours. you were the only person i could truly let my guard down and be myself with you got to see all of me the good and bad.

I wish i could change what happened between us but because of it i learned and grew as a person from it i regret what happened but i also appreciate it. You will never know how much of an impact you made in my life for the better. I wish you could've met the person i became because of you. maybe things would've went better if we tried again now but i will never know and i'm ok with that i've learned to live with that and let you go and just enjoy the memories we made together and the lessons you taught me because i realized that you aren't the same person either you also changed we met as strangers and became strangers again but i still appreciate you for coming into my life and leaving a mark on my life i want nothing but the best for you even if I'm not there with you.

-A.R

Love's Patient Chaos

———— ◆◆●◆● ————

I see love everywhere i go. it's always right in front of me, plainly obvious or lingering in the distance. it's never not there: always in a constant state of existing . yet i somehow manage to let one bad thing overcome the heaps of love all around me. i need stop to hear it in the laughter of my friends, i see it in the fields of green, i smell it in the flowers that are fresh in the fields, i feel it in basking in the presence of the warmth of the soothing sun. just take a look around: love is everywhere. I also think that love is quite similar to peace. a lot of the time it is mistaken for being something that disturbs that peace. yes, love can be scary because you trust and give your all to people - in any shape or form - in relationships, friendships , the love you put into yourself and your hobbies and talents everyday. it's terrifying to put that much power in others whether you aren't ready to trust them or are worried others will see you fail by putting so much love into simply just trying. however it is the best thing to put all your love into people, the things that you do and everyday life because it is who you are and you should

211

never let anyone take away your love. as in the end, it is better to have loved and lost than to have never loved at all.

- Rachel Galapin

Confused Love

—•◦•—

I guess it's about by love lost but I met her in November and I met her at a out patient area and I remember the first words we had with each other was her asking me for my number and then her friend was like "wow w RIZZ" and I said "oh yeah w RIZZ" and she laughed at me and would make fun of me for saying that but in like a nice way Yk like a loving way so we started texting and like i felt like we clicked the first time we talked she was so sweet at first and funny and we just were the same person but in different fonts anyways but I also remember that are first hangout was like my favorite time I got to spend with her we were all nervous and we got to go star gazing and we but a ginger bread house together and we just talked and talked and talked for a good 1-2 hours on her trampoline about like personal stuff and all that and then sadly a couple weeks later our relationship started drifting apart a little bit so I started to overthink and like question things and I got hella Emotional with her cause I thought I was gonna lose her and the bond and connection that we had but we ended up not breaking up but our bond had a little crack in it and then the bond started getting

213

bigger and bigger and bigger cracks which made like overthink so much and then I had this gut feeling that she cheated on me and I was right sadly women's intuition sucks ass but yeah and I asked her about it and she got defensive so I knew I was right and after that like we broke up but then we would like watch each others posts and story's and all that so we were still like drawn to each other but we knew we couldn't be together which made me so sad cause like I didn't know if I did anything wrong for her to like cheat Yk? Anyways but like we would watch each others stuff and all that and then one day she texted me again and we tried again and it just repeated over and over again so that's how we knew knew we couldn't be together. So we we did no contact and that was the worst feeling. Ever but fast forward to now we still talk as friends but I miss what we had and we just don't connect like we used to but I'd give the world to be with her again but at the same time I'd give the world to have never met her cause we both went through so much pain while we were together so I lost her and it wasn't even her fault half the time it was also mine we treated each other so badly that we fell out of love and yeah I do miss her but I also know we can only be friends which shatters my heart.

-Mari

FIRST LOVE

Everything started in that damn stupid Spanish class that i didn't even want to be in first i remember i just ended up switching into that class 2 semester of freshman year because i wanted to get that Spanish title, but i thought at least i have my friends in that class and that random kid who i saw the first day of school and thought he was really cute but later on realized he had a gf so i completely forgot about him as soon as i found out about that, fast forward in that Spanish class my friend happens to know him and be friends with him so we would talk every now and then but nothing too crazy because i respected the fact that he had a girlfriend , now it's April and for some reason they ended breaking out and i realize bro starts bring flirty with me and i was low key suspicious at first cuz he has just gotten out of a long term relationship and was probably not looking for anything serious. Tennis season start and most of the time i don't have right due to my parents working almost the whole day and I was freaking out already because practice was about to start and i still didn't have a ride , and then there was him so i just walked towards him and asked him for a ride, he was skeptical at first but later in agreed, and who would've though that little moment was gonna change a lot of things for me. This turned into a routine, he would take me almost everyday to practice and as you can assume some feelings started happening in both ways. and then one of those days we kissed. and that's when i started really falling for him. but then a little issue started happening as suspected because he she's out of a long-term relationship, but wasn't looking for anything serious and was just talking to a lot of girls to the point that he even went to one of this girls house and kissing and due to all that stuff, we just stop talking. now summer starts. I'm still hurt due to him because I was really falling for him but oh well I was starting to move on even though it wasn't that big of a deal until me and him start talking again he apologized and we're going on dates we start hanging out almost every day of summer. He made my parents and I was really really falling for him. I have never felt such a feeling like that towards someone summer was lovely there was still some issues, but we ended up talking them through and I was really falling in love with this guy words cannot explain how much I love them until he tells me he's moving to another school, which is completely 40 minutes away with messing with everything due to distance and he moved houses before summer ended so even though he moved 40 minutes away, we were still hanging out and we were still obsessed with each other. We loved each other or at least that's what I thought and then he started acting differently He started being distance with me. and then I suspected he ended up breaking up with me around October and you would think the story answered but no it ended here but sadly it didn't Football season all the school American dream activity is happening and suspected one of those games

216

after we broke up and then ended up talking which lead to kissing which eventually led to us talking again back to this point it was toxic. He was not the little cute romance we had back in summer . He wasn't being serious anymore. He was not being completely loyal between other stuff so fast forward to December we're still talking even though still toxic by this time but it was difficult seeing each other because his car broke down so he didn't have a car so there's was no way to see each other, and it turned into a situationship because we would only go back to talking and it seems like we got back together but we never fully got back together and sadlyI realized i was just way too attached to him to the point I just can't leave anymore and that's when I should've left because he was just not healthy and i knew this but i just couldn't. now it's January And out of nowhere we just stop texting, stop calling, it was sad how it got because it got to the point we're only snapping each other and that's when you know it's bad and we both end up agreeing in no contact and i was skeptical at first but he reassured me it was only temporary because he was getting a car in march, he was telling me to wait for him. which i did i still hopeful knowing all the love i had towards him which he assured me that he did too so i was willing to wait for him because he wasn't just my FIRST love , he was sadly my first LOVE, even though it was only on my part because he just saw me as one of all the girls he has talked to and nothing more serious than that the problem was i was way too delusion to realize this back on January because of how deeply in love i was with this kid and I'm calling a kid because he was never matured enough to even call him a man. fast forward to the first week of February we start talking again barely but wr are calling again, etc he

217

even tells me what i want for valentine's day which brings my hope to another level but sadly this isn't a happy ending love cutesy story , it's valentine's day the day my dumbass really though he was gonna try to come over and spend the day with me but poof he stops texting me with i though it was a little odd until i go in my fake acc which i follow him and i see he posted a story would you look weird for me because I remember one in my main and didn't see anything there so I go opening it thinking it's nothing serious. That is just a little thing as soon as I feel my heart shattered, I have never felt such an amount of pain and dropping in my life, though this is kind of exaggerated, but that's how I felt in the moment was so shocked and so heartbroken. I couldn't even cry. It was just so painful and I remember just like calling my best friend right away. I was sobbing already because of how much of a shock it was and she told me to calm down and then it was more of a shock because i knew he tried to hide it even though his try was worthless. So i sent him a screenshot of the story and told him that he lost me forever and the gaslighting started, he started saying that it was because i lived too far and that it wasn't what it looked like this and that and we just kept going back and forth until i gave up and sent him this last message "i always went back no matter how bad u fucked up because i loved you, and you took advantage of that, i really wanted us to worked out pero now i see how. it was, it was js me the whole time, i hope that you realize one day that u actually had someone that loved you more than you think, that actually wanted something real with you, y estaba dispuesta to work things out, and it's not the fact that u didn't do anything w her marcos it's what u didn't do with me, the fact that you gave her all that without doing anything with her just shows the

218

way that you see me because if you really wanted me you would've done that with me from the start but sadly that wasn't the case, pero esto it's not something that we can talk about and give it time, because you made me realize there was never no us. but i'm not going to be here for you anymore" and as soon as i sent that i felt my heart drop again and then he said nothing. literally nothing he only said that he didn't know what to say to that and that he hoped that one day we would find our way back to each other, like what??? after you put me throughout all that pain you really think imma even consider going back to you?? the thing is i did consider it because of how much i loved him even though i knew it was not gonna happen and that me loving him wasn't worth it but how they say "loving someone is never a waste" but in this case it definitely felt like it.

-Ajc

The Cheater Who Pleases
Everyone But Me

arly June 2014, it was before college exams before graduation, I met her on a social media video chat room site that was called WorldWideAsians.com, which no longer exists anymore. Kinda like facebook but for asians. It was her eyes and smile that caught me. We're both filipino, so we could relate with one another. But she was in Edmonton, AB Canada, while I was Toronto, ON, Canada. It started as video chatting on the site about 3 times a week growing to every day on Skype.

We shared from personal intimate details, to our greatest faults to our greatest losses and failures, to which we both exchanged sympathy and care with each other. Our feelings for each other grew and bloomed to the point we made commitments to each other and started our relationship. We were in love with each other. We did everything over Skype. Sexted out of pure genuine love, said our "I Love You's" before going off to work, virtual kisses, showed each other our cities and favorite places to eat and hang, sent each other mail, and cute corny little love packages like photos and stuff.

Talked about our parents and pets. We would skype and phone call overnight while we slept to replicate as if we were sleeping side by side with each other almost every night. Late August 2014, it was my graduation. We skype'd during my grad and I was the only grad who was pointing my phone around everywhere while we walked in the theatre in two uniformed lines to our seats, as if I was live streaming before live streaming became a thing. She was happy for me and posted me being called and accepting my certificate via Snapchat and on facebook. A few weeks later, she went out with her girlfriends for a friend's birthday at the club. She ended up getting hammered and grinded on some brown guy and kissed him closed mouth. I was not happy.

She cried and begged forgiveness and I gave in. STRIKE 1. Around December 2014, she bought me the latest GoPro and mailed it as a Christmas Gift. I mailed her a large teddy bear and my high school Rugby Jersey. Later on, we would start to miss each other because of the distance and she would question when I would be able to visit and cried. Around September 2015, we planned on how we would see each other in Edmonton by getting a room for rent for a week like a little escapade for use two without her parents knowing.

I got on a Greyhound bus for about $250 traveling from Toronto through all provinces between to Edmonton. The bus ride was 2 and a half days and I smelled like shit. When I arrived, I was in complete shock to see her at the bus terminal waiting for me. We finally had our very first kiss. I still remembered it being soft and warm. My dick however, also became warm but not soft. We had sex with each other about two hours later at the rented room. I was her first. I couldn't cum because I was too focused on looking at what I was trying to do right. We tried again the next day and she made me came. I remember we had a scare moment of the fear of getting her pregnant.

She took Plan B, we visited the clinic as extra precaution for PAP Test I think. And luckily nothing came of it. I also remember I had to do a lot of sneaking around with her parents whenever the opportunity of them being out of her house cane up. I got to see her house in person for the first time outside of Skype. We banged in her room and the living room couch. I got to meet her girlfriends, got to meet her cool aunt who kept the quiet about the ordeal we had, went on a double date, and she showed me around the city while trying her favorite spots and foods.

When it was time to go, we were both in heavy tears and gave each other the tightest of hugs and the longest of kisses. I remember crying on the bus for a good hour. I had never cried like this before. The rest is a bit fuzzy but I remember she cheated behind my back 2 more times and I was so in love with her that I didn't want to lose her and kept forgiving her. STRIKE 2 & 3. Eventually her parents got to meet me through Skype under the impression that I was born and raised in Edmonton and was out in Toronto for work. Around September 2016, this was it. I moved to Edmonton. I moved into her house in the spare bedroom with the approval of her parents. Work transition was wasn't too hard, but a lot of paperwork to process. For us, this felt permanent. To further establish our trust for each other, we exchanged passcodes and face recognitions of our phones to show neither of us had anything to hide with each other. But at this point forward, she either starts to lose interest in exchanging nudes with me or sends me nudes with less effort.

I remember her dad being pretty chill but her mom was strict and controlling over her. It was then when I first hand learned that her mom would become a burden on our relationship. Almost everything had to revolve around her mom and her little cousins. Over the course of being with her, I slowly learned that she was a people pleaser to everyone. I had my birthday once at her house and I invited people of different dynamics and she was more concerned of who wasn't going to flow with who and trying to please the guests all the time. Cant remember when, but she came and joined me to go home and finally met my family.

I showed her Canada's Wonderland. We had a fight because we spent most of the day in the water park and ran out of time for the rides, especially the biggest roller coaster in the park. She was really upset, she's an adrenaline junkie for this type of stuff. Another time she came to visit, we did it two days so we had enough time for rides. I showed her Niagra Falls, we had another small fight. While she wanted the front row of the tour boat, it meant breaking the rules a bit. There was a few times she asked me to do her college homework for her and believe it or not, I actually paid about $3.5k of her schooling when she had debt and maxed out her card. She paid me back, but still left owing me $2k. For this next part, I'm not going to go into specifics just because I don't feel comfortable about what I did in reaction but I'll just say I did something that made me look bad in

223

front of her family and I was shamed, when I thought I was acting in good intentions.

Around Christmas 2017, her family was consciously accepting gifts for the less fortunate for themselves while they had the ability to pay for unlimited internet and insurance of 2 vehicles. So after the shaming and all, I was still infuriated of her family cheating the system like that, so I went out to Toy R Us and purchased $500 worth of toys to donate. Another time she showed me a secretly recorded conversation with her mom saying that she couldn't see giving her blessing to me to marry her daughter. That was hurtful to hear. I really was planning to marry her to be my wife.

On a different occasion, I remember there were times I was trying to initiate sex with foreplay, but understandably she was under stress of school and debt and wasn't feeling it. She complained and asked in annoyance, "Why are you always so horny all the time?". Remember this statement because it'll come handy later. February 2018, it's my birthday. She's asleep on the couch beside me while I was "helping" with her homework. Next thing that happens, she gets a notification on her phone on the coffee table. A guy's name I don't know. I'm sure you can guess what happens next and what I found. Worse case scenario come true. 4TH AND FINAL STRIKE. A bunch of sexts and nude photo exchanges with this one guy that she has significantly put a lot more effort into than the ones that she would send me. Further digging, I find more chats with guys she's been talking to. About 6-10 I believe.

One conversation with a guy asking about how I don't know what's been going on and that I didn't deserve her and with her agreeing. Then another conversation that ended with her telling another guy that she loves him. At this point in indescribable words, I was traumatically heart broken. And keep in mind, it was on my birthday. I started crying, she wakes up and finds her phone in my hand and gets furious in .25 seconds.

Asking why did I have to look and that I should've just left the notification alone as if she was telling me to play along and go with it and not ask questions and not stick my nose where trouble was to be found. I was questioning all things at this point, I was hurt. I knew this was the final straw and enough was enough. About a half hour later, she was trying to justify the cheating. Saying she things we got into a relationship too fast. And she doesn't know what is wrong with her but that she needs sexual variety. Remember earlier when she complained about me being horny all the time? Funny how that works. Another half hour, I go upstairs to my room and sit on the floor in corner against the wall tucked behind the bed and the dresser so I wasn't visible from the door. Still traumatically in tears, I start chugging a bottle of vodka.

She comes up and find me on the floor drinking, she sits beside me and comforts me and keeps saying sorry. I remain silent. She takes the bottle and places it on the dresser and helps me up to sit on the bed. She's on her knees and starts crying, saying sorry and begging for forgiveness. A week later, she asks if I would consider an open relationship, trying to keep me around while she is able to do her dirty laundry.

I end up finding a condo of my own in another part of the city, we lasted for another month slowly making our contact more distant.   Early May 2018, the last time I was with her, we had our very first slow dance in the living room of my condo. And I never saw her after that. Except when I almost bumped into her at my work. After that, I slowly trashed any remanence that was tied to her by fire from a lighter and deleted her from all social media. A few weeks later, she tries calling me, but I ignore all attempts.   She then leaves a condescending voicemail threatening me that I owe it to her to call her back. I don't. September 2021, I finally develop myself individually to get back on my feet to move back home to Toronto for good.   Before I do, I thought I'd do one last thing as final closure. Forgiveness. Mailed a letter using a name from a favorite movie of ours and thought it would be fitting to use the return address of the bus terminal where we first laid eyes on each other for the first time.

I wanted no reply.   No response.   No contact whatsoever. Just seal a chapter in my life finally closed for good. In the letter, I hand wrote in the centre of the page, "I forgive you. Take care." My nice way of saying I forgive you, good riddance, don't talk to me ever again.   Another few weeks later, I get another voicemail not knowing who it is. It's her. Clearly not taking a hint that I wanted nothing to do with her anymore. Says she received my letter, how clever it was to use the name, and starts to strike up general friendly conversation talking about covid.

Voicemail deleted. Number changed. From then on to present day, I still remain single. I've tried looking, chasing, and now just allowing it to genuinely come when the time comes. A part of me thinks her family has placed a curse on me to never find love again as funny and corny as that may sound. Her family is illocano, from Northern Luzon of The Philippines, where voodoo and witchcraft is common there. To this day, I don't miss her. But I do miss the experience. There were times she hit and punched me, even in front of her family. And she knew it. She knew it was wrong. And coming from her, it will always stain with me that my genital size is never big enough. I have never loved another woman as much I loved her. This is my love story.

-Juice from ON, Canada

Searched And Destroyed

◆◆◆◆◆

This love story is about searching so hard that i thought I found love because of how hard i was searching and losing it and having things spiral into the ground. It all started from an unexpected place, which was roblox. it was just one of those nights, late nights sad music blasting and wishing i had someone to talk to or to be with. and ill never forget the song that was playing it was cigarettes by juice wrld and i just remember like tearing up and i starting praying to god about being lonely and not wanting to do this anymore.

About 10 minutes later i found myself in a random roblox game and i was just standing around and this girl walked up to me and started talking to me. after a while of speaking we added each other as friends and kinda went on to do other things for the night i think she said she was gonna shower or something. so i asked if she had a discord because i felt a connection with how we were talking and the depth of our conversations.

We eventually added each other on there and thats when the sparks starting flying i remember the first night we talked for 6 hours straight about all types of things we even found out we only lived an hour away from each other, we had a lot of the same interests and we were both going through the same thing with being lonely and trying to find someone and it was just amazing. fast forward 10 whole days we started dating, in those 10 days we spent the entirety of them talking and texting all day and eventually i just asked her and she said yes. now at that point ofc after praying to god about it and crying and begging i thought i was blessed from the angels above in that exact moment and things were solved all problems and everything just magically disappeared.

Well throughout this 10 month relationship of nothing but love there were things that were said and done that tore me down as a person and my mental health drastically. one of the main things was the past. she had a past with a couple of other people and that ofc affected me a lot. if i could take myself break myself and reshape myself i would from just how insecure i was about everything and just stupid.

I wanted her past to not be true i wanted it to be fake but it was real. it wasn't necessarily the fact that she had done things with other people it was more how she would just casually tell me and expect me to be react in a positive manor. it used to break me down to my core hearing her tell me some of the things and wonder my mind was so gone. i wish sometimes i could take back the thoughts i had at the time that haunted me throughout the entire relationship. another thing in the relationship that tore me down even more was the ex trying to get back to her. now that I've had all these months to heal and reflect on everything if she really didn't want him to contact her she would've made sure it was that way. id tell her to block him on ig, but shed leave him unblocked on iMessage and vice versa. fast forward 10 months to the end of the relationship, one night her ex texted her trying to "apologize" and make up for being a bad person and whatever else. i couldn't help but think any guy who waits a year to do something like that only has sexual intentions in mind.

And the reason i say that is because she said after they made up about everything else they started talking about sexual things and all the things they did with each other. as you could imagine that sent me to a place of mental health I've never been at before. she never apologized she never said anything. as I've matured and had time to find myself again, I've come to realize that no apology or no response serves as a response too.

So for me that took a lot for me to accept considering how long we were together how much love we shared to just one stupid text and it was all over just like that. I've since been trying to heal from it all its been about 8 months but something still kind of feels wrong maybe its how alone you become when you isolate and heal but i feel as though I've overstayed my welcome and wish to actually find what i was looking for this time. which is actually the reason i follow you and watch all your videos bc in that time of healing and wanting to find love again i saw your videos explaining why we feel what we do and what not to do when it comes to craving love and everything and they have helped me a lot since

230

then. so thank you for that. hopefully this story can help someone out there or let them know they aren't alone and things really do get better.

Maybe In Another Universe

This is about a boy that I thought was different from other guys and we all I have thought that before, for me he was the sweetest guy ever I was obsessed with him in attached and he was not just my boyfriend he was my best friend like he was the only guy I felt like I could trust and I was so comfortable around him and I loved him so much and still do and like I want to hate him but I can't hate him cus at some point he made me the happiest person ever and i still think he will come back and I am still waiting for him but a part of me says that I have to let go of him because it is hurting me that I am still holding on to him and I want to hate him cus he took the lover girl inside of me but I just can't hate him no matter how much I try and I know that I won't ever love a guy the same way I loved him unless if it is him, and he will always have a place in my heart, and I hope one day he realizes how much he hurt me, and I have so many questions on why he did that like I loved him with my whole heart like was I not enough or what?, like I always tried my hardest to make him happy and I still don't understand what I did wrong and I know that no other girl would love him the same

232

way I did, and the day I found out he was with a other girl my heart stoped because like why would he cheated on me? I thought he changed because he even acted like he changed but I guess some people have a mask that doesn't show there real them and I just have to live with that for the rest of my life and even after all he was not different from other guys.

My first situationship

I was going through a rough breakup where i did end up getting cheated on, through that break up i reconnected with an old friend it was so unexpected since that old friendship was end on like bad terms, we go close and we caught feeling it was so out of the blue. Since i was still hurt from my breakup we decide to take it slow , at the start they were kind and so nice they understood my insecurities and my pains. until the summer was over it was like they had a switch, they were on and off.

Some days would be good some days would be bad. some days i was their favorite person some days i was just another one of their many girls. it messed with my head so much but i push through it because i thought the good days were enough for me, at the time it was enough for me. i loved hearing them calling me their girl their pretty girl i loved their attention and affection.

But the lack of actual title bothered me, i made it known i was ready for the next step, actually being their girlfriend, but the more i made it known the more they pulled away the more they distant themselves, but until one night we were so close and was like how it was at the start, but the next morning they cut me off, just because their was rumor going around about me, i was hurt really hurt. I lose myself and lost a part of me, it took me awhile but i tried to heal myself to find myself again, it was painful but i was trying , until out of the blue they texted me the iconic "i miss you" text, i was dumb enough to fall for it, thinking maybe this time will be better maybe i will be worthy enough to their girlfriend , and i was for awhile it wasn't official but i could tell they wanted to actually try, until i found out they were in communication with their ex, i found that out a week before i birthday, i made it known that i knew but i didn't want to speak about it til after my birthday, i didn't want to ruin my special day.

My birthday finally came and it was amazing, even though i knew they was in communication with their ex i did still invite them to small dinner, they didn't come nor show up, i noticed that while texting they were distancing themselves , i was hoping they wouldn't ruin my day, but turns out they did, they ghosted me a day after i never got a text back nothing, i was hurt i was so hurt that i led myself on again that i let someone do it twice, but i was also grateful because they taught me a lesson they taught me to first not to be naive but they also showed me how love felt even if it was for a bit they showed it to me and for that I'm forever grateful even if it hurt me in the end.

-@neroangelii

Unpredictable Storm

A t first, she was my friends girlfriend, who later down the line, they eventually broke up because he was caught cheating on her. Let's call her Millie. Millie was super nice at first I actually snitched on my own friend because I hated to see someone as nice as her being cheated on in front of my face me and my friend stop talking because of that reason and me and Milly started being really good friends. I was very oblivious to a lot of signs, but I knew she had a small crush on me, but I was just too blind to it, we talked on the phone a lot not realizing the signs she eventually gave up and a friend of mine had to tell me that she had a huge crush and I was being stupid.

I finally asked her out on a date I was so shy at first there was no attraction. What is a screw into somethings so special, because I found her to be attractive in every way after that after completely getting to know her we started dating for three months, and everything was smooth sailing. Then the turbulence came one day she abruptly stopped texting me and I had to call her about a couple times for her to finally pick up. She sounded like an entirely different person. She acted like she didn't want to talk to me crazy attitude, and I had to finally force it out of her why she didn't want to talk to me and it's because she was very scared of opening up, she had some past trauma and love and she did not want to get hurt again. We both cried on the phone for a while promising we would be there for each other. This happened on and off for the rest of the relationship where I didn't catch the red flags she didn't like me meeting her friends I never met her parents. She was scared of me meeting anybody close to her eventually started to notice.

This was a pattern either I was being cheated on or she genuinely doesn't like people knowing her business. It was like I was trailing on ice she would blow up on me if I even got close to her job, and sent her food or flowers she had secrets. She finally confessed and told me that she had a mental disorder because of her abusive stepfather. She was diagnosed with dissociative identity disorder. Explain the mood swings and everything the weird behavior she had a memory lapses. She had a lot of anger eventually me too naïve to understand. She broke up with me on all hallows eve before our anniversary on November 3.

She had a friend walk her after work she used to work at express in the mall and I met her at the malls food court around 7 PM and she sat down and she just told me it's over and through the ring I gave her and anger I threw it right back because I didn't understand why she was doing this. I left the food court with my heart, pounding, my legs, shaking my hands sweaty and I had to call my friend Mitch to come pick me up because I

237

had basically fell to the floor and in pain people around me were staring when he came he just picked me up and took me home.That night I couldn't sleep the day after on Halloween's day I took out my anger on sending in basically going to a party in Miami, where I drank and smoked all all night with friends, and eventually blacking out. It was very painful. I wish I could tell her. I could've saved her from her abuse. I wish I could tell her. Thank you for breaking it off but honestly, I still feel hate towards her now and now most recently learning to love her and just being OK we were 18 she now lives in Orlando and has two daughters and she's repeating the cycle again with her husband.

-@kavmvn

Last Forever

She was my 'BestFriend'. She would be the first person I would go to about everything. She was my big sister. Last year it felt like I was doing all the work in the friendship. I talked to her about it but she did not change till January. For it being so sudden I decided to take a break. She respected it, but it hurt so much. Her friends were my friends. So there was no avoiding her. After some time it now feels like I can talk to her without feeling weird. I will always support her and her future endeavors even though we are not as close as we once were.

Cover In a Storm

I grew up quite lonely my only friends where animals and racing I grew up pushing well above my weight in all of life but especially motorsports considering I had no team no money no help. l'd also ask my parents why life is so hard why I have no friends, as a kid I always dreamed of just having someone a friend just my person. In early 2023 I met this girl called M me and her instantly hit it off and i was feeling all these new emotions as l had my first friend and I was the happiest guy alive but life is never that simple we had to overcome a lot of problems very early on knowing each other she grew up without a family she'd been abandoned by them so she could never trust me But we slowly started talking more and I caught feelings and so did she she would always call me "her handsome boy". I'd always been called handsome and physically fit but never by someone who actually meant a lot to me. I won't lie to you the first time she called.

-@george_ruffle32

Nothing Last Forever

For background contest went to a 6-12" grade School, so lie had long going friendships that last 6-7 years. During those years I lived across from one of my Classmates and I mean directly across. Not once have me and her talked looked or t done anything involving one another except our junior year. Junior year We had every class together still no interaction.

Until the mid year our physics teacher assigned us to sit next to each other. We were quiet at first our differences were t great and far from each other to make conversation.Despite that I was noticing something day after day, she Came with different shoes and with my fascination with shoes got me curious so l asked, "Where did you get All your shoes from? " From there we became friends, then I close friends ends after that. We told each other many things basically almost everything about each other.

A thing she never talked about was a love or romantic interest so I didn't think she had anybody in mind. Then I fell hard for her because she wasn't like anybody I met before, but she didn't know l hid it from her. Eventually around Valentines Day asked her out unfortunately she said she didn't fell the same. I chose to ignore this because i didn't want to ruin what we had. Summer came and were texting and calling everyday. We have a mutual friend and he also talks to her about things so after I asker her out during the summer she caught feelings. Then our senior year Came around and we are still friend she never Said anything about her catching feelings. After a few months of being just friends we were closer than ever so I decided to just ask her if she wants to something but take it slow.

This time she said yes but she wanted to keep it very private which felt ok with me because as long as i'm with her I was happy. That was around December. After a few months around February and on a Friday, I remember this day clearly it was raining and like 65° so it was cold morning. I get a text from her saying if I wanted to go late to our first period together; Which I said yes too obviously. Usually she was happy but this time she wasn't. I asked her about it but she said it was family things, I didn't want to push it so left it.

Later she wanted to meet up at a place we had just for us and I went at the time she said. She told me she had to break up with me.I was confused because everything was perfect on both of us and how we felt mentally, emotionally, and physically, but she said her parents found out and she wasn't allowed to date anyone. That was that the weekend passed and no text or anything but Monday morning following the break up. Im at school a bit early but was going to 1st period late because she's in all my classes and I wasn't ready to see her. The bell rang and someone tapped my shoulder and its her she

242

said, " going late again?" I Said "Yes". She replied "can I stay with you"? And I said of course. We ended up skipping 1st period and talking throughout the whole period and we ended up back together. After about a week or two her mom found out again and made her lose contact with me no social media, messages. The worst thing is she didn't want is in the same room and classes as each other.

During the talk we had I did mention me introducing myself to her parents but she said no and her parents wouldn't like that and I kept pushing it but she said no. After all that craziness about 2 months passed and school is about to end in a month but I didn't want to end on what happened. My only way to contact her was a note, I had my friend take it to her. She wrote back. We were communicating thats what mattered the most. After a week we made time to meetup and talk in person. We were talking in person more I more without the risk of anybody worrying that we were talking. Then prom was coming up. Her parents wouldn't let her go and I didn't want to go unless it was with her so l stayed back.

But I wanted her to have the experience of being asked out to prom, so I gave her a proposal with the sign, a small bouquet, and shoes which is what we bonded over first. We still weren't together & just needed her to feel like she deserved the world. After a day or two we got back together. 2 weeks before our school end we go on field trips everyday so we used those days to be together for the time loss. Everything was good especially leading up to graduation. Grad day comes and we take pictures in the back of the stage we are happy whatever. Around, early June she calls me wanting to break up because her parents. She Said whenever she listens to The Weeknd and J. Cole she thinks of me and I helped her listen to them more becoming apart of Dreamville and XO. "What we have is forbidden love like your favorite artist J Cole's song Nothing Last Forever. You introduced me to that song and the verse about all the times they tried. That's Us. I felt soul bonded with you. I'm sorry. I love you" she said. And now her and I are strangers again. But she reminded me that our love wouldn't go away because We had tags which We put all over our school and neighborhoods that wont go away for a long time.

-@don.dg40

Big Brown Eyes

Those big brown eyes

The first night I cried

How I tried and I tried

But no one compared

The brown twinkle In his eye

How I smile

Every time i hear his name

The bane

Of my existence falling in love

But no reciprocation

If only I tried

Feelings might die

But those big brown eyes

Will always make me feel

More alive

But

My blue eyes

Make no dent in his heart

As I fall apart

Hoping he'll reach out his hand

To grab the pieces

Before they fall into the never ending existence

I only want to exist with you

I cry

Silence

Is his reply

-s.v.f.g

Winter's Warm Embrace

His scent was covered with new winter snow,

The charming auditory in his voice hits my soul gracefully,

the apricity in his smile so pure,

Everything about him excites every inch of my heart,

Making its rhythm flow like the chimes in the could winter breeze

-A.L<3

Fond Memories

My love story. I never really knew what love was until the day I met a beautiful soul through distance, but oh how distance can be a blessing and a curse. A blessing because you get to know someone so well and deep. You get to connect with one another in a way that is so pure, but distance can also be a curse because there's only so much you can do when you need each other in time of need. when things get hard and you want to be there for them physically but can only comfort them with your words. You can be as beautiful as you want on the outside but the inside is what truly matters.

Love is such a simple word but can mean many things and in my case it meant falling asleep on the phone and waking up not even saying good morning to each other but moaning or groaning to each other as a way saying I'm awake but also half asleep. its asking each other "did you eat yet" with a gif after of a character squinting. its being on facetime for 8-10 hours or more on our free time watching a movie, show, or playing a game.

Its sending TikTok or Instagram posts showing how much they appreciate and love you to each other when you least expect it . its sending a paragraph of how much they care, love, and appreciate you with a gif of a couple kissing because its the closest way to show your affection to one another through distance. its being on facetime for 8-10 hours or more when were both free and watching a movie or playing games together.

-@bobbyheadpicasso

First Step

I found my first love in 7th grade it all started as a casual day of school until the class was paused to introduce the new kid and it ended up being a girl and when I laid eyes upon her I was blown away I felt something in my body that I have never felt before and haven't since she looked so beautiful. I was utterly shocked and amazed and so me being me I thought to myself I can't get this girl she's too beautiful and pretty but over time life had different plans for myself I came to school regularly sitting next to a friend of mine who befriended my crush and she asked me "do you like her" and I said "no" but after she told me that she liked me and I was shocked inside outside I wasn't very much expressive and I began to confess my feelings about the girl so she encouraged me to ask for her socials number whatever and I'm not the best and the most confident about that stuff but over time I would do nice jesters for her at school eventually she would be the one to ask. We eventually talked for a few months and got into a relationship together both happy we went on our first date and it went amazing and began to go on more and have good times with each other but over time things became ugly we began so happy and in love still in-love later in the relationship but ugly towards each other a bit and the longer it went it declined slowly leading to our inevitable breakup. I learned a lot from the relationship and focused to become better for myself and my next relationship whenever that'll happen.

-714.isaias

Waiting

My love story isn't the best but basically, I found this guy when I felt like my world was settling but in the end it wasn't. (t started off mutals we became friends, and when my world fell apart he was there. We became closer, soon he became my best friend, it became more the that. He had healed me and gave me my spark back. He told me he loved me and I loved him. He fell first but I fell harder. Soon I've found out there was another girl. I was so crushed that when I asked he got mad at me. The next day he became distant.

We went from being nothing to something to everything just to be nothing again. He took my heart after I gave it to him and I thought he would keep it safe. On new years eve right before 2024, he left me and we went into no contact. I was crushed, I felt like my world was over. I felt my heart ache and yearn for him, I had so many questions. In June we went back in to contact but we never gave each other any answers to any question. We acted as tho we never knew each other.

Soon I thought I had him back he proved there was still another girl. Then he started acting differently to me, he proved to me that he was js like every other guy. He asked me for nudes and then love bombed me for the second time. I'm still I'm contact with him but my heart aches for who he was. I healed myself just to be hurt again. Now I learned that he was nit meant for me. Now I'm waiting for him. I can't help but hope for him to come back as he was even tho I'm aware he won't nor will he ever be the same. My heart doesn't want anyone else. He's changed me so much I don't don't recognize myself anymore.

-Noor

Falling Petals

I didn't have a really stable life growing up, so it was super hard for me to open up to people, and she had been mistreated alot of her life and had a terminal illness from way before I met her. She was beyond words and I fell in love with her. I swore to always be by her side and make her a priority, and I did. I spent so many nights in the hospital with her that it became my second home, and she showed me what it was like to be loved. But we both had our flaws that seeped into the relationship. I was co dependent, and she couldn't stay in one place. One of her last words to me were she loved me, but she wanted to see if she could find better. Her new boyfriend wouldn't let her talk to me and eventually she had to cut me off. The last time I saw her she was in the hospital, and she told me how I still made her the happiest. We had this thing where I'd call her mamas, and I hadn't seen her in months so that was the first time I called her that in forever. She literally teared up. No more than 2 months after she cut me off she passed away. And I look for her in every woman I meet, and I try to learn from my mistakes, and love other people, but they'll never be her. And I learned that selfishness kills love, and you can give someone your entire universe, but if they aren't ready for you it doesn't matter.

Long Distance Kills Fake Love

When I was halfway through my Junior year in Ecuador this new Colombian girl joined 4 months till the school year was over. I didn't think much of her cause I didn't really know her well at that time plus she didn't seem attractive to me because we never had a conversation, we used to say hi to each other from time to time but no further from that. Actually my friend had a big crush on her but she didn't pay much attention to him although he tried to give her signals.

Since then we kinda created a known person connection but just there. One day a mutual friend of ours introduced us to each other. Then I got to know her name and where she was from, and I was also Colombian From My mom's side so we really had a bunch of things in common. Later on like a month later the whole school was told to divide into groups to make a project of a specific subject so for a coincidence me and her were put into a play and it was about the Odyssey from Homer.

I got the role of Poseidon and She got the role of

Athena (they were a couple in the book) So we had about a month to prep scenery, costumes, practice the roles and everything. She helped me do the balloon backings and we joked now and then so I started to kinda develop feelings. This one day we were with few friends on the classroom and she put some salsa on her phone and suddenly she asked me to dance so I agreed. then my friend left us alone there to get some privacy and that's when the feelings started developing further, that moment was beautiful since I never danced with someone and she had a bunch of patience with me. But we just left It there until the day of the play presentation I arrived early with a friend and didn't see her there but that was not a priority since I had a hurry to get ready.

But then suddenly I peaked through the classroom window and saw her dressed up and she had her hair done and everything and that was her true real Beauty. Now that's when I really fell in love with her, but I didn't express much feelings when we were in the first play. When we went backstage I just sat on the floor waiting, then she was sitting next to me on the floor and just leaned her head on my shoulder, I remember getting butterflies and just leaned back too.

At the second play when it was her turn to speak I did a funny face and she bursted out laughing in front of everyone and it was embarrassing for her but cute for me. The we did a few more plays and everyone went home. I remember the moment I got back from school that. That day I screamed of joy and anxiety on my pillow since I never fell in love with someone my entire life because my life has always been a disaster for me and it was full of hate and chaos and violence (that made me start

257

martial arts and now I'm a South American Kickboxing champion) So that was the very first love I felt and I wanted to invite her to the movies the next week I made a whole plan and everything. But I asked her friend and suddenly she already had a senior boyfriend so I really felt disappointed and sad I remember that every day I recess I stood watching them together from far away and that just made me really sad.

And that was for a whole month. But I stopped seeing them together and I kinda knew what was going on. She used to spend time alone in the lab when it was time for recess so one day I decided to approach her and talk. I asked her about her boyfriend and she kept quiet and changed the subject. Then I got told that they broke up because he wanted to do "stuff" with her and she refused. So we hung out almost every day on the lab and we texted each other after school and created a super strong friendship / situationship between us Since I was fighting for money in a illegal place I used to get injured a lot so she Saw me like that at school and just held me in her arms and massage me to kinda relieve some mental and physical pain.

And that's the first time I felt truly loved unconditionally. One day on bring your own clothes to school we both agreed to dress up as cowboys so she borrowed a hat and a shirt from me They took pictures of both of us and nominated us as the best couple dressed that day (even tho we weren't). Then one day my parents took the house keys and I couldn't go to my house so I didn't know what to do then she told me that I could go to her house until my parents came back So I agreed then we arrived and her mom already knew me because she told her about me before she fed me then left to buy some groceries so I was home alone with just her. Then we watched a movie on the bed, I kept respectful and was on my own space Then she put her hand on my heart and laid on me and we hugged and spooned together till her father and family came back So we just pretended to do homework like nothing happened hahah then At midnight I took and Uber to my house and when I was about to leave we hugged and gave a kiss on the cheek to each other. I was really happy after that day then she texted me saying that her parents wanted to invite me to watch a movie in her house again but this time with snacks and everything so I agreed and bought things for her and her family

Then after that day I invited her to make cookies an stuff That day she told me that she had to go back to Colombia with her family. That was like a warning to not get too attached because she knew it would hurt me but I didn't listen. Then on the last day ceremony something told me that it was gonna be the last time we saw each other so when it was over and she came to say bye to me I hugged her tight and didn't want to let go but the hug was so hard that it started to hurt her and she pushed a little so I let go and she said she would text me when she got home But I never got a textNext day at 5am I received a text that said she was on the airport about to leave to Colombia forever

I could answer because I was asleep soy when I saw it I broke on tears that day. And I was really depressed since then and we texted from time to time. But then like 3 months later she was being ultra dry and not wanting to text me anymore. She changed both physically and personality wise.Then we used to speak once or twice a week then once a month and that made me sad because I was the only one in love and she lost feelings just like that. Then one day I couldn't take It anymore and declared my love to her.

Long story short she said that she did had feelings for me but she didn't love herself at the time so she cannot love someone else and that she was not ready for a relationship. She asked me to be patient so I accepted but idk if she was being honest or if she didn't want to be in a relationship with me. So we really stoped speaking and regained contact like 3 weeks ago. I moved to Colombia because of my situation. She somehow knew and asked if I was here.

I said yes but in another city. She said that she wanted to see me and talk about things. I'm not really sure If I should see her but part of me just wants to run into her arms again but another part of me says that she only wants to see me because she felt bad for everything that happened here.

-Bruce H.

Payne

Both young adults shared a turbulent on-and-off relationship throughout the years, marked by moments of intense connection and equally intense misunderstandings. Despite their deep feelings for each other, the man struggled to meet the woman's emotional needs and be the partner she deserved. Over time, she grew weary of the unfulfilled promises and lack of effort and love, ultimately deciding to leave him for good. Before walking out of his life , she sent a message telling him, "We'll always find our way back to each other," a bittersweet farewell full of hope and resignation, following up the few days of them both messaging from what would be the last time they would speak to each other . The young man had the courage to finally step up and love her yet it was too late. Now, with her gone, the man is left with deep regret, realizing too late how much she valued him as lover and a human being and is now reminded everyday of how he failed to reciprocate that love. The weight of missed chances and unspoken words haunts him, a poignant reminder of what could have been.

Ego

I made my ex break up with me by making her believe I cheated on her because I was insecure during long distance. She would go out to the clubs a lot with her friends and I didn't want to tell her how I truly felt. At the time my ego was through the roof because I was in college surrounded by females that were showing me attention. I stopped replying to her messages and posted a fake pic from Pinterest of another female on a private story that only had her in it. She couldn't handle it anymore and finally decided to give up on our relationship. She was my first actual relationship and we had been together for 3 years. She didn't deserve what I did to her. She ended up deleting all social media since then. Till this day she still doesn't know the truth. Sometimes I contemplate on apologizing and telling her the truth but I feel like it'll do more harm then good because she's now with someone else.

Point of no return

I was heavy into drugs. I couldn't go a day without getting incredibly stimulated; & on top of that...I was extremely lonely. I remained pure to the hope I swore to hold on too on love & connection. Every fear I had I would fade away like wind & dust when I had just a crumble of hope in me. One day I decided to go on this random chat to have a lil convo with someone, & I came across this girl who was struggling also. We chatted up and we vibed so easily; i was free-flowing the convo so easily and brought me so much joy and bliss. We was really vulnerable & gentle with each other & decided to exchange numbers. We rlly clicked like we had already known each other for years. Then, my phone died and I just sat in my room...feeling like my soul & sense of self just vanished. Weird, but I'll never forget that. I slick feel like I'm cursed from forming long-lasting bonds. But, there's still hope....

Lost in Her Feelings

———————— ◆◦◆◦◆◦◆ ————————

If I was asked what is love, I'd say love is the way her green mix with brown eyes would make me melt and how the smile of hers turned everything around, love is her, her with brunette hair or not, its her love is everything when it's this lips telling me so, it might be loyalty over love but where's no love there's no home, a home to which we can turn to, a home that deserves quality time spent , communication, compassion, comfort, honor and respect. Those eyes, this smile, those laughs everything that would create love meant more than anything it was her long ago.

-@n40m118

Shooting Star

I wasn't looking for much during this time of my life. i simply wanted to have a good last year of high school essentially THE senior year. but then you came into view during that one fateful day that i honestly will never wash out of my head even if i wanted to but i know i will never want that . i was speaking in front of the class and you were in the first row, first time id ever seen you and wondered why have i never seen you before. it didn't matter though cause now that i had seen you, i knew i wanted to be with you. since i first saw you, you have stayed with me and i carry you every moment in my life. after that day, i looked for you in the hallways, anywhere i felt id get to see you to simply get a glance at you. fate struck again cause soon it was just us in a classroom for a project, i was never good at starting conversations but you i tried so hard to do so and we talked for hours. from that moment i knew you were a shooting star, my dream.

Track

◄◄●►►

W e met as high school kids, at a track meet and mutual friends brought us together. Surprisingly she was the one who shot her shot. First we exchanged phone numbers and social medias and began talking and it was just instant chemistry. we would talk on the phone for hours on end every single day at every possible moment that we were both free. The only problem was that we went to different schools and we lived half an hour away from each other. neither of us had a job or a car so naturally the relationship became stale as we could never see each other in person. we both acknowledged the problem and realized it was just"right person, wrong time".she once told me that i will always be her first love and "you set the standard for all future relationships that i'll ever have." it was a bitter sweet moment but i understood what she meant. we clicked so well that i set the bar so high for somebody else, when the whole time i wish we could have just stayed together. after that we just talked less and less no the point that we hadn't talked in a few years. then one day i something told me to search her instagram and she a new post from her only a few hours ago. it was her pregnancy announcement and she was already 8-9 months along and was expecting soon. i was heartbroken but happy for her at the same time. i wish her nothing but the best.

Gracias

So there I was, thinking how in the world could I have met the love of my life. Well it happened when I was in my Teletubbie costume, she came without confusion nor chaos. Her smile lit up my heart every time I laid eyes on her. I never knew that love could hurt so bad tho. She was stricken by the type of person I was, a person with no drama, no hate and nothing, but my kindness was taken advantage of and scared her off. To this day she is the most perfect woman in my eyes. Ella estará para siempre en mi corazón.

The Roller Coaster of Love

At the time we met I was a senior and she was a sophomore, both in high school. We met in April through a mutual friend, so I was already on my way out of high school. Naturally we exchanged social medias and contact info. I didn't know this girl would be one of the biggest and most painful roller coaster ride of my life to date. At first we just texted here and then. I saw her as a friend, wasn't really interested in her at the time. She was about my height, long brown hair, beautiful brown eyes that shined in the sun, voluptuous lips that went from light pink to brown. She had light skin and freckles too.

At the beginning we texted from time to time. After about a month she starts calling me FaceTime. This was something she preferred to do over texting. I wasn't used to it since I never really called anyone often but in time it became the norm with her. We're in September now, she's a junior and in those 4 months that have passed I've learned so much about this woman. I learned her mental state was bad, real bad. She dreamed of taking her life but wouldn't do it as it would hurt the people close to her. Her father passed away when she was about 6. When she was 14 she started dating this guy around her same age. He was very toxic. They had an on and off relationship for 2 years. They argued and fought a lot, he even threatened her with killing himself if she left him. And of course with my "hero complex" I wanted to save her. At around October she left him. I was happy about it not only because it meant she got out of the toxic relationship but also because by that time I had fallen in love with her and wanted to be with her. To this day I don't understand what made me fall for her it was just something about her, maybe it was the sense of danger she brought to my life, I don't know. Around this time I became close with her best friend who's around my age, Let's call her Jane. I'm still in contact with Jane to this day and I love her very much.

November, her birthday month. Our friend group wanted to celebrate her birthday so we went to a restaurant to sing her happy birthday, I even bought her a cake. We went to the movies afterwards. During this movie she started laying her head on my shoulder, touching my arm and I her lap. It was pretty clear we liked each other. Later that night we talked about what happened and basically confirmed we liked one another.

After that the FaceTimes became an every night thing, I would even wait for her outside the school everyday so we could at least spend 10 minutes together. December comes around and I start to notice she calls and texts me less frequently, I asked her several times if everything was okay to which she said yes. During winter break (December to mid January) she basically ghosted me. I asked her best friend Jane if she knew anything and she told me she was ghosting her as well. Early January I confronted her over text about the ghosting. She said she's been avoiding me since she doesn't know if she's ready to be in a relationship with me because we're very "different" from each other and she just got out of a relationship. She was afraid to be something with me and for our differences to cause arguments. This was all coming from her previous and only relationship where they would argue and fight.

I told her I understood and that I would be patient, but genuinely didn't understand the part where our differences would make us clash. I explained that if anything comes up we just talk it through and sort it out. She agreed and we got over it. After this we still didn't talk like we used to but we did talk more. Fast forward February and all of a sudden she starts calling me and texting me like she used to. I'm surprised but glad we're talking again nonetheless. But this time something was different, she started talking to me in a more intimate manner frequently.

I didn't mind it, I embraced it since I had been waiting on her all this time and she had been a bit cold in that aspect of things. The problem with this, which I realized much later, was that anytime I wanted to break through to her (like talking about how she felt and how her day was) she'd just say "fine""good""it was okay". Me caring about her, I wanted to know more like how she was feeling, etc, she'd just get defensive and started getting intimate over the phone with me. I realized that was her way of "shutting me up". This continued until late February where I confronted her about it and asked her what we are, what's happening between us and

271

overall wanted to understand what our relationship was. She later told me that she hadn't gotten into something serious with me because she felt uncomfortable about me being "pushy" with asking her how she was feeling and why hasn't opened up to me and that she just doesn't open up and it's hard for her to do so.

I believe that after spending almost a full year with a person, being intimate with them and basically talking every day with them you'd at least tell them about how you feel from time to time. But sadly she didn't see it this way. I responded by telling her "I genuinely love and care for you, but how am I supposed be there for you when you don't let me, when you can't even tell me how your day was" and I also explained my reasoning. Her response? "I am what I am and I'm not changing, so you choose".

I felt sad, angry and bitter all at the same time. How could this woman whom I love with my entire being not put in the same effort I was and refused to compromise for me. I had given her everything of me I could. I took my time with my response, I didn't even know what to say, but as much as I didn't want to I know I had to end it even if we weren't going to be friends after. That very night I told Jane about it, she was sad but cared a lot about both me and her but she was on my side. While we were talking about it Jane went on instagram. She has the girls account, meaning she could see who she was texting and what she was doing in. Turns out she was texting her ex about our situation, going in detail. This surprised and infuriated me because she was actually opening up to him about how she was feeling and telling him about our problem.

Jane decides to scroll up on the conversation, going even back to their texts in January as she was suspicious about something. Surprise surprise, that whole time she ghosted us during December and January? She was texting and calling him almost everyday. She laughed, flirted and told him about her days and feelings. Every single thing I asked from her, she gave to him, the person that's been causing her anguish and problems for months on end. I was angry, bitter and sad at the same time. So that very night I sent her the screenshots of her conversations with him.

Told her what I just said. The next morning she was angry, obviously. She tried defending her actions but I just couldn't... The problem was that she lied, told me she couldn't open up to me yet she did so to someone who caused all her pain. Remember that love can at times blind you. If I saw the signs earlier I probably would've stopped. But I loved her so much that even now, knowing everything that happened, I'd do it all again. The experience with her taught me a lot, now I know what to look out for next time. Don't give up on love just because of one or a few bad experiences. Heal first and don't let your past experiences define new ones. Each one is different and will always be, that said, use the knowledge that you gained to do and find better. To this day I still don't feel resentment towards her, because love is not angry nor bitter. Love is kind, giving, caring and letting go even if it hurts. A special thank you to Jane for being by my side through all of it and still being by my side to this day, I love you like a sister. Thank you for letting me share my love story. Peace be with whoever reads this. Love and guidance.

   -Marc Cayere @marcus_antonius_2055

Long Distance Lies

When I was 14 I met a boy. I fell in love with this boy. And I was so utterly obsessed with him. And he didn't feel the same way. He said he did, but he didn't. He cheated on me multiple times yet pinky promised during the whole relationship that he didn't, lied, and even made me jealous on purpose because he thought it was funny. He would post other girls with heart eye emojis on his story but wouldn't post me when I asked. And then he posted himself in bed with another girl. That was my breaking point. I literally felt my heart break and my stomach churned. I loved him so much and he never really cared about me. Life tip: don't do long distance relationships.

-@kinl.eyxoxo

Love Across

The story starts last year when I met an exchange student from Mexico in my university class. We sat next to each other in the first class and immediately started talking to each other. We also were placed in the same group for a project which meant that we were able to spend some time together and getting to know each other better during the weeks that followed. I felt really comfortable being in her presence which is weird because usually I am a very closed off person who doesn't allow new people easy in to my life.

We learned about each other's cultures and talked about the differences (because I'm from Europe). Obviously there were a lot of differences and a culture barrier but we could understand each other perfectly plus we have the same sense of humor. We also started taking salsa classes together. A connection started to develop naturally without forcing anything and after going on a couple of dates I finally asked her to be my girlfriend and she said yes. The only problem was that she would go back home in 2 months so we did our best to enjoy this brief time together.

We went to Christmas markets, cooked for each other, took trips to different cities, watched movies together and got to know each other on a deeper level all while seeing the end date coming closer and closer. She is really kind, caring, empathetic and we had a special connection. But sadly as of writing this our time is already up and she now lives in Mexico again which means that there is little hope of a future together. Maybe in another life...

Fading

I was in a no dating for a while but one day I bump into a girl in fresno. I was on a trip and only staying there for a few more days and she was pretty, her presence was like a swan in flight with a morning dew and the sun rising. I asked if she was okay and she said yes I asked where she was going cause I wanted to see if I was going to the same place. And it was a no go so I asked her for her insta and she gave it to me. Later that night I was in a hotel with my roommates and they were messing around while I was texting her.

She was pretty cool and we had a few same interests and it felt like we clicked from the start and after a few months of talking I finally asked and she said yes. I was so happy but after that it kind of spiraled down. We started arguing and it kept being a recurring thing I really liked her too but it just wasn't clicking anymore and so I broke up with her. It was a bad night for me and her and she thought I was cheating when I gave her my passwords to all my accounts.

And I kept saying "without trust we can't love each other" but she said that was BS so then we parted and I

278

blocked her. Then one night she texts me if I'm up I said yes cause I was awake at the time because we lived in different time zones and she asked me what was I up to but I was just being straight forward and gave small answers. And then she told me she missed me but I didn't like her back so I told her I wasn't interested and I told her I was going to block her but she kept texting me on other things. So I blocked her on all things and then it stopped. It was over and now she probably hates me.

Loss

In late 2021 I had recently lost my high school gf and was going though a bad breakup. It was my senior year so all I did was school work and actual work, I still saw friends and tried not to go deep into a depression but this was the worst heartbreak I had at the time. I was alone mostly, I smoked a lot of weed and hanged out with my one friend. Worked all the time doing 12 hour shifts on weekends.

Couple months later I started to get to know a girl at my school, it actually was the first time I had made a real friend at my school because most of my other friends went to different schools and the rest I knew before. We would hangout all the time and smoke, skip classes to just talk and hang it was nice. In April 22, while I'm working, I see her walking w a friend I use to work with and they come over to say hi. They were hanging out w someone else but he didn't introduce himself, I only said hi to her and my friend. Then they left. I wrapped up work 2 hours later and went home.

As I was walking home, I made the split second decision to make a right and go towards the lake to go smoke instead of straight home. Then I ran into my friend hanging out with more people. They stopped to say hi to me again when they saw me and this girl named Julia (not real name) came up to me flirting with me heavy, it was so obvious that she was into me and I immediately liked her too. We all decided to start hanging out and I got to talk and get to know Julia a little more, as we talked we agreed on the same things and had the same interests and it all just clicked perfectly. We decided to go to main event and that's when I got to hold her and we talked more.

Was nice. Then after we all hanged out she came over and we made out in her car, got her number and that's the start of my 2022-2023 relationship It was a ok relationship, we really jumped into it because we were so young and attracted to each other so we had our problems but we genuinely loved each other, we did mushrooms together and smoked weed during sunsets together. Spent each day with each other, it was a great relationship. But I still had problems from my last relationship, it was really toxic so I had picked up a lot of bad habits that I didn't fix which I severely regret.

I never meant to hurt her but I would do things based on instinct and me being scared. We had our ups and downs but I couldn't get myself in order and eventually she left. I lost my job and started running out of money so we couldn't do much, I tried to still see her but It got hard, I was stupid and kept something I shouldn't have and she left. I always wish I was different and that things were different. I'm better now tho.

Rekindled

It all started in 2023, my platonic love... One day I was coming back from a road trip when I got this friend request about a guy i knew back in my childhood, in that time I really liked him but never saw him again. We weren't really close but i was getting pretty close with his sister. Till this day we are good friends me and her. Well during the pandemic a friend invited me to a zoom meeting to paint and there I saw him, thru the camera, I was excited to see him but I knew he wouldn't remember me.

But back to the road trip day.. When I got the friend request i went to his profile to see who it was and bam it was him, I was freaking out cause I thought we would never talk again. (It was 5 years ago we talked and saw each other) I accepted him follow request and then I receive a message from him saying, "hey how are you? I don't know if you remember me but my mom follows you lol" I was like woah he texted me so fast But I told him that yea I did and if he also did, but to my surprise he said he didn't remember me much, I was like well makes sense but we started to talk and asking each other questions about our hobbies and music artist we like, there was a lot of things in common. Like for example we both like the same songs. He was really nice with talking with me, then i asked for his sister how she was doing and if she had insta or snap to text her. But he told me no, so I gave him my phone number to pass it to her and well then he asked polity if he could also save my number, and of course I said yes.

We started to chat in insta, snap, and phone number. We had 3 different conversations haha, but we were having a blast talking with each other. We would also FaceTime and call each other once in a while and it was like talking with a person who I have known for years, it wasn't awkward or weird talking with him. I didn't like him anymore at that time, but I never told my parents who I texted, so then later on after a couple of months we had to stop talking to each other.

I was really sad because he was the only person who understood me and was a real friend for me than any other person I knew for years. I still talked to him for a while before we actually stopped talking..... :(well to make this story more understandable and short I had to stop talking to him and that broke me, I started to notice that I couldn't live without him, he was the only one getting me to be happy. It's almost going to be a year without talking to him or calling him and I noticed I loved him a lot and that I would do anything for him.

Even through we don't talk anymore, I know that by heart we are still connected and one day we will see each other again. We will have that connection still like we used to, and maybe even share the feeling we have towards each other one day. But I just know that I never stopped liking him I just put that to aside because I just wanted to be friends. But a love towards someone you have never goes away. In fact it grows more stronger, to the people reading this I hope you guys learn from my story and don't wait to tell someone your feeling towards them, because you never know when you guys will stop talking or ever see each other again.

I would've loved to tell him how I feel towards him and never let him go. If you ever read this, Getting to know you was the best thing that ever happened to me, you were my everything and I just want to say that I love you and I will always be your number one supporter in the world!! This is how my platonic love story was, a love that will always stay in my heart till the day I die.

Unrequited Crush

wWell, a year ago, when I was 15 to 16, I had a crush on a girl who'd never talk to me. I was so delusional because of my feelings that I was obsessed with her, and I used to think she was superior to me. I'd do favors for her even if she didn't want to, and I would be nervous every time I went to school because she'd be around. Even photos of her made me extremely nervous, and every time I heard her name or someone mentioned her, I'd be nervous as hell. She'd never talk to me and this led me to follow weird and blackpilled YouTube channels saying that I'd be more likely to have a girlfriend if I dressed and looked well. I would get ridiculed, not for following YouTube channels, tho, but because I was different from everyone else. You know what? She ended-up unfollowing me on Instagram and removing me from my followers. Also, this isn't the account I used to follow her.

285

Healing

Hello so my name is James and I've kinda been putting this off because what I thought was love it wasn't. So do you know how they say you will never forget your first love well I thought my first love was in high school with the person I fought for when the girl I wanted was my dream girl but wasn't emotionally there for me when I was there for her and she just couldn't be there when I needed her but I was always there when she needed me but this is not if that story this is a year later with the woman I truly truly ever loved.

I felt as if she completed me but the only thing that was empty was the fact that we was long distance but still in the same region. She had her life and I had mines which couldn't be more better. We called every day she sent pictures of her self every day of my asking and I did the vice versa but then it hit a point where she got distance and I wasn't sure of what to do.

She came to me tho and talked it out with me and that made it certain that I wanted to…. Marry this woman , she was all I could ask for honestly and things was going great for month till dec I told her I was coming to visit her on my birthday which I took a whole week off of just to see her and at first she sounded very excited but after a few days I got text saying she didn't wanna do this anymore. I feel as if I lost another part of my self that day but I had to act like it didn't hurt when it hurt like hell. I was so distraught that I couldn't think of nothing to say but "I need you please" she said she loved me but was this a act of love or jealousy I don't till this day and I don't want to know anymore.

A New Friendship

Once upon a time there was this girl at the park name Aleah and she was playing on the swings by herself because she didn't have anybody to play with while she was playing on the swings. There was this guy that said hey, can I sit next to you ?, when she looked up she saw this nice looking guy. She said sure you can sit next to me so he did he sat down. He started talking with her they were talking about books. What's your favorite TV show? What kind of music are they into.

And they were playing tag for hours but soon she had to go home so he asked if he could walk her home and she said yes that's fine. While they were walking home he was talking to her she found out that his name was Hector, when she got home, they exchanged numbers and he left when she got inside the house. She was jumping enjoy her heart was pounding. She had butterflies in her stomach . she decided to take a shower when she got out the shower, she checked her phone and saw that he texted her He asked hey are you still awake? It was 10:30 PM it was kind of late since she had school

288

in the morning she texted him back saying yeah I'm still awake.

I just got out the shower. but I'm pretty tired. I have school in the morning. He responded with. Oh I see that's fine. Good night I'll text you in the morning. She responded back. Good night sweet dreams when she woke up. It was 7:15 AM. She went to go brush her teeth and her mom was making breakfast downstairs while she was getting ready. She got a text from him he said good morning how did you sleep when she saw the text? She smiled and she had butterflies in her stomach again she responded. I slept good. How did you sleep? He responded back.

Oh I slept amazing. I was thinking of you all night when she saw the text message she smiled. She even started blushing . she went downstairs to go eat since it was already 7:30 and had to leave by 7:55 when she was done, she said her goodbyes for the day and went to school. When she got to school she hangs out with her friend Maria they were talking for 20 minutes but then everybody started surrounding the class door when she asked her friend who's that she said, I don't know when she saw she got surprise.

She saw Hector Hector, just transferred into her school, and one hector saw Aleah he said. ALEAH HEY WHAT ARE U DOING HERE in excited voice she said oh I go to the school and he sat down next to her and they were talking for a little bit until the teacher came in and started teaching the lesson when lunch started, they all went to the cafeteria, and Hector was looking for Aleah, but he couldn't find her so he sat down by his self until a group of guys came in and started talking to him later on, he ended, making new friends, his friends name, or Angel, Roman, Alfredo, Danny, mike and Marcus they all became good friends later that day he saw Aleah walking home and he said Aleah wait up and she turned around and said oh hey, what are you doing here and he asked of he can walk her home and she said oh ok while they're walking home they were talking and laughing.

He told her on how he made new friends and she said oh that's good and he smiled and said yeah, that is, but you're still my best friend she blushed a little. When they go to her house, he said goodbye and gave her a hug and he told her I'll see you tomorrow and she's giggles and said OK bye when she got into her room, she started blushing so hard and laughing and jumping she thinks that she likes Hector, but she couldn't tell him yet because it was too soon so she took a shower and went to sleep.

Lost

All my life I've felt like a burden, like I wasn't meant to be in this world. I would pass back and forth, muddled amongst people that are glue to their screens, searching for the one. When I first saw her, I was mesmerized, thinking surely she is the one for me. She had smile that lit up the sky when I saw darkness. She had a scent that children normally had, which reminded me how much I wanted her to be my baby.

She had me tongue tied whenever we spoke. She was perfect, my queen, the one I'd been searching for all my life….. or so I though. A week after we started dating, she ghosted me, and at the time I was lost since she was the only one I looked forward to talking to all day, the one that stole my heart thinking she'd guard it with her life as she claimed, but in the end I just became a memory. She had a boy best friend she would mess around with more than me, she would have lunch with him and go out with him instead whenever we had plans but I couldn't leave her, she is my first love.

I had no one to talk to since she made me cut off all of my friends for her and honestly at that moment I realized that I was more lonely than ever. I wasn't thinking straight so I just found myself a girl best friend I would hang with since she wasn't with me anymore and it made her jealous. All I wanted to do was make her feel the pain I felt when she was with her so called "BFF" I WANTED TO BE HER BFF but she brought the worst out of me. Countless times she tried cheating on me with my friends yet I stayed through it all. She ever tried getting together with a female. I guess I wasn't enough so I went and started dating the person she hated the most to send the message that it's your loss.

Now this girl was the female version of me, I considered her to be one of my homies and she paid attention to me, loved me and gave me love bites, however everyone – especially me – is flawed. She kept comparing me to her Ex's in whatever I do I understand there's nothing wrong with that but the way she talked about them it is as if she missed them. Fast forward 4 months later it's the last time I see her and I'm moving away from her, she wouldn't even kiss or hug me, I guess she was devastated, just like me but I really wanted this to work even though we were oceans apart.

We called each other every night as if I never left, but slowly it seems as if she was letting me go, she too became sick of me just like everyone else does until she just stopped talking to me like I was her boyfriend. We just stopped talking, the relationship (friendship included) died just like every other one I have ever had. Now I lay on my floor like a fallen angel, thinking of what we could've been but I guess they never really care until you died...

White Feelings

---

*O*ur time together reminds me of the color white. It was simple, sweet and easy to mess up. He broke my heart but he didn't cheat, break up with me or lie to me. He broke it because when I told him about my trauma and most times he didn't care, changed the topic because he couldn't comfort me. But I thought it wasn't bad. I was completely blinded by love until everything started to feel like white. White feelings. He was everything to me.

He meant the world to me. But he's not the same person. Every time something went wrong in his life he seemed distant from me. And he got mad when I wasn't able to help him. White feelings. White. Not a color but a tint as some may say. White meaning blank, a clean piece of paper no one has used yet. That's how he made me feel.White feelings. In the beginning everything was fine but slowly I started to notice things that I didn't before.

I felt like there was a big sign covering my eyes from the toxicity. What really made me distance myself was when I told him about something that happened to me and he blamed me for it. Said it was my fault and I deserved it. This made me feel so hurt. This made me start feeling white except it wasn't really white, it was the colors slowly fading away. I stopped feeling those colors so it turned white. Making what we had, white. White feelings.

My Unrequited Love

"Love you— I love you. Okay? I love you."

March 31st, 2024, 1:18 a.m. If you had told me in August 2023 that this would be our future, I would have never believed it. We met unexpectedly, and I took no interest in his daily "good morning" and "hope you have a good day" texts. But as I got to know him more, I realized it was the best risk I could've taken—until he left. The first time he left, I was hurt, of course, but not heartbroken. It was what it was, and I couldn't change that. Then he came back. "Do you believe in second chances?" he asked me.

I do, but I wasn't going to let him back in so easily—until I did, two days later. This time, things were beautiful, or so I thought. Then he left again. This time, I fought for him to stay, but there was no stopping him. December came, and I was entering a healing stage, one that was very necessary for new growth within me. But I was unsuccessful. Out of the blue, we came into contact again, supposedly for "closure." But I gained no closure from that call—only heartache and frustration with myself. Soon enough, I started to heal again.

"New year, new me," as they say. He reached out again. It was brief, but it meant something to me that he checked in. March came, and one night, I got drunk and was vulnerable enough to pick up the phone and call him, just to hear his voice. It wasn't my intention to start "us" all over again, but that's what happened. This time, I was so sure it would last, and for a while, it felt that way— until I began to recognize his pattern. I knew he would leave again, and in a couple of days, I would receive yet another "I'm sorry, but you deserve better. You have to forget about me" text. I may have jinxed it, but I got the message the next day.

This time, I chose not to fight it. Later that same night, I was getting spammed with calls from an unknown number. I knew it was him, so I picked up—silence. For 23 seconds, nothing but the noise coming from his TV. I let it pass and put my phone on silent until I felt the urge to turn around. This time, it wasn't an unknown number—it was him. I was right, and so I answered. He explained that if I had any questions, now was the time to ask, in case this was the last time we talked. "Is this the last time you want us to talk?"

"No."

"Then why are you doing this again?"

"It's out of my control."

"It's not, though. You're doing all of this. You have all the control."

I asked very few questions, crying as I heard him answer. He asked, "Why do you try with me? What do you even like about me?" I began answering, but before I could finish, he interrupted and said:

"Love you— I love you. Okay? I love you."

Then he hung up. Those were the last words he said to me.He got into a relationship a couple of days later. In that moment, I felt betrayed and not loved at all. He used to tell me he wasn't ready, that the distance between us would make things difficult. They were long-distance. What did she have that I didn't? Why take the risk with her and not me? I got so invested in their relationship that I took no time to heal myself.

I see him in everything I do, every second of every day. I'm no longer waiting at the door with open arms for him to come back. It's closed, though it will forever remain unlocked. My promises to him will stay, along with the plans we dreamed of doing together. I never said it back, but I did love him, despite everything. I think I always will.

-T

Warnings I Ignored

The story about my love who broke me in pieces, doxbin and three important warnings I shouldn't had ignore. (TW: leaking, abuse, sh, sa, suicide attempts)

I always was the opinion that I don't need my love to be in my life yet. How could I? I wasn't really looking for it. But one day, I met someone on omegle. (Ironic I know) He was the sweetest person on earth and first time in my life I felt understood. We talked everyday, he made me much compliments, we met when we could and the love glasses never seemed to fall off.

Until after some time he couldn't stop screaming at me, harassing me and making me feel bad about myself. Yeah, I was sad about it but the only one who could comfort me was the one who hurt me. One day my love asked me to go on a call with a guy named Joseph because he was really drunk. My love didn't want to stay any drunk. My love didn't want to stay any longer because Joseph was getting really offensive but I stayed with him because 1 recognized he wasn't doing well. When I wanted to go because my love was really hurrying me for a weird reason Joseph said you don't even know what kind of person your love is" I asked him what he meant and he answered „marie comes everyday crying to me"

Marie. The girl where my love said that he didn't know her just from his friend. I asked Joseph further about Marie and he told me that they were together for months and even slept with each other. Her pictures got leaked and everything about her on a side called „doxbin". <My love didn't leak her tho.

I went to my love and screamed at him crying asking him why he would lie at me.

For the first time he was really cold to me. I had a really gut feeling. He asked me almost bored „what do you want to know" on this evening we had a huge fight. After that day, in the morning, I asked Joseph the whole situation. I even got to know Marie. He cheated on her, while they were still together he was already texting me how pretty I am. I also got to know how bad my love talked about me. That I was one of his hoes, I sent him videos, and he didn't even want to be together with me. I cried. I didn't stop crying. This day. After all he had done to me. After multiple times I needed to throw up because of his words and lay on the bathroom floor I left him. Not for me, but for Marie because he cheated on her.

My love kept asking me from where I know all this stuff since I told him not only Joseph gave me so much information so he doesn't get in trouble too much. At first my love did actually let me go. But suddenly he blackmailed me to leak the pictures of Marie when I don't tell him who the people were.

Wait. He got the pictures of Marie since they were together, they broke up, he was together with me and we broke up. He had the pictures of another girl the whole time we were together.? Marie was again for her life in a hole, she already had a drinking problem because of the doxbin leak from her another ex but now new pictures of her getting leaked? That was her low point.

Luckily me and Joseph established that he didn't leak the photos of her. But my heart broke into pieces, how could I love such a monster? When we met the first time I already felt a cold in his eyes that left me shivering. But I didn't listen to my gut feeling. Even my mom said that she hadn't had for such a heart rushing feeling for her whole life and she was scared from him. I know my mom, she wishes me the best in my life and she would accept any relationship. So that was the first and the most importing warning.

Maybe I should've listened to my gut feeling when he had got really weird friends who were just leaking, harassing and hating people. Just typical losers who are online

the biggest but when you meet them in the city you just see people with pimples, bad style and looking down from everyone. I didn't believe that my love was one of them.

Yeah sure he got a bit (ahem) similarity? - with them?

Or when he controlled me but the sick way?

The pictures I needed to take down because they looked „too good" the male friends I needed to drop because he was feeling bad about every single of them, the female friends because they were also having a gut feeling about him and when he wrote down every single follower of me at every platform so he always know who I unfollowed and followed new? There is so much more where he stalked me, and all this sick stuff being in his notes but that is a different story.

Should've that been my second warning?

What should I say? I wrote him again, just because I was alone and I missed him. And yeah, I catched feelings again for a person I didn't even know. Now that was a good relationship! He didn't harass me anymore, he didn't scream at me anymore and he was just a pretty good boyfriend! The only problem that I was the toxic person this time. I had borderline diagnosed and everything exploded, I was hard to love. I always blamed and screamed him for everything, I'm still sorry for that.

And he recommended me a break from the relationship so he could focus on school and I could handle my borderline.

I did that more for him than for myself. I went to therapy, tried to calm down when I had my borderline rages and switches and it worked! I got really better.

But suddenly. He was going away from me. I asked him if I did something wrong and what happened. He found a girl that he liked while I changed myself, my borderline, for him. But I accepted it, I let them be. Yeah, it hurt a lot but what should I do? I wasn't a good girlfriend and he was always bringing joy in my life so maybe I should let him get his joy, even if I'm not the one.

They broke up. He wrote me 2 hours later that he always searched me in her and that I was the perfect girl. Yes. We got back together again. I was a good girlfriend, but suddenly he got.. a lot more toxic. The most toxic person I've ever seen. It's like he's a completely other person. No. He didn't change, he was always like that but he was sick of pretending after a year. He was sick to other people, sick to me, I began to harm myself again because I was scared if I hurt him at my borderline switches or rages that he leaves me again so 1 did it on myself.

After I was brave enough to tell him that his only reaction was cold, like it leaves him cold that his girlfriend was suffering that much. I did mention to him a long time ago that I got sa and he was a completely other person to react to these kind of informations. It's like, he had no empathy.

When he wanted to leak Marie's photos he also said that it's her fault and he doesn't care if she ki//s herself.

Fun fact, I had a suicide attempt when we were in the relationship. I always told myself that it was because of my mental health and my mental disorders (that I have enough from) but it was because of the relationship. Of the manipulations, lies, and gaslighting.

After some time I had enough that he was so weird to me and of the gut feeling. So l searched for something. I didn't know what but I searched in hope to find something to tell me what is going on with him. Until one day there was a girl that went in my eye.

I wrote her nicely if she knew my love because we were together and he was acting weird and she told me to leave him immediately. Damn. Again? He isn't that pretty to act like this. Bro left me for an online girl- now that's the guy I spoke from at the beginning. You know? The one with dimples? Yeah. That's him. He's like an online loser like the others. He was messaging other girls while we were together and while I gave him everything. It was like built him so damn up for him to really think he was everything.

I showed that girl what he looks like and she was in shock that someone like me took a guy with this looks and this personality. I broke down in pieces. I didn't only like him. I loved him. No matter what he looked like, no matter how much I got jump scared whenever he sent me a face snap (I'm sorry).

When he found out that I showed someone a picture of his face he went CRAZY. He wanted to leak all my photos, my sa story, my suicide story, my self harm infos (wtf?) my full name, the full name of my family, everything. That bro was nasty. I was a minor on that point and he was already 18 god damn.

We both decided to never talk again. He keeps everything to himself and I don't show pictures from him anymore. That was the third and last warning I had to take to finally accept what kind of emotionless, sick, psychotic loser he is.

-Letizia

A First Love Loss

The craziest part is I don't even remember how we met. I just remember us having some classes together and having mutual friends. We'd play video games in those groups and we slowly got closer to each other our sophomore year of high school.

Junior year was when we met in person and had half of our classes together. At the time I didn't think anything of it I was just trying to enjoy high school and live my life. When I had found out you had a crush on me that's when I had really started to notice you. We slowly started hanging out more and finally made it official. At the time I didn't have much money or a car.

But I was determined to get you all of your favorite things to ask you out. I asked a favor of a friend to get roses and your favorite candies and snacks to put into a basket. After first period I was the most nervous I've ever felt about anything but once you said yes I swore I couldn't stop smiling for the rest of the week. I might your parents a couple weeks later and we both went to the dance together and you looked beautiful in your maroon colored dress. I miss talking to you.

Not about anything specific just pointless conversation where we'd make dumb jokes or just act our true selves and be happy. Our senior year came around and I could feel myself slowly declining mentally and I was growing more depressed by the week. I didn't know how to express myself at all to you I was scared of looking weak to you. I wish I had to learned to talk about my emotions than just bottle it up inside until it isolated myself from you completely. I could never forgive myself for hurting you countless times. As I started getting better and wanting to fix us you started pulling away. I figured if I gave you time maybe we can rekindle things after we graduated or so.

You started hanging out with the people you swore you despised and that hurt me. I later found out that you and him had something before we did, you just never told me, I wish you told me. Anytime I started to think about you and him my eyes would start to tear no matter where I was at home or in class. One day I wanted to talk to you in your car like we used you. You agreed and I was happy for a bit. I began to ask you if any guys hit on you or if you hit on any guys. You then told me that there was multiple guys that hit on you and it shattered me I just couldn't show it.

There was so much I should've said or done. I should've apologized for being a terrible person to you. I didn't know what I was doing it was my first relationship at all and I was still learning how to love you and myself again. I'm sorry. Weeks went on and we finally were going to graduate.

Watching you walk across the stage made me both happy and sad at the same time.

You looked so beautiful just as I had imagined. I tried texting you over the summer but you were dry with me and I can sense you still pulling away as I tried fighting for us back. I had a graduation party and I seen your story on instagram.

You were in the passenger seat. His hand was on you thigh, it was someone new, it felt like you wanted me to see it and get hurt. I can't blame you if you felt that way. At that moment I felt like my chest caved in and my heart rate exceeded going faster and faster. I couldn't breathe and I wanted to bawl my eyes out. I had to force myself to stay strong that night. The social media stories and posts of him. You removed me off of everything and tried texting you, I remember the exact words I said. "Please just talk to me", I seemed so helpless and so weak. I hate that feeling.

You left me on read that night. The rest of the summer I couldn't eat, I couldn't sleep, everyday it was the same pattern of going to the gym and crying myself to sleep later that night. I lost the weight I had gained in the relationship. In fact there was several things I accomplished I wish you were here to witness with me. Getting a car, a job, my first paycheck. I would've spoiled you I just know I would have. But that's all in the past now. I still think about you to this day, how I ruined everything and how I hurt you. I'll never forgive myself and I'll never ever regret loving you. You were the best thing to ever happen to me and I was happiest with you. I hope you get everything you want in life. Maybe one day we can get back to the way things were.

-    DAVID R

Journey of Love

S he was my angel and really lit up my world even while factoring in the low moments. She, in the grand scheme of things, made my life so much better. I've been with this girl for around the last two years and it's just been an experience and encounter of love and being cared about for me. She taught me what devoted love felt like, the kind that didn't mind staying when there's nothing left to give. The day we met, it happened with me crashing a stranger's birthday party.

March 14th, 2023, the day I consider my relationship anniversary. The week before that day, one of my friends came up to me and told me how they were going to a birthday party. She was worried, since their ex was going to be there.

Their relationship ended off, not on such good ends. She asked me to go, and I did feel weird at the invitation. I mean, I didn't actually know the person who was having the birthday. I thought about it for maybe a day, but decided to go. It sounded really fun, and it was going to be at a roller skating rink. I showed up at the roller skating rink that day.

Everybody was already inside and I may have been 10 minutes late. I walk in, pay to enter, and get some roller skates in my size. I've never skated before, so it was all new to me. Honestly, I was barely able to walk to the actual rink without holding onto something. After practicing how to move slightly on the carpet floor outside the rink.

I eventually decided to actually get to doing my version of "skating". Hopefully being able to catch up and find my friend and the rest of the group that came. The details get fuzzy from here. I remember getting in and lots of falling. Figuring out how to actually make it around for a couple of laps.

Later on in the night, I'd already found them and I was struggling to keep up. After some time though, my friend decides to take a break with some of the other people. I didn't feel like stopping, and besides I was having fun. So I kept going with just myself. Without noticing I was, although still poorly, making laps around the rink.

Then a girl pulls up next to me. She has this brown curly hair that falls to her shoulders. She's a little shorter than me, and her smile was so pretty. She actually knew how to skate, which totally wasn't embarrassing for me every time I knocked myself over. The girl introduced herself to me, her name was Angelina and asked if I needed help. We talked and then we held hands.

Sure, she probably did that in the context of helping me not fall, but I still thought it was cute.

Angelina was really funny, and was definitely bold.

She made fun of me, in a nice way, even when I was just a complete stranger to her. I felt comfortable talking to her. We go through the night, just us. Sometimes she would stop by to talk to her friends, but she'd catch up and we just kept going. I almost messed up everything. I didn't have the intention of asking for her number.

I don't think I was confident enough at the time. She stopped me though. She pulled me aside while inside the rink still, and Angelina asked me for my number. I'm so glad I went to that party.

I obviously took her number and texted her the next day. It was great, we would call and text, learn about each other. She was really energetic, and had all sorts of interests in different shows, characters, and art. It felt like Angelina never ran out of things to talk about. She was obsessed with dogs. Her favorite fruit were cherries and loved sunflowers. Angel adored sea animals and thought snakes were cute. Weeks would pass by, and I decided that I just want to take her on a date.

I would take her to this relaxed restaurant for lunch that was around my town. It wasn't anything fancy. Traffic made her a little late, but Angel showed up. She was gorgeous, and I definitely tried my best with what I had.The date was simple and was just fun. There was the usual talking and those weird moments, but it was good. The tone of the date was so unserious, we joked around and had a great time.

At one point, we decided to scoot our chairs next to each other to watch a movie on my phone before it died while waiting for food. I even kissed her outside that restaurant. All those things are good, but the main thing that caught my attention was how long we stayed. Hours passed by, we had finished our food and were just talking to each other. I felt bad for the employees, of course. I mean we were basically loitering. I never expected for someone to stick with me for so long without getting bored.

We started dating afterwards, I took her on more dates. The aquarium, museums, arcades, anything that I thought would make us happy. Live those adventures type of mentality. Each one, there was this common theme happening.

These dates would last the entire day, not just hours, she stuck with me even when there was nothing left to do.On our aquarium date, we had such an amazing time. We went around pointing out the dumbest looking fish or which one looked like the other person. The souvenir shop had tons of fish themed hats for us to try out and take photos. We both even snuck into this dolphin show, since we didn't have tickets. Only to find out we didn't even sneak into anything since they weren't running the dolphin show that day anyways. Eventually we traveled through the whole place and there was nothing new left to see. We started looping around the same places. We could've left, although I didn't wanna leave entirely, and I asked her if she wanted to go. Angel agreed to leave, but before we headed out I noticed she was acting strange, like she was upset. Come to find out that it was because she didn't really want to go either. It was ironic and I honestly felt special to her when she told me that. We stayed all the way till the aquarium closed. It was empty and we had a whole aquarium to ourselves.

There were these flat escalators that went above this fish exhibit, and we started running up and down on them. Treating everything like it was a little amusement park. This date was what did it for me. I realized I was really in love with her, and not just the way she loved or treated me. I loved how we would have the same interests or hobbies, or how unique she was to me. In my life, I've cared about people who wouldn't say the same. That wouldn't give me the time of day, let alone look out for my needs. The way Angel treated me, the way she loved me showed me something. That this is the kind of love I want and that I won't give my all to anyone who would do less than this.

This story of mine doesn't grab the whole picture, my relationships have had lows and bad moments. Times where we didn't treat each other like we care. Times of misunderstandings and personal problems we have as individuals. This all is just small parts of it for me though, so I personally see it as just small bumps in this hopefully enjoyable road that leads to her.

I also just want to say to anyone who over stress whether you're doing enough for your partner, when we love certain people we want to give them everything we can. The thing is, you don't have to, you just need to have faith. Have faith that your effort and time is enough. That the only thing that's keeping them there with you, is the fact they love you. You're more than what you bring to people, you can be genuinely loved for you.

A bad relationship is like cancer it only gets worse if you don't cure it

---

My first love has started with love on sight , As a young man with no experience with women I had all the courage in the world to ask for her number.The night before I asked for her number I was planning it out I walked her to her moms car after school for the past week or two I when I started developing feelings for her ,The Friday after school I started to panic I was getting all sweaty and nervous then it happened everything else around us is quite I keep eye contact the whole time I asked and…she said yes! A week goes by after continuously talking back and forth for hours on end talking about ourselves and each other and before I know it I'm ready to ask her out I'm confident enough.

I started off with small talk and smooth my way to asking her out she said YES ! My heart dropped with excitement I had a smile we set up a date. We set up a date for the mall and it went great but she invited a lot of her friends kinda ruined the mood . We walked around the mall aimlessly I got her ice cream and a bracelet and in return before we went home we took some pictures at the booth and we went in for a kiss it changed my life!For the next Year of my life I was in pure love maybe a little too to much.The first 6-7 months went smooth like butter a little arguments here and there but after that the next 6 months in our relationship was me wasting my summer waiting for us to do something together just waiting and waiting and I was soon to realize she hadn't met my parents and it felt that she was putting it off every time I brought it up my family convinced me that I need to do something I would get out of school in the worst mood there wasn't a time we didn't fight about something stupid and pointless sometimes I felt like I was fighting myself at some times.

After a year and a half of dating I needing to do something... On a Friday the best day of the week getting done with the gym and everything relaxing. My friend invites me to a party so all day I'm excited but getting mood killed by a pointless argument over something stupid all the arguments sucked our relationship dried over time.

The time for the party reaches I head over to my friends house and we get a ride over there having a good time the perfect time for my phone to be at 10..GREAT no charger around at all so I tell her and she says "k" the most heartless thing to say , I have lost all hope in texting back we stay at the party till midnight I'm having a good time I go to check if my mom texted and my phones dead so I wait so we go home to his house but no charger at all... we go on a hunt for a iPhone charger finally I find one...I plugged in my phone and dry messages no life in any of them I got fed up of fighting over and over I did it I put down my foot and broke up with her I left Her...I feel empty...scared...relived.

-Collin Kraich

Why me?

In early 2022 I met this boy who would soon become my first ever boyfriend. One day at school he had announced his new relationship with one of my good friends. I was upset at first but learnt to hide my feelings. I became a supportive friend, listening to her continuously talk about their relationship and even help her make a little bracelet that she later gave to him. 6 months passed and she was off, moving house and schools, which soon led to their break up.

I'll never know how much she meant to him but I remember how much of an impact "not knowing" had on me. Constant stalking, comparisons and dreading each time she would post, knowing that he would see her again and maybe even miss her. - In December 2022 the new Avatar movie came out and I decided to ask him to go with me. It wasn't a great first date as the movie went for 3 hours and we had never

hung out before, making it very awkward. Now looking back, I realize that was the only date we went on the whole time that we knew each other. And I was the one to initiate it. I was the one to plan every time we

317

would hang out. And I continued to convince myself that it was okay. those 10 months of a "situationship" before he actually asked me to be his girlfriend were the most "loving" and happy parts of our whole time together. He would come over to my house once every 1-2 weeks on a Saturday. We would play games on my ps4, watch movies, sometimes even bake some sweet treats. But my favorite part was when we would just sleep, holding each other, while songs from our playlist played quietly in the background. It was so so so peaceful and the way he looked at me made me feel so special. He would call me pretty and beautiful and would ALWAYS kiss me on my forehead. It was our thing. He was my first boyfriend, kiss, date, and all those little intimate stepping stones that slowly made me into this person I don't recognize.

I never thought of those intimate activities as gross or too much as I thought we loved each other and I thought he enjoyed it. Every time after he left, I got that feeling. That gross ashamed feeling. It felt like it was wrong. I thought it was because I knew my parents would kill me for it, but I think it was because deep down I knew it was too

soon, and I was too young, too innocent. I'm not going to lie and say it was his fault and that he pressured me, because no he didn't, it was my decision every time, and he would always triple check to see if I was comfortable. And that confused me more. Maybe I was ashamed because he was addicted to porn and maybe it was because of the way he talked about girls with his mates. I pushed those bad feelings away thinking "all teenage boys are like that though." But I know that if he did love me, he wouldn't of ever talked about or watched other girls in that way as if I didn't even exist. -2023 was a long year. April 1st was an important day. It was when we shared our first kiss. Funny timing right? Maybe that was a sign from God or foreshadowing. I don't remember exactly what happened that day but he would always tell me he remembered everything.

From where we were standing in my room, to how we were holding each other, and even how the kiss felt. We had kissed a couple more times that day and before you know it, it progressed, and now I can hardly remember doing anything else other than that. He gave me his Notorious B.I.G jumper that was at least 5 times too big for me, the sleeve cuffs covered in holes and his silver scent cologne lingering around the collar. And he even gave me his turtle necklace that he wore everyday.

My friends started saying "oh so he just gives his necklace to every girl he talks to?" I felt like a second option. Maybe I was a rebound. Maybe I was his second best option, just to temporarily fill the void that she left. But then why would he say that he loved me? -It was September 23rd 2023 and this is the day he finally asks me to be his girlfriend.

I was so excited and happy, telling my friends straight away. I thought that because he didn't ask me over text, it meant that it was special and heartfelt. We were cuddling in my bed while watching a movie. I think it was "10 things I hate about you". I was so warm and comfortable. I heard him say "hey you want to be my girlfriend?" I looked up and smiled, I said yes. It took him 10 months to ask that simple question, and lots of coercion from others, and even me. But I didn't care. We were official now.

He didn't have to pretend that he didn't know me when he saw his mates in public. I remember one day when we were hanging out at the park. I had pointed out his friends as they sat down right near us. He freaked out, and ran away to hide behind a building. He told me to hide behind a bush so he could go talk to them. So there I sat, behind that bush, watching him tell them a cover story about why he could possibly be talking to me.

I cried. He came back eventually and acted as if he had no idea why I was upset. He acted all sweet and loving to me, giving me more forehead kisses. I truly believed he had good intentions. Although he only ever cared about his reputation and looking "cool." His priorities were very clear the whole time. And I wasn't one of them. I just couldn't see it. -The last three months of 2023 were going well for our relationship. November 3rd was his 15th birthday. I didn't have a job, yet I used all of my left over birthday money to buy him some presents, and I even spent hours making him a rose made out of ribbon.

I had made him many things over the years. I didn't do it because I felt that I had to, I did it because I loved giving and I loved to show love. I loved seeing him smile. His slightly crooked front teeth that slanted down a little to the right. His big cheeks that hugged his eyes and formed little lines underneath them. And my favorite part were his small dimples. His left one more prominent then the right. It was rare to make him genuinely laugh or smile, so when it did happen, It made me feel so accomplished. Making him the happiest was all I ever wanted. Because that's what made me the happiest. Unfortunately the happiness didn't last very long. Rumors started spreading around.

He had gone out with his friends to this small lake nearby. He picked up an easy and acted out inappropriate movements while saying another girls name from our school. I wasn't even sad when I heard about it, I was just disgusted. I broke up with him for this. Although I never counted It as a proper break up because I took him back the day after.

We met up at our usual spot at the park after school. I cried and he comforted me. He looked like he felt guilty. Which is what I wanted. That one day of not being able to talk to him scared me. I realized how attached I was, and that made me believe that I needed him. So we were back together now. My friends were disappointed in me, which I understood.

I never told my friends the good parts of our relationship so they wouldn't get it. but no, it was me that didn't "get it." If one of my friends had been treated the way that he treated me, 1 would've noticed the red flags. I would've also told them to leave. And yes I would've gotten mad when they continued to complain about him, but then stayed anyway. But I thought with me it was different. I thought he would change after seeing me hurt. I believed him every time he apologized, saying he wouldn't do it again.

They never change. -New Year's Day passed by, and my parents had made some new rules. My boyfriend wasn't allowed in my room anymore. I was almost 16

321

and it was the most unfair rule I had ever heard of. I used to blame my parents in my head. I thought their rules and the strictness of their actions is what broke our relationship apart.

This was just a bullshit excuse I made up to validate his new attitude towards our relationship. He never put in effort, never tried to see me in his own time. And made countless excuses on why he couldn't buy or make things for me. I never cared for money or expensive things.

I told him that all of the time. I just feel like I was worth at least one flower for my birthday. Even just writing a card for me would have been way more than enough. His excuse was "my handwriting is bad" or "I'm not creative." So I continued to tell him I didn't care about the imperfections because they make it 100 times more special. If he didn't want to make or buy me anything, that's fine. I just hated the excuses and lies, when I just

wanted the truth. -Just like that it was my birthday again. 20th of April 2024. I turned 16 and still everything was the same. He wrote me another paragraph. Not too long, but at least I didn't have to persuade him to write it this time. Although my parents new rules were annoying, we still hung out as much as we could. Seeing that we weren't allowed in my room, we had to sit in the lounge room. We couldn't close the door, and we couldn't even have a blanket over us even though it was cold. We sat there for 2 hours. Watching his favorite movie, Star Wars. My parents were constantly checking in and staying close by, making it impossible to have a private conversation.

I couldn't hold him or kiss him. It was like our movie date back in 2022, yet this time he wasn't enjoying it. He sat there on his phone with his AirPod in, quietly listening to music and watching Tiktoks. I lay there, desperately wanting a sign from him that he loved me, to show me that he would rather be awkwardly watching this movie with me than being at home, playing Xbox with his friends. I wished that we were back in my room, sleeping, playing with his hair as he lay on my stomach. But that would never happen again.

I tried to make him smile that day. The whole time he didn't even say a word. He looked the most bored I had ever seen him. I felt so guilty for making him so unhappy. I had that empty pit feeling in my stomach that made me feel nauseous. That was the last time he came to my house. That was the beginning of the end. -June 9th 2024. The day that changed everything. At around 9pm my boyfriend texted me saying "I'm gonna walk to IGA." At the time I didn't think much of it, but why would he want to walk to the supermarket at night by himself? He didn't text me for 3 hours. I was paranoid and nervous, waiting for him to snap me back. His older brother added me and began to interrogate me.

He thought his brother was at my house, but obviously he wasn't. I was sent a video of my boyfriend and his mates drinking at a random party. I was angry, very very angry. He didn't tell me he was going to a party. He could've just told me. I blocked him to show that I was upset, yet he somehow took that in a different way. That night while I was worrying myself to sleep, he had decided to get into bed with a girl in the year below me from my school. They cuddled each other, made out, and he even gave her forehead kisses.

That was our thing. Others walked in on them, asking my boyfriend what he was doing, saying "don't you have a girlfriend? What happened to you and?" All he could say in response was "we are complicated at the moment." We weren't complicated. I was rightfully mad at him for lying and sneaking around.

He decided to sleep with her that night. -The next week on Wednesday the 19th of June 2024 is when I first found out about the cheating. right before we left school to go to sport my friend pulled me aside. She had heard the rumors. She said "apparently your boyfriend got with at the party two weeks ago. I don't know if it's true but I just want to let you know." I didn't believe it. I couldn't. I thought people were making stuff up as a joke. Not my boyfriend, he's not like that. That's what I told her. That's what I told myself.

I laughed it off and even texted my boyfriend letting him know that people were spreading lies. He told me he didn't know who that girl was, so we agreed to hang out at the park after sport. If only I knew this would be the last time we spoke in person. The last kiss, the last hug. That afternoon went on forever. We fed the birds, filmed videos together, planned a date for the upcoming weekend, and right before he left, he picked me up and spun me around, continuously kissing me. It seemed like a genuinely great time.

He laughed and smiled and I felt so much love in that

moment. In our last moment. Then he was gone. -That same night, before I was going to sleep, my friend sent me a long video, explaining everything that she knew about the cheating. I couldn't stop shaking. I was so angry. For about an hour I was sitting there in my bed texting back and forth with my boyfriend, confronting him. He lied through his teeth about everything, so 1 had to get proof. I added the girl that he cheated on me with and asked her about it. She told me everything, so I sent screenshots to him. Only when I showed

him proof, that's when he admitted to it all. And only then after talking to that girl, I found out about the second time that he went to her house. He switched up his answers so quickly after I had proof. He tried so hard to excuse his actions. Saying he still loved me and that he didn't tell me because he was scared to lose me. So I blocked him that night. -We were no contact for 2 weeks. It was the weirdest, loneliness and quickest two weeks of my life.

I distracted myself with my friends, which only helped temporarily. Seeing him at school didn't help. That day after we we broke up, I saw him. He seemed fine. It was like we were strangers. I tried so hard not to be upset, but it finally hit me. I cried at school in front of so many people. That afternoon I cried the hardest I ever have in my life. I couldn't breathe. I knew I couldn't be alone so 1 ran over to my best friends house. I sat in her room crying my eyes out while her and her mum held me.

I'm so so thankful for them. -After 2 weeks of no contact, I began to unblock him and we started talking again. It was a stupid idea. We called for hours, talking everything out multiple times. I cried and I even heard him cry for the first time ever. Hearing him upset made me happy. It feels bad saying it, but it's true. I thought it meant that he still loved me and that he regretted what he did. I promised I wouldn't tell anyone, and I didn't. Even though he broke my trust a million times, I would never break his. He promised me many things that day. That he would never go to a party unless I was with him, that he would never lie again, and that he would stay loyal to me. He broke that second promise as soon as he spoke those words. -Ever since the start in 2022 I was loyal to him. I didn't talk to a single boy the whole 2 years that I talked to him, I removed every boy off of my phone for him. I only had eyes for him. Whereas he continued to talk to girls on his phone.

His ex that I was once so jealous of, His past talking stages, random adult females that sent nudes, and even the girl he cheated on me with after he promised he would change. He continued going to parties even after he promised he wouldn't. But I didn't have the strength in me to leave him for good. Every time I blocked him I always purposely left multiple ways for him to contact me. He never did. He showed me that he didn't care about me by never reaching out, but I didn't want to believe it.

I always contacted him first to see if he would respond, and he always did because he loved the attention and the power. I hoped that it was because he still loved me. I now know that he didn't. So maybe I was a rebound, or maybe I was just conveniently there. In the back of my heart I still hope I was his first love.

326

Maybe he did love me for real. Maybe he just changed. I wanted to change him back, but that was impossible. That's just who he is and I have to accept that and part ways with it. I have to accept the love I deserve. And I will. I now have him FULLY blocked on everything and I am not going back. I saw this quote not too long ago saying, "keep going back, until you hate them." Idid that without realizing. It was a long, painful and draining process, but it worked. Maybe it will come back to haunt me in my future love experiences, but at least I'm no longer stuck. I'll forever long for an answer that I will never get. And that's to know, "Why me?"

-@abbier.priv

Two side of love

E veryone knows the typical childhood stories of a prince falling in love with a simple girl from the village in the kingdom

They meet deep in the woods, shared a moment under the stars

Dancing gracefully

Locking eyes as they both find rhythm not only with their body but their hearts

After that night they continue to see each other

Falling even more and more deeper in love

The prince's heart just longing to share his happy ever after with her

Showered her with words of affirmation

Gifts, flowers, hugs, kisses, laughter and love

They planned a future together

A home just for them and their future children one day

The memories they can't wait to make

The prince was ready to get down on one knee and to turn his dream into reality

One day, the girl left without a word

No slipper or no letter

A happily ever after turned into a future to never happen

A broken kingdom

She's gone

Was all that ran through princes head

He just felt his heart fall to ground and shatter in a million pieces like grains of sand

He wrote letters far and wide for his fair maiden

He wrote pillars of paragraphs for the beautiful girl, sent knights and hunters to find his love

Days, weeks, months went on by

As he fell more deeper into heartbreak and depression the kingdom was falling as well

The streets filled with crime, screams, crys, the sun never shone, and was never safe to go out at night

As the king was losing his heart, soul and mind the kingdom did as well

There was night he took his most mightiest sword and want to perice through his skin to never feel the pain inside

The prince longed for his love

Every morning and every night crying for his true love

hoping she would appear

Sadly, The kingdom became lost

Moving on

———— ✦•✦•✦ ————

I'm sorry this is out of nowhere. I've been thinking that because It has been such a terrible week, moving and dealing with everything has been a lot lately. Learning how to be on my own and just separating myself from everyone; I know you said I have people to talk to and friends, but it has never been the same, and talking to those same people that you call my friends made me feel worse because I thought I never fit in no matter how much you said they care about you and worried about you.

The reason why I'm saying this to you is because I always felt like you were my best friend, my only friend, and it's just so hard dealing with it alone while everything around me seems to be falling apart, and I don't know what to do about it. And especially moving on from you, it has been hurting so much and taking a toll on me, but it's for the better; it's what I must do. I am not asking for you to reach out and help me, and you do not have to worry about if I'm suicidal because I'm not.

I'm doing my best to heal from everything, and

saying this too, you will lift the weight on my chest, and you probably don't understand why I am going through this when friends made me feel worse because I thought I never fit in no matter how much you said they care about you and worried about you. The reason why I'm saying this to you is because I always felt like you were my best friend, my only friend, and it's just so hard dealing with it alone while everything around me seems to be falling apart, and I don't know what to do about it. And especially moving on from you, it has been hurting so much and taking a toll on me, but it's for the better; it's what I must do. I am not asking for you to reach out and help me, and you do not have to worry about if I'm suicidal because

I'm not. I'm doing my best to heal from everything, and saying this too, you will lift the weight on my chest, and you probably don't understand why I am going through this when I'm going to see you for college, and we will be able to talk. Honestly, I just grasped everything, and no matter how much I say I'm fine or over it, my heart will say otherwise, and it's been like that for months. But I hope you understand and I don't take up too much of your time when reading this. This is how I am trying to heal, or at least the only way I know how to.

A love that I can never have

———— ❖❖❖ ————

I fell in love with him very softly and slowly, it was not overnight but rather, subtle. At first I did not want to admit it, he was one of my best friends, someone that I just hung out with everyday, I can not possibly like him, can I? Reality hit when he was the last person I went to sleep thinking about and the first person I woke up thinking of.

He made it exciting to go to school, I would even dress up just for him. We seemed to like each other, however, when he asked if I liked him, I denied it because I was scared of losing him and ruining our friendship. And that was where I messed up. The next week he was already talking to other girls, trying to find the one. I felt betrayed because how could he move on from our friendship so easily? I guess because we never dated he did not get as attached as I did. I never usually have regrets, but this is definitely the only one. The next months were hell, he showed me girls he was talking to and I had to be supportive because "I never liked him".

Now he's dating a really pretty and nice college girl. I have to watch them be together while he never even talks to me anymore. His new girlfriend's suspicions are right about us but it made my worst fear come true, I lost him and our friendship forever.

-Mariah

Too much going on, way too fast and out of control

———◆●●◆———

This story is based on what it is like to be a person with insecurities taking on the challenge of romance and failing miserably. I'l be writing this passage from the first-person perspective as l represent a hopeless lover who was over-consumed with limerence and tortured himself into being way too protective and supportive of his ex-girlfriend. The magic all began on the 15* of December 2023 when I met my love playing Overwatch 2 and there, we started flirting for fun. It felt like we were meant to be since we got along so well.

Then again, all romances start well and everyone who's ever been lovestruck believes that they found their soulmate, don't they? We added each other on Discord, an app that I barely used at the time, which had suddenly become the app I lost sleep to. So up until the Christmas Holidays, not only had my bland life finally become somewhat more enthusiastic, but everything was under control.

Each morning, I went to school having only my future

career in mind, made sure that all my assignments were complete, and once I had time to spare, I'd text this charismatic girl who wouldn't dare to reply late to any of my texts. Not even for a minute. The more time went by, the more I started taking her seriously. The responsibility of being a good boyfriend had come to me knocking on my door as if they were some unexpected guests. Not to mention that I had to cope with an odd feeling of loneliness and companionship at the same time as the relationship was long distance. Nevertheless, since I had school to deal with, I had my distractions.

Then came Christmas. To this day, I can't recall any other Christmas that had ever felt so warm. Even when I used to believe in Santa Claus, it never felt as fulfilling as the onel passed last year. I had a target to aim for at school. I met a friend who I consider a brother, and I felt proud of myself all over. Now, with a girlfriend added to the mix, I couldn't ask for more. Life was life-ing, as some people might say nowadays.

"Ma chérie", the nickname I had given to my love ever since day 1, was nothing short of perfect from head to toe. Her music taste alone was astounding given that the songs she added to our playlist, all felt divine with instances like "Salvatore" by Lana Del Rey and "Take Me Back to Eden" by Sleep Token being the top 2 songs that still remind me of her even after several months of no contact. She was extremely caring, ensuring that every day, I'd wake up with thousands of adorable TikTok videos waiting to be watched.

Imagine a good morning kiss, just way better. White living so far, (exactly 3,144km away), she somehow had this radiant energy emitting from her to which I was spellbound. I could've talked to her for hours and never got bored. Of course, last but definitely not least, she was gorgeous. Where do I begin? Her hair imitated sleepy beauty, yet it carried the weight of Maleficent. Her eyes were blue and green, embodying peace and life yet they petrified me every time I looked at them. Her lips (How could l ever forget her lips?) were blood red, in color, almost begging me to kiss them yet only to lure me closer and reveal the sharpest fangs that were hiding behind their softness, eager to bite me and drain my life away.

She was a demon in a woman's body. So, moving on back to school, everything around me seemed grayer. It felt harder to focus on school because I was too busy thinking about my love. Even when I texted her, her character changed drastically. She just didn't seem to care for me anymore. I started sending her good morning and good night texts, I kept checking up on her, for every song she added to our playlist, I would add 10 or 20 more songs. Every time invited her to a game of Overwatch, she'd always find some excuse not to join me. From accepting all my invites, she suddenly started declining them all. It was obvious that eventually, she'd stop getting involved with me like the way she had done before, and I mean this in a form of acknowledgment.

I wouldn't want her to be obsessed over me but the way she acted at the time, gave me the impression that she had lost all interest. What had tormented me most was that I had no idea how to change it all. I thought that I had to do something to get her attention back, but I only made everything more twisted for myself. And what's more, the fact that I could only recall moments in which I was sweet and supportive of her, drove me insane.

How could someone like me who's so loving, lose anyone? Perhaps women do like a guy who has no emotion, cares only for himself, and is willing to leave everything behind if he just so happens to get bored. Looking back now, I feel so embarrassed. I understand that I had to leave her alone and continue to improve myself while in the relationship. Both of us have lives yet I threw mine away just to invest more in her. This is also the message that I would like to convey. While it is good to show your lover that you care about them, it is also necessary to give them space for the relationship to grow. You can't just water a plant every 3 minutes and expect it to become a tree the next day.

It all came down to a week before Valentine's Day when I couldn't handle ridiculing myself any longer and so 1 asked to break up for the infamous reason of "focusing on myself". To this day, I feel so ashamed for not knowing any better than to be obsessed with someone. It's an act of immaturity, wouldn't you agree? Limerence is all that it was. Many people have told me that it was logical since my ex was my first-ever girlfriend but even if I have managed to forgive myself after that, I still consider it unacceptable. It's like not knowing how to communicate at all even if it's your first time making a speech. As for the aftermath of the breakup, I'll keep it simple. I fell into a state of depression as I had lost someone very dear to me from my own mistakes. Not being able to control my emotions, added more weight to this situation and

339

further exposed this sense of disappointment up to the point I nearly grew wings and flew to another land.

All my progress at school was destroyed, my relationship with my family got way worse and three of my teachers counseled me since they'd "seen how [I] act" at school. I'm not a popular student at alt but to have even the teachers talk to me, you can guess the level of gossip that had been going on, right?

Bringing an end to this story, I somehow managed to climb back up from my own personal hell. Of course, without an abundance of help, I wouldn't be here to tell the tale so I must thank the teacher's who showed interest in me as well as my dear friend who always emitted positivity brightening up my mood as best as he could and i absolutely must thank the "Therapy we all need" chat. If it weren'tfor Cadey mentioning her discord chat, I wouldn't know how to act today and would probably be lost to time. I would like to add 5 pieces of advice as an extra part of this passage for anyone who would read this.

These points include:

Having patience

Being self-aware

Loving yourself

Learning to communicate

Working with what you have

Just by following 1 of these points, one will notice a drastic change in their mental state in a way that they can feel more relaxed while in the relationship and balance their current life with their romantic lite avoiding any moments of overthinking, engaging in pointless arguments or straight up falling into a void of endless questions starting with "What it..." Hope that this passage delivered an intriguing scenario in the reader's mind and has helped them with an issue that they could be dealing with.

Unexpected

My love story was an unexpected one but never would i have imagined it would've been the greatest impact on me. our story was unexpected but i will forever cherish every moment we had. the spark was there as soon as we both made eye contact on that soccer field on a Thursday night. as i wasn't looking for a relationship and was just focused on school and soccer, he completely changed my perspective. we didn't get the chance to say goodbye to each other but still had each other in mind.

after that same night I received an insta notification saying i had a new follower and as i looked at the name and looked through the highlights i knew maybe something was about to happen. we talked for hours and as days went by we caught feelings for one another, 3 months went by and that's when he popped out with the question "Will you be my girlfriend?". i couldn't express myself as all the emotions were still flowing and of course said yes. as he was my first boyfriend he ought to become my first everything and oh my was i in love alright. as every second, every minute, every hour, every day and every month went by did i come to think that i would forever love him.

my family loved him, most of my friends enjoyed his presence, my dog loved going on walks with him, everything was absolutely perfect. we indeed did have our differences but all relationships do, but it can always be resolved no matter what as long as you don't give up on each other. everything came to an end as my what so i called "best friends" decided to interfere with our relationship and lie to him because of a grudge they held against me, they didn't like seeing us together and one of them liked him. told him i was cheating, talking to multiple guys and just so many things that hurt him and his overthinking and trust issues took over him, we took a break focused on ourselves and tried things out again but as the girls continued saying stuff he just wasn't the same, he couldn't handle it anymore and wouldn't wanna talk things out.

I did indeed keep trying my best to still keep us together but no matter what i did it just wasn't the same so i thought the best choice was to end things although it wasn't what i wanted. we took 3 months off still kept in touch from time to time and while i still kept thinking the spark would still be there because of all the little things he would do, i decided to express my feelings once again to him and he felt the same way or so i thought.

It took me 2 months to realize that he wasn't the same person i knew before, he had changed and it was a shock to even his own friends that he ended up being like that. after telling me that he would be fully committed into us, put effort into us and that he was all into me, apparently during those 2 months he had lied to me. he was caught picking 3 different girls up at different times, talking to multiple girls from nearby schools and just so much that it in fact hurt me so much. i still wonder to this day how can a guy that was so in love with you at one point just end up switching up? after everything we went through, after fixing and healing together, was it just not enough? sometimes i wonder if maybe i was the problem or if maybe i did something wrong because i honestly don't know where everything went side ways.

I still think about him here and there and i will continue to as he has and always will have a special place in my heart because he was my first love and i'll look back into it later on, he was the one person who showed me what real love felt like. during this process, i learned to forgive but i will indeed never forget his non regular actions but this was the best way for me to learn from a new experience. i thank him for that and as i've learned to let go, i know that this will be a forever lasting hurtful memory from my first love.

-@pt.3yn

A Heartbeat Away

I met this guy name andres. we were both 13 at the time. I met him on February 26 2023 at a birthday party that was for my cousin they were best friends so i asked my cousin for his number. he had a gf but on September 17 2023 I found his contact we are now 14. I forgot who it was so i gave him a texts. we eventually realized who was texting who. He had a girl friend but my cousin told me to keep in contact with him because he knew they were gonna break up soon so i did.

A couple week later they broke up. He came to my volleyball game one time before we dated. We eventually decided to hang out. October 13 2023 we went to a corn maze and haunted houses even thought we weren't dating we hold hands, walked off away from everyone, took pictures together, him resting his head on my shoulder. i felt like nothing mattered anymore and i was safe with him. October 20 2023 | invited him to a school event we had. I got to meet his mom and step dad and sister he also met my mom and dad that night.

That night he asked me out, best night ever. I will never forget that night. We went tick or treating together on halloween and he was a panda and I was a shark. I let him meet my second family at the halloween party. I had a fear to go to the fair again after something happening, some how he convinced me to go with him which i'm glad i went. We had a blast! and after we went to go get chillies together and our parents got to talk to each other that night and meet each other. We would face time almost every night no matter what. We always made time for each other and it was like nothing matters expect me and him. It may seem like a cute teenager love story. But all behind this was fighting over little things all the time fighting. If we were together there would be no fighting. but on texts there was fighting all the time. It's now December Christmas week.

We been together for about 3 months. We been fighting a week, he was out of town with family. I felt like i was always having to texts first for that whole month so i didn't texted first to see. I got no texts and got ghosted for 2 days he never even texted. I got so mad and upset I texted him on Christmas eve saying this long paragraph and the one thing i regret saying is "I'm done" because i didn't want it to be done. He took it the wrong way and we got into another fight and when i saw the texts he sent saying "then we should break up" i felt like everything fell apart.

I love him so much. I texted my cousin 2 days after the break up hoping he would understand and i said how i missed him and i should texts him thinking it was a silly mistake and we could work it out until my cousin said "he dating someone else" something along those lines. i was shocked 2 days later he was with some one new. I lashed out on him and we got into another fight..

346

He sent me screen shots of him about to send the "i love you" texts but he never sent them. Then he blocked me after sending me those 2 screen shots. I loved him so much i still do and knowing he moved on that fast completely destroyed me. I got him to unblock me thru texting him thru another app, he has blocked me 3 times now. He always told me we could try again later so I waited and now 8 months later we're going into high school and he talking to another girl again.

Everyone says how crazy I am but it's not that i'm crazy it's just he was my first love and no one understand me when i say that. We started texting today but it was different like nothing felt right. but i also had that gut feeling telling me something and i don't know the message yet. but knowing he going into another relationship soon and i been waiting so long makes me so upset at myself how he doesn't care a little bit. maybe he does care and just doesn't show it. but andres i will always love you and come back to you in a heart beat. Yes of course i dated someone after 7 months because i told myself he wasn't coming back but i still know there some chance out there.

I will never forget all are memories we had together. I hope everything goes well for him and he gets treated right i will always love you. After reading this story your probably think "why would she go back" and the answer is that we were in young love still learning how to love each other we both made mistakes. If him and this new girl work out i will be so happy for him. I thought i was over him but after these last 2 days of texting him I have realized it gonna take longer than 8 months to get over him. End of story i'm still blocked on everything expect for instagram on his private acc. He apologized to me before i started writing this and I just wished he would apologize when he not about to get into a relationship. I really wish me and him worked out but we will see where god takes us. I love you andres.

-C

The sacrifices you make for love

A couple years ago I had a big friend group and we basically knew each other since we were kids we all went to the same school and always hung out. There was this one girl in the group that I would spend most of my time after school hanging out with her. Her name was Emma and Although she was still immature at the time she still was a smart girl and I found her the funniest person to be around.

I know I had feelings for her l just didn't express them wit her and I never ended up telling her. She also had feelings for me but l just didn't know it then. The one thing I'll regret is not pursuing her because I moved on and had feelings for someone else and getting with them. That broke her in ways I never knew and I simply didn't know how much I meant to her. I broke up with my girlfriend at the time and emme was still in my corner helping me get past everything.

Idk how she did it but she did. We were basically inseparable. We both had feelings for eachother and for some stupid reason we never told each other. She had her own boy problems and I always helped her when she needed it. She eventually got a boyfriend and we got distant. And I got a new girlfriend who made me basically choose her or Emme and the friend group. And I'm young and a lover boy so I chose my girlfriend and it kinda just ruined everything. They stopped talking to me a lot and my girlfriend ended up cheating on me. As much as I tried to fix what I had with Emme and the friend group it was never the same. But Emme did have a soft spot for me so me and her would still talk from here and there. Emme knew she still had feelings for me while with her boyfriend so she told her sister to start talking to me in hopes I would talk to her sister more so she could eventually lose interest in me. And unexpectedly I started gradually Drifting my feelings for her sister. Maya was funny but still young and at the time pretty immature. But I was too cuz I wasn't much grown at the time.

We ended up dating for a crazy 8 months for it to end because she could have "sworn" she saw me texting a girl when in reality I was playing a game on my phone. She was my first real relationship I would say and it hurt a lot. And I didn't really have much support at the time and I embarrassed Myself by begging for her back and we got back together but we never ended up working cuz she ends up kissing some other guys and talking to her other exes. And to be honest 1 just get placed in the worst situations possible.

I haven't dated since then and that was December 2023. I met a girl in my new school. Poured everything I had into her cuz I thought she was my everything just for her to lose feelings and not want a relationship 2 months in. Which just happened while I'm writing this. So to end my story I think what I wanna share is that be careful with your love and put yourself first before anyone else. Your love can be taken for granted so don't give it out so easily.

-@klokjit

Lovers

So during the school year I felt alone n in need of company, like I just wanted to be loved again so I got in a relationship wit an old ex who left me, be she had her own past relationship which didn't go well n then I decided to try again n it was going really well n then everything just started goin down hill, we always had arguments over stupid stuff i didn't like, n I wanted reassurance which I never got, n it got to a point where it was non-stop arguments n the relationship went down hill, n we always brought up breaking up, n I was genuinely trying to save our relationship, she really never tried to save it, she used to say she was but she was just making it worst. It got to a point where she didn't want to be in the relationship but stayed and acted like she wanted to stay n apparently she had lost feelings n then she broke up with me, but there was something about me dat didn't care or feel anything, n now she's been talking crap about men cussing me out, its a hole a different person, n it really just shows us how people really are. Ive dealt with it tho, dats it tho hope u understand wha happens i know it ain't long but it's something n it ain't the only story. But I blame myself for everything. They should of never met me.

-@gabe.hoopz

A Love To Hold Dear

It was around freshman year of high school when I first met her. Out of respect for her family I'll keep her name out of it, but she was the kindest person I've ever met. Everyone that had the privilege of interacting with her became her friend immediately. She was sweet, hilarious, and the most beautiful person I had ever seen. She had the most striking blue eyes that reminded me of the sea and beautiful golden blonde hair. She was everything.

We became really good friends quickly and the more we grew to know each other, the more we fell in love. I never understood what she saw in me. I was a bigger kid, awkward, a massive nerd, and pretty antisocial overall. But she saw those traits and made them beautiful to me. She had the uncanny ability to bring out the absolute best in me and I still thank her today for that. It took me so long to ask her out. I mean it was MONTHS before I got the courage to do it.

The second I did, the first thing she said was "took you long enough" and I was floored. My dream person, everything I ever wanted, she was right there and in my life by my side. We spent time together every day, I'd sneak out on weekends to go hang out with her, I'd pretend to go to a friend's house some days but really I'd be with her. I woke up thinking of her and I went to sleep thinking of her. It all sounds so cliche but I really mean it when I say I met the love of my life my freshman year of high school. My grandfather used to give me and my brothers two dollar bills, we always thought they were so special but really it's just cus it came from him. One day she folded one of the ones he gave me into a heart and told me to keep it with me so I always knew how she felt about me.

Again, cliche as hell but we were young and it's still one of the most meaningful gestures I've ever had towards me. We had been together a little over 8 months when I got hit with a bad depression. I was in the middle of a med switch and I had one of the worst lows of my life where even she couldn't help bring me out of it. I struggled to get out of bed every day, let alone talk to anyone and I recognized that wasn't fair to her.

I don't know why I thought it was a good idea, I don't know why I imagined it was for the best, but I asked her if we could just take a week break so I could re-regulate. I planned on taking off school and disconnecting from the world until I was back in a healthy state and I did my best to explain all that to her. She was really hurt, but she agreed because she knew I thought it was the best idea for me. I told her I loved her one last time before I left school, and while I'm glad I did I wish I had given her a hug or a kiss goodbye.

Just one last memory of her physically as well as verbally. I got word 3 days after that day that she had committed suicide. She had texted me the night it happened saying "I love you, and I'm sorry." I knew she had some mental health problems but I never imagined it would've come to that. It broke me. Entirely broke me. I blamed myself completely for pushing her over the edge, and so did her parents.

They didn't even let me go to her funeral. I wish I could say that I now believe I wasn't at fault, but some part of me will never let that idea go. I still grieve her to this day. I can't look a person with blonde hair and blue eyes in the face without remembering every moment with her. I do nothing but search for her in every girl I meet, but I know they'll never compare, and to be honest I don't want them to compare.

She was my one in 8 billion and she always will be. I still believe she visits me even after death, whether in dreams, or in the butterflies that land on me, or in the brief moment of beauty I get on an awful day, I believe that's her telling me she's with me. I always get flak, even now, when I speak about her because people like to think I was too young and didn't understand love or even who was right for me. But standing here now about 7 years later, I can say that even if it wasn't real love, it's still as close as I've ever come to it.

She permanently made me a better person and I know she loved me to the end. And the two dollar bill she folded for me? It's been in my phone case ever since I got it. I only get clear cases just so I can always see it and remember the light she brought, and will always continue to bring, to my life.

-@Isaac.deno

Thank You Thank You

Recently I was in a relationship with this girl who I never thought I would end up with. In class, we were both quiet and kept to ourselves. She made the first move to talk by texting me on Instagram. The more I got to know the more liked her. After a little over a month, I want to ask her to be my girlfriend.

She said yes I asked her with flowers I felt so lucky to have her. The date 06/24 now meant something to me. Things were going great we saw each other whenever we could. Always laughing and having fun conversations. It hurts knowing that everything was going great. We both had a family trip to Mexico I spent a week while she spent three.

I don't know how people manage in long-distance relationships was miserable. We didn't have good service so talking was hard. We both felt distant but we both still had feelings. We talked and agreed to go on a date when we saw each other again. I had it all planned a nice picnic, checking out vinyl stores, cruising around, and more. On National Girlfriend Day she decided it was better to stay as friends. The night before we opened up and had a deep conversation. I tried being there for her when she needed comfort.

It's important to remember communication is key but understanding is everything. I apologize for not seeing it from her point of view and I'll work on it but it was too late. I blame myself for the breakup I know things could have ended differently. For the next three days, I tried fighting for her back and checking up on her just to be left to see. I took a hint it still hurts that someone you talk to every day just stops talking to you. It might be stupid but I still have hope that we can fix things and get back together. I've been in relationships but this girl made me feel something no one could in a month.

We had a deep connection. Music was our thing. We both liked similar and different genres of music. She sounds like music fun fact. I miss her. After everything she's been through she has a heart of gold. She left a part of her in me that I'm grateful for. If you're in a relationship, please love your partner with all your heart. Go out on that date, buy them that thing they want, and surprise them before it's too late. If you're like me you're not alone. Don't give up on love time heals wounds. Do you but just be careful. We're all humans no one perfect. Thank you Thank you.

-Francisco V

Desideratum

You say one thing then do the other. You tell me you love me but you show someone else that love. You say it's not lust, that you care for me more than just my body but the only times you seem interested is when it has to do with my body. You say you love me too and you'd do anything for me yet you do that for her and leave me on the side. I see how you look at her, I see the genuine love and care that you have for her, yet when I ask for that all I get is unrequited feelings and a deep hurt left in my chest. Why can't you think of me that way? Why can't I prompt love songs from your heart, given to me and only me? Why can't I be the one you're reminded of every time that one song comes on?

You don't even know how much you hurt me. You think everything is just okay with us and then you continue to confuse me. You think I don't hurt from this. I swear it's like a rollercoaster ride with you. So many ups and downs, so many random turns, and the funny thing is we're not even dating. But you still pull me along as if there are strings attached. Why am I so hurt? You have no obligation to me yet you continue to come back and talk to me. You continue with the I love you's and the wanted touch and the excitement of everything but when it comes to true feelings you push them, or me, away.

You say I deserve so much more than what he did to me but Frankly this hurts so much worse, because you know I want you yet you continue to tell me how you miss her. The yearning you have for her can never add up to the yearning I have for you tho. I've been wanting a connection like that with you since we met and I know it's my fault that I couldn't Pursue that connection because I was in a relationship, but I really truly hoped that you would wait for me. I wish you waited for me.

You're genuinely so amazing and I can't express that enough, but damn you really hurt me. This hurt isn't like others, it's excruciating. It lingers inside of me with no explanations, just here to stay. I can say tho, when you do give me the attention the hurt goes away. The false hope sets in that I'll one day be yours. That one day you'll care for me like you do her. That can only last a moment tho.

I wish I was her.

I wish you loved me like her.

Fuck, you confuse me.

-@olive888tree

Broken Promises

He basically got mad at me for being on the phone with one of my friends for 2mins bc he had to vent about something to me. He ended things again, but this time i cried once and then i realized that he isn't matured yet and that once he has then it will he more easier to talk to him, but for now i can see i really matured from the last time he ended things. I'm not worried about it anymore if i get an answer i get one if i don't then thats the closure i needed. I'm at this point where it is what it is.

Like i used to be waiting like a 2year old for their dad to come back home, bc it took so long for him to txt me back when shit like this happens but now i muted him on everything left my phone on dnd from now on and i don't even check to see if he txted back or nothing anymore. I'm at peace right now bc i realized that i was the only mature one in the relationship and he wasn't secure with himself and still picked the smallest things to get mad at me for.

But now I'm over it the delusion is gone now and i realized if he really wants me wants the relationship he will mature and become better for himself. man one action changed my view on things made me more mature made me decide to not let my guard down bc if he can do it once he can do it again. until he matures and actually wants to talk shit out ima keep working on myself and keep myself at peace, yes i do love him but he isn't secure with himself. I cant have that in my life that is goes to show he isn't ready and isn't mature enough to be in a relationship so till then I'm leaving him alone. in time i did learn the hard way but now I'm at peace. i was tryna make friends and shit happens, I lost the person i love so much be of my actions shit i do.

Not like he would believe a word i say so theres no point so for now ima just leave him alone and maybe one day it will come around and he will wanna talk things out but for now it is what it is. maybe in future we will fix things but if not then i wish him nothing but the best my bad i hope you are happy and move on in life...

   -@_.xo.des

For Who You Are

———————— ◆•◉•◆ ————————

I think the hardest part about love is letting go and allowing yourself to see that person, that career, that thought- for who and what it really is. over the majority of my life, i've loved my best friend. we've known each other for years, watched each other grow up. at first it was friendship, then around fifth grade it was romance, then it devolved into a slight balance between the two after around freshman year; closer than friends but being in such different places that you can't really imagine kissing them.

Not sure how to explain it, but it makes sense to me. i didn't really think it was reciprocated. but any time the thought of there being an "us" was brought up, he'd never give a definitive answer. he cared for me as a friend but was protective like something more. yet even with where we are now, i'll always have a soft spot for him; which makes things harder for when he disappoints me or falls short. for a while, i struggled with what i've now learned to be limerence.

i'd put him on such a high pedestal that when he inevitably hurt me, i'd start to grow resentment towards him. but with therapy and a few years of self reflection, i learned how to see him for who and what he was the good and the bad. i realized that while not everything he did or didn't do was a direct attack towards me, he was a person, and sometimes people can fuck up- pardon the profanity. there were and still are times where he'll be an asshole. he'll make a joke at my own expense and embarrass me; he'll refuse to communicate even after begging him to; he'll treat me one way one day and a different way the next; but most recently was when he lied in my face after i came to him in a moment of vulnerability. i asked him what he thought of relationships in high school and if they were worth pursuing. since i'd been struggling with that loneliness in my own failed romantic endeavors. he said they didn't seem worth the drama.

"maybe if you're looking for something short-term, but i don't know". he opened up about his fears with time, saying that he wishes he had enough time to fall in love while also focusing on his career. for the first time, i thought i saw him. the entire him. and he saw me. we saw each other. then a few weeks later, he got a girlfriend. this sweet, amazing girl who i've known for almost a year now. for the slightest second, i was happy for her. i knew she deserved it. but then it dawned on me that everything he said that night was a lie.

How could he? i was hurt, i was angry, i felt stupid. not because he was with her but because now, i felt like he meant relationships weren't for *me*, not that they weren't worth the time in general; and for the first time ever, i felt every right to be upset. he's still my best friend and i'll always have that love for him, but i'm realizing he hurt me. he's not this perfect, amazing guy who can do no wrong— he's human. i understand that, and i'm still upset; i'm allowed to be both. that really was the nail in the coffin for me. we romanticize the things and people we love so much without even realizing it. we hold others to such high pedestals and then beat ourselves up for doing so when they disappoint us. but once we allow ourselves to see both the good and the bad sides of each other, then we can really know what's real and what's not.

we need to let go of that make believe image we have, as loving and comforting as it is. we also need to let go of that scornful image we have, too. we're human and we fuck up. doesn't make it justified, but it makes it understandable. after we do that, then we can react and know what ourselves up for doing so when they disappoint us.

But once we allow ourselves to see both the good and the bad sides of each other, then we can really know what's real and what's not. we need to let go of that make believe image we have, as loving and comforting as it is. we also need to let go of that scornful image we have, too. we're human and we fuck up. doesn't make it justified, but it makes it understandable. after we do that, then we can react and know what we're feeling is real.

-a.j

My Relation

O ne day i went to school and this was the first day of school, as soon as i walked in my classroom i laid my eyes down on this one guy and so did he. We both noticed and started talking throughout the day of school we were together and talking every time u til one day he just confessed his love for me, i knew he liked me but i didn't wanna say anything to him cause i liked him too.

After he confessed i confessed to we both weren't shocked as we both knew we liked each other then he said he would like me more if he dated me i didn't think twice and said okay and then we were dating.i was so happy u called my friends told everyone but they were scared for me they knew things i didn't like he liked many other girls while dating me and stuff i was scared but didn't think much of it one month went by another month went by then suddenly one day after school one of his friends came up to me and said be prepared i was like what?

Then on the way home my bf (now ex) messaged me calling me fat and ugly and other very rude things and broke up with me, i was sad intact really said that my own bf broke up with me then he told me "i only dated you to play you, you think u actually liked u?" that broke my heart.! left him and got over him easily as it was fake live but then after a long time of being single one of his other friends came up to me and started talking to me, i didn't know how to stop but I started liking him he was sweet, handsome and so much more he valued everything of me. then we became bfs shari hg slit of secrets laughing e.t. then on a random Wednesday he said i have to tell you something i said uhhh sure he told me he liked me i said me too i didn't know what to do and so did he, then u said why not we start dating but take it slow he said okay.

The next day everyone at school knew and this went on for sometime maybe like 3 moths then he suddenly said he had enough and broke up with me i was really sad that u git broken up with again but a week goes by and said he regrets it and got back this happening roughly around 9-10 times breaking n yo and getting back together. after the final time we broke up we stayed as friends and for a long long time. And as friends we talked about the past bringing up us dating we made fun of it until he asked me do u like anyone? after he said that u had a feeling he liked me so i said yes then he said me too then the next 3 hours we were talking straight about our feelings for each other and what to do again.

He said to date i kept on saying no cause i was scared he would break my heart AGAIN so i declined his offer after a bit of thinking i said okay but don't do what u did last time he promised me he wouldn't... guess what happened he broke up with me... on the same day he said i'm sorry i was pissed off blah blah blah and stuff let's get back idk what was running in my head i said okay then we were fine until just 3 days ago he broke up with me again for good that was final. After that i am still trynna move on and focus on myself now we are staying as friends and hopefully just friends.

Metamorphosis

I'm in the beginning of a relationship, and there's something to say about 2 people being aware of the excitement that clearly exists, but also the patience needed so we can move forward without having any mistakes or accidents derail what we've accomplished so far. And I'm not just talking about what we've accomplished together, but more importantly individually. The inner work, which should always continue, where we need to support when possible. The deeper layers that one needs to feel safe with. To be vulnerable again and feel free. We've been been in relationships where we each thought and felt we had our person. And life, God, the universe, shows us different, and we both chose to work on ourselves instead of blaming another person, working hard on not holding resentment. We loved these people in our past. And despite the pain that went into those relationships and the rips, our hearts learned to love so much better. We embody love now, instead of looking for it in others. We are becoming the best versions of ourselves, and I pray we see our story through. We trust the process, we communicate, we listen, and do the work, we are passionate and compassionate, all the makings of another great love story.

-Jose

Narcissistic Notes

So I met this person my senior year of high school definitely my first love or so 1 thought, I had met her at this park with some friends, I thought it was love at first sight everything was perfect for about a year, we even almost moved in with each other, I was with her every day of my life outside of work, I met her right after I had broken up with the mother of my child so I wasn't looking for love in any way shape or form when I looked at her i definitely had thought she was the one at that time in my life she was my everything I devoted my life to her this was the most obsessed I was over a girl in my whole life but all things must come to an end everyone around us would constantly nag us about the things we were doing that were not good for each other constantly letting outside noise mess up our relationship at one point in the relationship I had felt nothing for this person we had constantly been fighting every day over the smallest things that shouldn't have even mattered. Around Christmas I had try to rekindle things with her because I even mattered. Around Christmas I had try to rekindle things with her because I genuinely was so attached to this person that I thought that I could

371

physically not live without them, so we fixed things started communicating and everything was going good for about another 3 months, then they started laying hands and screaming at me when they'd get upset with me or when they wouldn't get there way, I had caught this person cheating on me multiple times thru out this time period and still went back because i thought I could fix them, but the biggest lesson I learned from that was 1 can't change someone who doesn't want too. Shortly after are 1 year anniversary I had lost all feelings for this person and had tried to leave them but they just kept promising me things that they would never keep there word on so 1 eventually got tired of there games n had just blocked them on everything because I needed to find peace in my life being with them made me hate everything about myself and I'm still stuck struggling finding who I am without them but everything because I needed to find peace in my life being with them made me hate everything about myself and I'm still stuck struggling finding who I am without them but I know there no good for me I know to never let someone hurt me that bad mentally or physically ever again, domestic violence can go both ways.

-Nathaniel

Love and Loss

ack in 2021 i had a girl ask me for my snap on TikTok and me thinking it was sketchy I said no but then she asked again and I gave it not a week or so I went on a school camp not knowing she was worried about me after a week I had finish the camp with my school I got back home and i saw messages saying she missed me so I said the same and while we talked for weeks and weeks she ask me a bold question she said why I haven't asked her out yet I then asked her out she said yes for the first stage it was easy not much arguing going on no nothing now moving on to the second stage things got complicated we argued a lot but we worked things out but stage three had a lot of things going on and as I man I take responsibility and accountability I was greedy for more and I lost the only one that cared about who I was and I regret that and I know words can't comprehend the amount of damage I did to our relationship and that was wrong and selfish of me now I'm wishing i could redo what I did now I lost her forever and there was a lot of crying and a lot of emotions going on and now I'm trying to become a better person so I could treat the next person right but I know I'll still live with the guilt I did to her and as a man I know not many guys care about cheating but mine was greed and I take full responsibility of it but I will love her from afar.

Summer Camp

I grew up always wanting to go to summer camp in the states so when I was 15, my parents broke the news that my brother and I were being sent overseas for camp. I was ecstatic. My dreams of lake swimming, the making of life long friendships, making art and a possible summer fling were becoming real. After 5 flights I found myself 9,687 miles away from home at the most picturesque campus I'd ever seen. I was so nervous I arrived late the first night of camp and missed orientation so I knew no one until I met my roommates Lillian, Nina, Maya and Lucia.

They were my rocks and we bonded so fast nothing could break us up. The first day of camp I immediately noticed him. We were in the morning sing and I was standing opposite the most good looking boy I'd ever seen. I couldn't stop looking at him and I really wanted to get to know him. That day the 1st of July was his birthday and he was freshly 16, without even knowing him I liked him and told the girls. Nina knew him from camp the year before and after some encouragement I told her to tell him I liked him.

A few days after she told him, he came up to me in evening painting class and asked me to paint with him. I couldn't contain my smile and my friends gave me knowing looks as we went off. We sat on twin rocks talking about nothing and everything while we tried to paint but were too distracted by each other. After class he took me up to the roof of the sing hall and we watched the sunset as we talked about living forever and what we would do if we knew we couldn't mess up. We kissed that night on the roof and I ran back to my dorm so fast to tell the girls about it. was so happy every time I thought about it I couldn't stop smiling and with the time difference I called all my friends back home to tell them about the boy.

We moved quickly and the next two weeks were filled with kisses on the roof, in the music rooms, by our dorms and the field house, sneaking back into our rooms past lights out even though the dorm heads knew where we'd been. He was perfect, from his deep blue eyes, his nose, his lips that always smelt of mint chapstick that made my lips tingle, his hands fit just right with mine. I'd never been this close to a boy before and never kissed anyone as much as him. Part of me knew that eventually the camp would end and there would be no more kissing, no more lying on the jetty with my girls and I'd have to go home to where this experience only existed to me. I kept telling myself to not get attached but how could I not?

He bought me a little gold heart necklace one weekend of camp and told me it was so I wouldn't forget him but he didn't understand how unforgettable someone like him was. I had many firsts with him, so many perfect moments. The last night of the camp we had a dance and we snuck away to be alone together for the last time. Our noses kissed like they had so many times before, except this time I breathed in every second wishing it could last forever. The next morning was filled with happy reunions with the parents and our mums took awkward photos of us together.

I wrote him a letter the night before and gave it to him as I left. Leaving was like leaving a part of me behind and my whole being wanted to turn around and run back. During my last week in the states he took the 6 hour bus ride to Manhattan to give me a letter and kissed me one last time. Every time now I think about the camp it feels like a dream, like it never really happened. How could an experience be so perfect every single way possible? I will always have my memories and my little gold heart to remind me it was real.

-soraya

Algorithms to Love

I thought I was breathing as beautiful as I desired to breathe

I've made mistakes in committing to searching for something that couldn't recognize me.

It's true your extortionate in by my heart was I only able to afford you.

The smile you give has no analog, nothing I can

think of could create the picture of your smile.

I thought I had the algorithm to your love.

I know I'll recover but the pain is all I want to know.

but what you've given me shall walk along side me forever.

My heart denies the credence of loss

It can't withstand not hearing its counterpart calls.

-@poetic_tay Donte

Things written cant be explained

—— ◆•◆•◆ ——

There's things that can't be put into perspective Things I try to find words for and create because my heart won't rest until it feels like it spoken searching for a quote that puts my feelings into words I lack to find it I can learn every language and read every word ever written but ill never find what's in your heart. if I said I miss you. I wish you asked which parts of you do I miss. so I can have you explore how I loved each part of you. Each part of you as a individual member. We say love is a beauty, I myself cannot deny Beauty is one of the rare things that do not lead to doubt of God. The best part of beauty is that which no picture can express. there's things in my heart that has no choice there's things in my heart that's been given no voice there's things in my heart with out a name there's things written that can't be explained.

-@poetic_tay Donte

Moon

I like to look at the moon, wondering if you are looking at it too, imagining that my gaze travels Miles to your window and whispers in your ear all that I didn't have time to tell you. Maybe the moon I see from my window reflects in yours. Are you with someone else, watching it reflect in your second-floor window? I like looking at the moon, but it wasn't the night, I was looking at you.

Toxic

My love experience contains in bipolar disorder, attachment issues, maybe a little of narcissistic abuse, and manipulation. There was this girl I meant on social media one night hanging out with my family, and I had seen this girl I add her she add's me back you know how it goes obviously. I start texting her she gives me her number and we play iMessage games , I left her on delivered for a week I finally responded back and she brings up how it's been a week since I messaged her back we start flitting with each other , I start to catch feelings and start talking to her I would tell her I love her (in the talking stage) bazaar right? But she would tell me she loves me back.

It was my first time in love. she was my first love she didn't know what I looked like, I was anonymous , I had stopped talking to her because I missed my ex and talking to my ex didn't last long at all. So I had made her a rebound technically, I fell in love in love like obsessed couldn't get her out of my mind For one second it was always her her her . She showed me a lot of things she made me who I am today . Fast forward like 3 years later

382

long story short in between those years we were always on and off.

I had figured out she had a gf and I didn't know it broke me into a million pieces but i still loved her I wasn't gonna give up or let her go . She got caught up a few times I think I can't recall this was so long ago. But each time I would get played I would stay no matter what , even if she treated me like shit put all the blame on me (although sometimes it was me A LOT) she would try to make me think it was all my fault but her actions caused me to act out and block her like a thousand times I wasn't crazy she was just a player who I thought was in love with me with only a little clue that she gave no fucks about me and was only there for the attention I gave her she loved that I chased her , it was so toxic but addicting , I was so blinded by her love and it was my first time Involve . We both overdosed bc of each other that says a lot , I know it's messed up but I didn't care when she odd and i regret it a lot till this day I should've cared more. I got my karma because when I did it she didn't care either I guess it was fair.

I always felt as if she just played with me like I was a dog and just step on me over and over again and I would allow it. I wanted us to have a love story I saw her in my future I saw us getting married having kids and being in love , but that wasn't realistic at all . So much shit happened that I probably forgot about . So up until now August 4th 2024 we don't talk to each other anymore our spark has burnt out forever ago I still love and think about her till this day I am bipolar so when I fall in love its not typical love its obsession aggression and a lot more.

383

but I just kept going back until my mind and my heart gave up and decided I am actually better alone so today I am trying to work on myself and build the life i wanna have without such a toxic person in my life putting me down for there actions. I still wonder if it was all a lie if she ever cared about me or loved me even a little bit I'll never truly know but all I know is my love for her was real I was all about her I would do anything for her but it isn't reciprocated. So I had to let go . this is my love experience in a short story it was great while it lasted.

Elaine

In high school, my life revolved around soccer and school. Everything changed when Elaine transferred to our school during sophomore year. We got paired up for a group project in English class and spent hours working together, talking about books, music, and dreams. I quickly realized I wanted to spend more time with her. We started to hang out after school, going to parks, shops, and even each other's houses. Elaine had a way of making everything feel more vibrant and exciting. It wasn't long before I found myself deeply infatuated, always yearning for our time together.

One day, as we were sitting on a bench in a park, I decided to tell her how I felt. My heart was pounding and my palms were sweaty, but I knew I had to say something. When I finally blurted out my feelings, she just smiled and said she felt the same way. It was like a weight had been lifted off my shoulders. We started dating, and those were some of the best months of my life. We did everything together. She introduced me to her favorite books and movies, and I showed her my favorite spots around the city and even attempted to teach her how to play soccer, though she wasn't very good at it. Elaine became a constant presence at my soccer games, cheering me on from the sidelines.

Her support meant everything to me, and I played my best knowing she was watching. After games, we'd often go out for ice cream or just sit in the bleachers talking about everything and nothing. It felt like I had found my person, the way I could see it at that age. Everything seemed perfect.

Then, one day, she started acting differently. She became distant, showing little desire to hang out, barely texting back, and avoiding me in the hallways. It felt as if she completely hated me she ended ghosting me days at a time, but I still loved her, so I put up with it. Always asking what she needed and what she wanted with little no care about my feelings, she had things going on at home so I always tried to make her feel as she could rely on me but it didn't matter to her.

She continued avoiding me for months. I started skipping class, going on walks instead, thinking about what I did wrong. My grades dropped and so did my happiness. My friends noticed and tried to convince me to break up with her, but I put it off, hoping things would change because I loved her even more than I loved myself so I continued to suffer. Nearing the end of the school year I couldn't take it anymore, an I finally broke it off. We never spoke or seen each other again as she moved schools right after. I still miss the feeling I had when we were together smiling telling each other everything ,loving each other.

Fragments of a love once whole

I t's 1:17 am on a Tuesday and I can't sleep because you're weighing on my mind. You were my first everything therefore part of you means everything to me. My heart heavily misses you it's like the ghost of your presence is haunting me and seeing our favorite color green, love songs, and even sunsets reminds me of us. I cherish the beautiful persona of love that you taught me. We've worked on ourselves and became better people before and I'm confident we'll do it again. I've known you since we were 13 years old and I'm still yearning for the outer worldly boy I had a crush on. I know you're moving this summer and I may feel distant but I'm wishing you the best from afar, my love. October 15th, 2024 in H mart we opened a fortune cookie that said "Spread your good feelings around" You then told me you loved me for the "first time" (of course I said it back) then asked me to be your girlfriend in the rain. May our everlasting love at 18 lie between these pages until we return to each other. Missing the sound of your laughter, the touch from your hugs and kisses, and your beautiful smile a little extra right now. I hope to hear from you on my 19th birthday, we're

387

almost the same age again! I love you bear. Thank you,
Kd Amidon.

Sincerely, Sj

Buchanan

I wish the overthinking didn't get to me

I wish i told you everything

I wish i did it right

I wish i didn't wait too long I wish i bought you the flowers you deserve I wish i made you smile more than i made

you sad I wish i was there for you always

I wish i took you on dates

I wish i was seeing you smile right now I wish i was texting you wondering when i

can see you again

I wish i could hold your hand I wish i could hug you and say I'm sorry

I wish i was with you I wish i realized this before i lost you completely...

Lasting Pain

I've tried rewriting this multiple times. Words can't exactly describe how it was w us. But I tried my hardest. I was in 8th grade. I know that sounds so stupid cause how could two fourteen year old girls be in love? But I really truly believe I was in love with her. I met this girl while I was in another relationship. I was at a new school and didn't know anyone. She had a crush on me. I didn't like her back at first, but I got out of the relationship I was in and I started to fall for her. She fell first, I fell harder.

She kissed me for the first time on my birthday in the school bathroom. I barely remember it but we were on and off for my entire eighth grade year and the summer after. I told her everything about me and to this day she knows more about me than my own mother does. She made me love myself. I have an anxiety disorder, and back then it was severely unmanaged, and she would help me through every panic attack and anxiety-induced episode I had (even tho most of the anxiety was caused by her) She was there for me always. She would promise me things, and in our minds, promises were the highest level of trust and you had to keep them.

We spent so much time together, and when we weren't together, we were texting or on the phone constantly, falling asleep and getting ready while on FaceTime. She kept breaking it off, attempting to stay friends, then friends with benefits, then we always went back to liking each other. When we were friends, we knew we liked each other. When we were back together, we acted like friends in front of other people.

We even got together when we were both w other people, having the mindset of 'it's not cheating if we don't like each other. I knew she wanted me the whole time, but she never admitted it. I found out later I was right, and she told me the reason she kept breaking it off was because she kept losing feelings. I found out later that was a lie. As many times as she left and as many times as she changed her mind, I always went back. The bad was bad, but the good was the most amazing I'd ever felt.

For Valentine's Day, she wrote me a love letter every day up until the actual holiday, where she was planning on asking me to be her valentine. I ended up not being her valentine, as she got w her ex gf before she asked me. but she gave me five of the letters a few months later. I still have them. She was very secretive about us, which I had no idea as to why but I later found out it was because her mom hated me for no reason other than the fact that she was able to.

Her mom had worked at the school, and if anyone knew about us, she would have inevitably found out. This was the same reason she broke up w me. Because of her mother and her unjustifiable resentment for me.

Her mom had a lot of control over her all her life, and my ex couldn't find a way around her. She acted nice to my face, and I never would have had a hint of her not liking me if someone hadn't told me. We only actually dated for ten days, to which she broke up with me using stickers, over messages. I didn't tell anyone about the breakup for days. In my mind, saying the words would make it real.

I wasn't ready for that. I was still so in love w her. For months after, I watched her care and love me less and less. I watched her get with other people, and each time it killed me a little bit more than the last. I watched her turn herself into someone she's not, just for the validation of her friends. We still texted as friends. It wasn't the same. The thing that killed me the most was how much I loved her and how much I would've fought for her. She is gave up on us. Months later I wrote a letter to her mother, never intending to send it but I wanted it just to have it.

I got into another relationship weeks after me and her broke up, with someone who didn't really care about me that much. The girl I got with after my ex played me a few times, we dated in the beginning of freshman year, which was fair because she was an unintentional rebound to me. I took her to my homecoming, which was convievently on my exes birthday. She broke up w me over text after a month and a half of being together, and I found out she might have cheated. I never found out if she actually did or not. During that relationship, she didn't want me talking to my ex. I was so afraid of losing her that I obeyed, and tried to stop talking to her as much as possible. Me and my ex weren't together, we were barely friends, but we were still in love with each other from a distance. She admitted she was in love w me during an argument about my at-the-time gf not wanting me to speak to her. I look back at those screenshots between us and I don't recognize myself. I regret being so mean to her.

We are both in relationships. She is w a girl. The relationship isn't healthy by any means at all. The way they got together was fucked and their relationship now is soooo toxic and just awful. My ex is not allowed to speak to me because her new gf said so. I resent the girlfriend every single day for not letting my ex speak to me, but I can't hate her as much as I want to because I get it. I hate myself more for hating her.

My ex still reaches out from time to time, and when she does it's for a few days then I'm blocked again. She is not the same person that I loved, she changed herself for the validation of her friends, but sometimes I can still see the side of her I fell in love w come out when we talk. Ive been holding onto that for dear life. She still thinks of me, she says. She looks for me in crowds she knows I'm not in. And it sounds like bullshit but for some crazy reason I believe her. I know for a fact I'm on her mind a lot, she just can never act on it. As much as it shouldn't be, that fact is comforting to know. She's always tried to be there for me. It got to the point where I felt as if she didn't care about me, she was only contacting me out of pity. I was absolutely sobbing in the bathroom at school because I had relapsed. She didn't really care. Just looked at me and let me cry, went on her phone and asked what was wrong in the most monotone way. She pitied me. I would've pitied me too. I'm so desperate when it comes to her and it makes me look stupid every time. I don't know how to finish this.

This paragraph is so scattered and not very detailed, and I apologize for that. I'm writing what comes to my head as it comes, so it's a bit unorganized. I'm slowly trying to work on myself and try to convince myself that it's over. I've been talking to someone for a little over a month now. I like him a lot. But I still am unsure about everything.

About Love Lost

As a 16 yo male that didn't think high-school romance lasted through marriage most of the relationship I've been in I just counted them as practice for real serious relationship that's what I thought until I met this one girl 2 years older than me that I met through a friend she was perfect at first caring, smart, kind, respectful, loving, works out with me she was literally just a vibe to be around a good friend and partner had our first date ofc it was with some friends couldn't just be us alone we watched a horror movie but I'll tell the truth for most of the movie we where fooling around if you know you know we spent our first birthday's together it was amazing made me think that I could actually marry someone I met in high-school until 6 months into our relationship I just didn't feel the same and she could've seen that I wasn't messaging the same I wasn't loving the same I wasn't acting like the me she fell in love with. Then on that fathead day she called and asked "do you not love me anymore" a lot of tears where shed on that day a lot of feelings poured out but too sum it all up gave her this example "one time I didn't have a phone and wasn't able to talk too her on a regular basis and I tweaked I cried about the thought of not being able to talk too her.." and not long before we broke up I lost my phone again "but this time I was alright without being able to chat with her I felt free not having to talk to her and deal with her that's when she decided to break up with me and am not mad as am the one who fell out of love for her but I wish I'd gone into a relationship with her when I understood myself more i feel like I lost the love of my life because I didn't understand my emotions enough I feel it that problem could've easily been solved that's my story thanks for giving me the chance to share it.

-@shehatesderrick

Broken Dreams

ummer of 2023 ends. I remind myself that my academics and outside work is in the high end of my priority range. Though at the of August, I met someone. Things were going pretty fast but that didn't bother me because it was apparent that we both had a similar kind of interest within one another.

I felt like my feelings with this girl could be compared to those paper lanterns that couples would go out their way to see, as one. I felt like my heart was opened, similar to how you would open the moonroof to your car, just to see the stars, gleaming in a joyful night. I felt like this person brought light out of me. I fell in love, I consistently thought, and I repeatedly dreamed about her. Whether it was through the day or night. We had a lot of plans for our futures with one another. All dreams having endings… Summer of 2024 begins.

I lost myself, drunk in love with this girl. In May, before the events of the ending. I've worn out from the disrespect, mistreatment, manipulation, and the insensitivity she'd display onto me. Love with this person masked my true feelings. It blinded me from

397

seeing my splintered heart. It felt as painful as seeing a lonely male swan. It felt as deceiving, wolves trying to befriend sheep's, it never has a great ending. It felt like I was as ignored as the fans that felt the doubt of never getting recognition from their idols. Loving her felt like a never ending fever dream. I fell for someone I knew wasn't ever going to love me in the way I would've wanted them to, but I appreciate them. I learned to never give in to the physical but give in to the soul and mind of a person, your connection with be stronger that way.

To Mutuals

Me and this girl fell out but had reconnected and our bond became stronger she also went to the same school as me and it was pleasant for a good couple weeks we called walked with each other and jus had genuinely talks and interactions we had such strong feelings for each other and I was starting to fall in love and it grew but then she said she needed to heal mentally and I gave her time while I talked and supported her and I tried complimenting and show her affection but I guess that was bad because one day we called and everything changed and she had connected with someone else I was upset and wasn't sure what to do and we just became mutuals after that she then told me they fell out and one day we decided to go to the mall and when we were at the arcade she kissed me on the lips and we had been mutuals and I wasn't sure how to feel and I still loved her but then she said she didn't mean to lead me on and so when we went home we kissed two more times and that was it no more contact.

-rj

Heartfelt Goodbye

I met her on June 10th. I didn't know if I liked her at first, she seemed a little weird to me. I talked to her for a little bit and she was actually a pretty normal girl just slightly misjudged. I invited her over one day and it was really awkward at first but we started talking and got to know each other. We hugged and she went home and we called all night and day. I never thought I'd find someone again after the first couple mistakes.

I had been going through bad mental health issues and couldn't figure out what I wanted to do at the time. I tried everything to make it work but I couldn't get a grip on my own life. I told her I couldn't do it and she begged me to stay, only then it was I realized just how much I cared about her. I told her I wanted my things back and we couldn't talk anymore. She begged me to stay over and over but I couldn't take it back now. I cried for hours, I threw up from anxiety, and I thought about suicide many times. The following day at 9:19 pm August 3rd she texted me, "I brought you your stuff, it's sitting outside your door."

I went out and grabbed it, met with my sweater, a redbull, and a note. I sat down, took a deep breath to prepare, and started reading. Not even half way through the first page I start crying again. I get all the way through it and I'm in shock, I can't move, barely can breathe, going through all the stages of grief again. I lay down in my bed and send her a message. "I'm sorry" it reads. We talk for a while, I apologize for everything and she assures me it's okay and she understands why I did what I did. I lay in bed right now writing this in my notes, sobbing, wondering if I'll ever have her back.

Confusing

onestly I had a different image of love than I have right now. Before my first ever love experience with someone, all I thought about was what love really felt like. All I really knew about love were from movies and how my friends relationships were like. To me I had a image that love is about two people getting to know each other through the good times and bad times, being there for one another. Cute little dates, gestures you do for one another, being happy and at peace with that one person your partner.

I was always the person who was looking for love from someone trying to see If could ever be loved the way I thought of it by someone else. There came a time where I stop looking for it in some way I gave up. I started to just really okay with it. But as time went it did get pretty lonely, even though I had friends, and hanged around them, I still had that feeling of what it feel to have that person who you can just come to. To talk about your day and experiences.

I remember I had a conversation with my mother about the topic and I described the person I would like to

402

be with in a relationship. Idk if that was weird, as a joking way as a joking way I was telling my mom I want a girl who's kind and loving, cute, smart and independent but very caring, curly hair well cause I always liked it. Crazy enough the exact same person who I describe to my mom appeared like a month later, as a new co worker at my job, and I honestly forgot about the conversation I had with my mom. Just that when I saw her all I could think about was that I seen her before, like I met her before, and that's were it hit me, she's the exact same girl I described to my mom that one day, I was shocked to see her.

I was scared too Ngl lmao. We interacted eventually of the bat I felt comfortable her we had a great conversation about funny experiences about our previous jobs and getting to know each other I developed a crush on her but was very shy to say anything. At the time there were others who also had a crush on her and liked her, so eventually I kinda gave up cause I wasn't really confident within myself.

Months later there I find out she has a crush on me, and that even shocked me more. We ended up going on a date, and got into a relationship for 1 and 2 months. There was the honey moon phase which was the first ever experience of love like I imagined it, it felt great, it just felt like home to me a safe place.

But like all relationships there were problems overthinking, understanding love languages, lack of communication and understanding, it was getting overwhelming for me part of me wanted to leave I was ready to leave when I had the chance, she knew she told me to not leave that she will change that I'm best thing that has happened to her that she loves me a lot. So I stayed told her I'll never leave her or treat her bad like the others did. I stayed to show her what true love looks like, someone who doesn't give up on something, someone who will always care for her and her safety and happiness, someone who will spoil her with many gestures, words of affirmation. And roses love letters. I gave everything, I loved her maybe I loved too hard. I started to lose myself and who I was, I started to overthink because I felt like I wasn't getting the same love that I was giving but I didn't want to say anything cause I was worried to hurt her feeling or being selfish. I was so in love, but when things hard and I needed reassurance from her it would always turn into a argument.

I didn't want arguments from her all I ever wanted was the reassurance i gave her that day that " I love you, I'll stay and fight for the love" but I didn't get that, it will just be arguing and taking space cause she felt overwhelmed. Eventually she left because it was overwhelming, when that happened it felt like I was betrayed She left me heartbroken, left at the moment I was very vulnerable, when I was begging for her not to leave that I will change my overthinking and emotions, when I needed her the most. It was hard to accept the new life without her all I could've thought about was why couldn't she just reassurance like I did, why did she give up when I wouldn't given up on her. We saw each other after 2 months after the break up, during the breakup seeing her happy and smiling made me feel like she moved on fast from that I was so easy to just forget. So when we saw each other again we decided to try again, another honey moon stage but when things got hard for me because I started to overthink things and have fears and start to feel anxious, she started to pull away she tried but my anxious mind and fears were too much for her and all I ever needed from her weren't arguments but reassurance from her but she would tell I'm not going to do it every time So at the moment as now our situation ship is difficult we still text and here and there, it's just I feel like I'm the only one fighting for it and putting effort while she doesn't. I know I have a choice to walk away but I find it hard to because I'm in love with her and her I'm not sure, right now that's my love experience even though we had a lot of great experiences together, but I feel she so focused on the bad instead of the good and I I'm stuck on fear of walking away and not knowing I can ever have what I had with her again. So to me this is my love experience, love to me right is confusing and hard.

Heartache

S o, i had met this girl some time in April of last year. we talked a lot. she was so beautiful and sweet. even as a friend, she had treated me better than any of my exes have. we both eventually gained feelings for each other. we ignored the feelings in case it would ruin anything. eventually, sometime in September, we couldn't hold them in anymore and started dating. September is my birthday month. she had made me a gift basket. inside was many things but my favorite gift was these little flowers and they were all my favorite colors. i loved them so much. i still have them.

Me and her were doing amazing. i loved her with all my heart. in October, we even matched halloween costumes. never did that before but it was so amazing. in December, i finally met her brother and sister. they both really liked me. then new year's eve, i met her mom and she met my parents. it was nice. we were on my rooftop and watched fireworks. that's where we had our first kiss. i loved it. it was so perfect. we had a spot on my roof for us. it was so nice. we even had a favorite restaurant for our dates. when i eat there i am always reminded of her.

our mutual favorite song was "fall into u by Oscar lang". i listen to that and just sit in my room. it's peaceful, rather than sad. eventually, i saw she still had her ex added on snap. i didn't think much of it though. she never used snap. it said they last texted around the time me and her got together. around late January, she got a snap from him. i thought it was super weird. she told me it was just a random thing. i believed her. later on, in February, same thing happens. i ask why he's still added and she says, "i don't know i don't use snap it doesn't matter". i thought that was super weird. i eventually found out they had a 15 day streak going on. i felt hurt. i tried asking her about it over text but she had ghosted me for a day. only to come back and apparently her phone was taken away. she had become super distant. it was hurting how distant she was becoming. in early march, i had talked to her about it again. that's when she just snapped. she told me she didn't want to be in a relationship anymore. she said she had missed her ex and it didn't feel right to be in a relationship. i agreed and i understood. a few days later, they were back together. that struck me so hard. i still can't get over it. seeina her smile with someone else. it's bad.

Hm

I think it was love but not meant to be he was there even if i would push away he was there even if i was the worst. i just needed to heal and he would wait for me still even tho i told them not to he was very stubborn to wanting to wait and help me heal, it was something i needed to do myself tho but he didn't want to let go at all he still wont. it might be love but it might be attachment which is why he needed to let go and so did i. we were to similar in good things and in bad we were just to similar to work out. yet he still wouldn't let go but neither can i.

All i know is that we need to let go and heal and love ourselves before we learn to love each other. theres a possibility to being perfect for each other but it wouldn't be possible in the position we are in because we needed to heal. She loved love even tho she didn't understand it. She craved to feel loved, protected, seen and understood. Time passed and she thought she was the problem with her love life. She didn't feel what she wanted to feel but still stayed and got left.

It made her learn that she needed to learn to love

herself first, she needed to learn how to understand herself and protect herself from things she didn't deserve to happen to her, loving herself was difficult but it ended up making her love life even tho she hated it and wanted nothing with it she fell in love with life and found out it isn't so bad if you gave it a chance. Life comes with challenges but she learned to not give up and love the little things. The sound of instruments and every note they play, art and the colors the artist put together to make something even more beautiful, the sound of rain falling onto the ground helping nature grow, the flowers and there colors and smells, hearing children laughing enjoying life without many problems or judgment, seeing and observing people to how they react to thing, making friendships, learning more about more people, having experiences without worrying much about what will happen because in the end everything will be better. Staying up enjoying time for herself with no noise no distractions, watching the sunrise ready for what the day may bring and sunsets remembering the lovely things the day gave her, seeing every color and seeing things differently than before, seeing that life is truly beautiful if you just sit and observe. Seeing that everything happens for a reason and for the better.

She truly fell deeply in love with life despite everything that happened in the past or what may happen, she really loved life and saw things from different perspectives to help her. All that is left is for her to learn to love herself but the more she loved life the more she learned to love herself, and the more she learned and understood about life she ended up learning and understanding herself more than ever. Things are always gonna happen wether good or bad but you just need to learn to see things from different perspectives and know that things will get better everything will just take time and in the meanwhile just learn to enjoy and appreciate little things in life then you will feel better loving not js people but life and urself.

So my love story starts off very young around 13 years of age I was in secondary school and there was this one one girl, we instantly clicked. We would have a lot of fun in class which would make me to start to have feelings for her, and those feelings grew bigger and bigger for about a year when I finally had the guts to ask her out so l did and I was very nervous because I thought she was going to say no and then it would be really embarrassing at school. But no she said yes and I was so happy because this was my first girlfriend and she just happened to be THE GIRL from my school. We went out together for about 5-6 and I thought we were really happy together like I would get butterflies every time we hugged or held hands. But also during that time my mother's health got worse because she has several brain tumors and it was and is really hard for me to cope with that. But when I was with my ex I would just call her and she would help me. But after those 5-6 months she eventually broke up with me and her reason was actually that she never loved me. She broke up with me just before the summer holidays which crushed my heart to peaces because it felt like everything was going wrong for example my mothers health that's really bad, my grandad that had just passed away and now her leaving me. I cried the whole summer holidays and then I got depressed for about 8 months straight. And then just to add the cherry on top my mother had a heart attack and then my father wasn't in a good state and he has

410

bipolarism so he was put into a psychiatric hospital for 2 months. But thankfully I found God around January which helped me so much and now I'm doing so much better, i'm very happy even tho my parents situation isn't the best I'm still very happy to be alive and very grateful.

-@Zacinio_

All Odds

OK, there was this time where I had seen this beautiful loving, handsome boy and me and him made eye contact. I felt something strong in my gut. I knew he felt something in his guts too between us. It was like it wanted us to be together but it really wasn't the right moment, walked away to go to another store and he had went to another store too.

It was the same store. It was like something was pulling us together like he wanted us to talk to each other so I made the first move usually girls don't do that but I was one of them that did me and him have been talking for two years and 12 weeks or days now to this day we had this promise that we made when we were talking where we wouldn't smoke, but he kept that promise for me and when it hits two years on a relationship for me and him being together, he told me it really hurt me bad, but I still had this gut feeling of wanting to be with him But I still stayed with him for who he was and I loved him for who he was.

I loved him with all my heart and I still always do. I hope to have something way better in a lifetime with him.

Yes, we may have our ups and downs, but I will still always love him, we had one argument that was really bad. He blocked me, but I got in contact with him on the game and I texted him and I started to talk to him. That was the only way. I asked him if he wants to play the game we did though he did not want to talk to me, but we still worked it out. He was all happy and we were laughing together we started talking again. Everything was falling back into place but very slowly out of very slow rate and speed then he asked me if I wanted to watch a movie and can worked it out. He was all happy and we were laughing together we started talking again. Everything was falling back into place but very slowly out of very slow rate and speed then he asked me if I wanted to watch a movie and can it be a date I said yes, it can then I made the move again. I said I love you, though something was telling me not to say that but I still did anyway because I will forever love him.

If he hurts me I may be some that I don't mean to say but I love him still with all my heart And I will forever, love him, no matter what I will always be by his side, even if we're not together for far yeah I know I hurt him in the beginning and I apologized. He lost trust in me, but still loves me and that's fine as long as I have them to be mine, I will forever love him with everything that I have.

Lost in Grief

I met her in high school we both notice each other around but kinda jus tested around we didn't really think about each other as relationship material we didn't know what each others intention were I had to make the first move we would go to the gym together we both had feeling at the time but she texted me when day if I was busy I was but we set a date for that Wednesday we went to get lunch we walked around after she kissed me out of no where I told her I liked her we kissed again we were falling for each other I had the biggest smile on my face but all things come to a end my cousin died he was extremely close to me it hurt I wasn't able to be mentally or emotionally available it hurt she didn't understand how I felt it went down hill we would break up n get back together I started to push her away I was hurt I wanted her to be able to comfort me she didn't know how to one day I couldn't handle it anymore I told her I wish I had my dead cousin instead of her I broke up with her I tried to get her back but it was something I wish I could take back she did love me it wasn't her fault that she didn't understand how I felt I was so focused on the people I didn't have I forgot about the people I do

have it hurt because I hurt her she only had pure
intention for me but I was mentally exhausted I tried
writing letters to her apologizing but it hurt her I regret
not controlling myself we dated for a year but it felt as if
we knew each other forever my last act of love was to
leave her alone I hope someone treats her how she
should've been treated.

Middle School Love Story

It all started on the first day of 8th grade. I wasn't expecting much since it was my last year of middle school, but I met this girl in my 7th-period class. We clicked instantly, like we'd known each other for years. Our friendship blossomed quickly; we laughed together, got kicked out of class together, and supported each other through tough times. She helped me through a toxic relationship and even caught my ex cheating, and I did the same for her.

One day, I discovered that she had feelings for me. I wasn't sure how to react because I didn't know if her feelings were genuine or if she was just my friend because of them. After a brief period of uncertainty, I apologized for my behavior, and we returned to our close friendship.

As the school year ended, my feelings for her grew stronger. I gave her hints about my feelings, and it seemed like she was responding positively. On our last day together, we shared a tight hug, and I realized how much I missed her. That night, we went to the mall, watched a movie, and tried to hold hands. We were

416

nervous but ended up having a wonderful time. I even got to meet her family, which was a nice experience. She surprised me by moving closer to me, and we started dating. Although it might have seemed rushed, everything felt right. However, our relationship faced challenges, including frequent arguments and misunderstandings. We broke up and got back together several times. During one of our breakups, I begged to have her back, and after three weeks, she texted me wanting to fix things. We resumed our relationship, and things seemed to be improving. I visited her home often, and we continued to share good times. On our four-month anniversary, I snuck over to her house, and we spent a great night together. Despite a few arguments, we managed to work things out.

However, as school started again, another girl in my PE class caused problems. My girlfriend became upset when she saw that I was talking to this girl, even though I had tried to handle it delicately. This led to more arguments and eventually, a breakup. Despite my attempts to reconcile, including talking to her mother, we ended up separating for a while. During this time, I was devastated, and my grades, friendships, and motivation suffered.

After a few months, I reached out to her, and we reconnected. It felt like we were back to where we left off. We spent time together, and I even met more of her family. Everything seemed to be going well again. However, she left for New York for the summer, and our long-distance relationship became challenging. We had more frequent arguments, which eventually led to another breakup.

417

When she sent me a message ending our relationship, I was heartbroken. I respected her and her mother's wishes and stopped contacting her, although it hurt to see her unfollow me on social media. Now, as I enter my sophomore year of high school, I still miss her deeply.

Betrayed Trust

———— ◆◦◆ ————

I was new to the district and so was the guy (i'll call him J) so me and J started talking after we both got cheated on and we clicked INSTANTLYY and i knew in that moment first ft call that i wanted to be w him. I think a week or two later we started dating everything was great i couldn't ask for more everybody knew about us and we were like the iconic couple in out school.

First guy i introduced to my entire family i also met his, i loved his mom and she loved me, we never had that "argument stage" because he was very understanding and kind and it was a new type of love that i never experienced. The point of this story isn't just to talk about the relationship more to focus on the person he turned into after the break up, i had been convinced to send him nudes and i did i also made the dumb mistake of letting him save it because in my mine it would "bring us closer" or "make our relationship stronger" it would make me "trust him more" or even love him more. Plus we were together for a long time so i thought i could trust him with that, i also opened up to him ab my

419

traumas and family problems in hopes to be understood and heard, and i was.

Well that's what it felt like. We spent 9 months together when i had a graduation party and since it was my party i was hosting and paying attention to other ppl aside from just J. Him and his mother didn't approve of that so they left the party early. His mom took his phone and didn't let him speak to me for about 2-3 days. When he got his phone back we had a huge conversation and i ended up breaking up with him. I thought that was it, it was done.That wasn't the case, the next day i find out he leaked my nudes and told everybody in the school about me and my personal life.

It broke me into a million pieces to think that the boy i loved and trusted most for almost a year betrayed me in the most imaginable way. Humiliated me, exposed me, defeated me and put me down like no other. I struggled with this for months even hospitalized because of how BAD it really got. J tho he moved on with his life and acted like nothing happened. It's been a year i haven't spoken to him since our last phone call, not an apology, not an explanation, absolutely NOTHING. The reason i'm focusing on this and not the "good moment" is to point out that one never knows who others really are until shit gets messy.

J proved me wrong and made it difficulty to communicate or trust ppl to this day. It's been 1 full year since our last conversation. I will never forgive him for the way he moved on like nothing ever happen got a new gf and everything turned the whole school against me and left me to figure t out all on my own to i forgave him to give MYSELF the peace he will never bring me back MY disturbed peace.

Love Story

What is my love story? My love story is romantic. How I first experienced my love story was very unexpected and it happened about a couple of years ago. The way I had met this old lover was odd and could been a one of a-billion chances that I know of. The way we met was on a high school field trip to Six Flags. We were both from two high schools that were hours away from each other. Our first interaction was late in the night on this field trip.

We first made a glimpse at each other in line for this ride that her friends wanted to go on. When she spoke she said how she was so scared to get on the ride and that she regretted agreeing to get on the ride with her friend. When she said that it felt so relatable that I included myself in their conversation because my friend had also forced me onto the ride. That was our first interaction with each other and before I could speak another word the workers had told me and my friend it was our turn to get on the ride.

Before the doors closed for us to get on the ride she told me good luck and hoped that I survive. When me and my friend got off the ride I saw her again and she was getting ready to get on the ride. I told her that I wished her the same luck that she gave me. During this moment I felt that there was some type of connection between us and I had this feeling in my gut that I should wait for her and see her again after she gets off the ride. When I felt that way I had also told her that I would wait for her to get the ride. When she got off the ride, she was surprised to see me because she wasn't expecting me to wait for her. After we met each other after the ride we went on a couple more rides and during this period when she was getting on rides with me and my friend she would put her head on my back a couple of times and during our last ride together she held my hand.

When we got off that ride she complimented me and it made me feel confused because I've never had any girl flirt with me so much when we just had met. I felt lost to the point where I was questioning if I was dreaming or if any of the interactions we were having were real. It felt as if it was our first date. When our night came to an end she walked me to where I had to be so I could get ready to leave. But before I left the park she bought me a gift. She bought me a Superman Plushie. I still have this plush to this day.

After we exchanged contacts we talked again a week after the field trip and we ended up becoming a couple a month after the field trip took place. During our relationship, we were long-distance and it was one of the most difficult challenges that I have probably faced in my life. We had a honeymoon phase like every relationship and I would say that you should never take that phase for granted. Once that phase was over we would have multiple fights and arguments that were dumb to fight about in the first place. But since we were long-distance having those arguments and fights was hard to deal with and hard for both of us majorly because not only us being long-distance is a challenge but being mad at each other and not talking to each other was damaging our relationship. But the more we argued and fought we began to realize that we needed to communicate better about our emotions and talk about what bothered us.

We even began to notice that our toxic side would come out of us and bring the worst out of us and it was damaging our relationship the most and I won't lie I was majorly insecure with myself because of my prior relationship and it made me very immature. We had learned to communicate with each other for the first time after multiple dumb arguments and fights. After finding out how to talk to each other and communicate our relationship became at its highest peak.

We had faced the biggest challenge that most relationships I have seen in my life fail and I was so glad that we were able to move forward and get past that challenge. I am so glad that we overcame that challenge because, during this period of my life, she was one of the people that kept me going and pushed me to be better. Even though I was young and still in high school I felt like she was my other half, that she was my soulmate. Not only did she push me to become better and kept me going, But she also gave me the mentality that I need to work hard so that when we have grow up and have a family together it would be easy for us and I would be able to make enough money to where she wouldn't have to work and I know that sounds like a fairytale but during that time it was like a superpower that she made me feel that I could be able to do that. The best thing that happened during our relationship but also hurt the most was when we saw each other again for the first time since the field trip.

We went to her high school homecoming dance and when I was heading to her I was excited but nervous. I made her a goodie bag and made a build-a-bear and homecoming poster to ask her out with when I saw her with her favorite Disney princess as the theme of it. But that night I also gave her a promise ring which I never expected that I would get to that stage in my life. But when I decided to buy her this promise ring it just felt right because during this time my gut was telling me that she was the one, she was the person I wanted to wake up next to every day, she was the girl I wanted to spend my days with even if they are good or bad. When she saw the promise ring she started crying out of happiness and I felt so bad but it made me want to cry also.

The best thing about that whole night was being able to slow dance with her. It was a moment that I had dreamed about doing with her for such a long time and I was able to live it. If I was able to relive that moment I would say that I would relive it again. The next day we went for a swim at the hotel I was staying at and went to the mall after. We took the most pictures we could because it was the only moment we had together that we weren't distracted and with such little time. The hardest thing about that day was leaving and going back home, that is what hurt both of us the most. We both craved each other's touch because it felt so safe and at home.

During this period, I had also started creating a bond with her little sister and I would help her with her times of need and advice.

I felt so special that she trusted me as the first person to go to for help. When she would ask me for advice most of the time I was truly able to understand her and it made me see her as a little version of me and sometimes I would even ask her for advice when her sister was mad at me. I would say I miss this bond to this day because I saw her little sister so relatable to me and I am thankful for her trusting me the way that she did and opening up to giving me a chance when she didn't have to. But after all the ups and downs during me and her relationship after her homecoming, there was the worst day to come.

On that day I went to go hangout with a friend of mine that she was jealous of that I wasn't aware of during this time. On this day I felt some type of way and I felt like I was being ghosted by her because I hanged out with my friend at the time. The reason I felt this way is because I would see her post pictures of herself on social media and when I would go back to our messages there would be no response. When I got home from hanging out with this friend she got upset at me and lashed out at me. Our toxic traits came out again and we didn't communicate properly like the way we used to and it caused me to shut down on her and this caused her to lose track of keeping her mental health healthy. I would say that if I were able to go back and change the past I wouldn't have went to go hangout with that friend during that period. But also even if I were to keep hanging out with that friend I wished that I hadn't shut down on her because I didn't express my feelings the proper way.

I wished that we both understood each other's perspective at the time because we both had different thoughts on the scenario at the time. But since we hadn't communicated the right way this made her do things that she would never have done during our relationship because of the pain that I caused her. This didn't just cause me lots of pain but she also was feeling this pain too and I just remember that I was in such so much pain that I cried out for my sister hoping she would come home from work faster and I wanted to call her so bad but I felt like I would've been a grudge to her being at work.

I would say that I regret not calling my sister because I wouldn't have felt this pain by myself and all I really wanted was for my sister to hold me and stop the pain and make it go away. I remember the words perfectly to this day, I said "I just want my sister" "I Just want my sister" and "I Just want my sister". Every time I think about those words I can just hear myself sobbing and crying my eyes out and it makes me cry every time because I never want to hear myself like that again and be so weak and at my lowest ever again. I never had felt so weak in my entire life and it made me feel so pathetic and I never want to feel that way about myself again. The Pain we felt caused the end of our relationship and I hate to say that not only the mistake of how we didn't communicate was one of the worst ways our relationship could've ended but all the mistakes we made during that time were the worst way to end the beautiful relationship we had.

What I began to notice from the end of our relationship is that she protected me from everything bad that was happening in my life and she kept a smile on my face when these bad moments were happening in my life. How I came to this realization is that a couple of months after our relationship I was dealing with rough situations and I started to realize that I was slowly giving up on myself and it was a difficult challenge for me to overcome but it made me realize that she protected me from so much during our relationship.

I sometimes still wish I had that protection from her still because she never failed to keep a smile on my face during rough times I was having even between me and her. Love could bring you the most happiness but it could also bring you the most pain you've ever felt and I am glad that I was able to share my pain and happiness with you the audience but with her also. I still have moments where I do miss her and I wish we were still together but I remembered that you can't change what happened in the past but what you can change is what is happening right now at this very moment. But even though I did experience the most amount of love I have been ever given in my life, it became a massive moment for my character development and growth on myself and allowed me to learn about myself and the flaws that I need to grow on and made me think about the person I want to be or become. My name is Salvador Madrid and Thank you for reading this and letting me share my story on my first experience of Love.

Dream Date

T his is my story about love lost. It all began in my sophomore year of college, in my American History class. I wasn't very talkative or social upon entering the classroom. There's was always this girl, Lala, who would catch my eye. From her underdye, her floral fragrance, but most of all her sense of fashion. That was actually the opener to our first conversation. She complemented my cardigan lol. I was too afraid/shy to ask for her for her socials; so i went on later in the day and asked for her snapchat through the canvas student app. Thankfully she was cool with it. From that point on, we quickly bonded over music taste, food, life, goals, etc. Fast forward May 7th, i decided to take her on a date at our local park. I specifically remember this day because i sold my Uno the activist ticket in order to fund the picnic i had planned for us. We listened to music, laughed, painted pictures on canvases, and ate from a charcuterie board. It was the dream date with my dream girl. However, i screwed things up a few weeks later. I expressed my feelings towards her; but got rejected. I tried to get her to view herself from my eyes and heart. But it simply didn't work and i scared her away. I hope she is doing well, and whoever love her treats her right. I hope she'll read your book one day and remember us...

Invisible string theory

I never thought the invisible string theory was real. I always believed it was some gimmick people only talked about related to movie characters, books, or a feeling they imagined. Longed for, but never reciprocated. I was a troubled child. Never thought I was deserving of love, or that a person would want to love me. But I grew, and grew, and grew. Like a beautiful weed, I became aware of a new type of love. Self love. Once I found that love inside of myself, I realized that is what I needed all along. In order to love someone, you have to love yourself. I met a girl. Well, we never truly met. At least, not yet. When I first set my eyes on her I felt her beautiful soul shining from inside out. We were strangers. Eventually, our souls met again. This time, We were friends. She saw that light and love inside of me, and I flourished with her by my side. Over time my weed sprouted flowers unfamiliar to me. Flowers that opened my heart even through all of my tangled roots. I poured these flowers into a beautiful bed for her. She wasn't just a friend now. We are lovers. We were strangers, We were friends, We are lovers.

The invisible string theory.

431

The One That Got Away

W hen I was first catching feelings for this boy Matthew who was a family friend for years, our older sisters are best friends, everything was so perfect, we would call every night, text all day, see each other on the regular. We would go to church together and spend hours with each other, that was until we started having arguments over dumb things, and we got blind sited by all of the harsh words we used, we would call each other names we didn't mean and say things that were just awful.

And after a while of us just arguing and me getting dry responses, I left, I walked away for a good 2 months. I even started dating someone new to forget everything and move on from the past, but that relationship alone was toxic and drained me and broke me even more, it exhausted me and I could quite literally feel my soul being deteriorated. After things with the relationship ended, I had saw a notification on snap from Matthew, I added back just to see if he wanted something, and after I did almost Just 5 minutes later I get a message from Matthew and it's his friend using his phone, I ask his friend to let me text Matthew, me and Matthew start texting and it turns out things weren't as they seemed 2 months ago.

I wasn't healed from trauma, he wasn't healed from his fears, everything felt as it was before everything ended, the long nights felt shorter, the birds were chirping before I knew it, time flew by butbit felt as if we could talk for hours on end.i felt all my troubles went away, like a huge weight was lifted off my chest and allowed me to finally breathe.i could feel our souls attaching in that moment.We were both misunderstood by each other, now things between us has been even better, we've learn to grow for each other, and give each other that reassurance, and express our feelings the best we can with what little we know. The progress in him had changed drastically in such a short amount of time, he's trying, after his past he's trying, to me that's more then enough.

Childhood Dreams

As a child i used to tell myself i was un lovable. all because my parents would say that the soonest i could get a boyfriend was when i couldn't pay for my own rent. that would make me even more excited about it. i hated having to wait so instead of thinking about that i would think about how i wanted to be loved how i wanted to be talked to and how i would love him back. of course i only thought about the good because i didn't know what people were really like.

I saw my parents relationship as pure genuine love that never died. but i was wrong. i would catch my parents fighting. and when they saw me they would immediately stop and pretend like everything is okay. but as i got older they stoped caring. they would constantly be fighting over my dads drinking and gambling problems that he still has to this day. he never cared enough to fix them but he always told her he would. i hated that. i hated how he lied to her so easily without even hesitating. i knew my mom didn't believe him anymore because it would happen so often but she would agree and smile anyway.

434

I hated how she went along with it just to make him happy. then when i was older, i started to like people. there was this boy in my class who liked me. i wanted to like him back but i didn't. instead i liked a girl. she had short brown hair with beautiful brown eyes that matched perfectly. she had braces and was shorter than me. i thought i wasn't allowed to like her because we were both girls so i tried to shut the feelings out. but they only got stronger. and eventually they were eating me away from the inside out. i felt like i was being tortured so i confessed. to my surprise she felt the same way. and we started dating. at first the love was pure and genuine the kind of love you want to wake up in the morning the kind of love that gets you excited and smiling just thinking about.

This girl was my everything. i loved her with every bone in my body, with every muscle in me, with every drop of blood, with every breath. but that love wasn't given the same. she didn't feel the same but decided to date me anyway. i had no idea at the time because i was to overcome by my feelings for her to realize it. but she didn't even try to hide it anymore. and it took everything in me snd more to end things. i hated myself for it and blamed myself for not being good enough. but since then i realized it wasn't me. it was her. she didn't like me and thats okay. I've accepted it and moved on. but i still think about her. i wonder how she's doing. if she still dates people for "fun" as she said one time. and now i think about it and I'm grateful. i wouldn't change a thing about it. I'm lucky i got to experience that fir my first love because i learned what people are like. others might not want that ti be there first love. but i really am thankful for it and it helped me grow.

The Pain of Letting Go

ive months ago, I let someone go, someone I thought I needed to release. The pain was like a fresh, open wound, taking me back to the little girl I once was, longing for the love I never received. Every man I've fallen for seems to mirror my father—rage with my mother's eyes, and each day feels like I'm rotting in bed, smiling through the tears to keep them at bay. No one will ever know how much I cried that day, feeling as though no one truly cared. I lost something so pure, yet so painful.

But as time went by, I held onto the belief that if it's meant to be, it will be. The gut-wrenching pain of watching him fall in love again almost made me want to throw up, but somehow, I found my way back to him. He painted memories in my mind that I can never erase, and colors in my heart that I could never replace.

436

A Second?

I was playing board games with close friends, and a girl who has only met me three times sat next to me. We were inseparable all night. When she hugged me, I felt a profound, unconditional love that reminded me who I am. It felt greater than romantic love.

Since you left 5/18/24 22:50

———— ◆◆●◆◆ ————

Love as strong as the hold of a black hole So great that delirium and love are identical Charmingly Compelling and frighteningly dangerous, the comprehension of my love is unobtainable and frustratingly euphoric A double edged sword, quick to reaction, in spite of harming the very one wielding it Sworn to protect and willing to the destruction of this world had it come into contact with my love My love, you are my love, you are what love is, the very thought of you is love, defining my love would be to define you, to take you a part cell by cell atom by atom. Obsession so deep that nothing compares God given, gifted to hold faith in my obsession, untainted and crazed For you are my eyes. Without you I am blind Without you I have no thoughts because you possess my very mind and soul My darling you are the angel god sent before me my perfect piece of delicate imperfection For you I am an insuperable soldier obliged to protect you my deity.

-    Dominic Greco

Beauty

I have a girlfriend and she is so beautiful we always talk about we getting married one day and go on a date and buy her anything she wants but when I started dating her I had a feeling that she doesn't like me but now she does she show me her love and I show her the love she needed bc she said none of her family show her the love and I told her "I am her to show you all the love you need" and she always says she's fat but I always seen her beautiful and I love her so much I want to give her anything she wants bc she deserves it.

-Wendy

Chloe

'**I**'ve had several relationships in my life. But part of me will always love Chloe my ex. Me and Chloe started dating and everything was perfect except on our 3rd month of dating. I found out that she cheated on me when she left to LA on a family trip and me being so in love with her more in love than I ever been I forgave her. After that happened we dated for 5 months until one day she told me she wanted to take a break and so we did till few days later I find her with someone else so we just stayed friends for a few months till we got back together for the 3rd time. I've always been stuck on her cause i really loved that she was the one girl that stayed the longest. I don't blame her for hurting me. I'm actually grateful cause every time we broke up it made me stronger. I thank god everyday for making me go through all the heartbreaks and everything I've been through.

-Jesus

Waiting for Her

I went into high school with no intentions of having a girlfriend but then I met this one girl I liked but gave it time because I didn't really know how much I liked her .After four months I realized that I had a crush on her .In that time I was a very shy person or not shy maybe more introverted and she's older than me by 2 years but I gathered my courage and strength to ask her for her number . When I asked her I felt welcomed by her and she said yes and from that day on we spoke every day and when we didn't we would apologize time went by and she confessed her feelings of her liking me but school got tough for her and she didn't want to waste my time so she said that she can't be in a relationship. I understood and respected her decision but I told her that I fell for her and love her so I'll wait for the day she's ready and has time to be in a relationship with me . Nothing has changed we still talk to each other every day and check up on each other .Till this day I'm still waiting for her to be ready and I will wait for her until we don't love each other anymore because she's kind, caring, respectful and loving ,she's the first person I talk to when I feel down and she's the one person on

my mind every second of the day and because of all of
that I love her and I will wait for her .

-V.

Im Sorry

She gave me so many chances and she kept forgiving me and i kept telling her i will change but i always kept ruining the chances, until one day she decided to end it and break up with me. I told her i've changed and it was too late. And now i'm here regretting everything and praying for her to come back. It's been almost a year and i still think about her and sometimes cry at night. I'm still waiting, hoping for her to come back. I lost the only person who made me happy.

Missed Connection

I t started out my freshman year of high school. Sometime in October we had our spirit week and this day the school had us cosplay our favorite characters. This girl in my class was dressed up as Ash Ketchum and I noticed it at like the last second of class and wanted to say something but got extremely nervous. We also had a trunk or treat/bonfire going on later that same night. It was really fun I'd seen a few friends, got hella candy, played some games and everything. It got to the point where I had way too much candy and started giving it away to people as a joke.

And I was just walking around the school parking lot and something told me to go towards my left and I handed this girl a Twix in-front if all her friends, she was shocked to see it happen and I thought nothing of it and kept going on about my night. Probably 10 minutes later I see her again and we start talking but this time I recognize her as the girl that was dressed up as Ash so I complimented. Her on the costume and she ended up getting me some candy she thought I would like. For some reason I couldn't eat it because every time I tried

444

to open one it would fall out the wrapper . Anyway the night ends and I go home still thinking about my night. Not too long after my mom is telling us that we're moving to Arizona and I'm like damn because I literally just met this girl and I think she's pretty cool. I think it was my last day it that school, the girl and I are working on a project together and we're can't share the document with each other so we basically just spoke the whole time and I thought about asking her for her number so we could keep in touch but again I got too nervous and didn't ask. A couple months later now in Az I had just finished cleaning my room and now I'm scrolling on ig trying to not think about her because I'm thinking I would never speak to her again but something tells me to click on a celebrities page and look at their following(I think my intuition?) So I click on the following and I see her page on Instagram and I'm like oh shit.

My heart drops bc I didn't think I'd actually see her page and I just sat on it for a few days overthinking until one day I just said fuck it and dm'd her and we're catching up and at this point I realized that I forgot to tell her I was moving . She asks me if I loved school or something and I tell her what happened. So were basically keeping in touch this whole time for months. The school year ends and my Mom moved us back the the state we were previously in but she moved us to another city so I have to go to a new school. At this school I meet this new girl and I'm thinking that we're just friends because that's the agreement that we had. I'm still talking to the other girl and I ask her out not realizing that I couldn't go 4 cities over and accidentally ghost her but now I'm dating the new girl. That was my biggest mistake in trying to find a girlfriend ever . I still regret it to this day and it's Even worse because she still follows me even though we don't talk to each other. Midway through my junior year I move back to the school and I'm nervous because I know that I'm going to eventually run into her. The first day nothing happens but I do see her but she doesn't notice me bc she was with her friends, I'm fine. The second day, in sitting outside of my classroom because I was bored and seen her walk past me.

We make eye contact but she double takes Im guessing because I moved. So I wave to her and she says wassup. We never verbally spoke to each other but over the next few days I kept running into her on accident because I didn't know that she liked her hand around a certain part of the school during lunch and I didn't have anyone to each lunch with yet so I just walked around the school. Eventually I figured out where she be and I just avoid it completely by just going to the library because that's where I ate lunch my freshman year. I forgot to add it but it was also way More awkward because now she has a boyfriend that she met not long after me and the other girl starting dating but I guess fuck it. Learn from my mistakes.

Rebuilt

In 2021 in high school I met this beautiful girl her name was j and we had 1 period together and I looked forward to it every day a couple of months went by with my love growing stronger and I wanted to ask her out but I was scared of ruining our friendship but the one day we were on the phone and she told me she used to have a crush on me and I told her the same and we were shocked so we started to date it was amazing and everything seemed cool until 3 months later I was on her phone and a Snapchat notification popped up and I got scared so I clicked on it and to my surprise she cheated my heart broke And I froze I didn't know what to do I left her and I was in a dark place so l started following @imkd114 on Instagram and listening to her advice it was working so a month later after I felt better I decided to text her and she told me that she never meant to hurt me and she didn't want to do it anymore she wanted me but it was hard to try again so I gave it a shot she delete most her social media I did also and worked on us and now we are almost 4 years strong and we have the most amazing communication skills ever we trust each other l forgave and forgot about everything she did to me l love her and she loves me one day I want to marry this girl I love you J.

Love Lost

here was a boy who went to my school. i would like to keep him anonymous so I'm going to call him Gabriel. we never talked but he was friends with my sister and we rode the same bus. when i saw him for the first time i knew he was going to be the one, the one who made me happy, the one who i could talk to when no one else would listen. i tried talking to him but i never got the chance or the courage too. then a year goes on about me liking him but never talked to him. the summer goes by and i forget about him and i stopped liking him. when the new school year started i ended up dating a different guy but we broke up because of him cheating. then 5 months go by and i started liking Gabriel again. me and him started snapping back and forth on snap. then that turned into texting. i told my friend that i liked him and that me and him were talking but just as friends. my friend took my phone when i wasn't looking and texted him to add her back on snap. i didn't know she did that then she told him i had liked him and made a group chat for all three of us. i was so embarrassed when i found out she told him but then i found out he liked me back. and instead of talking as friends, me and Gabriel were talking as more than just friend you know. and we talked for a month then he started sitting next to me on the bus. and he would drink from my water bottle then after 2 months he asked if he could hug me before he got off the bus. i said yea and my other friend she took a picture of us hugging. during school me and him wouldn't say much but just small talk because we didn't want to really make it public because we knew people would start saying lies. then he asked to hold my hand. i said yes and i was so excited because no one ever made me feel the way he did. there was a time when he had dropped something on the bus floor and we had both looked. it might sound weird but it was actually cute because we just sat there holding hands with our heads next to each other looking down at the floor. and yes it sounds weird or funny but it was really cute. then after 2 months of talking we started dating for 3 months. everything was good. he asked to go though my phone and i let him because i didn't have nothing to hide then i asked for his phone and he had a LOT of girls and i mean his whole snap. i told my friend the one who took the picture of me and Gabriel and she said it was fine and i shouldn't worry about it. and Gabriel said the same, that i shouldn't worry about it and how it's just for streaks on snap or there just his friends. and i ignored it but it was at the back of my mind. then when we did hit 3 months there started becoming problems. he got distant and i found out he had been texting another girl. i was so sad because that meant everything we did meant nothing yk. and that girl he was texting he had hugged her during school and they were dating. then a couple weeks go by and then he would sit next to me like nothing happened. and it was just a cycle of him ignoring me one week and the next we were friends . i told my friend the one who took the picture. i forgot to mention her name is sam. i told her what he was doing and stuff and she told me i should stop talking to him or break up whatever we were. and i did. i told him that i didn't wanna talk anymore or date or whatever we were. he left me on opened so i got fed up with him and i had told him that he was doing to much and that it would be best anyway because we were both going to two different schools. after talking and arguing we both said fine and broke up whatever we were. at first i was fine then i started realizing i didn't wanna let those memories go. and i didn't wanna say goodbye. but i knew i would sound dumb if i said i wanted him back after breaking up with him. i told my friend sam what happened and she wrote me a paragraph saying how much i'm worth and that he isn't worth crying over. she made me feel better and she was there for me. then the next week at school he didn't sit next to me and he wouldn't even make eye contact with me except this one time he was in the lunch room and i was walking in there to see my friend and i saw him, and he saw me we made eye contact before he saw me he was smiling then when we made eye contact his smile dropped. i don't know how to explain how he looked. i couldn't tell if it was mad or sad or what. then that week on Wednesday we both had B lunch and his table wasn't far from mine it was a couple feet away. he texted me saying "we need to talk" i heard him and his friend talking about it. and i said "can you tell me right now if the talk gonna be bad.?" he said "idk" and so all i said was oh he then said "but i just needa talk" and i just said okay and let me know when and he just said ok we were on the last week of school and he said we would

450

talk on Friday. we didn't end up talking. he never said anything i got him to sign my year book. then we were fine as friends but we didn't talk. we texted after i left and he left the school, i usually rode the bus but my mom picked me up that day and so i didn't really see Gabriel. he texted me and told me how much he's going to miss me and that he kept saying it and that made me miss him more and sad. then after Friday i texted him on Sunday. i said hi he said hey and i said what are you doing and he nothing bored and asked me the same and i said nothing just same and he said #real and i missed him so i took the chance to say #canwetryagain? and we started talking and he you want us to try again and i said yes then he said how we going to see each other and i said idk maybe a park or something and we both said yes and that we would try again and better this time but it didn't even last a day. after that we didn't text at all. i unadded him on snap i'm not going to say why but just because i know i would text him again and do something i shouldn't. then after 2 weeks he adds me again i added him back and my friend who got him to text me told me to not add him back and that she will ask why he added me back and he said that he thought we were cool and u didn't say anything i just stopped. after a month i knew it was time to let him go and i unadded him and stopped talking about him i only talked good about him but i stopped mentioning him name. but i could never bring myself to delete the pictures of us. this might sound like the story wasn't a big deal or it wasn't even love . but you can't say anything until you go thorough it. and i have left out lots of details but yes it was love. me and him went through so much together he would always tell me he loved me and how he missed me when i wasn't at school. but just because someone says that doesn't mean they mean it or they will fall out of love. the end .

-@xosam.s

Love

I was in a point in my life where I thought love wasn't real, until I met her. We were always mutual friends, never close to each other in any way. I had feelings for her for a while and regardless of what everyone told me about her, I knew everyone deserves a chance and I took it. I asked her out and she rejected me, I took it calmly there were no hard feelings towards her. Then it was after a football game she sent me a message saying how she wanted to get to know me and have a talking stage. Turns out we didn't really talk to each other, we were both so nervous to so we never did. Until thanksgiving, I decided to send her a message saying that I wanted to make things official even though we haven't been talking much. She agreed, I thought that was the best idea I'd ever make.

But from that day on we'd talk every single day and we grew to know each other very well. I'd never had been in a serious relationship before, but I knew how to treat someone how I wanted to be treated so for the coming months I did that. I bought her random flowers, expensive bracelet for Christmas, random snacks she loved, complimented her every single day multiple times, made her a big poster asking for her to be my valentine, sent her random multiple paragraphs telling her how pretty she is and how much I loved her, i never once cussed at her or said anything negatively, ran across a college campus to see her sign into her new school, helped her when she was down even if I was feeling so much worse, tell my friends I couldn't hang out or get on the game because I was calling her or texting her because she would get mad at me for hanging or talking with them , I would treat her like she was a princess always carrying her stuff to classes because her backpack was heavy, pull out her chair in class for her, i never got the chance to practice basketball a sport I hold so close to my heart and It affected how I played, I would give her random gift baskets filled with her favorite snacks, give her stuffed animals, I cut off my friend girls because she didn't like the thought of me having one, I gave her all my attention even if it meant losing everything I had but I never got that from her.

I told her how much I loved being called handsome and receiving gifts or random paragraphs but she never did often, only like 5 compliments the whole 8 months, she never really said she loved me often even though I loved when she did, she never checked up on me even though I checked up on her everyday, she treated me badly she would cuss me out often, she would tell me to stop saying " I love you" to her because I said it so often, . I know it doesn't sound like a long time but I never felt so connected and loved someone as much as I did her. She would do things to me that hurt me so much because I wanted to give her all the love I had, I did but I got so drained and I needed her to return the love back, she never did. I would often cry everyday because I never felt loved , she never said she loved me, never hugged me, didn't want to hold hands, and I would tell her about those things but she said she wasn't used to it so I was just left unloved. Love is draining but it's worth it if they return it back, I learned don't settle for someone who isn't willing to return it and to have self respect. Because I didn't and in the process it hurt me, it hurt me really badly.

-JH

Did He?

I was and I'm still in love with the guy that hurt me. Ive been with him since i was 15 and now I'm 18. Its true how much people say that in the first few months of dating its all love and more affection. It was all going good until in August i found out he cheated on me with a girl and it wasn't just some girl but his ex. After confronting him he said he was so sorry and the reason he did it was because he couldn't see me during the summer, i was crushed because it was my first every relationship and it hurt a lot. The very next day i went back to him because i thought he would change, I loved him so much that i blinded myself and manipulated myself into thinking that it was my fault for not giving him the attention he was looking for.

When i told him i would take him back he said he would change because he wanted a future with me and i made myself that illusion into thinking that we can really make it work and be together for a long time. We were doing so good after that but then I found out again he cheated on me, September 6th 2023. This time it was a girl that was just starting high school and he was in his last year of high school. Once again i took him back... I was disappointed in myself because i lost all my self respect but i wanted to be with him because i didn't want ti let him go especially because we had reached 1 year together. I didn't want to meet other guys. I always took the good things from him instead of the bad. Was i not good enough for him. Am i not skinny enough? Am i not pretty enough? What is missing from me? When we broke up because he wanted to focus in school and family i understood and a week later a guy talked to me and I decided to talk to someone else now that i wasn't in a relationship. We were talking for a good five days and then he stopped talking to me. I later found out that my ex told him to never speak to me because I'm all his and that he should go talk to other girl but not me.

I texted my ex asking why he did that and he said because he loves me and can never imagine me with someone else. Later on we had an argument for what happened and he told me "at least i didn't cheat on you with someone you knew" i got so mad but continued to say sorry even if it wasn't my fault. Why did i stay? I am still with him, i am 18 years old and still here with him. I met his family and he met mine. Even if i met his family would he still hurt me? So many things spiral in my head but, he has progressed a lot but i cant forget what he did to me. I forgive but never forget. Did he really change..?

A Night

er name was hetzi she was my friends cousin i was invited to go to her birthday party that night changed everything we danced the whole night to cumbias and bachata i was the "party starter" person that got all her cousins and family to dance and i remember someone took a video of me and the cousin and when we danced we were both in sync then later that night i walked up to her and introduced myself and asked if she wanted anything from jack in the box she said she didn't but when we got back she wanted curly fries and i had curly fries so i gave her my fries we played tag that night with all her cousins and i felt this tension with her like safe in a way (she lives in la and i live in the high desert) after we played tag i asked for her instagram and we both just never stopped texting or calling with her everything was so simple and easy to just talk to her we would call every night and just talk and yap about everything our childhood , parents, future, conspiracy theories, favorite movies literally everything she has a flower business and her favorite flower was roses red ones. i wish i could go back to the first time me and her started talking maybe things would be different i don't know we fell off because it was long distance but i know in my heart she was my soulmate. but hey maybe in another life i wish the best for her always i pray for her and her family all the time or when i think of her.

Unexpected

I have recently fallen in love with this boy and even though it is really recent i just want to show how much appreciation and gratitude i have for him coming into my life. I am really grateful for him and simply just blessing me with his presence we really like each other a lot and i want to continue being by his side. He has made me feel emotions that i never thought that i would feel again and it really is an eye opener for me because he showed me that there are genuinely no limits on how I'm allowed to feel. We both struggle with our emotions and feelings so we want to create a safe space for each other to express and show each other every single part of how we feel to each other because even if he can hide them he cant hide them forever.

We want to experience new things in this world either with or without each other but i think its just about how we experience them. It was so unexpected as well because this is my first boyfriend like ever. I never am interested in people i just like testing things out and see where it goes but with him because i physically get to interact with him and stuff its really just different because it genuinely just blows my mind that i get to Love him and i get to call him my boyfriend and the love of my life because i don't want anyone but him to experience things with. The unexpectedness was real tho one minute i wasn't interested next minute he my boyfriend like WHAT!!. Only reason why i wasn't looking because i was grieving over Moms loss. I don't know how i did it but i really pulled through and then he popped up and ye shit happened I guess. My mouth so big too I'm quite literally loosing it over him. Im obsessed with every single part of him from his personality, his looks, his smile, how tall he is. This is my first time experiencing like romantically love and we both bond through music my thing is noise and his is like reading. Music is really big for us because every time we listen to a song we create a moment and then it just sticks. And thats how we be moving like glue we sticking together no matter what. I want to spend the rest of my life with him and i will make sure it happens. I love him very much and i am grateful and even words cant guarantee you how much i love this boy. This is my love experience so far and hopefully in the future there is more to tell.

-Renee

461

Ugh

I truly regret being so difficult. It's the only word to define me. Difficult in terms of my way of being. My way of thinking. I am so difficult to deal with, to love, to endure. Believe me, I know what I am. I want to stop being this way, but... I don't know how. I don't know what you expect from me. I don't know if I am capable of giving it to you. I'm afraid you'll get tired of me and walk away like everyone else. You have no idea how much that would destroy me. You came into my life and in such a short time, you became someone so important and in a way indispensable to my life, and that's what scares me the most. Losing you... is my greatest fear. I just ask that we fight together. I don't want to tire you out, even though I know I tend to do that.

Clarity

— ◆◆●◆◆ —

ver since i was little i dreamt about finding my
prince charming that i was always looking for. it
started in October of 2023, my freshman year. i
went to a celebration my school had every year and
made some new friends there also. one of the girls there
that i met that year told me that she had a friend that she
wanted to set me up with, me being a little bit skeptical
about it i still said yes. i got his snap and we started
talking for a good 2 mouth or so. Over time he got really
dry and i confronted him about it but he brushed it off.

I knew it was a bad idea to just keep trying to talk
about it to him so i blocked him. after he came crying to
my friend saying how he messed up and felt bad, but i
didn't give two shits. two mouths later i find out from the
same friend that set us up that he's now dating someone
else, i didn't real care but i was still curious. my friend
got a picture of the gf and i was in complete shock. the
girl that he was dating looked like another version of me.
i didn't care about him then but i was shocked by the fact
he wanted to date someone who looked exactly like me
when all he did was be dry to my ass.

they didn't last and broke up mid year. my friend told me there was a rumor started that he cheated but i still didn't care about him. a mouth after (may) he reached out again and said that he was actually gonna try and fix everything and make an effort. i was still skeptical about it but i said yes even tho i knew in my gut i knew i should've said no. we talked again for a good few mouths or so. bc we didn't live close to each other it was hard for us to see each other be of our busy schedule. and also bc my family wasn't found of me dating a white boy when I'm asian. despite what my family wanted i still wanted to be with him. no matter how much distance i wanted to be with him.

over the few mouths i fell in love with him and out of every guy i saw, they were not attractive to me. a little after a few mouths his true colors started to show, we started texting less and not saying much on call. we started getting distant from each other again and when i try to fix it it is makes it worse. i confronted him about it and all he said was I don't know. those three words had me spiraling bc i didn't know what to do. I've never been in love with anybody much less from a boy who doesn't even know how to express his feelings and also lives in another city. i started questioning things about our entire relationship and wondered if he was like this in all his relationships. it was my first one

but to him it was probably his 5th. i asked "why aren't your intentions clear? am i just another side piece u have while u fuck other girls in your city? u never had any of these issues in your past relationship bc u knew what u wanted so why is it so hard with me?" he just took it all and said nothing. i should've known from the start that i was is a pity fuck to get over his exes. i told him to fuck himself and i blocked him on everything again but i can say this time it hurt way more then i thought. i decided to push those feelings aside and get on with my life. first period the same friend came up to me and said "i know about you and _" i looked at her and thought damn he really beat me to it again. i explained my side of the story and she said that he knows he fucked un and felt so bad about it. i kept thinking he didn't care about me throughout our entire relationship. overtime i couldn't push those feelings away anymore and they got the best of me. i was at a party and i decided to have to many drinks and started crying bc i apparently i said i missed him. after that night i knew that i needed to get my shit together.

no matter what i felt i needed to get over it bc i knew damn well he wasn't crying over me. now it's been awhile since i even thought about him at all and despite all my questions i have like did he ever felt the same way i did? was i is another girl he can fuck around with? or was he deeply in love with me like i was with him? now i know that he was is a lesson and the more i think about it he was is lusting over me from the start. i know now to raise my standards bc i know now i deserve better then a guy who doesn't know what he wants.

Him

This is a story about me and a boy I like. I first caught feelings for this boy last October yet we both had no idea who each other were. fast forward to December when I had made the decision to tell him I liked him because his best friend told me he was moving schools. so the day before winter break I told him after 8th period. me and him had never spoken to each other and I was so scared but not of rejection I was just scared and nervous to tell him. so I told him and his initial response was "I don't really know what to say" and I told him it was okay that he didn't really need to say anything and that I just needed to get it off of my chest.

so then I start walking faster and he tells me "you have a really good personality" and that was all. so then we come back from break and he's still there at school. I was so confused but I just ended up asking for his number. I would text him literally every day but we never talked in person. one day I decided to tell him that if he didn't want to talk in person then I didn't know what to do because I really did like him. so we started

466

talking at school and it was actually really fun. we because best friends and would sit next to each other and laugh during algebra. sometimes my feeling for him would go away but they always came back.

this summer I decided I was done liking him. yet I found myself feeling love for this boy once again. he had his sweet moments and his sour moments but I still continued to like him. I don't know why I can't get over him.

-@nataviiiaaa

Involve

My girlfriend and I first met freshman year of high school. I was a quieter kid who kept to himself and had a few friends. I never had any classes with her so we only knew each through mutual friends or our schools powerlifting team. We gradually became closer as we started to eat lunch together and talk outside of school. She became my best friend and someone I could tell anything to. After school one day she asked me to stay after with her and she ended up asking me out on a date and I said yes. I'm not exaggerating when I say it was the best decision of my life. Everything about me improved when i was with her, my motivation, my happiness, everything just was better around her. I wanted to pay her back for making the first move, so I asked a friend to find out her favorite flower. I spent hours carefully folding, painting, and gluing tinfoil together to make her favorite flower, I asked her if I could have the honor of being her partner officially and gave her the flower. She said yes and we spent the day cuddling and talking. She goes to all of my football games and I go to all of her volleyball games. It's been amazing and we're still together, going into our Senior Year.

- Amari

So on

So it starts where I was at the skate park and then I get a message from someone and I didn't know what to say but it was a girl who texted me and I was in shock and she said that's she liked me and I got a little to excited and feel In love right away and I didn't know I wasn't supposed to fall In love but I just did and btw it was my first ever girlfriend and the next day I saw her in school and we barley even talked we were so nervous that we just didn't say anything but once I started to get comfortable with her and we talked more and more and more and it's been 3 months and I asked her out November 6th 2023 and I was In love and she was too but there was some problems that we had cause I had a girl best friend and my girlfriend didn't like that and I stop talking to my girl best friend and one day it just all went down hill and I couldn't handle her no more so I broke up with her and next few days I was balling my eyes out but next day we talked it out and got back together. And then we just kept on arguing and till we broke up again and again and again we kept on going off and on back and forth I couldn't let go of her but then we got back together one more time and we promised each other we wouldn't leave each other then she broke up with me the next week cause she was thinking about the past and didn't want to get hurt again and I lost the only person that made me happy and she was the best person ever she gave me sooooo much love no one's has ever gave me my first heat break and we didn't leave each other in bad terms but I told her if she still loved me she would always say yes but the next thing I know she got a job and I guess she liked someone at her job and I would always tell her if she would get into a relationship and she said no but she lied right in front of my face and my heart broke even more and more and more into thousands of pieces and I will never fall in love again.

Pain

I lost someone really special to me but yet i still don't know what to do every time i think about them, the relationship was kinda perfect but the thing i regret that i was always stuck in the sin of lust and rushed it but I know everything we did was genuine and the way i looked into her eyes and heard her laugh my pupils would widen and i would feel them do it, i always loved looking at her beautiful face and picture and adore her and i loved buying her flowers and going to watch the sunset in on of our spots like the park or train tracks. I also loved her amazing and caring personality and the way we always looked i to each other eyes when we just sat in silence and she made an adorable reaction saying "stop no don't look at me" and looks away which made me want to real her closer to me and hug her as much as possible and kiss her in the cheek and especially on her forehead. I loved how she always dressed cutely and try to impress me when literally everything about her was perfect. Oh how i miss spending time with her and how badly i just want to tell her i miss her presence and her laugh and seeing her but we broke up months ago because i made a mistake in the start of the relationship when we started talking and how badly i regretted it because the minute i laid eyes on her i fell in love immediately and wanted to spend my whole life with her but my mistake and actions had consequences and i paid for them with loosing the love of my life. I wanted to do everything in my ability to change her mind and keep her close to me but thats when i realized i was forcing someone precious to stay with me when I should've respected her decision and let her go and be with the person she wanted to be and support her and be happy for her. I also loved meeting her family and getting along with her father and brother and her family accepted me too and i hated loosing them too and especially her cat (my favorite was batman) But yeah it was hard for me loosing someone so precious and a blessing in my life, i was crying for days until my mom told me i should just cry for her and my father in their funeral and after a few days i learned that she actually taught me how to be loved and actually heard rather than just being told to just man up and keep my emotions to myself and not cry. I was so in love with her and it hurt me that she moved on fast and started talking to her old talking stage but i learned that thats how life is and it waits for no one, so now I'm few months in and learning to let go of her but i hate it because everyday in slowly starting to forget about her laugh and small details about her but yeah i don't know why but i keep having dreams about her being in them and her family and i hate it because it keeps me confused and lost and recently i had another dream of her but her face was blurred out like I'm already forgetting about her I don't know if i should be happy or sad that I'm forgetting about her and moving, I'm just lost on what to do and don't know what to do anymore because a part of me wants to text her and talk to her again and the other half wants me to not speak to her again and stay no contact bc of all the progress i have made. I been taking care of myself more and learning self love more each day since the break up and so far I'm trying to connect more to god and try to make a stronger relationship with him but i struggle but i trying to improve everyday. And I'm also starting to control my urge to sin and other stuff and finding a hobbies. I just wish one day in the future when we see each other somewhere we actually talk and stay friends at least a part of me wants that but the other just wants to be happy and not know nothing about her life.

-       K.R.C

Hi my name is Jaky here's my story. First day of 7th grade year it was a new school for me when I walked in I saw this guy he caught my attention and I thought he was cute few days later I told a friend about it and after I told her she went to go tell him but he didn't knew who I was so I was okay for now next day comes and after school that day my other friend told him and she pointed at me l got anxiety and quick went to my car but then I saw that he was excited so when I got home I texted her saying "what did u tell him" then she respond with "I js told me that you like him" my heart dropped after she said that I was so nervous to go to school l js minded my own business and just went to class I told my close friend about it since she's friends with him she told me that he didn't like me but he said that we can be friends and i said okay few days later i decided to text him on instagram I was home about to talk a nap then I texted him all i said was " hey" then I took a nap when i woke up I saw that he texted me so i opened it and it said " leave me alone " my heart dropped after he texted me that so I did and I unfollowed him after that I told my other friend let's name her flower I told flower about what happened then few days later she tells me that she went up to him after school and she said " do you know a girl name jaky" and he said yes then she told him " do you like her by any chance " and he say no then she is walked away when I got home she texted me saying she had something to tell me and to call her so I did and she told me what happened and I got mad at her so i hang up on her then she was trying to apologize but I was still mad at her for a few days later I didn't talk to her after what happened she was still texting me trying to apologize but I just left her on seen then she texted me saying " if your going to be acting like this then why be friends " so then i replied saying okay and then she acting like if noting happened she said like "why are you getting mad he's is a boy" but in my head I thought " but i really like him tho" but I just told her how I felt about her doing that to me then I blocked her on everything few months after that happened I started being friends with his friend and we be talking then my friend let's call her Dan she started being friends with my crush and now we talk as a group but so me and him talk now and i followed him on instagram and he followed me back so now we're friends.

Soultie

T here has only been a few people in my life that
I've had a very deep connection with and there
was a special girl that was one of them. we met
from friends of friends online, it clicked randomly one
day where she called me randomly and we started
talking, the night in October the one call that never
ended and the feeling of butterflies that never left. we
talked for hours about what we love and our passions
and we built a connection, i remember the next nights
convincing myself that it was that one night but there it
was again her calling me and my heart skipping a beat I
have never been so happy.

We eventually started talking about a relationship
and building it slow and steady, we wanted to make sure
that we would take our time. As the months went by and
we bonded closer she was the one who introduced me to
the spiritual aspects of life and the connections that go
beyond the physical parts of us. Soultie, it never made
me any happier knowing I had a deep and spiritual
connection that tied us together from distances. February
came by and I asked her to be my girlfriend, the happiest

moment of my life where I felt like this may be it she might be the one.

But as our relationship progressed it slowly started getting toxic, long distance was difficult I was a very insecure person 2 years ago and I didn't like a lot of things she did. People glorify some stuff in relationships that shouldn't and it drains you. I was so used to our relationship i stopped trying in it. I would accidentally leave her on read for long hours because I would get caught up in games and all she would want is some of my attention, and there it was again the night call. every night, we called every night. She gave up trying to talk to me often because i was always in my own world not paying attention to her.

And when I did realize what I was doing she started doing the same, doing her own things and it upset me because I was starting to try for her. When the calls started again i was always mopey and sad because she barely texted me, the same way i treated her. It drained both us heavily until the start of summer where she asked to take a break, I knew a break was gonna mean a breakup. And it destroyed me but I knew it was coming but in that moment of June, I remembered our soul tie the bond we had wasn't lost, I wanted to believe that I wanted her to still believe it that we were still something that I was still hers and only hers.

It only made my delusions worse when we would always end up texting each other as months went by, my love for her was not dented but there was a void left I tried filling that void with other people but no woman can fill that void only she could. Her, her her her her.

bella, she was only right for me. I learned and grew when I was with and wasn't with her. Eventually, we fully broke contact and we considered dating again, my joy was coming back. She was still the same though, dry and "never on her phone", to this day i will choose to believe her, but she wanted me to change, it confused me at first, it really did but l loved her so I tried changing. I really did try to change but I couldn't for some reason no matter how hard i tried it wasn't good enough, to add we used to make fun of each other as jokes but at some points when my insecurities hit I would make remarks that weren't funny and it upset her which was reasonable. And the final straw was when I tried communicating with her that i felt like she wasn't texting me enough and I didn't feel like she was putting the effort i was putting, she decided she didn't want whatever we were anymore, she outgrew me I was still so young in the brain and i wasn't mature enough. I felt like I was going into insanity was that really what a soul tie was like. Non the less she taught me very valuable parts of life and how to grow as a person and work on yourself and I'm forever grateful of meeting her, she's an amazing woman who deserves to be happy.

This dragged on till early 2024, we tried making it work but it didn't which disappointed me so much I would have this anxiety that wouldn't leave me for months. I eventually got better and tried moving on, but no matter what she will always be a part of me and its something I cant control its as if a part of her grew on me and makes me who I am today. I wish her Godspeed because I do still love her and I wish her the best in life. Even though it ended bad I cant look at her in a bad way, but whenever I do see her time to time that little feeling of anxiety would come back. Who knows if what we had was a soul tie or not but what i do know is that I'm glad i met such a beautiful soul.

-K.T

Maybe in The Future

I was a sophomore I had been you could say best friends with this guy let's call him B one day we asked to see each other as we were internet friends and we meet each other at a park around our house we live close to each other we fell in love that night under the trees I felt a love so warm it was like a love I needed I never experienced love before days go by we date and being with him was so amazing than he said he wasn't ready to date it was Nov of 2022 I was left sad heartbroken April 2023 we start to date again but this time it was different he seemed different the love wasn't the same I felt as I was putting in more effort he was more toxic with me I felt stuck and every morning I'll wake up thinking he'll break up with me due to the fact he'll want to break up every single time and tell me he's "not ready" than I remember it was June 21 of 2023 I'm a junior and he's a senior we were at the park we met for the first time and I have a really bad feeling he hits me with the question "do u want to break up" I couldn't do anything but cry we both cried together we both knew this wasn't working out we had too many walls build towards each other but that's the thing I didn't care what went on I wanted it to be him that's who I wanted to marry days go by we text here and there until I left for vacation and he soon said he didn't want to talk anymore and wanted nothing with me "no string attached" | was left heartbroken couldn't eat or anything months go by and I met someone amazing he's so gentle with me offered to take me home we would go out dance and have fun until I get the text from my ex and ofc as dumb I was I stopped talking to the guy and went back with my ex but this time with my ex he was getting too sexual with me wanting to do things all the time till this one day and this day I will never forget he graduated and he said I lost my touch and I said what do you mean he began to criticize on how I'm adding weight and how he doesn't like my black hair that my blonde looked way better and I started to cry because I was now starting to eat because when I was with him I couldn't eat due to how stressed out I was and he said why are you crying I said because you said I lost my touch he said it's okay there's always room for development and he told me "the only reason why I was so toxic to you it was so you could leave me because I know you'll cry if I broke up with you" I left and never once did I talk to him again it's been 2 months since that happened and now I know it's best for me to stop going back I guess I gave him so many chances because I kept giving him the benefit of the doubt because apparently his ex's treated him bad but he treated me like I was nothing soon I found out on my birthday he hung out with a girl 5 times and ofc she was blonde lol the color he wanted me to do on my hair again although it hasn't been that long but I feel good for once in my life that I'm not with him and about the guy that I talked to before we're friends now I wouldn't say he rejected me but right now isn't the time for us maybe in the future:)

-Lias

A Spell

I fell under the spell of Love at First Sight. The moment I saw her and started talking to her we clicked instantly and were happy together for 5 years. Unfortunately distance got the better of us and we stayed as friends so we would never end on bad terms. We still love each other to death and talk here and there, could I have done some things differently? Oh for sure, but it's too late now and the only thing I can do is keep my love for her and keep loving her from a distance until the time comes. There were some times where I wish I didn't love her from the start, she knew and she changed, not for me, but to better herself so she doesn't hurt anyone else again like she did to me.

@_ruben.velez_

True

———— ◆◆●◆◆ ————

You know some relationships don't last. Most of them don't. But, it's the times that you don't expect to fall in love, that really resonate. One day, I was just riding around on my bike with my brother, we do this all the time. I haven't been searching for anything with anybody. I thought maybe I should stay alone for some time. The park is alive and filled with people. Kids in the pool, people playing basketball. Then, suddenly, the most beautiful girl, I've ever seen, gets out of the pool. Her hair is long and dirty blonde. Her eyes are two different colors. Her smile is as beautiful and the luminescent sea. She goes to get out of her bathing suit, and gets ready to play basketball. My brother bets that she can't make a three pointer. She laughs and says, "watch me". I tell her to do it then, and I laugh a little bit. She then shoots, and makes it. She looks at me and smiles. I knew it was her for me. I fell in love, the first interaction.

-Bivian Humphries Jr.

Floating

I wouldn't say I'm doing good or bad but I been going through some bad relationships problems I lost someone very special to me a year ago and 1 still think about them until this day sometimes it's hard for me to move on from her because everything reminds me of her every since we broke up I try forgetting about her by doing things to avoid her but it's hard I just want to be loved every time I try talking to somebody new I get used or cheated people talk about how ugly I am and they only want me for the attention especially because I already have bad problems I'm at the point of running away I keep going to the hospital because I cut my arms too much. it's not right but it helps me sometimes I'm such a cry baby lover boy and clingy person some people hate it for some reason I try my best to avoid it but I can't I'm just so damaged and my soul hurts so much I wish I can have someone who will love me for me who appreciate the things I do and I know I should take a break but it's hard knowing me I just want to be in someone arms and having the feeling of knowing I'm loved but no matter what I wait patiently for that day to come nothing crazy happened lately just come nothing

485

crazy happened lately just chilling talking to friends playing Roblox while I wait for the true love to come to me you can show my name for this too I don't mind I wish one day I can truly get that love story I always wanted everybody has a an addiction no I'm not going to lose feelings no I'm not finding anyone better I love you with whatever part of my heart I have left I love everybody just for who they are but when will someone do that for me.

-Malachi

My Little Secret Andi

It's about my friend which we finished high school together even tho we didn't really talk to much with each other back then , later we had come closer than death it self , we have been in lot of trip's and life moment's that we saw each other happy and lost. now that i know him , how do i have to feel alive . I think he has haunted me Its just that we had so much joy being together for four years , he used to call me baby and we had this humor being so girly we used to smoke weed together drink and go to mountains parties and we did great i think. There were so many nights we decided to stand up till sunrise , we used to watch sunset too we used to exchange thing's shirt's pants our hand clocks.

We had such energy always when we saw each other a smile was made in our faces. Eye contact's at begging of friendship. Having touching mechanism was the best part where i found on him His big green eye's. Too And those big lip's And his pure heart that was to me. He used to tell me such thing's Which I'm being scared because I'm starting to forget him. But i still remember

487

that day in July when me and him went on ride with his motor because he love's them and i was high and i wanted to hold him so tight that moment and never let go of him , but yea life didn't want so. And just because i had to let him go. That didn't mean i wanted to. and now i tell god what i did today how i felt how my day was because now your not here anymore , the star that you pointed out and said to me it's brighter than any other star , i tell to that one Everywhere we been and everything we did , i get to walk on those streets that still linger's your presence on it , i still hear your voice and yet i feel like it was real. I think he will find me back even if returns thousand years later. I believe the Vicissitudes have changed so dramatically since that night when i decided to take the courage and tell you my secrets . So one night before we changed our pathway i told him I love you and I'm sorry because of this but i will love you even as dream even as shadow .

And perhaps somewhere someday at less miserable life we get know each other again , but i believe that theres another world and better world for us and i will be waiting you on there . Then you asked me that night what's your secret i stopped and whispered and thought for a moment . Look at those eye's and his puppies have been bigger than ever before I closed my eye's and kissed him and that moment was everything freezing even my soul and i told him I'm sorry that i love you And he said nothing to me but looked and stood quite for awhile later then we went home and we had to sleep together so i decided not to sleep but just watch him because i knew that that time was that day where i won't see him again.

So i stood in all those places and watched all times sunset and woke up most of the time's in sunrise because he became my sunshine . He walked away and since that day I never heard or saw him anymore and i wish he's doing great and that one thing i wanna tell him. Is that i did great and i wish you saw.

-Toni

Romantic Love That I Once Lived.

———— ◆◆◆◆ ————

I once had a very loving, kind, and cute girlfriend that name is Paola. If I remember correctly, it was between 2015 and 2016, so she was a typical love of children, there were no kisses with lips or anything like that, but the point is that she was a very cute girl with me, even though I was a bad boy with everyone, she changed me in many aspects.

We had to end the relationship because we were going to change schools in 2017, and after that, we never met again until today

Now today in 2024, I have no idea where she is or contact with her.

Sometimes love makes us want to be better, I changed because of what Paola saw in me, but when I lost her, it did not stop the love I felt for her, I hope she is fine and she will find peace.

Certainly, I still think about her for some days, I hope to meet her again one day or in the next life if possible.

Blinded by Love

I was blinded by love. Loved too deeply, loved too less. There wasn't a balance, o a measure how I should love. Simply because it can't be measured. The last genuine love I've experienced was when I loved deep. No limits, expressed fully. Lost who I was, blinded, simply. I've started setting boundaries nothing can go through. Felt I'm not compatible with anyone my age.

They say I'm too old fashioned, too mature for my age. My experience taught me to only look for wisdom. My boundaries are super high, but it's good because it is my standards. Went on trying without forcing, never worked. Up until I found that one person. Everything then changed. This person was able to provide what I seek. Inner peace, strength, happiness and genuine love I couldn't fathom. I felt lucky once again. An addition to my purpose, my living. No stress, negativity, but quite the opposite; only tranquility, joy and peace. Upon meeting this person, I've felt as if I've knew about everything about this person.

Best chemistry I've found yet. I've felt I've found the

perfect compatibility. This person knows everything about me. Provides solutions and not problems. Knows my strengths and takes out my weaknesses. Quality time felt like time was nonexistent. Simply because that person was myself. I've been looking in the wrong direction when the person was myself the whole time. Self love made me ambitious, driven and with purpose. All along the person was me. I've fixed my inner vision. I was blinded by love.

-@vincentnbriones

Good Luck Allyfalfa

O ur love story began with hopeful promises, only to unravel into a tale of betrayal. He drew me in with his charming smile and heartfelt words, and when he asked me to be his girlfriend, I agreed with a heart full of hope. Yet beneath the surface of our romance, he was crafting a different story—one marked by cheating and deceit. While I was faithful, he pursued another woman, growing indifferent to me.

His betrayal was a harsh wake-up call, but it revealed an important truth: I deserved far more than empty promises from a dishonest heart. As our relationship fell apart, it uncovered not only the depth of his disloyalty but also my own strength and resolve. From the wreckage of heartbreak, I emerged with a renewed sense of self-worth and a firm decision to demand better for myself.

So, our story ends not in quiet defeat but in a strong assertion of self-respect and new beginnings. What started as a hopeful romance has become a journey of self-discovery and empowerment. From the pain of betrayal, I have found the strength to move forward, ready to embrace a future where I am valued.

-Kim Tran (@kqmiiz)

Shattered dreams and broken hearts

July 29 2022 first time I ever seen her heard her voice seen her smile heard her laugh something about her made me fall for her found out my cousin was best friends with her and helped me out by giving her socials days later school has started and she was in my morning class and she was just in my head I had felt something for her...... that's when I realized I had a crush on her every time I past her I tried to get her attention weeks passed yet nothing until August 17 I swipe up her Instagram story and complemented her once I did that my anxiety levels went up and I was nervous I thought she would make fun of me or tell me she's out of my league minutes past yet nothing until an hour later i got a message it was from her she told me thank you and how sweet I was from their I started messaging her and she kept messaging me too that's when it all started we were in a talking stage 3 months later it was December i went on a school trip which is know as the happiest place on earth "Disney land"and she was their and we both hung out all day that day on December 10 2022 i wanted to and was planning to ask her out i had everything ready i knew what to say but I couldn't i chicken out and didn't do it until a week later i was ready we went out it was to a party later That night we took a walk around 10 minutes later we got tired of walking and we sat down on side walk of the road we where hearing romantic love music and she laid her head on my left shoulder that's when I told myself I have to do it I want to do it am ask her to be my girl yet I was still very nervous and scared 15 minutes past and it was time to go back before we did I stopped her and asked I finally told her to be my girlfriend on December 17 at 6:05pm she said yes she was my girlfriend afterwards i went in for the kiss and we kissed it was my first kiss and hers too it was my first relationship and hers too we. Started heading back and it was a felling I have never Felt it was amazing it was my first kiss my first relationship but weeks later...it started to fall we had our first couple arguments and so we had a talk and well she didn't felt about us being together well i told her don't say that and to give us and me a month and we would work and a month later we fixed our arguments and we were back 3 months later that's where it all started she started keeping secrets from me she didn't tell me stuff that in a relationship you would tell your partner it felt like she did have trust on me one day she confessed something that really hurt me bad where we were not in a good place and started more arguments two months later on June 26 2023 she broke up with me which really shattered me and broke me I never felt so much pain and hurt in my life I cried for ours and days and weeks but she broke up with me during those last days we had so much arguments she kept ignoring me she ignored me for hours and never wanted to fix stuff she acted childish so the day she broke up with me i told her straight up which really upset her and told me if it really effected

me then she was going to break up which she did end up
doing a week later she messaged me and we both
confessed our feelings to each other we missed each
other but she wast ready to go back so we texted it was
like a relationship but wasn't we where in a break but
didn't want a relationship months past till November I
found out something from someone and told me....
Something about her that really broke me more and lost
trust and hurt me so much and broke my heart and made
me go into depression she wasn't loyal and found out she
did something not right and was messaging another guy
and found out she did it three times while in our break
where she left the guy and went back so I called her and
confessed to her if it was all true and it was and that's
where I started to lose faith and lost trust she told me she
was Sorry she told me so many times but it didn't felt
like it I stop Messaging her felt like it was over and
didn't want to text her two weeks later she messaged me
to give her another chance and that she was Sorry and it
was a very hard decision I didn't know so I had to really
think about her till 4 days later I messaged her again and
said I'll give her another chance so we went out but we
weren't in a relationship just talking a month later she
started ignoring but now for days she was ghosting me
for days and days and weeks and I thought I have had
done something bad and kept messaging her what was
wrong or what did I do or what's bothering she finally
messaged me and told me she wasn't going to text me if
she didn't felt nothing anymore when I first read that it
broke me I really thought we would work but did t two
weeks later she messaged me and asked me if i was
home and i was i thought she wanted to see me because i
really needed her i was in a dark place she told me she
was outside I went with joy tried to give her a hug but

she didn't want too and that was the first time I have seen her in 3 months so I really needed her she came to drop off my sweater I had give her and from their i knew. What was going on once she give me my sweater I asked for a hug cause I was in tears already but she denied and said no and left I was outside crying for a good 20 minutes later I messaged her and she just told me she was done and was apologizing for not being as loving as me and so much other stuff she still app for what she did to me for hurting me but she wanted to end in good terms and also wanted to end stuff before the year ended which it was a couple days from new years and I told her what happened to the promises of never leaving me and all she said things change and from their I don't believe in promises for me promises aren't promised just like tomorrow ain't promised so she left and never came back till this day August 20 2023 I have seen her once at a party and messaged her that night but no answer but we still follow each Other on social and I always tell my self I meet her when I wasn't looking for no one and she left when I mostly needed her.

Liz

———— ◆•◦•◆ ————

When I was young, I always been alone. I had no friends. in every grade, I was always alone with my thoughts. thinking that maybe it was because i was not normal. In every way shape and form, I felt so ew. Even in my family, I've felt unwanted. Ever lover I've met, always felt the need to leave since for them I was "to much to handle". I never wanted to speak anymore especially since I thought my opinion and what I had to say was unimportant and irrelevant to anything. until I met him. me and him shared a bond, that I thought would never break. he made me feel less guilty and alone. hearing his voice brung the comfort my head was never able too. the only part was that, me and him weren't the best together . But we comforted each other right? The days felt bipolar. Like the toxic was the only thing going for us. I wanted us so bad, to where I wanted to mold myself into someone I wasn't. and then blamed myself when things went wrong. he was the only one who made me feel wanted.

-Lizlean c

Love

--- ◆◈◆ ---

Man where do I begin with her, We haven't truly talked in a while. I've done a terrible thing to her, and to myself. I'll keep her anonymous... but she truly was and still is the love of my life. God I was so dumb. But what happened, happened and I can't go back. I bestowed on her, truly a dumb but overall beautiful act. Cause it's life. Everyone makes their own mistakes and has to pick up their pieces. Put it like this, Fire and Water, knight and a princess, God, if u will. That's how it is now, I just want her to know how much I still care for her and, I still want her mine. We were kids doing stupid things. Truly, we were just sixteen. Hey that rhymed! I bestow this message, and even this poem coming up. To just signify such a feet I pulled her to back then... So this is for you...

Darling.

My beloved love,

What words to say.

To you, nothing more but meer love.

501

To the times of pink and forever true

I wish I would've pulled the que.

To sweep you from your feet and rescue you.

To anything that distressed you.

My love for you will never be far

My love for you will always be like a star.

Shining bright and clear forevermore

My sweet love, come back to my core.

Darling… my beloved love…

I miss you.

To our walk in City Park,

The day we reached our spark.

I know it's kinda cliche…

But what am I supposed to say.

I love you…

all I want is for you to stay.

Darling…. Words can't compare of what I've done. My spirit's fallen.

But the war is won.

You're probably thinking, how am I supposed to care?

Trust me my love, for you I will always be there.

My heart. How wretched of me,

To put my own insecurity onto thee.

You see… words cannot compare.

How much I truly felt in despair.

All I want is for you to care again.

How I've seen you get up and glow,

To even bestowing yourself, even in my own show.

Of love and light, what I see…

The feeling of you right next to me.

Such a child I am to myself and thee.

But even so

The chaos in me,

Will feel like it will all be gone when you're there next to me.

I will shine so bright, if you just bestowed me true sight.

All in the mind for the better reality.

Bro it's so hard to keep goin,

I don't know how life keeps bestowing.

Truly I think, I'm gonna run

But I don't ever put up the gun.

It's like I'm Ina constant battle with myself

When the answer is truly to myself

The answer is me, oh yes it's me.

So why do I let it all fall naturally :)

Love you baby.

Zozo

In the beginning year of my junior year in high school, I felt confident on pouring my love onto someone who was as committed to commit to a relationship. I've always been a fanatic of the law of attraction, so I kept to myself until the universe aligned me with that special someone. So I waited, waited for someone to appear out of thin air. It got to a point where I thought that the law of attraction was a baloney.

Until, it happened. Ashley L., we've been going to the same schools since elementary school but yet have never spoken a word to each other. Not until that one physics class we had together. It all started off innocent until she had let me in on a little secret, she told me she's scared to walk alone in the hallways because of her ex. She was physically and sexually abused by him throughout her sophomore/junior. Right then and there, I knew what I was getting myself into. I knew she wasn't ready to commit and sacrifice for a relationship.

Not only because she just got out of a relationship, but because she got out of a relationship where she was a victim of sexual assault. It's not easy to trust someone

505

after what she had experienced in her previous relationship but regardless of what she went through, I didn't think of her differently. So I did what I felt entitled to do. I gave in. I sacrificed my gentle heart hoping that it'll make her problems go away. But as time went by, I was losing myself in the relationship. I lost hope, I lost faith, I lost what I've barricading from others to protect my peace, myself. So I decided to put my foot down and told her that I was done. Deep down I felt like I was saying goodbye to myself , but I knew I had to do what had to be done. Fast forwards a couple months later the unexpected happened, she changed. To this day I still don't know what happened when I wasn't in the picture but I got to graduate high school with her. Now I'm going into college with my high school sweetheart, giving our love another chance to prove its value.

-@v00lin

The Line

T he line between love and heartbreak is as thin as this piece of paper. A boy lost in his emotions; lost in his journey finds love in two people. Both change his view on love and both impact his heart.

Its the end of February. Kai who's 19 doesn't have any drive or passion in anything he does. Now Kai has a friend, named Shayne, someone who he's been friends with since the 9th grade. And she's in college and she has it all figured out. She like a walking ray of sunshine. But one day Kai saw something that just didn't feel right. Almost as if she was hiding her tears and cries behind her smile and laughter.

She brushes it off as if Kai is just "looking into deep into things"and asked him "why do you care anyway". He says because you're my friend and i love and care about you.

Over the next couple of months Kai and Shayne really looked out for each other and really have a love for each other but not in the romantic form. It was so beautiful and warming that it healed both of them and they were so open and supportive of each other that they found a romantic love with other people while still being

507

platonically in love with each other.

In October that platonic love was tested when Kai met a girl named Sade, and Sade was the female version of Kai. They were the same person and they started dating in November. But every relationship has its up and downs, and in December. Kai and Sade got into an argument, one that required the guidance of his friend Shayne who said " if you love her, you will find a way to work things out, and if she loves you, she will find a way to work things out. But i don't agree with what she did and she shouldn't make you feel this way."

The problem with Kai and Sade's relationship was that they were too much alike and it caused issues because there stubbornness would make them bump heads...a lot. But when Kai and Sade weren't at each others throat, they were so happy, so so happy. Shayne could see this happiness and something started to change in her attitude towards Kai and Sade. She started to say things like "i would never do that to you." or things like "maybe you and her aren't meant for each other."Well one day she she made a slick comment about Sade and it bothered Kai to the point he told her never to talk about her again. He told her if she doesn't have anything nice to say don't say anything at all.

But sadly in February everything came crashing down between Kai and Sade. Her and her brother were moving back home and Kai was getting ready to start Med school. These were things that they talked about before they even started dating but when the time came things just didn't go the way they planned. They stopped going out as much, they stopped talking as much, and they seemed to be distant with each other. Kai had asked Shayne for a word of advise on the situation and she was helpful. She said " whats meant to be will work itself out naturally."

Kai took what she said and thought about it, so on valentines day he left her a basket of her favorite candies flowers stuff animals and perfumes bug also a card, and the card was more of an apology, then a love letter. And later that day Sade called him and they talked for hours and hours and hours. But by the end of this call Kai asked Sade, "if she's ok?" Sade says "yeah"but with a weak sound to it. She then asked if Kai was ok, he had a pause and let out a sigh and said " yeah, I'm ok."

He then asked her "are WE okay." And with tears flying through the phone she said "i dont know" and she cried. And hearing her so upset made him upset and she went on to say with everything going on with her moving back home and work, she's just been stressed out and its overwhelming for her, so they they decided to take a little break just to get everything had going on straight. (They never saw each other again)

02-13-24

Two years ago I was at practice and next to our courts there was an older group practicing. I saw these two guys and I couldn't stop staring at them. Some months later I saw them signing up for a competition, so I waited for them to leave to look at their names. When I got home I got on Instagram and started stalking them, but in a crush way not creepy.

509

Two years later I was at a competition watching a guy from our Club and next to me was my crush. He started a small talk with me while his friend was in the bathroom. And later that night he followed me on Instagram and we started talking. I was so happy and excited that he actually noticed me and after a while of texting we got each others Snapchat.

The next month I started in the same group as lets call him Kevin and his friends so I of course became their friend and joined their friend group.

That same month our club had a trip to a competition where we stayed at a hotel. I was of course the only girl there accept one of our coaches, so I had to sleep in the same room as her. But that night all of the guys had the same room so I was with them and while Kevin was showering I layer in his bed. We were all talking and when he came back he just laid in the bed with me and we cuddled while the other guys were making fun of us. That night I fell asleep in that room in Kevins bed and I felt so comfortable. In the middle of the night we woke up from one of the guys sleep talking and we both started giggling and then he went for it and kissed me. Our first kiss 02-13-24 I still feel the kiss on my cheek and on my mouth when I think about it.

When we got back from the trip we were hanging out non stop after school, before practice, every weekend. We were inseparable. One day we were laying in his bed and he asked me to be his girlfriend, I of course said yes. The only thing that was on my mind when we were together was that we never went on dates, out in public. So the only people that saw us as a couple was our friend

510

group. It didn't really bother me but it was always in the back of my head.

Fast forward 3 months, he became distant and dry. He wasn't really good at communicating so I was really trying to communicate with him. One day I felt like he had a weird Friendship with a girl so I told him and he had the driest answer and after that he became even more distant. I also wanted to tell him about my past of trying to take my life and self harming but I didn't because I knew he would be dry.

One week later he went to Spain and I told him I really wanted him to be open to me and he just bursted out all of it. He sent we a paragraph about how he felt like we were more like friends and that thing probably went to fast with us. And I started crying and my sister came to my room. I told her everything and she took my phone and texted him. I told her what to text him because my fingers were shaking too much. I tried to fix it but he just gave up and that night we broke up. I was crying in my room for four days straight my mom had to feed me because I didn't want to eat. Now it's been a month without him and last week I took of our matching bracelet we had. It happens I cry sometimes witch makes me feel bad.

I relapsed because of him witch makes it even worse. Sometimes I dream about how I could have saved our relation ship. The first week of breaking up I was stalking his every move and I realized that is not the way to heal. So now I'm trying not to think about him and if I do I just try to think how close of friends we came become in a while. I now have two exes and I heard this

511

saying that there are two types of first loves. The FIRST love, and the first LOVE. I now realize that it's true and I think I'm going to focus on myself for a while. And I think it's important to know that it's okay to cry even after a month of a breakup or even five months after one. It's a part of healing and everything takes time.

-@anna_ostrovska

Walsh

You know the love that gets described in the movies? I like to think I experienced that type of love, yet the memories i carry haunt me every night in bed. The bed he used to tell me that i was his soulmate in, the bed we used to laugh for hours in, the bed he was once in. I have to live in the room haunted with memories or him in every corner, I can't help but hate him for that. I don't hear from him anymore, do you know how painful that is? If you don't, you're about to find out.

You know that weird feeling you get in your gut when you're talking to someone special? First time talking to him I got it and I knew he was going to be a big part of my life.

I met him at a party and took him outside with me, we laughed about random things but before we could talk for longer my friends parents picked me up.

He got in contact with me that night and we started talking more and he started coming over at night time just so that we could fall asleep together. I shared my first kiss with him that first night he came over, it was

513

everything i had imagined. He was the first boy I felt comfortable with, when he was with me everything went quiet.

Finally, he asked me to be his girlfriend and I said yes with no hesitation. We started meeting constantly and then i introduced him to my parents, they absolutely loved him, how gentle he was with me and how happy he was making me.

Most nights we'd call but if we didn't, I'd wake up to a paragraph describing his love for me and how he'd never felt this way towards a girl. He was my person and I was his.

Day by day, I started making a connection with his little sister as-well, we'd call for hours and she was somebody who I could play with, something I didn't get to do much as a kid. I built a sister figure with his and she was so special to me, always will be.

Unfortunately, his eyes started wandering elsewhere, to his best friend. Somehow her giving him the right amount of attention at the right time made him leave me. I would text him begging me to love me but constantly got the cold shoulder. However, part of me knew this wasn't the end once his sister texted me saying, 'I miss u sophie'.

We went on a break and I heard from him a few days later. I spent those few days drinking and crying, that's all I can remember from that point of my life. I took him back in a heartbeat, sneaking him over to my house at night, giving up my body to make him want to love me again.

He would whisper into my ear saying how he loves me and only wants me, I remember asking him if he would hurt me again, his answer was blunt. No.

I found out he kissed another girl that same day after he met me and my heart crushed. I felt like I had lost all my trust in him and I did. He apologized over and over again telling me he made a mistake. I forgave him and took him back in a heartbeat once again. We got back together but it wasn't the same. With no trust there was no point to our relationship.

It started off bad, he felt like a stranger. It took a lot in me to forgive him but I made myself because of the potential I believed we had. I was correct, he gradually built my trust back up and we fell back in-love with one another. We would spend almost everyday talking to each-other and meeting. It felt perfect, and it was for a bit. Until I started noticing his comments, he would tell me no boy would love me for more than my body, that I got lucky with him.

Gradually, my self worth got worse and worse when he would say small things that would make me hate myself. Constantly talking about other girls, how I wasn't his type, how he wished upon unrealistic beauty standards for his future girlfriends. Due to other things in my life, my mental health took a toll for the worst, I needed him but I couldn't put him through what I had to go through when my sister got ill, so I pushed him away. Instead of asking me if I was okay, he would tell me he hated the person I had become and that i wasn't the same girl he once fell in love with, it made me hate myself even more.

Midday, sitting on the side of the road I had packets of pills. I took an overdose and I remember thinking it this was my last moments I wanted to hear his voice, I spam called him but no reply.

It didn't work, I survived. Opening my phone in the hospital, I saw the messages from him, it was paragraphs and voice notes like the ones he used to send me during our first relationship. I felt so much love for him all over again, but I was so ill. I knew it would hurt me but I had to let him go, I told him we had to breakup, I wish he had known if we stayed together I would've dragged him down with me. I didn't break with him because I didn't love him, I broke up with him because I cared more about his happiness than mine.

However, the day I got discharged from hospital he was with another girl, the same girl he kissed after meeting me. I felt like nothing to him. Was it worth saving him from

me when I now had a hatred so strong within me just for him? I wanted to hurt him how he hurt me, but all I could do was cry. A few months later, I gave him back hid clothes and wanted to have a conversation to leave us on good terms but it just turned into shouting at one another. We never sorted things out and to this day I still pray we have another chance. Since then, I have been trying to make myself digestible. I am trying to make myself easy to love.

-Sophie Walsh

Appearance

---◆◆◆◆---

When I was 16 I was dating this guy but he wasn't the nicest to me, and for some reason neither was his family. They clearly judged me because of my skin tone and made fun of my appearance. And it got so bad to the point where I felt like he was against me and so was his family. So I made a mistake and cheated on him when I should have just left him alone. Long story short he found out and told everyone, he also told that " I would never find someone to love me as much as he did." And I believed it for a long time. Until 2 years later I met someone else and he seemed really nice but out of no where he told me one day that he liked me and wanted to be with me and I genuinely was caught off guard because I thought no one would like me or even want to be with me. So we hung out for a while to get to know each other and after a while I figured out I do have feelings for him and I never felt that way about anyone in my life. And we started dating! We are now currently still dating and I just want to say that it's okay to make mistakes but its important to change the things that you did wrong and try to be better person and you will find people that actually care about you and won't make fun of you, people that actually care about you won't make you feel bad about yourself and your appearance.

-Myracle

It will get better

———————— ◆•◊•◆ ————————

I met this girl online six months ago. We started off as friends, but I liked her a lot since I was lonely before meeting her. She wasn't sure how she felt about me, so I respected her need for time and eventually, she felt the same way. We started talking more and eventually, I told her I loved her. She said she "had love for me" but didn't know how to express it and didn't want to be dishonest. Although it made me sad, I respected her feelings. Eventually, she did say she loved me, and our relationship improved.

However, one night, she mentioned she had a secret but wouldn't tell me what it was. After some time, she revealed that she had tried to commit suicide. I told her it was completely normal and that I was there to help her, but she said I "pressured her" and made her feel invalidated. She would also block me when she got mad. We took a lot of breaks, but our relationship was never the same. She promised she wouldn't talk to another guy, but I noticed her following a new guy (she used to only follow me).

Now I'm pretty sure they are dating. What I've

learned from our relationship is that a relationship goes both ways; one person can't put in all the effort while the other doesn't. It also taught me to enjoy the moment. I thought she was the one, but it just didn't work out. I was sad for about a month, but then I realized I have to move forward in my life. I'm much happier now and can't wait to see what the future holds. A heartbreak is one of the worse feelings but It definitely does get better.

Loml

I t was July 2nd, 2022 and i came across this girl's profile i found her very beautiful but i was too scared to say hi through text so i decided to do those anonymous replies stories, i asked what age she would go for in a guy she responded with "same age or a little older" even though i was younger than her i just turned 17 at the time and now i am 19 writing this story for you guys, i remember she posted a responded to mental health and i replied something in the lines of "no matter what never disrespect a girl who was always there for you".

Since that reply we texted ever since at first i wasn't interested but it wasn't because of her i wasn't looking for anything at the time and i got out of a 2 year relationship 3 months prior. so i was hitting the gym 5 days a week and had the goal of losing weight and focusing on myself. we exchanged numbers 1-2 days into texting and we did our first facetime call for the first time ever and i caught feelings right away because we clicked immediately she was funny, compassionate, friendly but also super sweet.

We always called on the phone every single day and never got bored of each other. a week later we met in person and when i saw her turn the corner of the street and saw her for the first time in my life i fell in love immediately. i knew i found her it was originally supposed to be a meet up at the train station where i once lived near by but i ended up dropping her off to work. my gut was telling me to not go home immediately and drop this girl off my mind was telling me "this girl is gonna be special to you" i told myself its either this girl is gonna be the love of my life or she is gonna be my biggest lesson, she ended up being both... she was a busy person and i saw her whenever she got the time to see me.

One day she found a new job next to her house and i decided to get her Starbucks her favorite order strawberry lemonade refresher with a chocolate croissant, it was a weird combo but I'm not the one to judge lol. we hanged out by the corner of her block and we looked into each other's eyes and shared our first kiss i will never forget that day i will always remember it. i knew i truly liked this girl and i wanted to go more further with her. the first 3 months was great super healthy for a situationship i wanted to take it slow we both wanted to, to be honest.

Until October came around i started to become emotional attached to her i became jealous as the months progressed but she didn't like it at all she never knew i was jealous until October came around. i thought i learned from my previous relationship but turns out i didn't. she thought about the choice to drop me when she found out i was jealous but she didn't choose to because she liked me very much so she gave me the chance to change and gave me so much great life advices. it started to get more worst than ever i would develop serious anger issues and would mentally take it out on her. when the new years came around she asked me to leave everything behind and make things right and i said yes because i really did like her that much. it would only get worst from there we took a break in January but i broke no contact because i couldn't spend a day without talking to her it was horrible she was my person i couldn't go without.

Valentines came around i didn't have any money back then i never had a job but i was getting an allowance by my parents so i saved my money that i would get to buy her the love birds lego set but we still had problems going on but we still tried to solve it out. Till this day i never officially celebrated valentines day with anyone like that it's kinda sad to say to be honest. i would treat her so bad and would fall into deep guilt it felt like i failed as a son, brother, uncle but also as a lover. i would try to take my own life 4-5 times by overdosing in pills from March-May out of pure guilt. My suicide attempts took a toll on her affected her very much.

We decided to take a break on April by then we didn't speak for 3 weeks after my senior trip she texted me and things got better there was a day where i was mad because i created a fake relationship in my head like if it was real and said i went to go see the ex and i guess she tried playing mind games with me. i was angry and went crazy and went to the ER having my dad watch me. i felt ashamed eventually we worked things out for a good amount of time we started seeing each other more often

523

than ever i met her mother a few months prior to that she is super sweet she loved me always talked about me. we started going on dates we were on a budget so it wasn't the best dates but all i cared about was the quality time with her. days before my 18th birthday she took my virginity and that day i knew i was in love with her i was being very sweet and kind as i could be to her but a day before my birthday she found out i was lying to her for a year straight about a girl that never existed in my life a fake relationship that i created not only that, i lied about a girl i used to have a crush on during my junior year of high school.

I lied about having a job at best buy i wanted to look cool. i never realized i was lying about my life until that day. I was too blinded by love to even realize it i felt sorry not for myself but for her i really treated her like completely shit. she blocked me for a few days and she told me the week of prom that she made out with 2 of her co-workers and it broke me severely mentally and emotionally. we were supposed to go to prom together and i ended up finding out when i was on the way to the venue alone i wasn't happy at all i hid all my sadness and guilt through a smiling face that entire night.

My sadness turned into anger and all i wanted was revenge on her. everyone at school knew what i did and i lost all my friends because of it. i basically ruined my own life with my own lies. my graduation day came and i wasn't happy i wanted out of the school right away. the girl texted me saying "hey listen we will work this out just give me time to work this through" and i believed her. that text kinda brought a little joy to me at least i knew there was still hope for us to work out. me and her didn't speak as often anymore after what i did but we still texted and stayed in contact for a bit longer. July 4 came around we were supposed to meet up but she told me to meet up later but by then i was already at her block. as i turned to my life i see her walking with her ex of 4 years it caught me super off guard. it was a worst fear coming to reality and it broke my heart down to the core. i acted like i continued walking but i followed them i still don't know why to this day but i shouldn't have.

She eventually saw me following her and told me to stop and slapped me. i cried on my way home that day hiding my tears until i closed my room door. she went to her ex's family party and drank with him. she started to crying her eyes out about me and everything we been thru. she said " i cant imagine what he is going through right now" that same hour i broke my door mirror out of anger and cried my eyes out for 2 hours straight screaming and crying. i deserved for what happen that day. i was filled with anger and rage for the next few weeks. that same week i invited over a friend of mine of 4 years and we kinda hooked up unexpectedly.

I told the girl what happen i felt guilty after that night and she wasn't happy but my evil side told her "i wanted to make you feel the same pain you made me feel" it was scary saying that. i wanted revenge and i got it but it only made it worst. it bothered her very much and she expressed how she missed me for the last few weeks but i was too angry to react. her bday came around i bought her two sets of legos for her bday. she loved legos. she had guy friends through the time we talked and it was the reason why i got jealous because they wanted something with her she was just too blind to see it and called me crazy and insecure, it hurt me bad. a week later i tried finding her and speak to her she wasn't answering my texts she ignored them.

She thought i was stalking her at first but i couldn't even defend myself about it. her co worker told me thru a phone call said "she don't fuck with you my g" and that was the closure i needed to let go for good. she wasn't responding to me anymore and i desperately send paragraphs day by day of me apologizing to her. it was in person i would last see her and i walked away from her for good. i left her alone and got the closure that i needed. August 2023, month went by i called her after my new job that i got. she tells me that she found someone new and tells me how amazing the new guy. it broke my heart to the core but i was truly happy for her.

Her name was Jessica and i will never forget about her. Sometimes you have to make heartbreaking decisions that will bring you peace and it did. its been a year now since all of this happen. i took the lessons and i stepped up in life. i got a job now. i got into therapy and I'm 7 months strong into therapy and i never been calmer and relaxed than ever. I'm going for a career in photography and i love it. I'm glad that i met you Jessica i don't hate you for what you did, i hope you found the courage to forgive me after everything. you probably will never see this because this will be in a book you probably will never find but if you do, I'm sorry it couldn't be me, in a different universe we would've been boyfriend and girlfriend.. guys please use my story as awareness to your mistakes because it will lead you to the same path I'm in, i hope you guys can learn from me i would leave my instagram down below if you need any advice I'm always here to talk to any of you, love you guys <3

@nelzonwdagrip_

May 17th

I never believed in unrequited love until I met her. It's been some time, but she still lingers in my thoughts, especially the day of May 17th, a day that feels etched into my mind. At first, seeing her in health class didn't mean much, but as I got to know her, I was struck by her kindness and attentiveness, which reminded me of a caring mother. She reassured me when I somewhat botched our first project.

The small gestures, like offering candy, reassurance, and eye contact had made me see her as more than just a girl—she became someone special, someone to cherish. We worked on more projects together, grew a meaningful relationship, and as the semester progressed, I realized how amazing she truly was. But I didn't rush to establish a deeper connection, thinking she was in the same grade level. I had thought there was more time. As the semester went by and I found out she was only a few days from graduating, I frantically searched for her Instagram. Under the suspicion that she might've already been taken, how could she not be? To no surprise, I was, unfortunately, correct.

I confirmed it by an Instagram highlight, which featured her significant other's gift to her: a bouquet of flowers. Our last meaningful interaction was on May 17th, and I never contacted her afterward, fearing it would be awkward on my end due to my unrequited feelings. Im not she knew what i felt, but now, I wait, focusing on myself, hoping to see her again by chance. Also hoping that then, that she is no longer with her current partner. I've never given up on her, but perhaps that's the problem. As much as I want her to be with me, I hate the thought of her feeling the pain I've felt losing someone like to that of her boyfriend to bad terms. Perhaps they part ways on good terms. Maybe then we meet paths, but until a day as such, the thought of "what if" will stay afloat.

-george._.bruv

Deprived

---◆◆◉◆◆---

The root of my story comes from the love of my two parents, my dad although big of heart had a lot of moments of pride at times within the relationship that led to conflict, my mother was good at arguing with him and making him feel bad afterwards. I thought this was normal to be put back at once place once you've done something wrong but I definitely missed the nuances behind the morality.

When I was 12 I had my first crush, for context I was very tall and looked older for my age (1m75). Her name is Salomé she was a year older than me. I used to homeschool with my mother (who used to be teacher), we had a nice group of friends and friends of friends who also we doing homeschooling and every summer they'd rent this vacation place for a couple weeks just for us to hang.

Salomé kinda had this seems mean but is soft persona, I think I related to her problems to some extent. I felt a bit unhinged at times. My parents (especially my mom) wanted me to be able to express myself growing up, to grow without fear, be good in my shoes. After an incident with a teacher in my first school that's how she took the initiative to homeschool me. The thing is it kinda made me a black sheep, I was tall, black, homeschooled and vegetarian by choice. All those things weren't trendy as they are now and meeting friends of friends would often make me a bit anxious. I had people who loved me for who I am, but some were downright bullying me and it was hard to stay calm even tho I did, I preferred crying instead of fighting even when I knew I had an advantage. That however boosted small kids ego so I made myself tougher emotionally.

Salomé who became homeschooled by how unhinged she was felt closer to home. Her however didn't really want to be homeschooled initially since her looking older with makeup gave her some popularity she seemed to enjoy. She was kinda narcissistic at times, I like to think life made her that way. She brought me into her trouble maker life and we were acting like adolescent in our pre-teens. I liked those times, and the unmindfulness of it all.

Things took a turn when we had a long dispute full of curses. She loved the spotlight so much that having that dispute in public was nor worries for her, she definitely enjoyed that. Separating people, making them debate, pick a side, she'd never lie but she'd manipulate chaos. I think she made me like that too.

On that one long argument a girl who had a crush on me stood for me, she told the parents and then even that made them pick sides. The friend group got crushed and we all entertained it.

Afterwards I became lonely I had activities that made me meet other kids but I didn't want to be vulnerable again, I just wanted to stay nonchalant. I worked out a lot to put my frustrations in something but it just accumulated in me somewhere. At the time with Salomé we were almost getting intimate and since that led to no where I feel like I repressed myself sexually for some time.

Years later I made my own group of friends playing basketball met more through that, I'd never fall in love again, and I avoided girls, maybe for the better. I almost got closed to one girl but I'd always repress my feelings every time we'd get close. I had a sex friend but I think she was in love with me but kept it for herself. Things stayed like that until I moved at age 16 in Rwanda. My farewell party removed the anxiety I had for the longest time, I felt like I was truly loved and maybe everyone felt that too.

When I moved in Kigali I started crying as I reached my new bed, it suddenly hit me that I'd not see my friends again, as I got into my first school in the American system I felt like I was too mature for everyone, I think maturity is not a linear concept however but I got back that black sheep role slowly. My first year I was a happy kid a bit too extraverted. The kids already knew themselves so they would kinda leave me hanging at times, I didn't care too much tho, I made friends in a new basketball team outside of school. Then met a lot more from it. My 17th birthday I organized a huge party when my mother wasn't there lmao I invited 100 people and they talked about that party for years, I then made people pay to enter my parties and I became the popular kid in high school super quickly, I think I didn't like the sudden change in behavior from them and started ignoring the people from my school. I repressed some of my feelings again.

When next year came I had to try hard for my last school year but I felt so lonely at home as an only child. My basketball teammates helped but school was draining me like crazy, my only friend in high school made the difference. I think I needed to see my mother more, or have a women by my side or something. It felt hard.

I succeeded in my exams but a twist of fate made my principal remove me from a class to purposely make me fail, I didn't know at the time but a student put some menacing texts all over her texts and she been suspecting me the whole time since I was the black sheep. It made me fail my diploma and I never wanted to step foot in a school again after this.

Covid came and it tested me a whole lot, I was having great time with my mother that I cherished to this day. I was talking to this girl named Sarah online during my last semester, she lived close to my previous hometown. We played video games together it was very nice but she only saw me as a friend. Me missing my exam in a way kinda grew us apart since she had a background that put so much importance in those things. We still friends to this day though.

Since it was my last months in the country before I'd move back I talked to 2 girls that been wanting to get to know me. One of them was Olivia, she'd often come to my parties and I could tell she was interested. During confinement we had s once and I realized she had a boyfriend after hand.

The second girl became my girlfriend for 2 years her name is Manzi. I needed a lot of affection at the time and Manzi was exactly the same, she could be a bit unhinged at times to other people I wouldn't interact with but everything felt good. I loved her so much it felt endless, I she had a good relationship with my mother and so I did with her mother and brothers I thought she was the one. I'd come every time she had a break from school. Her father though was an emotionally distant jerk, and I believe the neglect she felt with him turned her into an undiagnosed borderline person. Her mother's inaction between their bond wouldn't help. I think I had too much empathy but it became hard on my end.

When I came back in my previous hometown I had changed so much that I couldn't become friends again with the people I used to see. I became best friend with a person a bit too emotionally distant with his emotions but he is an overall great friend. I got into the habit of smoking weed it got bad, I was working and paying my rent just waiting for when I'd see her. We would FaceTime on and on, talk on the phone on and on, I had little time for friends. She wanted my whole attention and I gave as much as I could to my own detriment, I had dreams I wanted to work into fashion but I was spending all my time on her since she filled that hole in me. After the first year and a half pride took me and she posted herself with a dude she told me before hand who wanted to have s with her it made me so mad I blocked her out the blue. She definitely wanted attention when I wasn't giving her enough, it drove me crazy and she contacted me again only 3 months after. During those 3 months I'd miss her but not so much, I think it was childish of me but it felt right for how I typically was with her. I modeled a bit during that time and made a small progress towards what I enjoyed, it felt fresh on the last month. Then we got back together pretty much instantly but she wouldn't communicate her problems from here, it would be the start of the end in the peak. Every time I'd see some friends or do something else she'd get mad, She blocked me for going out late when I told her I would.

So many things would happen but we still had great times especially when I'd come physically to see her it's like nothing bad ever happened. I told her I had to go back home on valentines day because the tickets were cheaper but we would still be able to meet a month and a half later beginning of April. We spent good times together but then she felt neglect from me again during those times, there was a deadline for art school that took a tall on me and I ended up not making it out of cheer fear of getting unaccepted. All of march I was feeling ashamed and decided to smoke until I couldn't feel. I would avoid some of her calls sometimes or not have the camera because I didn't want her to see me like this. End of march arrives, I didn't faceted her at all, we'd call for hours. We can't wait to see each other. Once I arrive on the first of April I feel something odd and she avoids me, she cancel our plans to go to a party with her friends and I told her that it's not cool because we planned this for months, she argues that I'm guilt tripping her but I'd find out later that the guilt came from something else.

We see each other on the third and make out like we haven't seen each other for years, and then she admits she has a bf. I discover her dark side the next two days as we have s in the shower then in my bad but she wouldn't let me penetrate without telling me so before, during or after hand. She'd just act like nothing happened, and I was so influenced that I wouldn't say a thing. She invites me to her crib afterwards and I see her family for a bit, I gave her all the gifts I planned for her. Then when I ask for explanations she avoids me and blocks me, I didn't see at the time she blocked me I told her I'm coming to talk to her and waited at her window for hours with my phone with no power. I regret not intruding the house to talk to her.

She left me in the dark until June. Where I blackmailed her for some explaining, I regret having done this but I told her friend to tell her to talk to me if she doesn't want me to send her nudes to her father (I never had her dad's contact) we talked but there weren't enough explaining, she just felt the lack of presence, she just felt attracted to the guy, and I Expected more. I wondered if she ever loved me. Afterwards she blamed me for how her relationship is not being good and she cursed me a lot I wanted to end my life I accumulated bodycounts a lot and stopped caring for a while until I found a new relationship for 8 months, her name is Farah she had her own issues with males and s, it was tough to understand the objectivity of everything, she was a lot colder even though we had good times but somewhere in the relationship I had an introspective mushroom trip and decided on stopping smoking entirely. It destroyed our bond and then our relationship but it didn't hurt me this time.

535

The absurd wouldn't affect me anymore. I found self love again, I'd lose it and find it back, but ever since then I've been happier. I made better friends and accepted people for how they are and worked on my boundaries. At times I'm neglecting myself, but I discovered it's a state of mind and I shouldn't stay in it. Thanks to that I could explain all the happened more objectively and found my worth in there. I understood that many of my previous relationships we people who didn't really love themselves.

I discovered that my mother had father issues like many of those girls and how many of the things happening to me were rooted to the neglect I accepted to myself. I decided from that point on to aim more towards abundance. Towards returning people instead of feeling like I'm losing them, listening to the ego instead of repressing it and better manage it. But never being in a deprived mindset, or not to stay in it too long I'm practicing everyday but I'm definitely proud. Of my path and now I'm definitely more comfortable alone and with everything happening to me. If you take time to respond or don't include anything it's absolutely no problem ! It felt good to have this retrospective, I was kinda scared it would put me in a bad mindset but I felt confident and even more now that I went through it all again ♡

-@yungmiquella

Fallen Love

So it all began when we first met on TikTok, we started talking trough Snapchat, it started off with chatting everyday while having fun talking to each other, i had no idea how much we would love each other, I asked her out since she actually lived 30 minutes away from me. We decided to start dating and went out on fun dates and stuff, as time went on she started getting very distant, i kept on asking her "what's wrong what's wrong" yet she still didn't answer my questions, then one day she answered my questions, she said that her mental health kept getting worse and worse and that she needed time for herself, she said we will go out a week later, so when we went out she seemed fine but deep down i saw the message saying that her mental health was getting worse, i asked her what was wrong and to tell me everything that has been going on, she refused to tell me and we went on with our date, forward a couple week's further, i tried reaching her but i found myself looking at the call. Call forwarded screen, her mom actually called me a few weeks later saying she killed herself. It actually turns out she has been making suicide letters, her mom said she had made one for me, i came

537

over as fast as i possibly could, on arrival she handed me the note and asked me to sit down and read it to her, my name was on the letter and i began tearing up immediately, as I read it out loud it said "i promise it wasn't your fault it was mine, I should've told you before it came to this, i love you so so much and I hope we can be lovers in another lifetime" i bawled my eyes out and couldn't sleep for weeks, this happens 2 years ago. Really shows what mental health can do to a person. I still love her so much and haven't moved on. It's been 2 years and I still haven't found someone as loveable as her..

-xerv

Don't fall in love with your best friend

I'm 17 and I had this girl who I started getting close with in a time period of about 6 months. I had known her since we were 14 but we had stopped being friends for a while and just started to get close again. At the time she had a long time boyfriend that she had been dating for 11 months who I was also friends with bc we played soccer together. But they eventually broke up and ended on bad terms. He went to his parents country on a vacation and fucked another girl there, only his 2nd body after his ex-girlfriend.

This made her mad and she started calling him a hoe and they went back and forth for about a month and just said horrible things about each other. Throughout all this my girl friend was devastated as she was in love with him and I was there to support her through all of that and I saw how much pain she was in. Throughout this time we grew to be best friends and became super close. Eventually after about a month of her and her. Ex shit talking each other we started to develop feelings for each other.

This was the first time I really felt something for another person and what I would say is my first experience with love towards another person who isn't my family. We started talking and we were each others valentines and she was my first kiss. When everything was going good one week she started acting a little bit different and by the end of the week she told me she wanted to stop talking. She said it was because I don't believe in god and she is really religious. I was like ok and I wasn't too upset because I figured I would probably have a chance later and I would maybe try to become more religious.

Then not even a week after her and her ex went home together after school. And to this day she still won't tell me all of what happened but I know stuff happened because she told me later on some of it. I was upset by this because he had treated her so bad and we had just stopped talking. She told me she wouldn't let him try anything after the things he did and she would never get back with him. Despite this she got closer and closer to him over time. Me and her still stayed best friends and talked all the time but I could see it happening right in front of me. She went from saying she would never get back with him to saying she would get back with him maybe if he changed to she would get back with him if he changed etc. this led to arguments between us as I felt she was just playing with me and my feelings and she would always deny that she played with me and wasn't getting back with her ex.

Eventually they did start talking again and he eventually asked her out to be his gf. I felt like this took a piece out of me as I had watched it all unfold in front of my eyes. I had already been having a rough time because of stress from school and being sad that we had stopped talking. But seeing her go back to him just tore my heart out and was my first actual heartbreak. There are many many things that I haven't said because it's simply too long but this experience seriously changed me and my mindset about love and relationships. It's gotten to the point with the girl that we barely talk anymore even though her and her ex broke up again. Even though I didn't want her to go back to him in the first place, I didn't feel happy at all when I heard they had broken up, I just felt numb tbh. But I learned how hard love can be but also how good it can be at the same time.

Broken Trust

So in the beginning of 2022 I had met this boy that I fell in love with we talked for about 5 months and on my birthday December 2 he officially asked me out we dated for a while I was super In love with him I would always talk about him to my friends they were super annoyed about it but anyways we would always talk on the phone 24/7 we started drifting apart from each other in January we started going on and off with each other I ended up breaking up with him because I could deal with him anymore, a couple of months had passed by and I started missing him each day regretting breaking up with him I couldn't focus in school I had lost my friends because of my depression I had gotten into because of the break up. In June 1st of this year he had texted me talking about if we could restart I obviously said yes not knowing he was going to play me after all that happened we stopped talking and I had lost all of the love in me thinking I wasn't going to be able to find love anymore.

-@nanda_2oh9

Uncharted Love

So after my last relationship ended very toxic and hurt me deeply. I wanted to move from the state i was in and get away from everything. I was already going to move but i felt as i needed a new beginning and i figured it was the perfect opportunity so i did move. At the new job i was working at this girl caught my eye and we caught each other's eyes on each other. Couldn't tell if she liked me but she did indeed like me. We started hanging out after work , going on dates but one of us isn't ready for a relationship and the other is ready. I like her a lot and she's so beautiful in my eyes but as of now the time isn't right for us. she gives me a feeling i haven't felt for years and a calm/safe feeling when we are together . she doesn't have any red flags and is very caring. This was all i wanted...a new start and someone to make that start with me. As she has her doubts of getting into a relationship right now; We'll see what the future holds for us.

The art of disappointment

ometimes we mess up. And I'm not talking about
some silly little mistake that comes with an "oops."
Im talking about the kind of mistakes that make
your own heart hurt. The kind of mistakes that make you
punch yourself in the head saying "Why would I do that"
"Why DID I do that." These things aren't "mistakes".
"mistakes" don't hurt people you care about. "Mistakes"
don't disappoint people. Actions do. Learn from your
actions. Don't repeat the cycle. There is always a better
way. There will always be a plan B. There will always
be hope that you can do better. Disappointment creates
opportunity for change. Be the change you wanna see in
yourself.

-Cristian

Self Love Is Valuable

—◆◆●◆◆—

Well, the girl I was in love with was a great person. Our love was unlike anything I had ever experienced in my life—so genuine and real. After some time, roughly a year, we started to grow apart. I think it was mostly my fault. I began to change as a person as the relationship progressed because I feared losing her. In reality, she was there and wasn't going anywhere, but I was too blinded by the future and not living in the present. I was also too scared of our past, which I couldn't change for the betterment of us. As a result, we ended up breaking up after a year and three months. I was so frustrated that I wanted some sort of revenge. However, that wasn't the answer, and it would have just made things worse for me. Taking the wrong advice, I messed a lot up, but eventually, things got better. After a while, I learned to love myself and found god. I'm still learning to move on from her three to four months later. Loving someone and then having it crumble taught me that I can't love someone if I don't love myself, and that takes time. Now, looking back, I'm lucky to have been loved by such a great girl and to have shared the experiences we did. I wouldn't change a thing about it. She truly deserves a lot and the best love, but so do I and everyone else.

-Duran Hardin

A love beyond words

Well so at the time i wasn't looking for love and i always believed in it and searched for it but i was just doin me right working and staying in my own lane and one day i met her online thru insta and as we were talking we both bonded really well and i instantly knew that we both were matching energies and deadass i loved her w everything i never saw her or loved her in a lust way and i deadass thought i found everything i searched for cause its all i ever asked for she was telling me bout how we gonna have 3 kids in the future and we gonna get married and it was like only us understood each other i tried talking to ppl around me but when i would talk to her its like she immediately knew what was wrong like we both were spiritually connected we were basically meant to be we worked on our goals together and everything was going right there were times i even cried like how i would feel or be if i ever lost her and i was so afraid of losing her cuz i know in times like now its hard to find. you know and we would eat together be together all the time and she had told me i brought her spark back so as time went on she started getting comfortable and i would be left on seen or there were even times when she left and i cried i started overthinking i felt not wanted and she would tell me that everything's okay and i listened i felt so dumb but its the only way that made me feel good i craved for it and so one day she told me that everything doesn't last forever and that was the hard truth i told her we can last if we both fight for it and we communicate and she said it doesn't work that way and so one day i woke up and we were texting and out of nowhere she stop texting and i looked everywhere and i was blocked i lost everything i cried and felt no motivation to nothing i used everything she said as motivation and thats how i created 3 masterpieces become your best self and know whats right and wrong .

-@lilchasinmusic

How I Lost The Loml

When I was at the gym training for volleyball this guy kept looking at me everywhere I went he looked or I everywhere he went I looked but I didn't think anything of it when I was walking to the locker room we locked eyes and it felt like we knew everything about each other and saw the future when I was leaving the gym so was he he looked at me and held the door open I ran to the door and thanked him he was so shy but he felt brave enough to ask for my number I definitely said yes we texted everyday and every night we felt a connection we went everywhere together through thick and thin I knew he was the one even after hard argument but we would run back to each other and say we are sorry before I met him I was going through a lot of heart breaks but when I met him he fixed something that he didn't break he always took time out of his day or night to text me and check up on me he came to all of my games and I came to his it felt like unexpected love but when my ex figured out he ruined "Everything I tried to get a hold of him but I could never I felt so sad and hurt I thought I could never be loved but he texted me one day to talk we fixed everything and we take things slow again and now when where together we look back at the day my ex tried to ruin everything to get back at me but it never worked bc we knew it was true unexpected love"

-@sy.dsyd924

Changed Over Night

This story is about a love i lost , it effected me in every way. I was 12 when i met him. He was my best friends brother, he could not keep his eyes off of me. I was young but i was not in love , he was. I loved him to late. Years went.. I always hanged out with him and his family , they always invited me every where. At 14 i lost contact with him and i did not speak to him for 2 years. He changed , he was way more different. I was now 16 , and i did not like this him now because i know it was a front. It was just a play, this isn't him. He had went through so many girls , i did not understand because i was the first girl he ever liked and dated. How could he forget me like that? We came in contact in November 23.. i knew it wasn't good for me. He said how he missed me , and everything that happens he wish it happened differently. I trusted him. Then i trusted him with my body. I excepted him to be for real and in love with me back , i told him he was my first ever and he promised never to take advantage of that. He asked me to be his girlfriend. I was happier then ever. But the whole relationship felt unreal. I felt so empty. I did not eat. I could not sleep.My family noticed something was wrong with me. A month went by and it was almost Christmas. It did not feel like Christmas. I told him that. I noticed a girl in his following.. i clicked on her and she was posting all about him. I cried , and cried and confronted. He told me i was being dramatic and let's move past it and he would block her. Well i did move past it but it changed me in every way . It affected me in every way. Why was i not enough for him. It turned out he was seeing this girl through out are whole relationship .. i begged him to change , and to forget about her i thought. He said he needed time. In January he ended up blocking me and getting back with his ex. I was at my worst. I took time healing . There was not a time i didn't think about him. I had so many talking stages , but all i could think about is him. Months have went by , it is now July 24 and he comes forward and appears at the party i was at. He tried so hard to get my attention. That same night he texted me and he told me. " Would u want to get back with me". I felt so heavy. Although i thought about it , i knew it wasn't good for me , i did entertain him though. I did went to his house a few times. After those times i felt so safe, but it did not feel the same. This was not good for me , i had to get past it. I realized he's not the one i needed. He made me cry he made me want to die. I am 17 years old and today I'm healing from a relationship that traumatized me. I never thought i could be treated like this or be put through a situation like this. There's so many parts i left out. He changed and affected me in so many ways , i will never beg someone to change again.

-@marymariahhh

Challenged Love

O ne day i went out with my friends we were just chilling and then there was this fine girl passing by one of my friends said "i bet you cant bag her" So of course i took the challenge i guess u can call it that and went ahead and talked to her after a bit we were done talking and we shared socials. So we started talking more and more and started feeling/liking each other so after a few weeks me and her went on our first date it all went well until one friend passed by and wanted to stick with me since all his friends where gone.

I was in the middle of a date so i said "i don't know man" he said i wont bother you 2 I said nothing after that i was just like okay i guess then me and the girl where gonna hold hands and get more intimate and he (my friend) kept interrupting the intimacy so i told the girl i had to go because i was feeling weird she said "its okay i have to go soon as well don't worry." I took the bus once i saw she got in her moms car she texted "get home safe" i never got such a text it gave me a warm hearted feeling. I never even dated someone so it all was a first for me.

We continued talking but then she started being dry

553

started short answering and it hurt me a lot i kept beating myself over "did i do something wrong" i said "its probably my friend" in my mind and then we didn't talk anymore it hurt so much because i actually liked her at first it was all games but i started to know her better and feel how she would feel in certain situations and i stopped contact with every other female. And then i started doing bad i stopped eating lost a lot of weight and even damaging myself (self harm) i loved her so much i had to block her for my own good i kept seeing her stories and posts so i blocked her then somewhere in that time period i made a second account for my music (this account) and she followed me after 7 months of no contact so i was like why did she follow me after all this time?

So i tried figuring out not knowing what i would get into again. She got diagnosed with anorexia anxiety disorder she had to take anti depressive medication and she was doing bad stuff. But even iff she had all that i loved her still i always have a soft spot for her her name still hurts till this day she was my first love after all We started talking again And starting to like each other again then we went on a second date everything was going well but i had this feeling i had to cry and she told me "you look sad want to go apart from here so u can cry I'm here for u" so we did we went some-where else and i cried she did to because we were both still damaged from what happened and the things that came with it.

We went back heading hands and looking each other in the eyes. I still remember the look on her face the feeling her eyes gave off just how happy we where that we tried again even after all this shit we have been through. But then again shit went sideways and i was left again it hurt even more it hurt so much i wanted to take my life. I tried to. But i am so happy I'm alive. And i have to thank you for that Kd your videos saved me your advice and words your kind calming voice saved me. Your i love you at the end of the video made me feel loved even iff i don't know you at all it made me feel worth it to keep fighting for me and what i want. So yeah thank you ALOT. I learned a lot from you about love and things that come with it.

-Isa

An Open Door To A New World of Hope

———————— ◆◆◆◆ ————————

So I was 16 at the time- but I had just met this girl at drivers Ed , and I didn't know anyone at this school , and this girl I saw (shall remain nameless) she saw me sitting at a table alone all nervous and anxious and she says " hey you can come over here and sit with us if you want " and I smiled I wasn't expecting anyone to call me over , anyways we talked and I ended up catching feelings for her and she did as well , it was love at first sight , after the first year or two things started getting more complicated and we had broken up- been some of the hardest times in my life , but we had been on and off for the next 2 years after that , she ended up getting engaged to another guy and she was over me and wanted nothing to do with me, we're both adults now and we don't talk anymore and it's only been almost 2 years no contact , we both messed up but we were also not meant to be- it was a life lesson and it changed me for the better.

-Jf

How I Formed My Definition of Love

——— ❖❖❖ ———

L ast year summer 2023 I met my first love. He was an amazing boyfriend and it a totally new experience for me. He was special because I've always wanted to know what loving someone genuinely felt like. He made me feel seen, valued, and he was my home. Unfortunately, I didn't know how to love myself unconditionally and soon after traumatic events in my personal life I became extremely codependent on him for my happiness. Later I found out that I was anxiously attached and he was avoidant attached to me.

I made my whole life about our relationship and when you are that codependent you become sensitive to every little slight change in your partner's behavior. We ended up constantly breaking up and getting back with each other. But at the very end I ended up cutting ties because he became too toxic for me. He "didn't" know what he wanted, abused drugs, and our relationship became too lustful. Even though I knew we weren't compatible that's when I finally knew that I loved him... unconditionally. I now know what loving someone and

557

to be loved feels like. My definition of love was created by not having love reciprocated.

1. Love is Loyal. If hurting me doesn't hurt you then you don't love me, because I would never think of doing that to you.

2. You never stop wanting to make them happy. I shouldn't ask you to do things for me because I would do anything to put a smile on your face. I should never be put in the position to ask for the bare minimum.

3. Love is unconditional. I love you for not what u do for me or how u make me feel. I love you for who you are as an individual and your characteristics.

4. I accept you for who you are. I love you for who you are and not the version my mind wants you to be. I've seen every version of you and I chose to stay.

I knew I loved him because I was able to forgive him for all the shitty things he's done. Once I had God in my life it changed my heart. I am able to forgive others and let go. After my first love, I've been in 2 other relationships. The guy right after him was the first time I've ever felt like I received unconditional love from another. I appreciate him so much and I will never forget that. What i realized after my first love is that I have to love without being so attached. I have to accept the fact that there isn't forever and be confident that don't need anyone to be happy because I am full of love. That realization alone can be depressing because loving isn't exciting anymore because you're seeing them for who they are. But it's also the best decision you can make for both people. I believe that abundance and gratitude is the key to happiness. It is only the ppl with a full cup who can pour into others. And when your cup is empty you need to be that person for yourself and fill your own cup. At the end of the day it's up to ourselves to be happy, no one else is responsible. The most latest guy I was with was proof to me that healthy, mature, secure attachment and, long distance is truly possible. This man was truly a gift from God. God really rewarded me through all my seasons of isolation. He made and still makes me feel like a diamond even though we're not together anymore. We broke up recently because I noticed that anxious attachment was still lingering in me. I plan to meet him again if possible, but I will trust that God has a plan for me even if it will not be him. At the end of the day it's all up to God who gets to be in my life. What's meant for me will find me and stay.

-Katie Park

Goodbye

---◆◆◆◆◆---

My love story started a long time ago take me back to 2015 when I was 14 years old. I didn't know what love really meant because no one showed me until a woman came into my life name Lily. She was the most amazing person I have ever met in my life she was always a bundle of joy. Every time we would go on a date I would see her eyes sparkle and laugh. We would go on & on. Eventually things would take a turn. She would eventually move out of state. And eventually she lost her battle with cancer. but every time I see a butterfly I remind myself that We all have those moments in life where we feel lost then someone comes into your life and changes it all around I hope you enjoyed this chapter of A young boy named Brandon that once loved Lily. She was the spark in my life. I will forever love you & miss you.

-Brandon

The Love That Never Was

— ◆◆◆◆◆ —

So there was this guy and me and him were not really that close until recently, so when we started getting close I liked him but none really knew but my best friend. So then my other friend told me she liked him and asked for me to ask him if he would date her and he said "no because he needed to focus on school and stuff" sooo basically I told her what he said and she said " ohhh well I didn't like Him like that anyway " soooo when me and him started getting close I asked my friend if she was ok with us being close and she said that she didn't like Him and it was ok. But then all of a sudden she started not talking to me and distancing herself from me and then I realized that I really did love this boy because I was willing to give up my whole friendship for him. Sooo me and him started getting even closerrr and then his cousin texted ,e and was basically like " you should of thought about *my friend* happiness before yours " and when I got that it really hurt me It hurt me because my whole life I have put other people before me and I just got hurt in the end. Sooo I got overwhelmed by everything and decided it would be best if me and the boy just stayed friends. So I was really hurt because than that same friend that said she didn't like Him started liking him! Sooo I was hurt and got really sad because I had to hear her say that they were on the phone and what not when I still loved him! Sooo yea I felt like a bad person towards him and myself and I just became really insecure because my friend was really pretty and he really did start liking her sooooo yea now they don't talk as much, me and th3 boy don't talk at all, and me and the girl dont talk much. Andddddd I still love him buttttt I'm getting through it.

The lesson of love

I fell in love with this woman name S'ymone and she has a child of her own and I helped her take care of her child. I love her daughter like she was mine and I love S'ymone like she was my wife. She give me the feeling of warmth and passion. She made me feel like I was a great person to her but she still wanted more than I can give her so she started acting weird, very distance and careless of my feelings so she started texting other people and using them for the same reason she used me for. She use us for money, A place to live , A babysitter which I was most of the time. I felt hurt, angry, sad, confused and when I started to notice she would use reverse psychology and say everything is my fault so I became vengeful and got revenge and she became hypocritical fast but it got me nowhere but arguments and she just kept doing what she was doing and just got up and left me for a transgender woman to man but I still love her and her daughter from a distance and I still believe in love and always will. I've learned that love is hard, challenging, deep, upliftings. Love brings out the authentic you the strongest of yourself.

563

Now I understand and appreciate what she did and didn't do. Now I finally a have peace.

-@ jeremiah.garciadios

I Don't Love You Anymore

ecember 2022. was when i got a text from a person i never talked to and never thought he would text me. He was the boy my friends talked about. I didn't think much of it because he just texted me if i can help him get with one of my friends. We talked a little bit and then ended the conversation.

In summer 2023 after not talking i got a text from him. We started talking and really connected. We both had the same interest and talk about anything and everything. We were friends for a while but then i told him i liked him. He said he felt the same and we started talking even more. I thought that we could really be something but then he started showing his real side. He started being dry all the time and never started a conversation. I ignored all these signs and tried to fix him. There was one time when we had a long period of time when he didn't talk to me and blocked me for no reason. I always found a way to text him and asked for forgiveness even tho i didn't do nothing. He came back every time this happened.

But in 2023 December i got really drunk with my

friends and i started drunk texting him. He didn't like it and ended the conversation by telling me he lost feelings. He blocked me almost everywhere except TikTok. I cried for months and couldn't talk to anyone. He was the only person i could think of 24/7. I thought that i could never find anyone like him. I tried talking to other people but it wasn't the same. 2024 February was when one of my friends told me he has a girlfriend. I was devastated because i thought that i was getting over him but i clearly wasn't. I always stalked his reposts hoping he reposted something about me. After months of thinking less and less of him and not stalking his reposts i feel much better and happier. But not to long ago i looked at his reposts for the last time and saw that he's not doing well. From his repost i saw that he started taking drugs and not focusing on his health.

As a friend i wanted to text him on TikTok because i was still blocked on instagram. I texted him that if he needs anyone to talk to he can still talk to me. I specifically told him that I'm over him and that i don't want to start anything again. He replied almost immediately and replied with a dry text. After that i said to myself i wont text him anymore. I realized that just because i am in love doesn't mean that he is going to be the love of my life and that i still have a whole life ahead of me that i need to live.

What Is Important To You

⬤

There are many ways to be important, but in my perspective to be important is to be life-changing. Recently, around winter last year, I met my loving boyfriend. The majority of people I know or come across have always loved the idea of "high school sweethearts", I mean who could blame them? Being able to last throughout high school including all the ups and downs of maturing and growing up is what people dream of achieving with their significant other. As time passes, growing up into new people can be a breaking point for many. People change and that's perfectly fine. He and I have had many arguments even when we weren't officially dating, being able to sort out our differences and still enjoy each other is key to fixing the arguments. Always try to understand your partner instead of constantly getting angry at them for having different opinions; their opinion matters, and being in a relationship takes teamwork. He has changed me as a person, he's opened up many opportunities I've never had before. During my sophomore and junior years, I was on a rocky path dealing with the concept of love and boys. I knew what I wanted, but I never got what I deserved. He has given me what I truly deserve and I'm so thankful for him. He brings joy into my life. Every chance I get to see him, it always lightens up my day no matter how down I am. Even though we've been dating for a while, he still manages to give me butterflies. I'm glad I get to feel loving him over and over just like it was the very first time I felt love for him. People lose interest in their partner because they "move fast" or just date for fun. I don't understand why people do that, but I can never relate. I love many people, from my family to my friends, and obviously to my boyfriend. Unconditional love will always pour out from me, I love the concept of love; I love, love. I wish that no one loses what's most important to them whether it's a thing, a place, or a person. I hope I never lose anything important to me, especially my person. He is my person.

-MSM

Difficult Love

S o me and this one girl just broke up today and i
don't really know how i should feel to be honest
yes i'm hurt by it but i'm kind of happy she left
because she would leave me on delivered all day and we
would start texting at most 5 times a day i felt so sad that
the only person i had a genuine connect with didn't want
me anymore even though she was giving me signs all
throughout our relationship such as talking to her exes
even when she told me she would stop, she made me and
her go on a break to try and fix things with another ex,
and she stopped being sweet to be but i never wanted to
let her go because i really loved her and i have bad
attachment issues because i never really felt loved as a
kid but she made me feel different and she would even
send heart eye emojis to guys on ig but i never thought
anything of it because she would always reassure me so i
just forgot about it so yes i'm sad and really miss her but
i'm kind of happy i don't have to be stressed out and
overthink every second of the day what should i do i feel
like i want to just accept the fact i'm not the only one.
but i feel like she is going to change. She would say all
these sweet things only when i was upset and i just miss

her so much. even though i know i deserve better. she made my life so much better but she made my mental health terrible. also we were long distance so that made it worse.

Not So Happily Ever After

t all started around early September of the year 2023.i had joined this running club and met new people.I got close to this one guy in particular.I was going through a hard time that year and having someone there who understood me was to good to be true.We got closer over time and where best friends for a good while.Our friendship was the kind you see in tv shows.You know like the Nickelodeon victorious show cat and beck.yup it was just like that.He always made sure I felt ok he always made sure nothing was bothering and he told me he felt the need to protect me.Over time I fell for him.I fell harder then ever to the point where I felt like it destroyed me.

February 12 2024 was the last time I went on a run with him.we went to our usual place and after running 5 miles we decided to chill and hang out.we sat on the track grass while he put some corridos on his phone.we danced and he carried me just like in the movies spun around in circles and looked me straight in the eye. He told me while looking at me straight in the eye saying"thankyou for sticking around and being the best version of you, you've come a long way."He let me down and looked me straight in the eye and seemed like he was about to kiss me but he got nervous.He didn't kiss me and before we both went home he told me he could have the baddest girl out there but wouldn't date her because he was simply 'NOT READY'…it hurt because if he wasn't ready why did he lead me on and acted like he wanted something more than "just friends" February 14 2024 I was in the school hallways I seen him have a valentines basket I didn't think much of it because he didn't talk to me on the 13. Someone comes up to me and says "he brought something for you!" I was confused and ask what flowers did he buy since the person that told me said that there where flowers. She said they were roses I knew right then and there that, that basket wasn't for me since he knows I love sunflowers and has gotten me them be4. Moral of the story he lead me on and we still talk and he thinks I'm over him but truth is I'm not.

He talk about new girls and talks about how he talking to new people.He recently mentioned this girl he met and he sent me a picture of her and she was in Lingerie. I was speechless and couldn't say nothing but "Ouuu she's badd" it hurt so much and I'm slowly getting over it after 10 months there where nights I couldn't sleep because of all the questions I asked myself.it hurt me even more that I was going through sleepless nights while he was peacefully sleeping.to make things even worse he told me he still has the hand written letters I wrote him . I wonder why does he have them if he never liked me in the first place then why does he have them?

Unrequited Love

My name is ashleigh. there was this guy named kamaye, we met in 6th grade. we never talked but he ended up leaving the school later that year. we didn't talk still for years. and then randomly i decided to follow him on instagram. we talked and i actually ended up ghosting him for a while. weeks later, he texted me an iMessage game because he wanted an excuse to talk to me. we then started talking and on February 27th, 2024 we started dating. we were in love like no other. we shared a bond that we had never seen in our lives before. we played Minecraft, cooked, baked, painted, ate food, talked, and so much more. he was so important to me. a little later in our relationship, he started struggling with self hatred. i made sure i did everything i could for him but it was too late. he let his self hatred drown him and he became a different person. finally, on July 18th, he broke up with me. he told me that he can't handle a relationship and he didn't want to bring me down with his struggles. i understood and agreed. a day or two later, i decided to tell him how i didn't like that he changed and told him about himself. he got angry and cut off contact with me. he is very angry to this day. ever since then i've been praying that he cools down and takes into consideration of what i told him. we shared such a special bond and i will forever love and care for him. he will always be a part of me that will never leave. i pray to God every day that he will find himself and his faith. i love kamaye with all of my heart. i pray that one day he will return back to me.

-Ashleigh

Only For a Brief Moment

t all started one day I was working at a local gas station.A couple months into working here, this vendor that would come in he got my attention and I got his. I remember on valentine's Day 2024 he would complement me particularly on this day. I hadn't notice before, but I was attracted to him.One day unexpected he asked out for coffee. I accepted if only I knew then what would be the end of this I would have never accepted that coffee that day. To me it was like an instant connection. Someone could say a love at first sight. As the next few weeks passed by we kept on going on dates. In my mind, I honestly did think he did like me for me. But I was wrong so so wrong. Then suddenly I quit due to personal things going on at my job there. I remember thinking about him that day that I quit. I didn't even think about myself. I felt sad, disappointed in myself, disappointed in the people around me.

7 Months

this girl was my everything she showed me a side of me I thought I never would see again she brought out the real me she put a smile on my face literally everyday. I really did love her she was one of the few people I had that would actually listen to me when I talked about my day or how I felt or if I needed something/Someone to talk to but she cheated after almost a year in the relationship she was an angel on the outside but a devil in the inside she's now the reason I don't want to fall in love anymore she ruined me all that money and time wasted it's been a few months now (7 months) sense it happened I got closer to god I've been going out a lot more then I used too I really just started enjoying life when I got over it... (wasn't a lot cuz I didn't rlly want to relive/ remember it even think ab her)

Butterflies

My first day in kindergarten i came in the middle of the school year, and i got bullied by the other kids except one boy, his name was Adan, Adan had brown hair and gorgeous green eyes..when everyone would be playing at the playground id be sitting by myself behind a big tree, i sat there everyday twisting grass around my finger, there would be times Adan would come and sit next to me and had play with me, I had a crush on him..but then in 3rd grade i realized he treats everyone the same so I'm no different.in the end of 3rd grade i moved to another school..and in 8th grade, there was a transfer student.

every girl was falling for him, i was shy and always sitting alone but when i saw him i felt drawn to him, like if i knew him...he looked..familiar, we had pe together and we wore shorts and a t-shirt my shorts shrunk over the years so they fit me tight and shorter then they were supposed to, during pe our teacher mr.Fernandez introduced him..and it was Adan, the same Adan from kinder through 3rd grade. When i first heard his name my ears perked up and i look at him my eyes locked into his as the sun hit his green hazel eyes and we locked eyes for a second, my face heated up so i looked away.then Sunday comes around, me and Adan saw each other a few times he smiled at me a few times and so did i.but in the end i knew i wasn't different to him just another boring girl, but Sunday, i was at church before church starts theres food in the lobby and little chats with pastors and stuff.i was wearing my hair down a long tight white dress and black heels, i looked pretty that day, i was getting food at the table and i reached for a cookie and another hand touched mine, it was Adan. coincidence maybe?he smiled and waved, thankfully i wore makeup because my face heated up so much."sorry, oh your um "nat"right?we have pe together and english."Adan said to me, it took me a moment to respond"oh yea your Adan wow you go to this church?"i responded, we chatted a bit before we went inside as church started.

I sat infront of him the whole time i couldn't stop thinking of him, how he looked into my eyes..the way his eyes drifted to my lips once or twice, i felt a tension?i thought nah theres no way..I'm the only one who feels that way, i tried to ignore it and payed attention to the pastor, i felt a tap on my shoulder it was Adan again my heart dropped,"i like your dress, you look familiar now that i think of it."he whispered,"thank you and um yea i think its because we used to go to school together kindergarten to 3rd grade."i responded, his smile grew"i think i remember you, you'd get bullied and wed talk about tv shows behind a tree and play with bugs and grass"i was so happy to hear that he even remembered me.anyway..he asked for my ig i gave it to him of course the whole time i had butterflies.

Unrequited Love

⬥◦⬥

It was the first time I thought I had experienced love by someone but it was all just a one sided facade. It started my Freshman high school year, with a guy who was freshly out of high school, which should've already been a red flag. He was the son of my mother's friend. At first he was nice, and it seemed like he really liked me. I had spent almost two years with this person thinking that he was a good and trustful person, but I was oblivious to the fact that he was lying to me about talking to other people. I was hurt, and I blamed myself for not trusting my gut but I didn't really know how to express that to other people given the circumstances, I felt like I wasted so much time that I could've spent focusing on my high school career. I lost a lot over the course of the two years I talked to him, from friends to good grades, I was falling behind. I had to make the eventual decision to cut him off, which I had been so scared to do because I was worried that it wouldn't just effect my relationship with him, but my mother's relationship with her friend as well. But it felt like a weight was lifted off of my shoulders, I felt like I was free from someone who lied and broke serious boundaries. He was my first everything, and I regret it so much, knowing that I was just being used, but that experience gave me an insight on the people who genuinely care about me and respect the decisions I make and support me through everything. I now realize that the only genuine love I need to worry about is the love that comes from my dearest friends and family.

Jenna

e had started off as my guy best friend then tried out how it would be for us if we were to date. It was absolutely amazing and lovely while it lasted, I wish I had communicated how I felt about things instead of breaking it off. We still continued to talk afterwards but I had always felt something for him inside but I always denied it because I felt like he wouldn't have wanted to try again. Him and I still were very close and he was always there for me if anything. After a breakup I got with this other guy, who I shouldn't have dated because I knew it wasn't going to go anywhere.

Things later on got complicated and he wasn't good for me. Then my guy best friend came in and told me how this guy isn't good for me and I deserve better. I ended up listening and the guy I was dating and I broke things off. I was very very close with my guy best friend and it came to the point where we. would do couple things but still denied it when people said we still had feelings for each other. I always denied it because I was worried he wouldn't agree. Then I realized, if he's doing the same things I am wouldn't he like me back? So, one of our friends said something along the lines of "What are you waiting for just date?!" I decided to say "I'm waiting for him to do something" then he said "Really?" I got nervous so I just shrugged and it was left as that. Afterwards   he texted me asking if I was messing around or not and I said I wasn't. He later on told me how he has been feeling and he said "I've been telling myself I love you as a friend but it's begun to be so much more than that". We have been together for a while now and most people were not shocked we got together and we got some people mad that we did. We still joke about how we found out our feelings because apparently I gave a lot of mixed signals. I love him with all my heart and I know he's the right one for me. He has always genuinely cared about me and has looked out for me. Without him, I don't know what I would do. I just hope he stays forever. He always give me the reassurance I need and always makes sure I'm doing what I'm supposed to be doing. I love that we have so many memories together. He always does the most for me and never lets me out do him. My love for him will never be able to be expressed in words and I can never give back how much he has done for me.

-@_jnnhrnndz.52

K

I met this boy during track right after getting out of a serious talking stage. After that talking stage I told myself I'm not going to get into a relationship anytime soon but he showed up when I least expected and it felt like love at first sight. We would talk everyday and we'd always hang out together. We were perfectly happy for the first couple of months until what you would call the "argument stage" that lasted a lot longer than it should've. Most of the arguments started from overthinking about friends, intimacy, and the other person feeling distant. Me personally, I kept comparing him to his old clingy self to his distant self. He eventually got tired of all the arguing and broke it off after a year and 10 months. I didn't take it well and kept on texting and trying to get him back but he moved on less than a week from when he broke it off.

I kept thinking "how long did he have these feelings for this other person?" When I found out about his relationship I finally stopped texting him. I stopped eating and cried every night and eventually started going to therapy. But I wanted to see him so I tried to run into him at school knowing his classes but doing that hurt me more. 3 weeks after our breakup he texted me telling me that he missed me but he likes the other person as well. A week later he told me they stopped talking mutually. We both still have feelings for each other so we texted and talked a bit in person but kept our distance since his friends don't like me. Things started to get intimate and we became friends w benefits. I overthank that thinking he's using me. But he reassured me and we're now talking again. He's still busy most of the time so we don't get time to each other. My overthinking was mainly about him not making time for me and hanging out with the opposite gender. But now I still overthink time to time but he reassures me about it and texted me when he can when he's out with family or friends. We've been talking for 2 months now and I feel like we

583

understand each other on a deeper level. The arguments don't happen anymore and we're both learning and fixing ourselves together. He's everything to me. Some people might say were toxic but all I have to say is if it's meant to be it will be so don't give up on love. It might come when you least expect it.

Bottled Up

Okay okay let me tell you and thank you for listening to my story every time I bottle up my emotions and never tell anyone but Anyways me and my dad use to have a bond a daughter and father bond I don't really remember much of it because of how my mom and dad would fight a lot and he would yell at me for a little thing or hit me with his belt and my big brother too that would effect my memory of when I was a little girl but I do cry sometimes and I wish I could stay in the past with my family and how I would be best friends with my dad and with my mom I loved him and I never said it to him not even now i regret not saying "I love you" to my dad something I don't regret saying it because as a child I never heard him say "I love you hija" as am his only daughter it would effect me now not gonna lie I remember two memories with my father one time is when I graduated kindergarten it was the only graduation he ever went too but I was happy with my certificate in my hands And I was smiling at him taking a photo next to his car and he brought me out to eat I was really happy that day and then the 2nd memory is when the day of my moms wedding it was when my mom had to dance with her tios and brothers and my dad had to dance with my tias and sister and when it was my turn he look at me and said "what?" Because he never thought I was gonna dance with him but I was and he laugh and smiled at me I smiled back at him and dance with him I was happy at that moment to but now it's not like that I was his special little girl once and now he looks at me like if he hates me with hatred and maybe anger it's because there were so many problems between me and him he would always argue about me and always had something to say ever since I hit puberty he would talk about me in a bad way in front of my tias and they would agree I was sad about it because he would always judge me and what I wear he would call me a slut and I am 14 years old he doesn't understand to love his children i know because he also never felt love when he was a kid but that doesn't mean he can treat his children like he was getting treated as a kid. I would cry because my parents wouldn't give me their love their were too busy arguing all the time I would hide with my big brother in his room but my mom was the only person who would put a smile on my face but my dad always tried his best but not really sometimes My dad was the first ever boy to break my heart because I never got the love I wanted or needed from him I wish I could go back in the past and enjoy the time and moments I had with him when I was a kid.

Platonic

t all started in 2023, my platonic love... One day I was coming back from a road trip when I got this friend request about a guy i knew back in my childhood, in that time I really liked him but never saw him again. We weren't really close but i was getting pretty close with his sister. Till this day we are good friends me and her. Well during the pandemic a friend invited me to a zoom meeting to paint

and there I saw him, thru the camera, I was excited to see him but I knew he wouldn't remember me. But back to the road trip day.. When I got the friend request i went to his profile to see who it was and bam it was him, I was freaking out cause I thought we would never talk again. (It was 5 years ago we talked and saw each other) I accepted him follow request and then I receive a message from him saying, "hey how are you? I don't know if you remember me but my mom follows you lol" I was like woah he texted me so fast o

But I told him that yea I did and if he also did, but to my surprise he said he didn't remember me much, I was like well makes sense but we started to talk and asking each other questions about our hobbies and music artist we like, there was a lot of things in common. Like for example we both like the same songs. He was really nice with talking with me, then i asked for his sister how she was doing and if she had insta or snap to text her. But he told me no, so I gave him my phone number to pass it to her and well then he asked polity if he could also save my number, and of course I said yes. We started to chat in insta, snap, and phone number. We had 3 different conversations haha, but we were having a blast talking with each other. We would also FaceTime and call each other once in a while and it was like talking with a person who I have known for years, it wasn't awkward or weird talking with him. I didn't like him anymore at that time, but I never told my parents who I texted, so then later on after a couple of months we had to stop talking to each other.

I was really sad because he was the only person who understood me and was a real friend for me than any other person I knew for years. I still talked to him for a while before we actually stopped talking..... :(well to make this story more understandable and short I had to stop talking to him and that broke me, I started to notice that I couldn't live without him, he was the only one getting me to be happy. It's almost going to be a year without talking to him or calling him and I noticed I loved him a lot and that I would do anything for him.

Even through we don't talk anymore, I know that by heart we are still connected and one day we will see each other again. We will have that connection still like we used to, and maybe even share the feeling we have towards each other one day. But I just know that I never

588

stopped liking him I just put that to aside because I just wanted to be friends. But a love towards someone you have never goes away. In fact it grows more stronger, to the people reading this I hope you guys learn from my story and don't wait to tell someone your feeling towards them, because you never know when you guys will stop talking or ever see each other again. I would've loved to tell him how I feel towards him and never let him go. If you ever read this, Getting to know you was the best thing that ever happened to me, you were my everything and I just want to say that I love you and I will always be your number one supporter in the world!! This is how my platonic love story was, a love that will always stay in my heart till the day I die.

-J

Me And You

n the realm of fate, where stars align, our love
story unfolded like a celestial rhyme. From
September's warmth to August's gentle breeze,
our hearts beat as one, through life's joys and pleas. Her
and I, two souls entwined, in a dance of first love, pure
and divine. A bond so strong, it transcended time and
space, a flame that flickered, yet never lost its grace.
Through trials and tribulations, we stood as one,
weathering storms, beneath the golden sun. Our love was
tested, like silver in the fire, yet we emerged, our hearts
still entire. In moments of darkness, when shadows
loomed near, our love shone bright, dispelling every fear.

We found our way, through amounts of pain, and in
each other's arms, our love remained. To the world, our
love may seem imperfect, a tapestry of tears and
heartache, yet to us, it's a masterpiece, a work of art, a
love that's been tempered, like steel in the heart. Our
love is a symphony of laughter and tears, a harmony of
whispers, and sweet, sweet fears. We've made love,
we've made memories, we've forged a soul tie, a bond

that will forever be.

Through every downfall, every argument, every test of will, our love remained, a constant, a beacon still. We've risen, like phoenixes, from the ashes of our past, our love reborn, forever to last. Today, as we stand, hand in hand, heart to heart, our love shines bright, a guiding light, a work of art. We are soulmates, two hearts, one beat, a love that's been, and forever will be, a love that's unique, a love that's ours, a love that's destiny. In this journey of love, we've found our way, through every moment, every breath, every day. Our love story, a tale of forever, a love that's been, and will forever be, the most beautiful, heart-touching moments, we'll always see. With every breath, our love grows anew, a garden of devotion, forever in bloom. In each other's eyes, our hearts find a home, a sanctuary of trust, where love is never unknown. Through life's lessons and flow, we've learned to sway, together, as one, in every step, every way. Our love has been the anchor, the guiding light, the safe haven, where we take flight. In the tapestry of time, our love will shine, a golden thread, forever divine.

We've woven a narrative, of laughter and tears, of moments that whisper, I'll always be here. Joshua and Valentina, two souls, now one, a love that's been tempered, like the morning sun. We've danced with shadows, and bathed in the light, our love, a celestial music, on this earthly night. Our love story, a testament to the heart, a symphony of moments, that will never depart. We've loved, we've lost, we've found our way, and in each other's arms, we'll face another day. In this journey of forever, we'll hold hands, through every sunrise, every starry night's stands. Our love, a flame, that burns bright and true, a guiding light, that shines, just me and you.

-Joshua Matthew Galli

My First Love Story

◄◄●►►

I was a junior in high school who had never dated before. In all honesty, I had no thoughts about the very idea of even dating up to this point. However, that all changed swiftly at the beginning of the school year. I had a study hall class at the time, and noticed a girl that I haven't seen around before. She had brunette hair with blonde lowlights and eyeliner--along with wristbands and overall really stood out to me. I waited in the hallway before walking into class one day and introduced myself to her.

We were the only two in the hallway and the first ones to show up before anyone else, so then we continued our conversation into the classroom. I could tell almost instantly that she was interested in me and matched my energy. We got to know each other almost effortlessly and the spark was there, so I ended up getting her snapchat. We then were talking all weekend and I felt like the chemistry was undeniable, so I ended up giving her a hug when seeing her about a week or two later. She told me that her birthday was coming up soon and I knew that homecoming was about three weeks away, so I thought of an idea. I got a cookie cake asking her to go to homecoming with me and it was on her birthday. She was very excited and almost punctured a rib with how tight she hugged me. We became official that week and it was my first relationship. We parted ways two months later, but I'll never forget the magical vibes from the moment I met her and the first six weeks of that relationship.

- Noah Stickney @thatcobranoah

Victor

Once upon a time, in the shadowy corners of a bustling city, there lived a man named Victor. Victor was an ordinary-looking fellow, but he had an extraordinary obsession. He was deeply in love with a woman named Clara, who worked at the local library. Clara, with her bright eyes and warm smile, was the light in Victor's otherwise dim world. Victor's love for Clara was anything but ordinary. He would spend hours in the library, hiding behind tall shelves, watching her every move.

He memorized her schedule, knew which books she liked, and even learned the sound of her footsteps. Victor's heart raced every time she walked by, and he would often leave little notes in the books she borrowed, hoping she would notice his affection. One rainy evening, as Clara was closing the library, Victor finally mustered the courage to approach her. He stepped out from the shadows, his eyes gleaming with an unsettling intensity. "Clara," he whispered, "I've been watching you for so long. I know everything about you.

I love you more than anyone ever could." Clara's eyes

widened in fear, her heart pounding in her chest. She tried to back away, but Victor reached out and grabbed her arm, his grip firm and unyielding. "Please, don't be afraid," he said, his voice trembling with emotion. "I just want to be with you, to protect you, to love you forever." Clara's fear turned into a desperate struggle, and she managed to break free from his grasp, running out into the rain-soa. Rain soaked streets. Victor watched her go, his heart shattered but his obsession only growing stronger. From that night on, Victor's presence became a constant, unsettling part of Clara's life. He would leave flowers on her doorstep, send her anonymous letters, and follow her wherever she went. Clara lived in a state of perpetual fear, always looking over her shoulder, knowing that Victor's love was a dark and twisted shadow that she could never escape.

Reclaimed

---- ◆◈◆ ----

1 0th Grade, geometry class is where everything begins. With a normal day of trying to catch up in geometry just like everyone else. But there's peoples joking and laughing behind me. Kind of gets annoying in a way, so I do turn around and give them a stare. A white blonde hair woman, by the name of Anna looks at me, and starts laughing again. Thinking it's funny that she's being so loud. She's new to the US, moved here a year ago. I explain that I'm just trying to do my work but also laugh because her laugh is funny.

So is her German accent, her broken English even. We end up talking and doing assignments together. A friend names Jamarion starts liking her, at this time I did develop what some would call a "crush" on her. But she has no idea, and as a friend I encourage him to ask her out. He does and she says yes, we stay friends but then I move to NYC unexpectedly for family. I have no idea what happened to her or him.

1 1/2 years later I move back I start a new job and about a year after the new job and moving back, she sees me at the car wash, I had no idea and a few months later

I get a follow request on Instagram wondering who it might be. I accept it because why not you know? They message me "omg are you still alive?" And I simply reply "yes? Sorry I don't know who you are." She ends up revealing she's Anna and her and Jamarion broke up a long while ago. We start messaging and getting know each other. I end up realizing after all the time being single and almost forgetting about her it feels like no time has passed despite our accomplishments without each other. I also realize I do still feel the same, but when I notify her of that, she had feelings too and also feels the same. After about a month of talking we realize let's give dating a try, and ever since then both sides have been happier than ever. Finding partners that treat them like they want to be treated. Thankyou.

Wrong

—◆◆●◆◆—

In the middle of may I first met someone unexpectedly, in the moment we were both in a relationship knowing what we were going to do was wrong, which led us to both cheating on our partners. He had a very bad reputation of breaking people's hearts, and being full of lust but I put that aside to see how things went. We started talking more summer of 2023 when we were both single, things were great , we connected on a deeper level and I was so in love.

Until late August I found out he got back together with his girlfriend and I just felt so stabbed in the back. I was deeply attached and I thought the feelings were mutual. We were doing long distance but I thought if he really wanted to make things work he would. Around April of this year he took my virginity, after that I thought we were going to be together forever and we were going to have a strong relationship. Until he told me this was nothing serious and I should've known better. My heart shattered, I felt so much pain.

But I knew things were for the better, so I got my closure and he said this .. " "If u wanna be otp everyday n every night you need to know that I have a gf and I know what we did was serious but you knew it wasn't going to be nothing from the start. I have my own life with my own gf, I was really trna talk w you and understand but I have a life also n I'm sorry it has to b like that but that's just the way things are. This doesn't mean I don't wanna talk to you or be with you or anything but rn I have a lot going on so this is me just me really telling you how I feel" I felt so used and I felt unworthy to find love after that. But I've moved on with my life and learned that I wasn't the one for him. I still have so much love for him but he has taught me not to be so trust worthy in just anyone because anybody can just walk out of your life .

-@here.is.emely

Lover that became a stranger

She was a rainbow

But you were colorblind.

Hard to love

Easy to hurt

You made that girl believe that. Why?

Because you're cruel,

-and scared of your own self-

You destroy others because you've already destroyed yourself.

You're a liar too.

Every single word you say is a lie

-some more discreet than others-

But still,

I still manage to believe all these lies that you sing,

I believe these words that cut my heart slowly,

Slowly enough that I realize too late that I'm bleeding;

Bleeding for you.

Because the girl I was wanted things to work out;

She liked you somehow;

She gave you everything on a silver platter,

A guide on how to love her,

The exact coordinates to her heart,But the boy,

The one you are, Took everything-

And left it all at the same time,

Showing that you never cared,

And that you never will.

I still see you,

At parties,

-where we met-

Laughing with your friends;

Staring at me until your eyes meet mine.

And I see you smile.

-The kind of smile that reminds of the place I had for you in my heart-

You're looking at me like an athlete admiring his trophy,

Because that's all I'll ever be for you:

A prize.

You never deserved me.

Never deserved anything that I gave you.

You're just a unhealed boy thinking he's a man,

Hoping I'll run back to you,

But I'm not.

For you now I'll always stand still,

And I'll slowly forget you.

You can stare all you want but you'll never find my eye to look at,

All you'll see is a girl that doesn't like you anymore.

But she still hopes you'll finally find yourself,

Even though she won't be there for you;

Because without you she's the rainbow she was always meant to be,

And you're the boy who doesn't see colors because he doesn't deserve to,

And you better hurry to grow

Otherwise your mirror will be the only friend you'll have to cry to.

-@chri_anna.p

Once Lived

I once had a very loving, kind, and cute girlfriend that name is Paola. If I remember correctly, it was between 2015 and 2016, so she was a typical love of children, there were no kisses with lips or anything like that, but the point is that she was a very cute girl with me, even though I was a bad boy with everyone, she changed me in many aspects.

We had to end the relationship because we were going to change schools in 2017, and after that, we never met again until today

Now today in 2024, I have no idea where she is or contact with her.

Sometimes love makes us want to be better, I changed because of what Paola saw in me, but when I lost her, it did not stop the love I felt for her, I hope she is fine and she will find peace.

Certainly, I still think about her for some days, I hope to meet her again one day or in the next life if possible.

-Sau

Meadows

---◆◆◆◆◆---

I played video games a while back and i had few friends on there a the time and though those friends i met a girl, her name was celine.

Me and celine would play almost every game and spend all day and night laughing and talking till we fell asleep and then eventually we ended up audio calling and then that led to video calls.

A year into the relationship she was serious about coming to see me and she ended taking a flight over here to puerto rico and she stayed for 2 and half months cause we wanted to stay together but she ended up deciding she has to go back so she did so.

As time went on i was having more problems at home with my mom and it ended up getting in the between our relationship and i was just immature and didn't know how to handle anything at the time and i pushed her away and changed in a way that made her fall outta love with me and one day she just didn't wanna call just text me.

She expressed how she thinks we needed time but soon that turned to us not talking.

That same month my cousin helped me by bringing me out to kansas so i could ease my mind and make some new friends and i ended up deciding that maybe its time to get closer to god and start working on myself and build a new me Ever since then i made it an effort to get closer to my family and start working out a bit and that soon gave me a little bit of confidence and i started noticing things change around me and everything felt lighter and i felt myself enjoying time and actually appreciating life for what it is. The point is time is the best healer, I've changed a lot and found love in me and I'm still loving myself more and more everyday and being more social after so long of being antisocial. I appreciate her for what she did and the experience she gave me   because of that I'm able to see things differently and find love in myself, something i never had.

Shy Glances

I n a small town nestled between hills, Japjot and Deepika's love story began with shy glances across the classroom. They were each other's first love, navigating the fragile beauty of young hearts intertwined.Their days were filled with laughter and stolen moments, but as time passed, insecurities grew like shadows in the dusk. Petty arguments escalated into hurtful words, and tears blurred the promises they once made.As the year drew to a close, Deepika made a difficult choice. She knew they needed space to grow, to heal from wounds neither understood. With a heavy heart, she ended their relationship, leaving Japjot lost in a sea of emotions.The following year brought unexpected encounters. At first awkward, their friendship slowly rekindled, built on a foundation of shared memories and newfound understanding. They laughed about old fights, reminiscing about how young and naive they once were. Through late-night conversations and comforting silences, Japjot and Deepika discovered a love that transcended romance—a deep, platonic bond rooted in mutual respect and acceptance. They learned to cherish what they had, grateful for the paths that led them back to each other.In the quiet moments of their friendship, they found solace, knowing that some loves are meant to evolve, to grow beyond the confines of what they once were. And as they stood together, watching the sun set behind their town's familiar hills, they knew that their story was just beginning—a tale of young love tempered by time and transformed into something infinitely precious.

Hijabi

ummer of 2023 i met a hijabi muslim girl at work, she was beautiful and just so charismatic it had everyone talking about her like she's one of the greatest things to happen to their lives, so when she took a liking to me in particular I felt special, I was in love , but I was afraid to become something because I wasn't ready, for months I would purposely ignore her as she kept flirting, one day after work I couldn't take it, I confessed I liked her back and we kissed privately which is a huge "no" in her religion. she told her best friend who than told everyone and she thought I told everyone so she hated me for awhile, but after finding out her friend betrayed her she came back to me wanting me even more, I was hurt and broken and all I wanted was her more than anything. We tried to repair what happened but we couldn't hold our feelings back, so much pain, so much I wanted to end my life because if I couldn't be with her I couldn't live. We had a final coffee date January 2024 and I decided I should pursue my other true love , acting , so I sold everyone and moved 1000 miles away from home all by myself, I still miss her some nights and it's already July 2024 , I'm still healing, the entire situation traumatized me , I hope one day I'll be whole again.

-@donovanduranactor

The Next Stop: Heartache

————— ◆◆●◆◆ —————

I t's 10:34 pm. The train is half empty, but I choose to stand by the door, my back pressed against the glass. My legs have been throbbing with pain for the past hour or so on the ride back home, away from you, but every aching bone in my body refuses to sit, instead yearning desperately to feel the weight of my body pushing my feet against the ground. Strangers pass cursory glances at me; boys and girls have their eyes locked onto each other, half-convicted men sit with their legs crossed and their iPhones in their left hand.

What do they know about love?

The glass is black, and in the reflection, I see myself: eyes hollowed out by fuzzy visions, cheeks chiseled out by the sharp, concise fragments of truth, jaw sharpened by the appetite you deprived me of. I don't want anyone else but you to fix me because everything else doesn't make sense.

Next stop: Artarmon I think to myself, "So this is what pain feels like?" Pain is wherever this train is taking me because it's heading in the opposite direction of you. As the train rumbles on, the lights flickering like fireflies in the darkness, I can't help but think of the last time we were together. The memory of your touch, your laughter, your eyes, it all feels like a distant dream now.

The agony of longing! It's as if my heart has been irreparably shattered, leaving a gaping chasm that can only be filled by the love we shared. Every fiber of my being yearns for your tender embrace, your soft whispers, and your radiant smile that once illuminated my existence. Memories of our time together haunt me like a ghostly refrain, echoing through the desolate corridors of my mind. I'm trapped in a prison of my own making, with no escape from the bittersweet torment of remembrance.

The train's relentless motion only serves to underscore the distance growing between us, a constant reminder of the love slipping further away with each passing moment. The flickering lights outside seem to mock me, their ephemeral dance a cruel reminder of the transience of joy. The darkness that follows only serves to deepen the ache within, a hollow sense of loss that threatens to consume me whole. My thoughts are a jumble of fragmented images, a kaleidoscope of moments we shared now taunting me with their absence. The gentle pressure of your hand in mine, the soft cadence of your laughter, the piercing intensity of your gaze-all these and more swirl through my mind like a maelstrom, leaving me breathless and bereft. In this bleak landscape of heartache, time itself becomes distorted, stretching out the agony of separation into an eternity of longing.

I'm lost in a sea of sorrow, unable to find solace in the

vast expanse of my own despair. The pain of our parting has become my sole companion, a constant reminder of the love that once was, and the love that may never be again.

When Love Last

All my life when it's came to loving someone I never wanted to fully give my heart to someone because I could never say I fully trusted a girl, for me if I don't trust you I won't take you serious and my whole life I would shield women from ever even getting that close to my heart because once there, I give you the ability to hurt me.

This girl really changed me to someone I would have never thought to be, someone I can't even recognize, but it's been for the better without knowing it she showed me what real loves feel like and has showed me that I could love a women outside my family this much. This story really begins in the 7th grade, I was just going through my snap chat stories and I just see this girl with half blonde half black hair looking like 2017 x, and in my head I was like damnn she's bad but that hair is cringe asf like bro x does not know you bud. And plus she had a boyfriend so I didn't really pay her any more mind. But then fast forward a couple years later, this same girl followed me on instagram outta nowhere and I had already know who she was.

So in my head I'm already thinking we're together because when a baddie follow you that's just how it be y'all men out there know what I'm talking about. So when she first followed me I was just chillin, I didn't want to text her anything because I couldn't have her knowing I wanted her that bad, and plus it would make me look bad and desperate and that could never be me. But guess what she ends up doing yep... she unfollowed me and yea that shit hurt I can't lie, even though we never talked before I still felt like we was damn near already married. But I go on with life, shit happens oh well. Fast forward a couple months she ends up following me again and in my head at first I'm like yea I'm not following her back this time fuck her.

So then I have her on unfollowed for a couple of days but she still follows me and plus she's liking my stories I post of myself so, I'm really thinking like damn maybe this time she not playing with me and actually might fwm. Like mind y'all, this girl is like actually beautiful like frr one of the most beautiful women I have ever seen and I always had a crush on her like I was telling y'all since I had first seen her in middle school on Snap and mind you this is happening my senior year in high school. So at this point I'm just chilling, like we're liking each others story's back and forth but theirs no communicating at all just story likes. And one day I just decide like you know what, it's time for me to say some I'm tired of all this little kid shit it's time to make a move.

So I slide up on one of her post of her stacking rocks saying some bs like "how you do that every time I stack rocks I can never get that high". KNOWING DAMNN

WELL I HAVE NEVER STACKED NO FUCKING ROCKS. But aye you gotta do what you gotta do, you can't try to message a girl like that with some heart eyes or some lame shit like that because trust me it's you and hundreds of other guys saying the exact same thing a girl is not gonna take y'all serious, yall trust me when I tell y'all this. Yea so we were texting for like a day or two and guess what? She ghost me. Yea at this point I'm really tired of her bs like I was thinking everything was going good but I guess not, but she was still following me so I was super confused.

So fast forward a couple of weeks to senior skip day and me and a bunch of my classmates go to a park in Austin called zilker. When I'm there I'm just chilling having a good time then I'm just scrolling going though insta stories and I see the girl posting she's at zilker and I end up calling my bestfriend real fast to tell him on some what should I do shit, because she had already ghosted me so like I wasn't gonna text her again but also she was kinda of like the love of my life "she just ain't know yet" so I couldn't really just let us be in the same place and not do nothing. So we had just decided that I don't text her but if I see her I go up to her. So me and my classmates are just going around different parts of the park just going and hanging out.And she's not where to be found.

I just end up giving up and we were leaving at this point so like it was really over with. As I turn around to grab my belongings and get going I start walking and mind you I have glasses on, So I'm just looking straight and for some reason something told me to look right and guess who I see... her. And not only do I see her, she sees me where literally looking dead at each other for like maybe one of two seconds but it really feels like time slowed down for just that point of time. Were looking at each other and I don't really remember who looked away first but I remember me looking away then looking back at her and right when I look at her again I see her looking at me than she instantly looks away. And I know I said I would talk to her if I seen her but I folded. And plus the people I was with were already leaving so I just kept on walking. I thought about texting her that day but I was saying to myself nahh too soon let me chill.

I text her the next day. She responded with something like "yea I saw you at zilker yea I think I need you forever" type shii. That's not really what she said but that's what It felt like. So we end up continue texting and we had ft later that night and right after-that first ft call I knew that we would be together. So we officially start talking, but shit would happen and we would stop taking for like a week or two and this happened a few times but the thing is we would always come back to each other. I end up asking her out June 19th 2024 after we went to go see bad boys 4 life on a pouring rainy dark night, really was like the perfect way, in the car both soaked listening to music enjoying each other presence. And since then we have been together happily ever after yea we bump heads here and there but we know how much we love each other and no matter what is said or done we're never leaving each other.

Now we're literally inseparable, we're getting married like not right now but I know for 100% I am marrying this girl. WE WILL BE TOGETHER FOREVER and I love this girl more than anything. This is the story of how me and my blessing from the man above found love and became forever in love. I love you, cadence.

-@philipmara_

Mara

⬥⬥⬥

They say some people go their whole lives without finding true love some might even say it's not real. I've experienced many kinds of love; puppy love, painful, lying, pointless, cheating, and limerence in my life but never "real" I was hopeless. I was done being used miss treated lusted over I was done. I spent a long time being alone after years of disappointment.

It was the best decision of mine until Mara slid up on my Instagram story... boy how my life has been turned around and flipped upside down. At first, I was extremely avoidant of him as I was to everyone we would text then I'd just stop responding. Until it was the infamous senior skip day where all high schools in Austin meet and Zilker. That day I'd seen Mara for the first time in person and I knew the moment we locked eyes this was someone very special. I freaked out when I saw him and so no reason I didn't understand why I felt the way I did I ran to my friend "I follow him on Instagram that's Philip!!!" her sitting there confused because I'd never mentioned him at all.

I didn't stop thinking about him the whole day I was

just in my head debating if I should text him. A couple of days went by and tried to just forget about it because I didn't have time to fall in love and get hurt all over again. But the universe said differently. He texted me saying something along the lines of "You have a beautiful smile" I was in disbelief. I already ghosted this man and saw him at Zilker didn't say anything and he still complimented me??? I would be lying if I said I wasn't blushing. We ended up having a long conversation and we talked about Zilker and seeing each other. Eventually, we ended up on the phone the same night! I have never in my life clicked with someone so fast until I met him.

When we were on the phone we talked to each other like we had been friends for years. I kept getting to know each other and it hit me… I was falling in love. In my head after all the work I did to fix myself why would I fall in love and get hurt again??? So I started to avoid him. For a couple of months, we would talk and stop talking about 3 different times for some reason every time we stopped talking we would always find our way back to each other and it was so confusing to me I have never been the kind of person to do this. but he was just so different. He was so comforting something about him felt like home. He treated me how my dad treated me which is insane for me to even say. The last time we stopped talking was because I had actually lied to him about my past thinking that he would judge me it was probably our first time ever actually fighting with each other..

Weeks went by of us not talking all I could think about was him I even found myself crying about him. So I texted him telling him how much I actually loved him

621

and apologizing and wishing him the best in life. He apologized as well and explained to me that he would never judge me and a lot more but I don't wanna make this too long. He came over about a day later and I cried to him telling him how much feeling I really had for him and I was just so scared of feeling love for someone. We realized that we couldn't keep running from the way we felt. So I decided to completely fall in love.

We started going out more he took me on dates. I was realizing that this was right. He is showing me what real love is... June 19th we decided to go see a movie mind you this was the last month we had together before he was moving 8 hours away for college... but anyway, after the movie it was storming and we ran to the car in the rain we made it to the car completely drenched!! We were just laughing and out of breath and it got kinda quiet... he asked me to be his girlfriend. And I said YES. But before I could get too happy I asked "Are you sure this is what you want you are about to go to college" and he said he was more than sure and he wanted this forever... I don't know how I got so lucky with someone like him. this is the last thing I'd ever expect from man in this generation. forever?? He choose me over the "college life" he picked me.

The day came and he left to college and I was unsure how this was going to go but he reassured me we would talk everyday and that I have nothing to worry about. we FaceTime every day he would update me and reassure me all the time he is the first person I can say that I have completely given my trust to I can say proudly that I know he would never hurt me. He does everything to make my life easier treats me like a princess, we have had our issues but we've never had a problem that has gone unsolved he will always make sure I'm okay after any conversation. he loves me so soft and gentle. He treats me with kindness and care who would've thought that I'd be this happy in a long distance relationship a couple days ago he decided he's going to come back to Austin for good and this is where our story is truly going to begin. I've found my person and when I say I want this forever, I mean forever. I love you, Mara. If you're reading this a couple years later I'm a wife now.

@imkd114

Made in the USA
Columbia, SC
07 February 2025

52650346R00346